W9-BTP-091

RECEIVED
APR - 3 2007
By

No Longer the Property of
Hayner Public Library District

HAYNER PUBLIC LIBRARY DISTRICT
ALTON, ILLINOIS

OVERDUES .10 PER DAY MAXIMUM FINE
COST OF BOOKS. LOST OR DAMAGED
BOOKS ADDITIONAL $5.00 SERVICE CHARGE. BRANCH

The
Secret
Magdalene

The
Secret
Magdalene

a novel

Ki Longfellow

CROWN PUBLISHERS

NEW YORK

HAYNER PUBLIC LIBRARY DISTRICT
ALTON, ILLINOIS

This is a work of fiction. Names, characters, places, and incidents either
are the product of the author's imagination or are used fictitiously.

Copyright © 2005, 2007 by Ki Longfellow

All rights reserved.

Published in the United States by Crown Publishers, an imprint of the
Crown Publishing Group, a division of Random House, Inc., New York.
www.crownpublishing.com

Originally published in a different form by Eio Books, Brattleboro, in 2005.

CROWN is a trademark and the Crown colophon is a
registered trademark of Random House, Inc.

Library of Congress Cataloging-in-Publication Data

Longfellow, Ki.

The secret Magdalene : a novel / Ki Longfellow.—1st ed.

1. Mary Magdalene, Saint—Fiction.   2. Christian women saints—Fiction.
3. Women in the Bible—Fiction.   I. Title.

PS3612.O533S43   2005

813'.6—dc22   2006015275

ISBN 978-0-307-34666-7

Printed in the United States of America

DESIGN BY MERYL SUSSMAN LEVAVI
MAP BY SOPHIE KITTREDGE

10 9 8 7 6 5 4 3 2 1

First Revised Edition

F
LON

b17599878

This book is dedicated
to Shane Roberts,
with Love

There were three who always walked with the Lord: Mary, his mother, and her sister, and the Magdalene, the one who was called his companion. His sister and his mother and his companion were each a Mary.

— Gospel of Philip

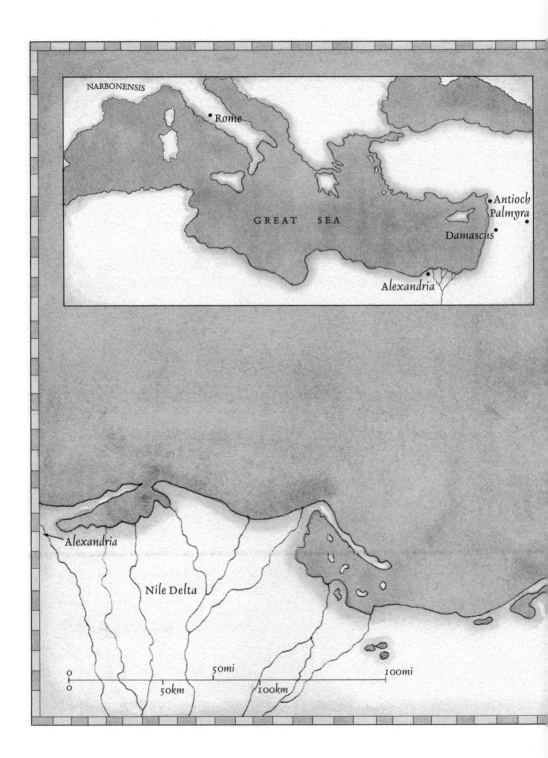

NARBONENSIS

• Rome

GREAT   SEA

• Antioch
Palmyra
Damascus •   •

• Alexandria

Alexandria

Nile Delta

0   50mi   100mi
0   50km   100km

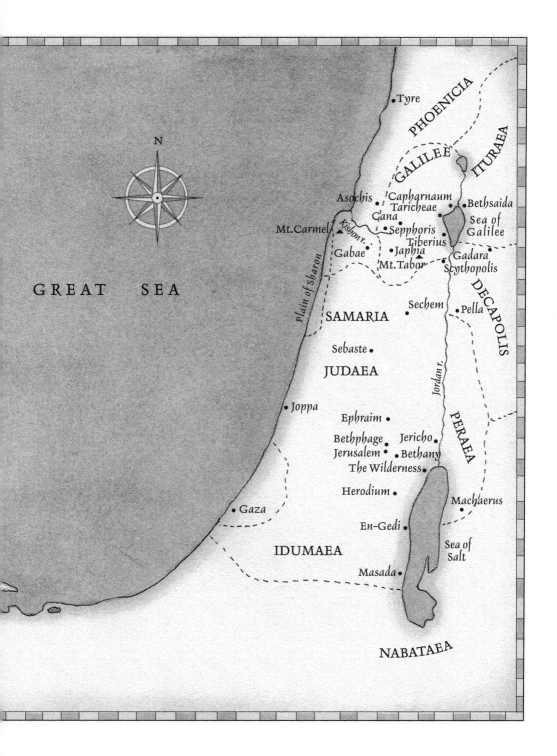

N

Tyre

PHOENICIA

GALILEE

ITURAEA

Asochis • Capharnaum
Taricheae
Cana • Bethsaida
• Sepphoris Sea of
Mt. Carmel Kishon r. Galilee
Tiberius
Gabae • Japhia Gadara
Mt. Tabor Scythopolis

GREAT   SEA

DECAPOLIS

Sechem • Pella

Plain of Sharon

SAMARIA

Sebaste •

JUDAEA

Jordan r.

• Joppa

Ephraim •

PERAEA

Bethphage • Jericho •
Jerusalem • Bethany
The Wilderness

Herodium •

Machaerus •

• Gaza

En-Gedi •

Sea of
Salt

IDUMAEA

Masada •

NABATAEA

The
Secret
Magdalene

It comes, at last, to this—I am changed from water to wine. I who was dead now live. I know my own name. I AM. These then are the thoughts of Mariamne, daughter of Josephus of the tribe of Benjamin. In the waning of my earthly days, I recount the life of the Daughter of Wisdom, who came in time to be known as the Magdalene.

As I know my own name, I know there will dawn a day when Yehoshua, whom some call Joshua and some call Iesous and some call Jesus but whom I called Yeshu, shall be seen for what he is: nothing so whimsical and so impractical as a god, and nothing so arbitrary and so transitory as a king, but as a great heart standing on the edge of the world teaching us all to soar by teaching himself. When that time comes, I too shall be heard again: she of the Temple Tower and the disciple known as John. Yet care I nothing if my name is lost to the winds, for my voice is raised only in praise of Yehoshua, son of Joseph, and of Jude, son of Joseph, the brother whom all called Jude the Sicarii.

I begin in the voice of the child I was, speaking of the day I saw Simon Peter of Capharnaum kill the Temple priest, knowing Seth of Damascus, always my most faithful friend, will arrange these things on parchment now that I can no longer do so.

The Voice

Because I have recently been ill unto death, Tata has taken me to Temple this morning—but only me. Father does not know she does this. Salome does not know. We go alone so that Tata might offer a dove unto Asherah, the wife of Yahweh. Tata would thank Asherah for my life, for I have not died in my tenth year, though it seemed I might.

We are pushing our way through the Court of Women, Tata keeping a tight grip on my hand so that I do not stray from her side. But the dove in its wicker cage distracts her, and for this one moment, she has turned away from me. I have turned quite another way, pulling so that I might catch sight of the God of the Jews hiding in his Holy of Holies, and as I do, Tata is forced from her place by a Temple priest who would move past us, his face full flushed with pride of station. I know this man. His name is Ben Azar and he has eaten at Father's table many times. I do not like him. I do not like his eldest son. No matter that I have heard Father say I might wed this son of Ben Azar, I will not.

Tata's bird fights to be free of its cage and Tata fights to hold it. But I am turned full round to follow the progress of Father's friend, the Temple priest. He has gotten no farther than a press of men who look nothing like those who might eat at Father's table. Nor do they look like men of Jerusalem. They appear wild men who think wild thoughts, and I break away from Tata's hand that I might see them all the closer. Ben Azar is turning this way and that way to pass, but no matter which way he would go, there stands a man who blocks him, and as they do not move, he pushes at one who is nearest. But from this crowd of wild men comes now a very bull of a man, a man whose eyes burn like the sun at the end of the day. And in this man's hand there is a *sica* with a blade as curved as a smile. I would scream, I would warn Ben Azar even though I do not like him, I would call out to the Temple police. But a hand rough with toil is clamped over my mouth and I cannot call out. I can struggle against the grip that holds me fast, and I do struggle—though it avails me nothing. It avails Ben Azar nothing. I can only watch as the man like a bull thrusts his knife into Father's friend, not once, not twice, but thrice. Hot red blood splashes my feet; it spills on the golden tiles of the courtyard. Bright red blood fills the surprised mouth of Ben Azar, the Temple priest.

It is done. Ben Azar is dead on the courtyard tiles. And he who has held me fast lets loose his hand. I whirl in place so that I might see his face.

There are two who stand behind me.

As alike each to each as Jacob and Esau, these two, who are surely brothers, have hair and beards as red as a criminal's hair, as red as a magician's. There is no mercy in the eyes of one, but in the eyes of the other there is sadness and there is pity, but so too there is a fierce righteousness. There is also, I think, a terrible pain. As I stare up at these murderous twins, the man who has killed Ben Azar of the House of Boethus speaks out in the crude sounds of Galilee, "It is done, Yeshu'a." And the twin he calls Yeshu'a replies, "Yes, Simon Peter. Come away."

They are gone. And it seems no time has passed. And it seems nothing has happened, for only now does Tata succeed in caging her dove. And I would think I had dreamed this terrible deed save for the still body before me, and the blood on my feet, and the sudden sharp scream of a woman who has, only now, seen what others begin also to see.

∝

Because it is my day of birth, Father allows me to dine this night at his table. How Roman of him! Even more exciting—how Greek!

Salome, who is also allowed, pretends she is not as excited as I am, does not think I notice the care she takes with her toilette or how cross she is with Tata and the other slaves who dress her hair. But I know my friend as I know myself. Is she not my father's ward and the sister of my heart? Dressing with more heed than ever I have, scenting even my feet with sweet oil—to dine at table is such an honor and so rarely conferred—I tell her that even though she has grown breasts, she may not act weary, weary, *weary*, as older women of our station do.

In return, she yawns.

But here we are, and there is Father laughing at something a guest is saying.

Neither Salome nor I have ever seen this man before—all oil and ooze, he names himself Ananias, and oh how he stinks. An Egyptian Jew, he claims to come from Alexandria, and when I hear this, I become all ears. There is nowhere so wonderful as Alexandria, unless it is Ephesus. He informs us he trades in the gold of Nubia and Parthia, and the precious balsam of Jericho, but that he relies most on his sponges. People will always buy a sponge.

Nicodemus of Bethphage is also at table. Being almost Father's equal in wealth, he is Father's oldest friend as well as a fellow member of the Sanhedrin, the Jewish governing body. Naomi, Father's new wife, is allowed this night at table too, though this I would rather forget.

As the men speak, I watch Ananias peeking at Salome's new breasts. Not that Father notices. Nor does Nicodemus. They are too

caught up in food and wine and the talk of sponges and money. Salome even leans forward so that the merchant Ananias might fill his
eyes with the shape of her "treasures." I am glad I have as yet no
treasures. But if I did, I would not share them with such as Ananias.
And if I did share them with such as Ananias, I would wait until they
were bigger treasures. I tell Salome this in the secret code of eyes and
mouths and hands we have used since I cannot remember when. She
tells me he has brushed her bare skin twice now. I would laugh out
loud if I could, but if I did, it would be a long time before we were
allowed at table again. Besides, as ugly and as aged as he is, the merchant has been many places, done many things. He is an Alexandrian! There are so many *ideas* in Alexandria! Though I do love gods
and though I love goddesses more, I love philosophy most. Tata says
philosophy is religion without its clothes on.

I keep my nose covered with a scented cloth as I listen to the
sponge merchant.

"I saw it with my own eyes," Ananias is saying in a voice a goat
might use if a goat could speak. "I was right there at Temple, no
more than ten cubits away when the priest was stabbed."

I sit very still. None here know that I too saw this killing. It is four
days ago now, and still I see it. But I shall never tell of it, not even to
Salome, for if any learn, Tata would face the lash for taking me to
Temple to offer a dove to her forsaken Goddess Asherah, once wife
of Yahweh.

"Whap! Whap! Whap! It was as quick as that. And there was the
priest, dead as a dog in the street."

Nicodemus is silent, his mouth turned down in disgust. I can see
him picturing Ben Azar as a dead dog in the street. "They are everywhere now, the Sicarii, these men with curved daggers."

"Everywhere?" asks Naomi through a mouthful of chewed cab-
bage. "Have the Romans crucified this one yet?"

"Crucified him, madam? They fail even to catch him."

Father's chest puffs with importance. "Oh, but they will. The
Romans catch all assassins. Their crosses line the road to Joppa."

"Perhaps this one will too," says Ananias, "and perhaps not."

Father snorts. "Does this new brigand think himself Judas of Galilee? And if he does, did the corpse of Judas not stink as any other? I say to you, this one will also rot."

I grip the stem of my glass. Father mentions Judas of Galilee! Judas was a bandit chieftain. Tata has told Salome and me of the great revolt Judas led against the taxes of Rome in the very year I was born.

Ananias smiles at this. "You have heard, my friends, what the Poor say? You know the teaching of the mad Baptizer?"

"As a Sadducee, I do not listen," says Nicodemus, picking his back teeth. But then Nicodemus is always doing something revolting.

"Who are the Poor?" asks Naomi. "What is a mad baptizer?" As is usual with a woman, the men do not hear her.

Ananias answers himself, "They say that we live in the End Times."

"Nonsense," says Father.

"And that the world will soon cease to be."

"How soon?" asks Naomi. But her words are swallowed at a look from Father, who then has this to say, "So that is what the Poor and the Sicarii are doing? Bringing the world to an end one priest at a time?"

The merchant of sponges starts. "Hah! There is a thought, Josephus! There is a thought! I shall make it mine."

Salome and I look at each other and I am amazed at how high she can pull her eyebrows. Mine sit like mice over my eyes, afraid to move. Hers rise and fall on her face like the sun and the moon, make emphatic remarks like learned scribes.

Nicodemus sits like a stone, but Father laughs like a Greek, even as his fat guest is saying, "The Poor ask if we are God's Holy Nation, how is it we live as Greeks and submit to Romans? They answer we are subject to Rome because we sin. But they also say that there comes a messiah who will redeem Israel, endure the End Times, which shall destroy all others, and usher in the Kingdom of God." Ananias helps himself to the olives, pops one into his mouth, then another. "Some claim he brings a sword."

Father finds this wonderfully funny. "And what shall this messiah do with a sword?"

I find it hair-raising. How shall all others be destroyed?

Ananias pushes back from table. "I imagine he intends to smite those who do not put aside the ideas of the Greeks and the yoke of the Romans, and all those who break the Law. He will smite the Soferim, even the Sadducee."

Father waves away mention of the scrivening Soferim, but his laughter thins at the mention of the Sadducee. I tap Salome's leg with my toe. I am saying, *By Isis, we are the others!*

"He will smite the Sanhedrin and the high priestly houses of Ananus and Boethus. Indeed, has not someone already smote a member of the House of Boethus? They say all who betray the freedom of the Jews by preferring to be slaves to the Romans will know his hand."

All evening I have been marveling at Father's patience, but it is worn away now that this guest mentions the Sanhedrin, and now that he mentions Father's good friend, the new high priest, Josephus Caiaphas of the House of Ananus. But mostly it has vanished now that he mentions Rome. The new emperor Tiberius is not the old emperor Augustus. The Roman presence here is not as easy as it was, and it worsens. Father stares at the merchant of sponges with an eye as hard as a coin. "Is it not true that these same men preach that giving all one's worldly goods to the Poor is blessed in the eyes of the Lord?"

"It is," agrees a now more careful Ananias.

"And do they not mean themselves, and not the poor of the streets?"

"They do."

"Well, does it not then follow that if I should give *all* my worldly goods to the Poor, then it is *I* who should be poor? Will the Poor, now being rich, give me back all my goods? If this is so, how long will it go on, this passing back and forth of a man's possessions?"

Ananias has no answer, but Father has still a question.

"Would you agree that this sect, these Poor, also call themselves the Many?"

"Some do, Josephus, yes."

"In that case, there are two things to say about the Poor, also known as the Many. They are not many, and they are certainly not poor."

If I dared, I would laugh aloud. I do sneak an admiring look at Father, who rewards me with a tender smile. But Ananias has gotten the point and so changes the subject. "Tell me, Josephus, have you ever visited Megas of Ephesus?"

I practically jump out of my skin. He speaks of the most famous oracle, no, *sorceress*, from here to Antioch! She who is also a sacred harlot—a whore! He asks if Father would visit a whore. *Yea Balaam!* The mood, already grown grim, darkens like a stain. Last year Tiberius ran all the magicians out of Rome. These days, if he catches someone practicing magic, and if his mood is black, he orders them killed where they stand.

All await Father's answer. Salome signals me: *Do not open your mouth,* she is saying. *Do not dare engage this oily old man in talk of Megas of Ephesus, no matter how much you would like to.* And, oh, how I would like to—just as she would.

And though Ananias says what he pleases, he can see when what pleases him does not please others. "Accept my apologies, Josephus, for talking of such things."

Now it is Father who surprises us all. "No, no, I must know. What is she like, this one? Is she as beautiful as they say, and as powerful?"

Being half Father's size and having half Father's lung power, Nicodemus cannot restrain him. But he can search the stony faces of our slaves, trying to know if what occurs here will leave this room. He will fail, for this is not a gift Nicodemus possesses.

But I do.

Two men of the north stand like pillars behind Father. The German bears fruit and the Celt bears wine. They do not look at me, though they know I am looking at them. I hear them immediately, for their thoughts are sharp enough to cause me pain. This has been so since my illness, though Salome thinks it will pass as the illness passed. There is nothing in them but the usual scorn for my father and his friends and, as always, a fear of Salome and of me. And yes, what they hear now will later be whispered into other ears. But as

Naomi is forever saying, what can one do since it is against the Law to cut out their tongues?

Ananias eats a fig and honey cake, dripping honey down his beard where it mingles with olive juice and wine. "Megas of Ephesus puts the Delphic oracle to shame. No rhymes and no riddles; even a fool can understand his fortune."

"But not even the wisest of men can change it," trumpets Nicodemus. "It is ha-Shem alone who writes what is and what will be."

This is typical of Nicodemus, forever calling YHVH ha-Shem, the Name. Others, not half so fearful, call him Adonai, the Lord. But all say that Yahweh would strike me dead if I named him. I do not believe that. Under my breath I say, Yahweh, Yahweh, YAHWEH!

It is then that I do something that changes everything.

I open my mouth before all at table and I speak.

"NOTHING IS WRITTEN BUT WHAT EACH MAN WRITES. IF CHANGE IS INTENDED, THEN CHANGED THINGS SHALL BE."

Father and Nicodemus and Naomi could not act more surprised had I climbed up on our table and piddled in the imported wine.

I am more than surprised. The voices have never, not once, spoken before any other than Salome and me. And no voice has ever said anything so strange, nor said it so loudly. I clap my hands to my mouth. Salome does not move an inch, but I can feel her as sharply as if she has slapped me. I feel as if I am ill again, as if the killing fever is back. Father's table and all who recline there swim in a sea of heat that is mine alone.

It takes a long moment for Father to collect himself, and when he does, he says, "That did not sound like you, Mariamne." His voice grates with threat. "What thought was that? Was that the thought of a demon?"

The head of Nicodemus has shrunk into his neck. "Josephus," he says, "my stomach has turned sour." He is afraid of me. All my life people have feared me. Naomi comes no nearer than the courtyard of my room if she can help it. Caiaphas, who is now high priest, has shunned me for half my life. One cannot blame him. At five I climbed up into his lap and named his deepest shame. From time to time, even Father's eyes roll at the sight of me.

But Ananias has sat up like a cobra, looking at me as if I were something he could sink his teeth into.

Father signals a slave to remove my plate. "Obviously you are not yet well. Go to bed. Take Salome with you."

Running into our room, I fall flat on Salome's couch. The sense of illness has quickly passed; to know it passes has made me giddy. Speaking in Salome's Egyptian tongue against those who might listen, my giddiness makes me say, "So near to your treasures, it's a wonder the Egyptian's cock did not crow."

Salome starts at this, then throws back her head and laughs. Like Father, she is very good at laughing. Father laughs whether he understands a thing or not. Salome laughs from understanding too well. "No matter how old they grow, their snake still lifts its head. Tata told me so."

Of course Tata told her. Who else would do so? From Tata we have learned much that would sicken Father should he know of it. In the house of Josephus of Arimathaea—a member of the aristocratic and priestly Sanhedrin!—we have been taught of Egypt's Isis, she who is Alpha and Omega, the beginning and the end. We know Babylon's triple goddess Mari-Anna-Ishtar, Canaan's Astarte, and the Arabian goddesses: Al-Lat, Al-Uzza, and Al-Manat, who are maiden, matron, and crone. We know too of sublime Inanna, and powerful Demeter, and splendid Aphrodite, and the delicious Venus. If Father were to learn she taught us of these, he would have Tata's tongue ripped out, Law or no Law. And do we not know these are all one Goddess come to us in her myriad forms for her myriad purposes? Even worse, we also know of magic and ritual power. Tata says that wise women have walked our land, and we would believe her even if Torah did not tell us so. She says there have been powerful women in Sumer and Assyria and Egypt and this must be true as well, for Cleopatra herself is only recently dead, and only the most abysmally ignorant know nothing of the seventh Cleopatra. And what of Megas, mentioned at table, whose love potions and magic spells are known throughout the Roman world?

As for men, Tata delights to talk of them. She speaks of their seeded staffs, their cocks, and a dozen other silly names. And the poems she knows! Some I blush even to think of. This one: *The king goes with lifted head to the holy lap of Inanna*—and so forth and so on— is almost more than I can bear, especially now that ever since she told it to us, Salome calls Tata's special interest a "lifted head." But this next one stirs my blood and is my favorite. Tata says it was written by a priestess of Ur two thousand years ago. *In the bed that is filled with honey, Let us enjoy our love / . . . My sweet one, wash me with honey.*

If Father only knew what manner of person he has given us as our bawdy nurse and slave! I bless his oversight. Tata has opened our eyes to many things beyond this narrow place. Because of Tata, Father's world of scripture and Law is not our only world. As females we are not considered worthy of an education, though in Father we are more fortunate than other daughters: we can read and write in Latin as well as Greek, Hebrew, and the common Aramaic. Like boys of privilege, we know the Five Books of Torah by heart. Salome has taught me demotic Egyptian and what she knows of her own Egyptian gods and goddesses. So, though we have no one but Tata and ourselves, our time in Father's house is full to the brim.

Sprawled on Salome's couch, I say, "Ananias has been to more lands than Father. He speaks of Megas . . . What do you think he meant by secret sects?"

By now Salome sits naked on a golden stool, looking at her face in a mirror of metal, and combing out her hair. "Palestine is full of secret sects, they come and they go. They hang in their hundreds from crosses along the public roads. But the Romans remain. And the common people remain, to whom all these sects are merely an annoyance. And the rich remain. No matter what happens, there are always the rich. Since we, Mariamne, are the rich, we ought not to complain."

I accept that. There is a cruel truth in it. Salome is very good at cruel truths. It is now she chooses to turn from her mirror, to fix me with what she calls her evil eye. "What did you mean by speaking as you did at table, letting them hear one of our voices?"

It was not one of our voices. But I do not say that. "I did not mean to, Salome."

She studies me, then shrugs her shoulders. "Don't do it again."

"I shouldn't dream of it." She does not know how much I mean this. I would be more than terrified to hear it again.

"Good. Now, let us play our game."

We do many things my father would not approve of, but the most powerful thing we do is play the game we have invented. Gathering favored stones and anointing each with Salome's moon blood and my spittle (as yet I have no menstrual blood to offer), on each we have painted a letter of the Greek alphabet. As a weight, we have hung a golden amulet on the end of a slender chain. To play, we arrange our stones on the floor, hold the amulet over the stones, and read out the letters as they come with the swinging of the heavy gold bobble. The letters become words and the words become sentences; that is how it had begun, our voices. For in reading the stones, we began to speak what we read.

The voices told us right away that they were not gods. Nor were they prophets. Neither were they the dark goddesses of Duat's fiery pits or the demonic Manes who live under Rome, or Keres, the winged Furies of death. They swore they were not *ba'al 'obot*, nor were they dead souls from the crevice of dust, which is Kur. But whatever they are, they speak of things neither Salome nor I understand. For instance, just after my illness, they said, "The One is coming."

"One what?" Salome demanded, which is how she asks most questions.

"One who will herald a kingdom of Light."

It was I who had then asked, "Will the One be another voice?"

"The One comes in body."

Since sickness and death took its leave of me, we have argued over what this "One" might look like, who he might be, how he might sound, and what in the world he will herald. We have never agreed on a single thing about him, save this: he will be a he. For as Salome says, of what use would the "One" be as a she? Who would listen?

I place the stones on a fine linen cloth spread on the floor. I fill the golden bowl from Thrace with oil of myrrh and I light it. We paint our eyes with green copper paint from Sinai like the Temple virgins, the daughters of Aaron. Salome snuffs out all other lamps.

She fetches the amulet from our cedar wood coffer and hands it to me. Chewing bitter doghead, we wait, and when the flames blur, and when we hear the sound of silence in our ears, we don our masks. At this point, I always realize how afraid I really am and how calm Salome is. (Though surely nothing could be as fearsome as that which was shown me as I lay ill. I have yet to speak of it, to anyone.) In less than a breath, the bobble is swinging wildly from stone to stone, so quickly we cannot keep up.

"Slow down!" Salome pinches me. I see she is straining to read the words that come at a dizzying pace. "Mariamne, will you slow down!"

I am about to protest that I have nothing to do with it. I open my mouth to say so, but out comes the Voice that has just spoken at Father's table. "POOR SPIRIT THOUGH HE SEEMS, THE MERCHANT ANANIAS IS SENT TO YOU!"

Salome snatches away my mask. Worse, she grabs a hank of my hair, pulls my face close. "Sent to us?" she says.

"AS A TRUE HARBINGER OF COMING TIMES!"

I slam my jaw shut in horror, hold it shut with my hand. Salome is staring at me through the masked eyes of Horus as if I have just broken out in sores.

"ANANIAS IS COME TO TAKE YOU HOME."

It is very hard not to scream. I think what Father would think, what Father *does* think: Is there a demon in me?

Pulling off her own mask, Salome spits out her doghead and re-lights a lamp. "That putrid old man? A harbinger? And I am the sister of Herod the Great." Then, turning to face her mirror, she speaks in a voice very unlike her usual voice. "What are you!"

Salome reaches out a hand, comes near to touching the metal surface, snatches her hand away.

I too look into the mirror and almost swallow my tongue. The surface shows not my face but the face of something akin to a man.

"You see it! You do see it! Is it this night's voice?"

I am thinking, by Isis and by Demeter, and by all the goddesses, have we conjured up a demon? At just this moment, the merchant Ananias walks into our rooms from off our private courtyard. How dare he? And what does he want?

"Is what this night's voice?" he says in that patronizing tone males reserve for females. And then, noting Salome, who has not covered her body with so much as a hand, he walks closer. Much closer. "What game do my fishes play?"

Before he can truly see us or our room—the riot of robes and scarves and girdles and tunics falling from our clothes chests, the bottles of Father's molded glass, the bracelets and anklets and pendants and headbands, the ointments and powders and creams, before he notes the pastes and the potions and the scrolls—there are scrolls everywhere—before he sees the word stones still on the floor, his eyes drop for one fraction of a moment to the surface of the mirror. Oh, how they widen in fear.

"Get out!" hisses Salome.

But Ananias is rooted, staring from the shape in the mirror to us, from us to our stones, from the stones to the bowls of water, the scrolls, the vials, back to the shape in the mirror, so stunned that Salome and her treasures are forgotten. His thoughts are pounding in my head. What kind of children are these, he is asking himself, are they full of sorcery? Do they practice *kishuf,* and do they conjure demons? I know he is thinking we are witches. He is struggling to control himself, to understand how he might use us.

Salome shoves him out of our room and I slam the door.

The Way

The merchant of sponges visits in Father's house for a week now. In this time he has happened on Salome and me every day, even if we are in our private quarters or in our small courtyard filled with the scent of limes and Tata's roses. The excuses he uses! Clever. Funny. Once even plausible.

Salome is vexed. I too would rather Father's fat friend had never come to our rooms, never seen what he has seen, but twice now he hints at some secret place he knows, where there are others who share our hidden interests. Ananias says they have much to teach us and would gladly do so, that there are women among them. But Salome asks why anyone would teach marriageable females. What profit is there in such learning?

"That old man is up to something," says she. "He may even hope to sell us into slavery." To which I say, "He would not dare! Father would pour pitch down his throat." "Josephus," she replies, "would not know we were gone for at least a week. By then we could be any-where, for are there not auction blocks everywhere?"

I find this thought in my mind: How long *would* it be before Father noticed us missing?

∝

Tata and Salome and I are out of Father's house and moving slowly through the sweaty crowds in the small market street. Pushing against the hot stink of poor people, I keep close my alabastron on its silver chain. There is a perfume from India in this alabaster vial, but very little. Even Father, a shipowner who owns a glass making factory, can afford only so much spikenard. As usual, Salome and I are searching for books to add to our collection, books that will teach us what we do not know, or show us something we have not seen, or make us think something we have not thought of ourselves. I do not know about other children, not knowing any other children save my cousins Martha and Eleazar, but this is what lives closest to our hearts and is our greatest joy, the seeking of knowledge.

Among Tata's many friends, it is Hermas, a man of far Ephesus, that we eagerly seek. Every kind of strange and fascinating religion flourishes in the city of Ephesus, every kind of fascinating person lives there. To this man goes most of Father's money, which is, in truth, my mother Hokhmah's money. At Hokhmah's death, which I do not remember, Father allowed her to bequeath the whole of her dowry to me, and he administers it scrupulously. Salome's fortune comes from her own father who is also dead, the victim of some foul Egyptian poisoner. Salome is very interested in poison.

Today I am eagerly buying a book of Egyptian *hekau* in Egyptian hieratic writing. There is in this book a magical spell, a *talitha kuom*, which might help hold the shape in the mirror that still waxes and wanes behind the shine of the metal surface, struggling to come or to go we cannot tell, but we have decided to capture it.

Plucking our purchase from the hand of Hermes of Ephesus, Salome turns her back on the buyers of fruits and vegetables, on the bleating of the penned sheep, on the hawkers of salted fish and fried locusts, on the beggars and the thieves and the afflicted and the incessant poor, on the loud and constant whine of haggling that goes on all around us. She stands under the umbrella of the merchant of magic and begins to read the spell aloud, and I am in agony that someone might hear. What if a spy for Tiberius lingers near?

"*Eeim to eim alale'p barbariath menebreio arbathisao'th ioue'l iae'l oue'ne'iie mesommisas,*" she reads, then switches to Greek. "'Let the God who prophesies to me come and let him not go away until I dismiss him.' Oh, this is good, Mariamne, listen! *Elpheo'n tabao'th kirasina lampsoure' iaboe ablamathanalba krammachamarei!*"

"Is there blood involved?" asks Tata, who has not understood a word, either Greek or Egyptian. "Blood is full of power." She is looking over Salome's shoulder, and at the same time shielding her from anyone who might take undue interest.

"No," says Salome, "but there is dung and there is spittle. 'Anoint your right eye with water from a shipwreck and the left with Egyptian eye paint with the same water. If you cannot find water from a shipwreck, then from a sunken skiff.'"

"Dung is good, spittle is better, blood is best" says Tata. It is here that a heavy hand comes down on my shoulder. Ananias! He has come up behind us, sneak that he is. His stink is so unique, I am surprised he has surprised me. Quickly, he reaches for the scroll, but quicker yet I shove it into Tata's basket.

Salome moves away, followed by Tata, who is followed by me.

Ananias follows along behind us, as we all know he will. I look hard at Tata. She is fierce and she is brave. Why does she not shoo him away?

Neither Salome nor I have the slightest idea how old Tata is, or who her people are. All we know of Tata is what she has been pleased to tell us, and she is pleased to tell us a great deal, but none of it about herself. We do know she is a Jebusite from the blood of the Canaanites. It is written that the Hebrew are sprung from the seed of Abraham and Sarah. It is written that David captured Jerusalem. It is written that David's son Solomon built the First Temple. But it is also written that long before David and Solomon, and long before Abraham's god offered him the Land of Canaan, Tata's people were here.

When Salome first heard this, and being no more than six years of age, she asked aloud how Abraham's personal god could offer what was neither his nor Abraham's, but Tata's?

Father first stared at her, then sent her to our rooms.

Unshooed by Tata, Ananias trots along beside us on fat legs, wheezing as he keeps up with the pace Salome has set. He looks ridiculous. And he never stops talking. "I despaired of the hope," he is saying, "that Josephus allowed his women out of his house." Here he wheezes, a long squeaky exhale. "But here you are and here am I, and if we could just go to the end of this street and turn left?"

It so happens that Salome, now quite a bit ahead of us, but within earshot, does turn left, but whether to please Ananias or by mere happenstance, I do not know.

We are moving up a steep street beyond the inner wall, each of us following Salome who now seems to be going somewhere, but where? Here the haze of cooking fires and the stench of man and his beasts, and worse, their incessant wastes, is less. We move toward the high white walls of the Temple Mount, which means that the houses crowded on either side of us grow whiter and whiter, which means richer and richer. Salome has turned right. Up ahead there is a terraced rise and on top of that a low wall and in the wall a small and private gate. I am amazed to see Salome pass through.

Ananias is still babbling away. "Yes, that's it, that's the gate. Now, do you see the third door along? Turn there." These hills are killing him. If we can just keep moving, he is bound to collapse in a quivering heap and that will be the end of this foolishness.

By now, my heart beats from more than Salome's fast pace; it beats from a growing fear that we shall find ourselves slaves in some foreign land, that Salome is walking us, no, running us into a trap. I catch Tata's eye. For once, it is she who knows my thoughts and alarm darkens her face.

A woman who waits at the gate has taken Salome's hand, has pulled her through into a dim passageway. I dash in after them—and come to a sudden halt. We are in a marble courtyard shaded by the sweetest of almond trees. There is a pool of water held in a shell of blue stone and near the pool sits a man as old as Father. A younger

man sits at his side. With bankers' eyes they watch us make our confused and unhappy entrance. What adult is interested in children?
Every day, unwanted pagan babies, sometimes even males, are thrown
on dung heaps, and only a few of these are plucked from death among
the garbage so they might grow into slaves. *Yea Balaam!* These two
must think we shall bring them some fabulous price.

"Are these the ones spoken of?" the older man asks Ananias.

"Yes, Heli, these are the two I promised."

I look at Salome and she looks at me; we both expect Ananias to
name his price now, to collect the money he has earned for bringing
us to this slave trader. The man, Heli, is pushing aside Salome's head
shawl. "So young," he says, "and the other, the taller one?"

"Younger," says Ananias.

"God's ways are God's ways. Addai, what do you think?" He asks
this of the younger man still seated on the stone bench. "Does the Jebusite woman stay or go?"

He means Tata, and finally, Tata's wits are about her. She slips her
hand under her cloak seeking the knife I know she carries there.

The man called Addai, says, "She stays. We have no need of scar-
ing children."

His voice is heavily accented. Is it a Peraean accent? Galilean? Big
of belly and bowed of leg, his nose is as flat as his face and his mouth
is as wide as a jar. As for his robe, it is poor. And his feet—bare. But the
man Heli is dressed in a white robe almost as fine as one of Father's.
Two such men speaking as equals? Such a thing would not happen in
Father's house, and that is a certainty!

Heli speaks to Salome. "Ananias tells us you are a witch. He tells
us the other one is also a witch."

Tata shoots Ananias a look of such malevolence it ought to make
his nose fall off. Salome turns pale and does not answer. Witches! For
all of Father's influence, if we are witches, Salome and I might be put
to death by stoning. For if we are witches, do we not practice *kishuf*?
Are we each not a *ba'al 'ob*, meaning two who allow the dead into their
bodies? Or so these men must think, for all who do not know feed on
what they think they know, making great leaps of dreadful imagina-

tion. A *ba'al 'ob* like Megas of Ephesus is almost untouchable. A magician and miracle worker like the great Hanina ben Dosa is almost a rabbi. But Salome and I are not either of these. Does Ananias hate witches? Is this why he mentioned Megas at Father's table, to entrap us? *Oh Isis!* Do we stand before men who would abide by the commandment in Exodus that thou should not suffer a witch to live?

I look at the man Addai; I reach into his mind. How his moon-eyes widen! He can tell I have entered him . . . and I am so startled, I pull away. He is a short man, but he looks as solid as a bullock. "If you would know what I think, little one, you must come out and ask me."

Unnerved, I stand as proudly as my knees permit. "Who are you?"

"I am Addai of Shechem."

"And Shechem is where?"

"At the foot of Mount Gerizim."

By the stars, a Samaritan! Father reviles the Samaritans. He says they are a mongrel stock, a horrid mix of Israelites and Assyrians. He says they accept scripture only up until Moses, but no further, and claim all later prophecy is false. He says—no, he shouts!—that they once built a temple atop Mount Gerizim they claimed was the true Temple. "The *true* Temple! Thank Yahweh that the Maccabees destroyed the thing, an abomination!"

The only time I worry over Father's health is when he discusses the Samaritans.

"What are you?" I ask this, this . . . Samaritan.

"A stone carver. I learned my trade in Samaria but perfected it in Galilee."

A stone carver? Father would haul us from this house in gibbering apoplexy. A lowly stone carver addresses the blood of his blood? I am my father's daughter, and as I stand in this house of strangers, I find myself full of his feelings and teachings, angers and passions. A Samaritan is worse than a Galilean, and as Father would say, a Galilean is bad enough. Even Father's slaves have more distinction than this man. "I know what a stone mason is," I say, knowing I insult him by the use of the word *mason* instead of *carver*.

Salome, high-handed as ever, asks, "Whose house is this?"

"This is the house of Heli bar Nehushtan who is of the Way."

Salome dips her head toward the older man. "That is Heli bar Nehushtan?"

"It is. And unlike myself, he follows an honorable calling, which means he amasses money. Like your guardian, he too is a merchant. Among other priceless spices, Heli exports the juice of the balsam plant. The woman at the gate is Dinah, his wife."

"What is the Way?"

"Ah, we come to the crux of it." Addai's voice is light. Amused, he says, "To know more is to endanger the innocent, by whom I mean you. Not to mention the guilty, by which I mean me."

"Why did Heli bar Nehushtan ask Ananias to bring us here? He has no right to bring us anywhere."

Addai looks back at Ananias. "You are right. These are not mere children. Heli asked to meet you because Ananias has sung your praises from here to Jericho."

"As witches?"

"Heli misspoke. Not as witches, but as prophets."

Salome and I shudder as one. More than the word *witch*, the word *prophet* rings on our ears like doom. Once, prophets were those who made clear God's wishes. These days, prophets are men of business. Where Ananias sells sponges and Father sells glass, prophets now sell visions; for a fee they answer personal questions. These days, the common people are as infected with prophets as a dog is with ticks. If they hear one marketplace crackpot, they endure ten, each one telling them they must follow the Law to its last tittle and dot, must strive for more moral fervor, or perish by the hand of Yahweh.

"Prophets?" My voice squeaks like a small hinge.

Addai laughs like the swinging wide of a great door. His warmth would melt stone. "To be a Deborah or a Miriam or a Noadiah or a Huldah? Is this so terrible?"

Says Salome, "There are no more true prophets, not since the Exile."

Heli rounds on her. "There speaks the ward of an influential man. The influential have no need of prophets."

I look at Addai. "But you are a Samaritan. You cannot believe in prophets?"

"What has been," says he, "can be again." And here he smiles a smile as wide as his wide face, and I cannot help it, I smile back. There is no maintaining fear and foreboding before him. I redeem myself by saying, "Prophets are as common as rocks. Why wish to be another rock?"

The people laugh. In the midst of this laughter, Heli of the Way calls forth a servant, a woman he names Rhoda, and in her hands she bears a tray. My laughter dries in my throat.

There are stones on the tray. There is a pendulum. Heli signals the woman to place the tray on a small stone table, saying, "Ananias has described these things to us. As humbly made as they are, I hope they will serve you as your own."

Tata has come forward, but Salome stays her, "You expect us to perform *kishuf*?" Her color and her voice are high. Not to mention her eyebrows.

"I had hoped," replies Heli, "you would favor us with your gifts."

"Hope is a flown bird."

But I find I trust Addai, stone carver and Samaritan. And if there is yet danger here, I have thought of something that will release us from it.

"I will," I say, and enjoy the surprise followed by the disapproval that clamps down on Salome's face, the shock on Tata's. I pick up the pebbles, arrange them any which way. I take the pendulum, nothing like ours in balance and weight. Everyone has gone quiet. The men lean forward. The wife Dinah leans back. With this, my Salome is returned. I can see it in the curve of her lip as she struggles to keep a straight face; adults have only three reactions to things they do not understand: they fear it or they worship it or they deny it.

Perhaps the first two are the same reaction. The third as well.

The pendulum does not move. I throw it down as if I am exasperated. I slip the silver chain from my neck with its small vial of spikenard. With a flourish, I use this for a pendulum. But this too hangs like a dead thing.

What comes is exactly nothing. Just as I meant to do. Nothing.

I swear I will not be stoned for a witch.

Ananias is ashamed that he has praised us so, and I am pleased to see it. So too am I pleased to see the disappointment of Heli bar Nehushtan and of Dinah, his wife. Though it does not please me that Addai might be cast down. But if not to stone us as witches, what then did they all expect? That Isaiah or Ezekial or Elijah had come among them as a female child? As two female children?

But Salome cannot stand it, she simply cannot. She snatches the alabastron from my hand, rearranges the pebbles in their proper order. What can I do? Salome is Salome. Right away the alabastron steadies under her hand, then begins to slowly swing, picking out one letter at a time. All lean forward in earnest, even the servant Rhoda. I wonder they do not bump heads. If they mean us ill, we are sunk.

The first thing the alabastron spells is the word *silence*. Then in a rush, "Lo, comes the Angel of Silence. Hear ye, children, hearken to the unheard." Salome reads it aloud so that they do not miss a word. I have not heard this before. I catch Salome's eye. Rather than pretend to fail, does Salome pretend to succeed too well, so that she makes no sense at all, thereby confusing and confounding? Ananias is repeating the words under his breath, "The Angel of Silence. Hear ye, children. Hearken to the unheard." Meaning what? he thinks. Is this great profundity? Or great foolishness?

But Addai of Shechem has been staring at Salome; instead of puzzling out the words, he has taken up the mirror from the tray. He has been turning it this way and that, and now he turns to me. The shape is in the mirror again. Something that seems a coiled snake moves like smoke across its surface. I gasp. Salome's eyes dart from the stones to the mirror. As do the eyes of Ananias. "See! Did I not say my little fish were full of wonders?"

"Salome," I gush, "where is the new spell?" I have forgotten that every word we say is witnessed. I have forgotten all but the mirror. We make Tata fish the magical papyrus of Hermas of Ephesus out of her basket, though Salome has to yank on it before Tata lets it go.

"What shall we do for eye paint and the water of a shipwreck?" ask I.

"Words carry more power than any of these things," answers Salome.

I nod—of course! Perhaps no magician would agree, but we have come to think it is not the trappings of magic that make magic but rather the *intent* to make magic that makes magic. But there must be power behind the intent. And it must be done in perfect confidence. Others might believe that this power comes in the form of demons, or from gods. Others might think one must allow a demon to enter one's body, to take on its power, but we do not believe this. We believe power comes from our own intent.

Salome and I quickly speak the words on the papyrus, not taking our eyes from the shape in the mirror, and I see that it responds to us—it responds! But Addai has stepped forward, he has taken the mirror from us, uttering two very foreign words, words that sound as the ripping of cloth. And with that, the mirror is clear. He says, "From this day on, if allowed, I shall care for these two prophets as if they were my own beloved daughters."

I stare at Addai. Salome glares at him. But Heli smiles. "They have endured enough of us," he says. "Take these children home."

As Rhoda ushers us away, as Tata follows a pace behind, I hear Addai speaking to Ananias. "You have spoken truly, my friend, these are indeed *bat qol*. Go. Tell our friends. Have our friends tell friends. But shun the collaborators. Shun even the Poor who await the fall of the Kittim."

I know who the Kittim are; they are the Romans. The Poor are surely those Father made such good fun of at table the night we met Ananias. But I am not sure whom he means by the collaborators. Does he mean Father and Father's friends? I think he does.

Just as we would step through the door, Heli stops us, saying, "Let me show you something." At this, he pulls back a woven cloth that hides the entryway into another room. "Behold," he says. And we do. We see a treasure of books such as we have never seen in one place. "When you return," he says, "you may read as many as you wish."

Return? We shall return?

On the way back to Father's house, I walk on air at the thought of so many books.

Eventually, I ask Salome why she would lead us to Heli bar Nehushtan's house. She answers, "I have no answer, Mariamne."

And so it begins, our new life. Not that we know it is our new life. What we think, Salome and I, is that it is a grand adventure, and that like all childhood's adventures, it shall pass and we will remain where we are and who we are: young females waiting for the day Father arranges our futures by arranging our marriages.

From this day forward, we pester Ananias to take us to Heli bar Nehushtan's as often as he can. Because we are so often disregarded in my father's huge house, it is as easy to do this as Salome once said it would be. And if Ananias cannot take us, then Tata does. Through Heli and Dinah's wonderful home come men of learning, the educated of all nations, men who teach philosophies, men who write poetry, men who wonder at the sun and the moon and the stars and who question the nature of the gods. And there are women! These are not many, but they talk as the men, debate as the men, teach and write as the men. My head spins with the thought of being a woman like these.

We escape Father's white marble house in the Upper City of Zion whenever we can. How exciting to bind our hair, to dress as boys, to follow Tata's instructions in how to move, how to lower our voices, how not to lower our eyes. I need no longer envy Salome her treasures. Tata binds them tight, tight enough to make Salome wince. We do all this so that we may go unnoticed as we make our way down from our high hill and through the streets to Heli's house. This goes on for many months, from the dry season of Iyar to the rains of Marchesvan.

We do not think of how it will feel when it all must end.

As, of course, it must.

I wait behind a door that opens onto Heli's courtyard on this evening in the month of the olive harvest and I prepare myself to speak. Israelites come from everywhere; there are members of a sect who call themselves the Congregation, there is the Brotherhood, the Yahad, the Covenant of Unity. There are the Friends, and the Meek, and the Little Ones, and the Dawn Bathers, and the First, and the Many—and just as Father said, the Many also call themselves the Poor. There is, of course, the Way, though as Addai says, almost every sect from here to Egypt names itself the Way. I have asked him why then do he and his friends do the same? He has not answered.

One can get a headache from all this, trying to know who is who, and why.

I peek out to see who is here. Tonight there are a few Haberim, whom the people call Pharisee, curious to see what the fuss is about, though these are careful to keep themselves apart for fear of being defiled by the touch of the *am ha-aretz,* or "people of the land," the unlearned farmers and fishermen and herdsmen and laborers and such. In return, the *am ha-aretz* turn eyes full of loathing on the Pharisee. I see countless more *am ha-aretz* than Pharisee.

There are a handful of scribes, and for one fearful moment I wonder if any of these know Father, or he them. Then I remember that here we are as boys. Even should they know Father, they would not know Father's daughter or ward in either of us. There are also two Doers of the Law, the Osims or Essenes, in white robes and girdles. Father laughs at the Essene; I once heard him tell Nicodemus that these are so devoted to the exact ritual fulfillment of Torah they do not allow themselves to excrete on the Sabbath. We have never seen one of Father's Sadducee here, but this is not surprising. Father and his friends are rich and powerful, so what need they of change? Besides, they do not believe in angels and rewards and punishments in the world to come. Though it is curious that they do seem to believe in demons.

There is now begun to be a group of scruffy, fierce-looking men who gather in the back, keeping to the walls of the courtyard, and always near the exit. These men wear the roughest of robes, and over their shoulders seem to carry all they own in leather bags. Salome thinks they might be Cynics, followers of the philosopher Diogenes, who believed in living as an animal lives, with great naturalness, and if so, she should like to know them.

I think that the more people who come, the worse the smell.

It does not occur to us to fear what is happening by making our voices public. It does not occur to us what these people might be thinking of us or what they might eventually want from us. We are yet children, and nothing occurs to us but our own happiness at having all these people think us boys, and that we are now listened to.

We make our way through the hot press of people, who hush as they see us, and we seat ourselves on the stone bench by Heli's shell pool. This evening it is Salome who speaks. "A spirit came to me," she begins, "and it said, 'You, son of man, though you have bound yourself in flesh, know that you are a being of Light. There are none who do not walk in the Light.' Do you doubt this?"

And right away a man bent by the years speaks up. "I, Ahad Haam, of the Yahad, doubt this. For he who would walk in shame and corruption cannot also walk in the Light."

We are used to these interruptions; the things the voices say always cause a ruckus. More than once Ananias has cried out for silence, saying that we were *nabi'im*, the mouthpieces of Adonai. People must believe him, because more and more come to hear us. The voice in Salome rises against the old man of the Yahad. "There is not a soul in or under the heavens who is not beloved in the sight of God. Even you, old man, are beloved of God."

By Isis, but comes such muttered concern! Some are full of hope that this is true, and some are furious, for what is the purpose of the Law if all are beloved?

I gaze out over the faces who stare at Salome as she is transported by the voice and my sight comes to rest on someone who is like no other. He is very handsome. He is very young, though not a youth. He has no beard, but shaves as the Romans and Greeks and Egyptians do. Like the Essenes, his clothes are white. His nose is bent. I like his bent nose; it makes him more handsome rather than less. I keep my eyes on him just as he now keeps his eyes on Salome. What is her voice saying? God loves all his creatures? I am surprised. No voice of ours has ever spoken for a god. For which god does it speak? It cannot be Yahweh, for he would not say such a thing. Salome and

I know many gods and goddesses. Would any of these say such a thing? What of the pagans among us who do not give a fig for Yahweh against their own Baal or Dagon or Milkom or Chemosh or Qos? Perhaps it is one of these?

"No!" shouts Ahad Haam, whose friends are urging him on. "This boy does not speak under the power of the Holy Spirit, for we all know that God does not shine on one and all!"

"Not on them, old man, but *in* them," says the voice in Salome.

"Blasphemy!"

"How do you know what is blasphemy and what is not? Do you speak for God?"

"I know what the Law says!"

"You may know what it says, but do you know what it means?"

Salome seems to be growing taller. She is certainly getting louder. But then, so is Ahad Haam. He shrieks, "In Jeremiah, the Lord says: 'I have heard what the prophets have said, who prophesy lies in my name!'"

Salome's voice overrides that of Ahad Haam as a river overrides a rill. "Hear me! He who presumes to know aught for certain knows nothing. And he who presumes to know nothing, stands at the brink of gnosis."

The heat of the people rises. The voice has used a Greek word, *gnosis*. Most do not understand it, but Ahad Haam understands it well enough. *Gnosis* means more than knowledge. It means insight into the divine.

I am not alone when I wonder who speaks here.

"I will not listen to this," says Ahad.

"You will not hear. And yet my voice is all around you. You will not look, yet my face shines in yours."

I press closer to Salome. The face of Ahad Haam is as dark as Father's face when he is crossed by someone of no importance. His breath is like the breath of a winded horse. Behind him, his friends make a show of threat. I catch sight of the handsome young man. His hand is in his robe. Does he carry a Persian dagger at his belt? I reach into his mind to see what it is he sees. I reach further . . . and further . . .

and then I no longer know if it is night or day, past or present or future. I turn away as fast as I can, only to find myself standing. I do not remember standing up. But I am on my feet and I am shouting louder than Ahad Haam of the Yahad or Salome. Much louder. "BEHOLD! I AM COME AMONG THEE ISRA-EL!"

Ahad Haam, Salome, the crowd itself, fall silent. At this moment, a dove winging home to Dinah's dovecote lands on the tall wall keeping out the steep and narrow street beyond. I see this as if I were no more than a cubit away, yet I am across the courtyard. I see every feather in its breast, the tender blue skin around its eye. A number of the big bearded men in the back are moving toward us, pushing people aside. There is an antique among them, an old man with skin as dark as wet leather and eyes as bright as the dove's eye. Tall as a ladder, skinny as a rung, he seems to push harder than the younger men, and when they see it is he, they step back as if he were a leper, or a high priest. My heart is throwing itself against my chest as if it would escape me. I do not want this shouting voice to come. It has not come at Heli's before. Wildly, I look around—there is Salome, as surprised as I. There is Tata and Ananias and Addai and Heli and Dinah and Rhoda. There is the handsome young man. I close my eyes, grind down on my teeth. I will not speak again, I will not, will not.

"HEAR YE, SONS AND DAUGHTERS OF ISSA-RA-EL. FROM THE MOUTHS OF CHILDREN COME I. PREPARE FOR THE COMING DAY. I SHALL MAKE MYSELF KNOWN THROUGH ONE WHO APPEARS AS A SHEPHERD AMONG LAMBS, THROUGH ONE WHO STANDS FORTH AS A LION."

What am I saying? I do not want to hear.

I look around me, the Voice of Voices strong in my throat, and I cannot move. "DID ISSA NOT WALK WITH ME? AND IS THE WORD NOT MY WORD?"

At that, I faint dead away. Later Salome, bathing my face and hands in aromatic oil, tells me that the first to reach my side was the handsome young man. He lifted me and took me to Dinah's private room. His name is Seth, and she tells me he comes from Mount Carmel, which is far to the north. He is a Nazorean, who are not the Many but the Few. But no doubt, this is a play on words, a jest.

As I am put into my own bed in Father's house this night, I ask Tata what she makes of the shouting voice. "I think," says Tata, fussing with my bedding, "that we shall have to find a new courtyard. Perhaps we might try Herod's amphitheater."

∽

Pinning up my hair so that I might seem a boy is a tedious process. Still, Tata manages it. She and I are about to walk out a side entrance of Father's house when I realize I have forgotten my stones. "Tata," I say, "run back and fetch them."

Salome, bundled against the cold rain in a hooded Arabic burnoose, is already outside. As is Ananias, wearing his thick wool mantle and head shawl. They are near the door in the north wall of Father's house, along which runs the side street that climbs up our steep and terraced hill to Herod's palace and the Upper Market. I remember something else I have forgotten, but Tata is already gone. I poke my nose out the door so I might tell Salome and Ananias to wait just a few moments longer even though Ananias is made nervous by the night. Our merchant believes in demons, and demons come out after dark, especially the Queen of Demons, Agrath, daughter of Mahlath.

Just then, a figure enters the street from below, to come striding up the hill, and oh, I would know Father anywhere. I am so terrified I think I might pee myself, but I cannot run away. Perhaps Father will not notice Salome and Ananias? But of course he notices them. What man of property would not take note of two robed figures lingering by his door as the night draws down? Father stops and confronts them. But neither Salome nor Ananias can answer him, for if they do he shall immediately know them. I feel Tata come up behind me; I feel her tremble with the same terror I know.

Ananias is Father's guest and he is standing in the street with Salome. Young females are not allowed out without escort, are not allowed out in the company of men other than their father or their brother or their husband. Father reaches out and violently jerks back the hood of Salome's burnoose, pulling loose her pinned hair. Did he think it was me?

I know what will happen now. What will happen is that my life will change forever. Salome's life will change forever. Father is a proud man, and quick to judge. Ananias is already condemned. Salome is already banished. I am already bereft. *Eloi! Eloi!* I would rush into the street and plead for Salome if I thought Father would listen. I would do anything to stop what is about to happen. But there is nothing I can do, so I do nothing.

"Defiler of children!" Father shouts. "Foul betrayer! Get away from my house. And take this, take this, this—" Father is so monumentally outraged he cannot find a word strong enough, bad enough. He spits, "this *female* with you before I kill you both!"

Ananias can do nothing. To tell the truth would accomplish naught but the betrayal of Heli and Dinah and Addai.

"Leave my house and never return. You, Salome! You will take nothing away with you. You will never speak to Mariamne again."

Salome does not cry and she does not plead. She does not bring up the name of her father, Coron of Memphis, to remind my father of his promise to care for her. She will walk away though she is only thirteen. Where will she go? And who will marry her now?

I can feel Father turn in his mind; the black and bitter rage centered on Ananias and Salome now looks for me. He wonders how much I have been involved in this abomination to his name and to his house. He wonders if I too have been defiled. He wonders what he must do about it.

I spin on my heels and I rush toward our quarters, not stopping to see what Tata does with herself. I tear off the boy's clothes I am wearing, kick them under a clothes chest. I work at my hair, pulling it down as fast as I can. I struggle into my night things, and I manage all this only moments before Father strides into Salome's and my room. I have never seen him like this, never felt him like this. Inside he is like a cave of winds; he does not want to banish me, I am all there is left of my mother. He is terrified that he must punish me as severely as his Law commands him to. A man cannot have the females in his house behave as he believes Salome has behaved. Father lives for the good regard of others. If he thinks I have also behaved in this way, or if I have been of help to Ananias and to Salome, then he has no choice, he must shun me.

I stand silent before him, my head down, my mouth dry, my skin crawling with dread. I could not speak now if it meant my life. I have never been more afraid.

Father has decided I am guilty. Over the years, there is nothing that Salome has done in our house that I have not done as well. I can hear him thinking—rapid, desperate thoughts. Salome is thirteen and expected to know what is moral and what is not. But I am yet under the age of twelve and therefore cannot be legally held to such a standard, and in this he finds a loophole. And a solution: he will pretend he does not suspect me. He will send me away. But not too far and not for too long. Though it shall be far and long enough.

"Mariamne," he says, and I know how much it costs him to control the shaking of his voice. "You will never see Salome again. In the morning you are to travel to Bethany. Tata will accompany you." I almost collapse; I was sure he would have Tata beaten for this. It is her responsibility to watch over Salome and me. "You will live quietly in my brother-in-law's house. You will be a sister to his children." He takes note of the books scattered over table and couch and floor. "There shall be no books!" He ignores my stricken look. "This comes from indulging you with books! There will be no more indulgences from an overly fond father! You will be gone by the time I awake. In time, I will send for you. And for Tata."

I find my voice. It is a very small voice. "How long, Father?"

Father does not look at me. "You will not be a child when you set foot in this house again. Nor will you be without a husband."

With that, he turns his back on me and walks away.

Not until he is gone do I feel Tata grip my shoulder and shake me hard. "Mariamne! Child! What shall we do?"

For the first time I realize how helpless she is. I am only a child, yet a woman asks me what we shall do. Not because she is not strong, not because she cannot think for herself, but because she is a slave and has no right to choose the events in her life. In the midst of all else, I am struck rigid by this discovery; I have never once thought of it. My poor fierce Tata, to be born both a female and a slave. Until now, I have thought nothing save what shall I do? Now I think: what shall we do?

Father's brother-in-law is the husband of my dead mother's sister, Rachel. He is almost as serious as Nicodemus of Bethphage. Their only son, my cousin Eleazar, is a sickly little thing. To live in the house of Uncle Pinhas and Aunt Rachel is to grow old while I am yet a child. Tata will be a slave among slaves, inferior to those who serve the master's own children. My father is rich and important; therefore my female cousin cannot ill treat me. But she shall certainly make Tata and me pay for the shame brought on their house by my presence. And Tata more than me. I have met my cousin Martha. I know this will be so.

And no books! Cicero said that a room without books is like a body without a soul. I cannot live without my soul. Still, to do as my father bids me is the sum total of my duty. What else can I do? What is Salome doing right this very moment? She is going to Heli of the Way's house, that is what she is doing. And then I think this thought: if Salome can go to Heli's house, Tata and I can go to Heli's house.

It is as if all the stars in the sky fall into my mind. I do not have to do what Father tells me. I can feel my heart beating in the tips of my fingers and at the roots of my hair and at the base of my spine. I love Father. I know he loves me. But Father is trapped in his Law and in how he is required to behave. And did not Addai of Shechem say he should care for me as if I were his own beloved daughter?

"Tata, pack a basket with whatever you value most. Then help me pack my things and Salome's things. We are taking as many baskets as we can carry, for we are leaving Father's house."

"To Bethany?" she asks.

"No, not to Bethany."

Tata's spirit would escape out the top of her head if more joy crowded in. Or more fear.

⊂∞

Tata and I arrive breathless at Heli's gate at the second hour of the night, to find all in turmoil. Immediately we are bundled from sight, sent to join Salome who greets us with shrieks of relief and delight. Salome and I cling to each other and await our fate.

In the fourth hour, we are told to rise up and prepare ourselves for travel.

We shall go as males. It seems we are leaving Jerusalem. Having no more to lose, neither Salome nor I object. So it is that we five— Addai the Samaritan, Ananias the merchant, Tata the runaway slave, and two "youths," both outcasts—set off east through the streets of Jerusalem, watched from the shadows by Heli and Dinah of the Way as well as by others we do not know and cannot see. Heli presses a book into my hand as I pass. It is one he treasures, and I weep to receive it. We walk toward the Gihon Spring Gate and the Kidron Valley.

Beyond that, I do not know where we go. I merely follow Addai.

We walk all through the night. Somewhere on the way down through the steeply dropping country to the east of Jerusalem, I fell asleep and Addai picked me up as if I were a swaddled babe. He has carried me now most of the way. Ananias and Tata have walked, a donkey between them bearing our worldly goods. Our worldly goods are not much. Salome has ridden a second, smaller donkey. Barefoot, Addai travels with all that is his, his tools and the female donkey Salome rides. He calls her Eio. Salome whispers that *eio* is Egyptian for ass. I am still surprised at the sponge merchant joining us. Does he not have goods to protect, servants to see to, the Queen of Demons to avoid? But there have been no explanations.

Where are we going? All I know is that we go east, and that the east is the Holy Land, for the east is the place of the coming forth of Helios, the sun. Addai leads us; we follow no path. Even in the dark I can tell the land we travel is as barren as Sarah's womb. From the heights of Jerusalem we have dropped down and down, following the folds in the hills, some of which are as narrow as the streets of Jerusalem and some of which are as deep as tombs. The rain comes and the rain goes, but never enough to wet us through. The night air smells of dirt once baked and now steaming with damp. Tata is not used to such walking, and Ananias frets that we are being led into worse danger than the danger we flee. They both grumble at the thorns that catch at their clothes, the abuse to their feet. Addai shifts my weight and I ask him if I should walk. "Hush, child," he says, "we are very near."

"Near where?"

But he does not answer me. We are walking down a steep *nahal* in the dark, a ravine of bare rocks rising to either side, and only a thin strip of stars to light our way. The air changes. The smell of the air changes. It stinks of rotten teeth. "Addai, what is that nasty smell?"

"Home! This is the land of Damascus."

Damascus? We could not be anywhere near Damascus. Damascus is a hard nine or ten days walk, at best, to the north. But I am too tired to bother with this puzzle. I lay my head back on his shoulder. We drop through a final *nahal,* and before us in the starlight, far as the eye can see, shimmers a still flat sea. It is the sea that stinks.

"Behold," says Addai, "we are where we meant to be."

I behold. Addai points to our left. Perched on sheer steep bluffs of powdery rock is a village. Or maybe it is a fortress. Whatever it is, it looks carved from the soft rock itself. If Addai had not pointed right at it, we might never have seen this place.

It is another hour of hard climbing before we find ourselves near. Addai has led us around a stone wall, and I think there is no gate, until there is. The sun is touching the tops of the mountains on the far side of the flat and stinking sea when we pass through this gate. We are in a courtyard, as deep as it is wide. Beside us rises a stone tower the height of many men. Over to our right, there are steps leading to a huge stone pool. And right in the middle of the court-yard is a simple sundial on a dais. Father's sundial is twice as big, but Father prefers that things of value be seen. Straight ahead there is another gate that leads out of the courtyard into what looks to be a narrow street.

Leaving our donkeys tethered to a post beside a small cistern, Addai leads us to this gate and through it. Where are we? Is there anyone here at all?

My question is answered a moment later.

Out of the shadows cast by the rising of the sun from beyond the stinking sea steps the handsome man in the perfect white linen tunic.

"How welcome you are, Ananias of Alexandria," says the man who has called himself one of the Few. "I see you have brought our children home."

Salome and I dart startled looks at each other. *Remember what the Voice said*, she is saying. *Remember?* Ananias is come to take you home.

I remember.

The Wilderness

It is more than a month from the evening Father sent us away. We are in the wilderness, lost to the lives we once lived, lost to the city of our childhood, lost to all we knew, lost to our very gender. More alien than the place are the people. We are children of wealth and privilege. These are poor nobodies! We are children of taste and gorgeous artifice. Here, our floor is dirt, our walls are skin and hair, our *dukha* is a stick for digging a hole in the ground.

Here, there is no one to fan away the heat that wilts us, no one to brush away the biting ants that torment us in our beds. No one comes to bathe us, to comb our hair, to clean away what we have messed, to bring us sweets. No one but Tata. But as we are now males and she is not, she lives with the women. This is nothing as it was at Heli and Dinah's house; it is not a grand adventure.

For the first time in our lives, we are bit by bugs, stepped on by camels, shoved aside by strangers, made to fetch and to carry, slapped by cooks, shooed away by potters, shouted at by men. And oh, how

we rush to the poor tents we've been given, there to stomp around
and to howl when we discover we can no longer eat whenever we
like or whatever we like.

In short, we are miserable.

We make Tata miserable. We cling, or we demand, or we complain,
until one day she rounds on us, saying, "By all the salt in all the sea,
how thoughtless are the young! If there is that which does not feel,
save furies of the body, and the spirit caught up solely in the self, it is
you two!" And then she tugs her skirts from our hands and walks
away. We do not see her again for two whole days. It surprises us,
even quells us for an hour or so, but it does not stop us. We remain
insufferable.

The merchant Ananias comes and goes on his travels. Addai spends
much time in Jerusalem working on the construction of the dead
Herod's Temple, a task that has lasted his kind for more than forty
years. But Salome and Tata and I never go anywhere at all.

We see no reason to climb down more than once through any of
the deeply cut nahals just to find ourselves on the shores of a sea that
stinks of sulfur and bitumen. There is nothing there, not even a wharf,
though boats go by below us daily.

Addai tells us we are fortunate to arrive in the season of the rains.
He swears that all through summer, day and night, one can bake
bread on the flat clay roofs, but for now the winter sun shines off the
smooth lime-stoned walls in light as white as linen. It takes days
before my eyes grow used to this, and to the lack of color. There are
only the pale yellows of the dry cliffs above and below us, the
pale yellows of the high flat shelf where the settlement stands,
the pale dusty green of the palms, and the lapis lazuli blue of the
pools. There seem more pools here than in the whole of Jerusalem,
and from each to each, sweet blue water flows through canals cut in
the yellow rocks.

As for the buildings within the yellow walls, some are as high as
three stories. The tower is higher than this and, oddly, has no entrance on the ground floor. But no building is a house. It is either a
meeting hall or an eating hall or a workshop or a flour mill, or it is

full of storage rooms, but never a sleeping chamber. People sleep in tents north of the outer walls. Addai tells us many more sleep in the caves that are all around us in the high and dusty cliffs. I shudder at the thought—no matter how hot the night, I would not sleep in a cave for my life. There are sand rats in caves. There are vipers in caves.

We have come to know the handsome young man with the bent nose, Seth of Damascus. When he finds us idle, he produces books from somewhere, and we devour them . . . we would read anything, and we gaze on Seth's books as a drunkard might gaze on a vat of wine. For example, the Book of Enoch. In Genesis it says that a thousand generations ago Noah and Enoch walked with God, but only Enoch vanished because God took him. But the Book of Enoch says more. "And I looked and saw a lofty throne. Its appearance was transparent hailstone, its wheels like the sun, and then the sight of the cherubim. From underneath the throne came streams of fire so that I could not look directly at it. The Great Glory sat there. His raiment shone more brightly than sun and was brighter than snow."

Though I have never spoken of it, I know what Enoch saw, for I too looked and saw a Great Glory as I lay ill, and I tremble in my skin to read another try to describe it.

Though he is young himself, Seth seems always at a distance, always watching, always weighing. Sometimes it seems he is become our shadow. He also becomes our uncle. If anyone asks, and many do, they are told I am John, and Salome is Simon, and that we are kin to Seth. This silences them immediately. Seth explained the need to remain male like this. "If you are female, you will be treated as females." That was all that Salome needed to hear. Young Simon and younger John have appeared as prophets in the wilderness, and we are both respected and avoided.

Tata has had a great deal to say on the subject of our being males, much more than when we merely went to Heli's house. Here we must learn how to stand, how to sit, how to make this gesture or that. Salome moans about binding her treasures, and worries about her menses, a thing that now visits me. But Tata has an herb for our monthlies. It does not stop them, but it makes them so much less and so much easier to hide. She makes sure our cloths are taken from us when needs be, that they are smuggled into the woman's camp and buried there. Tata also tutors us in our choice of phrase so that we do not say things as a female might, nor abase ourselves before our fellow males without thinking. Where did Tata come by all this knowledge?

Above all, Tata tells us, is the matter of being "cut." If the removal of their foreskin isn't the single most important thing, after the member itself, in a Jewish male's life, I don't know what is. It marks him as chosen; it is the blood covenant he has made with God. Salome says you would think if God wanted to mark a man chosen, he might have left this bit off their person in the first place. Now, *that* would be a mark.

Here in our wilderness, people are daily coming or going: old, young, men, women, children, whole families, Jews as well as Gentiles. Our small open spaces are so often packed with travelers and their animals, with asses and dogs and goats and sheep and camels, the encampments so swollen with tents or simple bedding under the stars, or the caves so filled to overflowing, it is like Jerusalem at Passover. These visitors seek out Seth or Addai or others we do not yet know. The travelers are ill, or they are wounded, or they are troubled in their minds. Some come to bathe in the large basin set aside for them. Some come for the prayer. More come for the herbs, or poisons, or potions that are traded here or grown here. All come for miracles. Some never leave but are buried in the cemeteries on the edge of the cliffs.

Yet not all who arrive are ill. Nor are they blind or crippled or possessed. Some are the men who stood recently at the edges of Heli's crowded courtyard, the hairy, wild-eyed men. All these are sons of Israel no matter if they are Samaritans or if they are Galileans or even Ituraeans. I am confused and confounded by them. Some are armed and some are not. Some men in the same sect carry knives and others do not. Ananias is certainly right: there are more divisions in an Israelite's belief than I should ever have imagined. And all spend much time arguing with each other! Each evening at table, we hear them. They shout, they wave chunks of bread, they turn their backs on each other. Salome says they speak much more of war, revenge, and righteous hatred than of the nature of their god. Or perhaps, adds she, such things *are* the nature of their god.

Meanwhile, though all who are Jews have the same god, not one of them can agree on how to approach him or to honor him. What they do agree on is that God, who is male, is the only God. By this they do not mean YHVH is supreme among gods. They mean that there are no other gods or goddesses at all. They mean that those that claim to be gods—Baal and Isis and Zeus and so forth—are demons. By the hour, they assure themselves that the One and Only God has singled them out especially. They swear they are *am segulah*, God's treasured people.

Salome and I have discussed this before Addai as we should never have discussed it before Father. In Father's house there was never much talk of Yahweh. But here it is as if he were only in the next city and were due home at any moment, and all were women crazed to ensure he would be pleased by how tidy his house, how obedient his children, how full his coffers. We question: if the Jew is the jewel of all creation, why did God bother with any others in the first place? Salome also asks what has happened to God's wife? Tata tells us Yahweh once had a wife, and one of her names was Shekinah, and another was Asherah, and another was Astarte. She tells us they lay together in the Temple's Holy of Holies as the Bride and the Bridegroom. But where is Shekinah now? Has Yahweh driven her from the marriage chamber? Is the Bride of God lost and alone?

Addai listens but expends no effort on answering us, save to say, "I once heard it said that none of us know anything, not even whether we know anything or not." Though he does suggest that perhaps my father's people were chosen because all other peoples turned him down. At this, I honk with laughter, but Salome laughs so much harder I have to pound her on the back.

The Poor make their home here, and have a council of elders who meet in a large room near the potteries. Save those who swagger about with knives in their belts and flint in their eyes, all are busy.

Some of the men fish in the river Jordan, the mouth of which is a few miles away, or set out over the stinking sea in small salt-encrusted boats to collect the rare and precious floating rocks, which is tarry bitumen. Some labor in the fields of barley and wheat and some labor in the smaller fields of madder and other medicines growing wherever there is room. This medicine is used by the ill who daily arrive, or decanted into small bottles and sent up to Jerusalem with Ananias, but the bulk of it is traded with the Arabian tent people whose encampments fill the mountains of the Moab far across the Sea of Salt.

One thing that does not occur here is the sacrifice of animals. Those in the settlement honor the Sabbath, they chant the Shema at dawn and at dusk, and they observe the Holy Days, but there are no priests and there is no Temple. Father would be baffled. Nicodemus would be incensed. Both would ask why a man should have to do his own praying. Are there not priests for this? Is this not what priests are for?

In Jerusalem, there is not a day save the Sabbath where people are not sacrificing some living thing in *asham*, a guilt offering as atonement for some infraction or other, or to make peace between this one or that one, or as an *olah*, a personal repentance, or to give thanks for whatever it is they feel thankful for. From early until late, there is such piteous shrieking and such helpless bleating, and there are days on end when the wind does not blow, and a haze of burnt flesh hangs over Jerusalem like a winding sheet.

But here, this is not so. The air is clear, and Salome and I are set to guarding a secret grove of balsam trees, for the "white tears" of the balsam is worth twice as much as silver. Seth has shown us its true gift; more than a perfume or a royal oil, it stops the flow of blood and it deadens pain. I begin tending my tiny crooked trees as I would my own scrolls. We have also charge of a grove of carob trees and date palms that grow far up a steep-sided wash of gravel. Leading nowhere, this ravine, or *nahal*, narrows as it goes until it is seemingly impassable, so is home only to a family of feeble folk, one of the four things scripture says are "little on earth, but they are exceedingly wise." Fat and furry, short of leg and small of ear, these hyraxes hide in the rocks, barking in alarm if we come near.

Here there is a small spring that waters our palms and our carobs, and a space of soft sand bounded by a huge rock like a bowl that each day is warmed by the winter sun until it becomes a thing of great pleasure to lie in. We cannot be seen from the settlement and no one from the settlement can see us. Of course, immediately this becomes our private place. *Kishuf* is a thing of horror to the Poor, so we keep our word stones and our magical papyri hidden not in our small tent in the men's encampment but here near the homes of the feeble folk. As Salome says, "Let their barking be of use."

As the days pass, we explore the desert above us and the Salted Sea below us. We have seen a thin red fox catch a fat brown sand rat, and once sat for hours watching big black ants devour some sad fallen songbird, until it was nothing but feathers and bones and beak. We have walked by the crystalline shore of the toxic sea picking up balls of gypsum, cracking them open for the yellow sulfur inside. The mud is black and stinks beyond words. Once we dared go farther, climbing for hours among the bluffs over the sea, and there entered a cave littered with shells and bones. In this cave we found three small figures made of lime plastered over reeds. They are all female and their femaleness is too evident for comment. Who made these things? No Jew would make such things. How old are they? We have wrapped them in cloth and hidden them with our other things up our private *nahal*.

We think perhaps we might go farther still, strike out for Jericho, the Moon City that Moses saw from the top of Mount Nebo before he died, or for Egypt, for if we are boys, surely we can go where we please? When the time comes, Salome has concluded, and I have agreed, we shall gather up Tata and flee. In the meantime, we shall prepare ourselves for a life on the road. First, we will learn the fine art of spying. And second, we will learn *kishuf* from Addai; not spells and magical rites but tricks of the hand and eye. Such skills will keep us from going hungry as we travel.

We take ourselves to our hiding place amidst the date palms and carob trees. Eio and the barking hyraxes on guard, we hide in the dusty heart of the fat brown trunks so that Addai might show us how to divert the eye, how to say one thing and do another, how to delude the mind. In no time, we learn to pluck objects from the air. Make things disappear. Produce scented oil or blood from the palms of our hands. Cause mirrors to cloud and sticks to become snakes. I revel in this. I practice for hours. I even think I might have a gift for *kishuf,* and Addai agrees. Though I suspect Salome's gift is the greater. I am sure Addai agrees with this as well. In any case, he tells us that the spirit in the mirror is more than the usual magician can do, and more than the usual magic.

We use our word stones. We talk as we have always talked, long and loudly. But we do not laugh as we used to, we are not indulged. We do not know where home is, or what will become of us. Still, I ask myself, is the life of a prophet to be preferred to the life of a wife and mother? Is the life of a poor male to be preferred to the life of a rich female? This is my answer: it is worth it. Though we are afraid and though we plan for the day we will run away, I have never known such freedom.

At supper this evening, one wild man has bitten off the ear of another wild man. Salome has leapt from her seat. Just as have I. Just as has every man here, some fierce in support of one wild man, some in support of the other, some in support of neither. Names are shouted out: "Athronges!" "Simon!" "Judas of Galilee!" "John the Baptizer!" And names are shouted down. There are cries of outrage and threat. The din in the dining hall brings more men running. *Yea Balaam!* I cannot believe I see this! I cannot believe its cause: the man who has lost an ear calls someone named Judah the Priest messiah; the man who has bitten it off calls someone named Zakkai the Hidden messiah. And now others name their messiahs. And all at the top of their voices and all at the ends of their fists.

Salome has darted forward the better to view this growing mayhem. I too would dart forward but am halted in my tracks. Seth has come from somewhere and grips my belt so that I get nowhere. Beside us, Addai, who was also not here a moment ago, pushes by in quick pursuit of Salome. He catches her just as she is climbing up on a bench between a man who calls down curses on one and all and another who shakes his fist. Salome too has her belt gripped and is pulled backward and away from the gathering melee. In moments, we are pushed from this place and out into the clear night air, as more and more men rush into the dining hall.

Though we moan to miss the madness, Addai chases us into our tent. He makes a small fire so that we might be warm and we might see. Seth does nothing but stand by the tent opening and watch him. Salome does nothing but grumble, but I watch Seth. How is it that he is near by night and by day, and yet we scarcely know it?

Nothing is said as Addai builds his fire, but when it is done, he looks to Seth, asking, "How long before our people erupt? This year? Next year?"

Shrugging, Seth seats himself. "These are the End Times, and if they are not, more and more men believe them to be so."

I ask, "Do you believe them to be so?"

Seth turns his regard full on me. "The Queen Bee speaks." Why does he call me Queen Bee? What does it mean? "And I answer her like this, the Poor claim the days are come when Good and Evil contend one with the other. They say it is now that Evil will bring the greatest misery to humanity, and more than misery to the Chosen of God. It is the time foretold for the coming of the Messiah."

I ask again, "Do you believe this?"

"God has chosen and set aside one nation of all the nations of the world, neither numerous nor powerful, to be the recipient of his laws—"

"The Jews," sighs the Samaritan Addai.

"And by observing them, to offer an example, a witnessing to all nations." Seth raises sparks with a stick. "But it seems a whole people cannot be expected to carry such a burden, so it has come down to an elect to provide this obedience. But of these elect, there begin to be those who are zealous and who look for a messiah in the form of a warrior king. In this they prepare for a war between Light and Dark."

Addai raises a brow. "This night they prepare by practicing on one another."

Seth allows himself a smile. I, who have never seen him smile, am dazzled. "But we are the Nazorean, and we do not prepare for a war between Light and Dark. Nor do we look for a warrior king."

Salome plants her feet in the dirt before Seth. "Tell me what you mean by Nazorean or I will go mad."

I did not think Seth of Damascus could laugh! When he is finished laughing, he says, "I would not see you mad, Simon who is called by Addai 'magician.' Therefore, calm yourself, and listen. The people of Israel became one under the messenger Moses. But after the long and terrible exile in Babylon there was sent to the Israelites not one, but two further messengers: first Ezra, then Issa."

I say, "Issa? The Loud Voice said, 'Did Issa not walk with me?'"

If Seth has heard me, he makes no sign, but continues, "Ezra chose certain writings and said these were the holiest writings, the only writings. These were Torah. Ezra's followers became the Jews. But Issa did not believe in the choices Ezra made, and those who thought as Issa thought became the Nazoreans. It is the belief of the Nazorean that it is they who are the true Israelites."

Salome, an Egyptian, is amused, but I as a Jew am shocked. "You mean Father and Nicodemus and Caiaphas are Jews, but to you this is not the same thing as true Israelites?"

Seth answers me most solemnly. "Ezra was then as the high priest Caiaphas is today. Caiaphas takes his power from Rome; Ezra took his from Persia. It was Persia, not God, who walked behind Ezra. Do you think the people of Moses would smile on Persia, and now on Rome? Would they see who serves the Temple and be content?"

Salome laughs. "I would not tell the father of Mariamne such a thing."

"But he *is* told," interrupts Addai, "as is the high priest, as are the Pharisee and the Sadducee. Many among the Nazorean have grown weary in their telling and become impatient, *more* than impatient. They begin to think of themselves as the soldiers of god. There are only a few of us left who do not see blood as an answer."

I stiffen in understanding. "The daggermen. These are Nazorean?"

Seth moves away from the fire. I can no longer see his face as he speaks from the shadows. "The Queen Bee asks if they are Nazorean? Only insofar as they attach themselves to the teaching and teachers of Issa. John calls these men Zealots for the Law and hopes to contain them."

I wonder, but do not ask, who this John is. There are so many called John, myself among them. I find a small voice to ask only this, "Why do you call me Queen Bee?"

"For the Voice within you. The ancients called such a one as you Pure Mother Bee, as they called all the queens who ruled in the age of the matriarchs." I would that I had not asked, for I clearly see that Salome hurts not also to be called Queen Bee. Seth speaks on, "I say the Sicarii are fools and I fear them, for by their bloodletting they would destroy us all, Jews as well as Nazorean. Because of this, we of the inner Nazorean keep to ourselves as much as possible. As for what those who have broken with us call themselves, most are now the Poor. Or they are the men of Issa, Issa-ene or Essene. They await the Anointed One."

"But the Nazorean do not await a warrior king?"

"The true Nazoreans look for the coming perfection of man, a transformation of being the like of which has never been seen on this earth."

I am dazzled by the thought of such a messiah. A perfection of man? I am suddenly struck by what the Loud Voice said, I shall make myself known to thee through the one who appears as a Shepherd among Lambs, through the one who stands forth as a Lion. Has a voice in me prophesied the Messiah of the Nazorean? Frantic that somehow I have something to do with such things, I signal Salome, but she does not see me. "This Issa," she says, "I would hear of him."

Seth answers her, "I will tell you what is said of Issa, to show what men make of a man who confounds them. There are those who claim Issa was born of a virgin called Mari, that he was not human but divine, that he performed miracles and raised the dead, that he was crucified, taken up into heaven, and that he will come again as the Messiah."

Salome shouts with laughter. "But as you are true Israelites and not pagans, surely you cannot believe this?"

"Issa was a son of man. As we all are. Is this not miracle enough?" Seth then turns his attention to Addai, saying, "It is not long before we must leave this place."

Later this night, as we prepare our meager blankets for sleep, and close the dusty flap to our small tent, I whisper to Salome, "It is not long before we too must leave this place."

A large caravan is in from the north. It is said this caravan will be among us for three days and three nights, and then will continue on to Gaza, the gateway to Egypt. Gaza is a Greek city, which means that though it is full of Jews, it is also full of everyone else. It is a cosmopolis, a universal city. In it live poets and philosophers and satirists. This is all we need to hear. When the caravan leaves, Salome and I mean to go with it.

On the second evening of the caravan's arrival, a strange cold makes the air seem solid, as if we could step off the cliffs over the Sea of Salt and walk away on cold alone. In the third hour of the night, Salome and I sneak as close as we dare to the fire of the camel drivers and the muleteers. These are camped outside the west wall and the hub-bub they make is more than the entire wilderness at its noisiest. We shelter behind the bulk of a sleeping camel, huddle against its flank for warmth. *Yea Balaam*, but camels stink! We peek over its skinny curve of a neck. There is more than one fire, for this is a large caravan. There must be five or six fires. There are women and children around one, what seem fairly wealthy merchants around another, simple travelers around a farther two, and off near the cliffs there are three tents that stand by themselves. There are camels with *hoodahs* on their backs, the largest of which is shrouded all in black. We should certainly spy on these first, all three tents look finer than any Father has, and as for *hoodahs—Eloi! Eloi! Eloi!* What do I see! The daggerman who stabbed the Temple priest is mere cubits from our camel!

Like a great tree, he stands planted before the sparking campfire, the skin of his thick legs and his thick arms and his thick neck and

his fat cheeks above his black beard as ruddy as a roasted calf in the
fire glow. Before our eyes, he boasts of his killing. He describes the
stabbing of Ben Azar to a circle of seated men, all leaning toward
him. We hear the man's name: Simon of Capharnaum. In a voice
thick with the unpleasant accent of Galilee, Simon of Capharnaum
shouts out that he has killed other priests in other towns. He proclaims that he has killed Roman soldiers. He has burned whole villages of those he thought loved Rome. He killed a man in Jericho
because the man was a Jew and would not be cut. He swears he
would kill any Jew who polluted the Law, any Roman who sup-
pressed those who kept it. "I have a brother and a son and a dozen
cousins who would do as I do!" So shouting, he pulls a man to his
feet, a man who looks nothing like him and is a full head shorter.
This man glances round as if someone would kill him, and is speechless at the prospect. "This is my brother Andrew, a man every bit as
righteous as myself!" Simon shoves his brother back down again, and
here he stops his shouting long enough to glare about him. There
comes a dreadful moment when I think he can see us behind our
camel. No one moves; no one dares say a word as he tells them that
the Lord will bring about the Last Days and that is certain, but he
will not bring it with plague or with flood, no! He will bring it
through the righteous anger of his Sons of Light. He tells them that
he, Simon of Capharnaum, does God's work, and that he waits for a
man, a very king! "And then! And then! 'We will make the people
drunk with the Lord's fury!'"

   I see men listening who have long argued that no man can act for
God. I see the ear biter who has forever sworn that the Anointed
One has already come and he is Zakkai the Hidden. I see the man with
one ear who claims he is a certain Judah the Priest. I see men who
love John the Baptizer. Any moment, one or all of these men will
surely leap up and run to Jerusalem in a night so that they might
smite a Roman.

   Now he is telling them what occurs up in Jerusalem, and as I listen my throat closes in fear. Simon and his brother are not only stabbing priests in the Temple, they are breaking into the houses of the

rich. Simon swears that soon they will not just plunder the rich, they will kill them, and he laughs that the priests and the Sanhedrin and Rome stand helpless. I am frantic with concern for Father. Simon promises the robbing and the killing will go on until all righteous men will take heart, and arise. Then they will drive Rome and men like my father, children of the pit, from the land. The men who hear him snarl and shout out curses. Their hatred thickens the air until I cannot breathe.

I reach into the mind of this Galilean daggerman. It is as hot as his breath and as red as his rage. But to steal a man's life and call it good? Father taught us no such thing. Our reading of philosophy has taught us no such thing. My heart tells me no such thing. Are these men right and all others wrong? If they do God's work, has God gone mad?

I feel as if my illness is with me again, I feel as if I will once more sink into the heated dark where the shouts of this world become whispers.

"Come away," Salome hisses. "We will wait for the next caravan."

In that instant, a hand comes down on my shoulder, and I see an arm go round Salome's slender neck. "What is this!" shouts the owner of the arm. The hand on my shoulder is a vise, its grip so strong I think my bone must break under it. We are shoved forward, out into the light of the campfire.

And all we can see is Simon of Capharnaum.

His hand is instantly under his mantle in threat. There must be a hundred fevered men here, and of these most are not his men, but men from the settlement. "And who are these among you?" he asks.

There comes a great stirring among the men of the settlement. Most of them know us; all know Seth and Addai. I cannot follow so many minds at once—what are they thinking? Simon has asked the men holding us to bring us closer. "Mere boys, eh? You would hear the talk of men?"

Salome does not dare to open her mouth. If this man were to find we are not boys, but girls, what should he do? What should all these men do? Simon turns his huge face to mine. I am close enough to smell his breath, made rotten by the stump of a broken eyetooth. I am so close he can poke me in the chest, saying, "Speak up, boy!" As he touches me, there comes over his face a puzzlement. His thoughts have not caught up with what the flesh of his finger is telling him, but they might.

"Tell me your name so I should not forget it. And tell me the name of this other, so that I might not forget his name."

Salome finds the strength and the wit to say, "His name is John of the family of Seth of Damascus. My name is Simon of the family of Seth of Damascus. He is my brother. Why do you question him?"

I am amazed at how she sounds—like a proud youth caught in a prank.

At the name of Seth of Damascus, the eyes of this Simon narrow. "Seth of Damascus," he mutters more to himself than to us, "how comes young kin of a Maccabee to the wilderness?" And then, with a suddenness that catches me completely unprepared, he grabs my upper arm and shakes me, glaring about the campsite, picking out faces in the intently listening crowd. "Is there a Maccabee here? Is there another who is blood to such?"

My thoughts scramble for grip. Seth is a Maccabee? Our Seth is come from the Great Family of Heroes who took back the Temple of Solomon and seized the throne of Israel for the first time since the days of David and Solomon! By all the stars, how wonderful! Is not Hanukkah observed to celebrate the rededication of the Temple by Judas Maccabeus? And yet how sad. For the Maccabee were later sought out and killed by Herod the Great. No wonder Seth is held in such high regard!

A great fuss comes among the men of the settlement as someone pushes forward from the back. I pray it is Seth, and breathe again as they make room for his coming because it *is* Seth. Right behind him walks Addai. And though my joy at their arrival is immense, I find that I am still privy to the thoughts of Simon. This Galilean is a jumble of contradictions. He is both brave as a bull, yet craven as a stoat. He believes himself a man of vision, yet longs to see. He would follow the first man who promised him what his heart desires, but he could not name his heart's true desire. He is full of hatred, yet yearns to know love. I pity him. I am afraid of him because he would crush my pity if he knew it. To him, Addai as a Samaritan is not worth a single thought, but he knows Seth. He fears him. He wonders: Could this man lead to the coming king? Could he be that king? Should he align himself with a Maccabee? Or shun him?

I have never touched a mind so calculated and so conflicted.

"I am kin, Simon Peter of Galilee," says Seth. "Is there reason you find fault with John and with Simon? If so, I shall answer for them."

With a gesture, Seth requires Simon to loose his grip and I find I am as well released from Simon's thoughts. The relief could not be more profound. As Addai gathers us up, pushes us away, my last glimpse of Seth is as he speaks to a man who has stood beyond the light of the fire, one who comes forward, and places his hand on Seth's shoulder while all others give them room. Eloi, but I have seen him before! I have seen also the one who shadows him, as alike to his brother as one grain of millet is to another. The brothers have hair and beard of Thracian red, and I saw them last standing near to Simon of Capharnaum as he stabbed the Temple priest not once, but thrice. As I am pulled away, I hear Seth name them in greeting: Yehoshua and Jude.

When we are once more near our own tent and he is sure we are not followed nor overheard, Addai rounds on us. His voice is low but his passion high. "What you do and who you are affects more than your own skins!" Salome hangs her head. By this, I know she knows his anger is just. I too hang my head. "If you are found to be females, what would happen to Seth who has spoken for you?"

"It would not go well," I say to him.

"Not well! It would go badly, very badly."

He closes our tent flap, commands that we remain inside, that he will be back, and until he is, we are to speak to no one. All we are to do is to wait.

And then he is gone, and Salome and I are left gaping. Salome says "Why do Addai and Seth do this? Who are we to them that we endanger them so?"

My very thought. Indeed, why should they?

Daughters of the Nazorean

Though the camp and the caravan settle in all around us, though fires burn low and it is sure by now that everyone sleeps, Salome and I are frantically whispering. By Isis, where shall we be tomorrow? Still here, waiting for another caravan? Should we choose other than Egypt? We cannot go back to Jerusalem for Father would not take us back into his house. Perhaps north to the true Damascus? Or better yet, Tarsus! I long to see Tarsus, the city of Posidonius, the great astronomer, who devised a machine to show the workings of the sun and the planets and even the stars. Were Tarsus ever mentioned in front of Nicodemus, he would sputter. "Mysteries and abominations!"

Oh yes, I should love to go to Tarsus.

I am suggesting leaving it in the hands of a god or a goddess when Addai suddenly pokes his head into our tent, completely unexpected. "Hush and rise up. I have someone I wish you to meet."

I shut my mouth in the middle of a hissed word. "Who?" asks Salome.

"A great teacher," he replies, already walking away.

A teacher? Immediately we throw warm mantles over our youth's tunics and hurry after Addai. We reach the same gate in the wall we reached the first day ever we saw this place, and enter it. Once again we are in the courtyard of the small sundial. Near the tower he stops us. "Sicarii," he whispers, pointing up as we press ourselves to the stones. I look up. Above us, a watchman by night passes along the edge of the top of the tower. But this is not Sicarii; this is merely a zealous man. Suddenly, I am chilled by understanding—all of them are Sicarii. They are all terrorists and killers! This is why there is no easy entrance to the tower, why there are no houses or bedchambers here. This is why our camp sits high on a cliff set back from the Sea of Salt. How foolish I have been, not to have realized this sooner. These are the very men Rome would seek out and destroy. *Eloi! Eloi!* We are in a seething nest of them.

When the daggerman moves away from the lip of the tower roof, Addai edges along the tower wall, around the jutting of a small storage room, then slips through a door in a farther wall, and we slip through too. We find ourselves in a perfectly square room that is mostly a set of steep stone steps leading up to the tower roof. Here, it is darker than the moonless night. Following Addai, we move quickly through this square room of steps and into a long rectangle of a room that lies on the opposite side of our entrance. Addai holds his finger to his flat nose and stands waiting. It is not long before we know why. Seth comes in out of the dark of the evening. He does not look at us. But I look at Salome, and she agrees. He is still very angry. A moment later, Tata steps into the room. Tata? What great goings-on are these? Tata glances our way but makes no other sign that singles us out. I fully expect Ananias to enter as well, but he does not; instead comes a woman whose head is covered. The woman lights a small earthenware oil lamp, cupping her hand round the flame, and by this, I see that her skin is as black as pitch. I poke Salome, but Salome is glaring at Tata, offended that Tata betrays us by keeping a secret. But what is the secret?

The woman as black as the night guides us to a door. Behind it there are only steps hewn into solid rock. The steps lead down into rooms below, storage rooms lined with bins full of foodstuffs, things that are better preserved by the chill and the dark. By the flickering light of one small lamp, no one of us speaks, no one moves. Are we hiding? Salome and I glance at each other; she makes one of our signs: *if so, from whom?*

The woman of the south walks forward, toward long-necked jars of oil and baskets of last summer's grain. She and Seth together move a certain heavy pot and then the larger one behind it. Behind this is a wall of stone, rougher and older than all other walls. Seth moves this stone and she that stone, and then, to my utter amazement, a door opens through which he and Tata and the woman I hear them call Helena promptly disappear.

"Go," we hear Addai say. "It will take you where only the Few may go."

I duck my head and wriggle through the hole in the wall, Salome right behind me, to find that we go not to another room, but into a tunnel, a bore going down through the stone in which there are very narrow and very steep steps. I keep hold of Salome until we reach a bottom, far underground. It is cool down here and sounds echo. Addai shoos us along another tunnel after Seth and Tata and Helena whose light is far ahead.

We follow them, passing other chambers to our left and to our right, until we come on one that is perfectly round. Instantly my heart races with joy. I care nothing that there are stone benches here, or that lamps are placed high in the round walls, or that there is a round bath in the middle of the round room. What matters are the books halfway from floor to ceiling. Books! Here is where Seth finds books! And here I notice the ceiling. A vaulted dome, round as the heavens and full of painted stars. There is the moon and there is the sun, both shining in the sign of Pisces, the Fish. And in the middle, a sign. It seems also a fish, but a fish made of two circles. What does it mean?

In this vaulted chamber wait two others. One has the face of an actor—there is certainly an actor's conceit written on it. But the other stands as tall as a ladder and as thin as a rung and I know him immediately. He was the ancient who pushed himself forward in the house of Heli of the Way when the Loud Voice spoke. Salome kicks my ankle. By this, I know she knows him too. We both think, Surely this cannot be the great teacher?

The old man folds himself onto one of two stone benches at the edge of the pool; the others sit here or there. There seems no ordering of class or worthiness. There is only the feeling that since the old man has seated himself, so too shall the others.

But not us.

Addai signals that Salome is to remain on her feet, that she is to continue silent. This too I must do. Then he himself takes a seat near to Tata so that my friend and I now stand alone. I am jumping with nerves. Where is the great teacher, the sage, the *tzadik*? Will he appear from one of the tunnels? In my mind's eye, I conjure up someone greater than the magician Hanina ben Dosa or the sorceress Megas. Will he strike us dumb? Or will he answer our questions? Will he tell us whose books these are? Beside me, I feel Salome tremble.

Seth now does something very surprising. He stands, he places himself before the ancient and then he bows with his palms pressed together like an Arab. "Things have not gone well, John," he says. "Our children have made themselves known."

The old man's mouth is as small as a pebble. "Nothing goes well. Though it goes as it must." He lifts a bony hand to point at himself, but he speaks to me and to Salome. "I am John of Kefar Imi. Few and Many and many more call me John the Baptizer."

By the moon, Addai has brought us to the madman of the river, who, by his terrible accent, is another Galilean! Salome and I are made to stand before the infamous John the Baptizer, he who so inflames Father and all his friends? I cannot help it, I gape at this rung of a man talked of in every house in Jerusalem; John the Baptizer gapes back. "Come here, girl," he says.

Girl? He knows my sex! I creep forward until I am only a cubit away from John of the River. He is buried in his robe. Covering his head is a cloth of brown. His beard is a wild thing. I follow the hard fold of skin from his nose to his mouth.

"I have seen there is a *bat qol* within you," says he. "I saw this at the house of Heli bar Nehushtan as I now see my own hand." He thrusts his hand in my face. "I saw this as I see the toes on my foot." Glancing down, I see his feet are as camel's feet. I spend a moment fearing he will thrust his foot in my face as well, but he does not. "I know you are a Daughter of the Voice." He plucks at my clothing, pulls me closer. "You know what is said about those who are visited by a *bat qol*? It is said they are mad and will only grow the madder."

I think, John the Baptizer ought to know, is he not a prophet too, and a Galilean?

Seth startles me by speaking. "Socrates once said our greatest blessings come to us by way of madness."

"Socrates was a Greek." John has turned his head slightly in Seth's direction, though his eyes remain on me. "But he knew a truth or two. As for you"—and here he turns his face toward Salome— "Seth believes you have the mind of a great scholar. But from what I have heard and seen, I believe you to be willful, devious, and vain, daughter of Coron of Memphis."

I feel Salome stiffen at this, as do I. Of course she *is*, but who is he to say so?

"And I am well taken with you."

Salome is not like me; she will not be silent. "Where are we?" she asks. "What is this place? I have heard many things about you. I have heard you do more than wash away sins, that you wash your god into souls. Are you the great teacher Addai promised us?"

Yea Balaam! Salome's questions are my questions! I wish her courage were my courage. In the face of this flood, the old man holds up one finger, one only, and Salome swallows what more she would say. I am amazed. I have never seen her do this, never. Over John's face, a change has come. There is a lift in the brow, and a light in the eye that was not there a moment ago. I have seen lifts and lights like these before: they show in the face of Addai when he savors magic, in Seth's when he debates philosophy, in Father's when he contemplates profit. It is the light of the fanatic talking about that which he cherishes most. But this old man's light is blinding; the very air seems suddenly charged, as if dark clouds were gathering over the hills. What he says next comes like a blow to the heart. "But even as you are Daughters of the Voice, you are also females alone in this world. What else is there to say of you? You are nothing." Without moving, I recoil. The words that follow are not blows, but chains; they weigh me down link on link. "You have no brothers or uncles or fathers to protect you, to give you value. What man would marry you now? If you were not here, where would you be? What would you do with yourselves? There are those who would say you are not worthy of Life."

I am rooted to the spot; I am frozen in the bone. My belly cramps like a fist. Though I have taken my eyes from his face, I know he stares straight into me as he says, "Look about you. What has become of you?"

I look about me. I am in a pit deep underground and I am dressed as a boy. My name is a boy's name and no man claims me as his own. What has become of me? What will become of me? I do not know, and I am sore afraid. I am listening to a heartless old man, a prophet, tell Salome and me that we are not welcome in the world, not as a man is welcome. This is not the first time I have ever heard such a thing, but it is the first time I understand it. Salome and I are females. We are less than animals or slaves without Father. Or brothers. Or husbands. Oh Isis, Queen of Heaven, what shall become of us?

Salome would never cry, but I cry.

I bow my head and I cry for the small thing that I am, and will always be. Fleeing to Egypt is suddenly dust in my mouth. I cry until I feel a cool hand on my forehead, so unexpected. I open my wet eyes to find I am looking into a face no more than the space of a palm away. I jerk back in surprise. It is a woman, a stranger, dressed as a traveler, and with a pearl at her throat worth my Father's house. As well, there is a hauteur to her I have seen in no woman, except the promise of a Salome to come.

"I have ridden a long way to see you, a very long way. And what have you seen that makes you weep? You could not be seeing what John sees."

I only cry the harder. I am shameless in my woe. But the traveler stands before me, her hands now folded into her black cloak and on her face a look of vivid expectation. Beside her, but back a step or two, stands a clean-shaven man. This one's brow is as arched as the smile of a lizard and his thoughts are as plain as brushed words on papyrus. He is the son of the woman before me and his name is Izates. The dust of the road clings to the hem of his cloak just as it does his mother's, whose name is Helen. Izates is wondering why he has traveled these past days and nights, two weeks of days and nights in a caravan of merchants and murderers, to meet children. He is not sure if John's madness is sent by God or is a demon's touch, and he hopes he will discover the answer for himself, and soon.

From his seat, John speaks again. He holds up both arms as if he were blessing his watery flock and he talks as if he were speaking to legions, though he speaks only to Salome and to me. "Behold, Mariamne, daughter of Josephus of the tribe of Benjamin, in you there dwells a brave and manly mind. I say the same of Semne, known as Salome, daughter of the Egyptian Coron. In your actions and thoughts you are as men. I see that you are good and brave and that your souls are blessed among women. So I ask of you again, as you are a man and not a woman, so that boldness and understanding rules your mind, look around you."

Though his voice now softens, I barely hear him.

"But, though you are men, you are yet boys. How could you see when I have set about terrifying the female in you? Seth, you should have stopped me."

"Who could stop you? You are as the miracle worker, Empedocles, the disciple of Pythagoras, who was always yelling at the top of his voice, and by his own loudness convinced of his purpose." Seth turns to me and to Salome saying then this astonishing thing: "You are where you intend to be, for all that occurs is intended."

By raising an arm, the haughty traveler interrupts him. "I and my son have journeyed from Adiabene. We will hear this one speak." She is pointing at me, and I should be driven to flee at these words, but Adiabene? Adiabene is farther east than Palmyra, farther than Babylon, farther even than the river Tigris. By the heavens! This one comes so far to see me? The woman continues to speak, but what has Seth just said? We are where we intend to be? To a Jew, prophecy is everything, and if not prophecy, the Law. I have heard no Jew speak as Seth speaks. All that occurs is intended?

What is John saying? "You, Mariamne, daughter of no one, and you, Salome, daughter of no one, you are Daughters of the Nazorean."

Helen of far Adiabene steps between John and me. She lifts up her chin, holds up a hand, and by so doing commands the very air to attend her. She looks directly into my eyes. "Did Issa not walk with me? And is the word not my word? I came to hear this one speak, John, and I *will* hear it speak. I am Helen, Queen of Adiabene, and I would hear through the Voice that is within this child that you, John of Kefar Imi, are the One."

I stand as if held up by rope. Queen? The Queen of Adiabene's voice sounds in this round room with its domed ceiling as God's voice must have sounded in the heavens over Moses. But John has caught her in the white light of his regard. "Woman," he says, "on this earth you are a queen, but before God you are one soul among many." John of the River is not shouting, but the authority of his person shines forth as I am told the great beacon of Alexandria shines forth, and before it Helen lifts a hand to her face, seems almost to shield her eyes. "You will not demand of God what is God's to give. You will not command the voice God chooses to use."

Salome, who has been standing all along, trembling with what I have thought is rage, sits down on the bare stone of the floor and on her face there is nothing but rapt attention.

John has turned to me, and in his turning, I feel my knees weaken. Will he speak to me as he has spoken to a queen? But no, his voice when it comes is soft and it is mild. "As Seth tells me you are the Magdal-eder, you will speak as you will speak. That is the privilege of prophets."

Magdal-eder? I shake my head. I do not will the Loud Voice. It tempts my illness, makes room in my blood for fever. I would put it away forever, would swallow it, would spit it out! Yet something rises in me; pushes up from my chest. And I do *not* will it to come. "COME I THROUGH THE MOUTH OF THIS CHILD!" My arms begin to raise themselves as if another owned them. "THE ONE WHO COMES IS HERE. THE ONE WHO COMES IS THE VOICE THAT CRIES IN THE WILDERNESS. WHO WILL HEAR?"

"It is as I knew it would be," cries Helen. "This long journey is fulfilled."

Now I understand. I am thought to be proof that John the Baptizer is the messiah of the Nazorean. I could not be more dismayed.

Seth speaks. "I think, John, they would do well for a time in Egypt."

Queen Helen gives out a great sigh. "If it is not one land that calls to you, Seth, it is another. You would break my heart."

And this from her son, Izates: "Get yourself to Egypt, brother, before I break your nose all over again. We endured you three years on top of a mountain. We endured you following John. But there will be no suffering you until you see Egypt."

A thought from Salome flies through my head and I catch it. *All that occurs is intended. Did we not intend Egypt, Mariamne, and does it now not come to pass?*

∝

I look up. The night seems no more than an Ethiop's hand across the face of Glory. The moon is an Ethiop's eye. I think Cicero right when he says, "Beyond the moon are all the eternal things." *Oh Isis!* I am going to Egypt!

I lie here awake, buried in thought. If what occurs is intended, Salome would have been born a male and I should be a great philosopher. Or a great mathematician. Seth once named mathematicians, and I was astonished, not for how many there were, but for how many were women. If I could truly be anything I intended to be, I would be a philosopher and a mathematician and a magician in one huge person and I should laugh as I strode up and down the halls of the Great Academy I would found and name with my true name: Mariamne of Jerusalem. That is, if intentions were more than wishes.

It is a fact that no one would intend to be born a cripple or blind or poor or one of those wild people who live farther west than Italia. Surely no one would intend to be born a savage Celt? And yet Salome and I intended to go to Egypt, and here we are, going to Egypt.

"Mariamne," whispers Salome, "are you awake?"

"What?" She has surprised me. I thought her well asleep an hour ago.

"What do you make of John?"

I think for a moment and then I say, "I think he is either full of wonder or he is full of camel dung. Either way, I will find out."

Salome answers immediately. "You will find he is full of wonder."

I come awake to a world that shines. When shall we leave? How shall we travel? What shall we do when we get there? We pester Addai and Tata with questions the whole of the morning. But it is not until the woman from the south appears and whispers to Tata who whispers to Addai that they finally answer us. We shall go tonight! And we shall go with only three others. Tata looks at Addai and I understand something I do not want to understand. Salome is first to cry out. "But you are going with us, are you not, Tata?"

Addai's voice is firm and it is flat. By this, I know his heart bleeds. "You will go with Seth and with two who follow John."

Two who follow John? Who are these? The sun seems to have stumbled in the sky. Salome cries out, "But John of the River? Are we not to know John?"

Tata takes Salome in her arms, smoothes her hair as she did when we were very young. Addai says, "In time you will know all that you will know. But for now, know this, I trust my chosen daughters with Dositheus as I trusted him with my own daughter."

"Dositheus! *Who* is Dositheus?"

"You met him last night. With John."

"That man! But he has the face of an actor!"

Addai smiles. "And why should he not, as he is an actor."

An actor! If I have thought the work of Addai beneath notice, what is there to say about a man who would stomp about on a stage making faces and shouting? But wait—Addai has a daughter? Addai has a wife?

Before I can ask this, Salome asks and, as Tata packs our few things, receives this in answer.

Once, long ago when he was yet young, Addai dwelt in the city of Shechem in Samaria. As his father had been a stonemason, so too he was a stonemason. As his father had been a lover of the Law, so too was he. And all was well with Addai and his wife, until came the day she would birth their child. Abihail died that day. If this was not grief enough, the babe was a girl, and a cripple. Addai named her Jael and cared for her tenderly. It was Jael who shook his faith as harvesters shake an olive tree, for by the beliefs he held, if Jael's twisted body was not God's doing, then a demon was in her. Addai knew no demon lived in his innocent child. Therefore, God had cursed Jael. But why?

Jael grew into a maiden as brave as Esther, as loyal as Ruth. But she was shunned by those around her, for who would not shun she who was cursed by God? And the father Addai saw all this and was helpless before it. He could not stop it and he could not endure it and he would not have his child endure it. So he gathered up his daughter and he left Shechem. He did not curse his god nor did he curse his neighbors, for such a thing was not then and is not now in Addai, but he put them both behind him.

Salome and I have averted our eyes from the faces of the ill and the crippled and the poor. Have not Father and his friends always said it is the Law that no one but the pure in body might enter the Temple? When they said such things, did I think anything of it? I think of it now.

Addai and his daughter wandered throughout Samaria and west to the Plain of Sharon. Then came they unto Galilee and the city of Sepphoris for there was work there, and in Sepphoris he met his fellow Samaritan, Dositheus of Gitta, who had gone to be an actor. When he came out of Galilee, his new friend went with him, for each had grown fond of the other.

A man who does not stay in one place is mistrusted. If he is not

Hapiru, a roving brigand or a bandit or a misfit, he is surely an exile. But like traveling philosophers and cooks, traders and healers and high-class prostitutes, Addai and Dositheus were welcomed. For three years Addai found work for his capable hands and Dositheus acted out battles and romances and the agonies of the gods near village wells. If neither of these skills were wanted, Addai would perform his "tricks" of magic. There was always a warm meal at the end of the day.

It was not a terrible time, it was not a time of hardship, but they traveled as aimless as clouds. And though Jael grew stronger in mind and in spirit, she grew daily weaker in body. Then one day, when the sun beat down like a woman beating a rug and Jael could stand to be carried no farther, they found themselves on high badlands looking down into the forested green valley of the Jordan River. And there they saw John the Baptizer for the first time. And here John singled Jael out from all the hundreds who were there that day and he cried out, "Behold! Many and many are mistaken. There is no demon in this child!"

A miracle occurred: The eyes of these thousands were opened. They saw there was no demon in the daughter of Addai.

And then John said, "Behold! Many and many are mistaken. This child is blameless. Where is the curse?"

A second miracle! The people opened their eyes and saw God might wager with his own self-doubt, which the prophets call Satan, but he would not curse one without blame. Addai and Jael and Dositheus followed John until Jael died three years later, and Addai and Dositheus have followed John ever since.

I wonder at a father losing his only beloved daughter, and then I think of Josephus of Arimathaea, and I stop my wondering as pity for Father fills my heart.

There are still hours to fill before the coming of the night, and of Seth's coming to take us away. But if Addai has a tale, so too does Tata, which greatly surprises Salome and me. She has never spoken of herself before. Not to us.

"My mother," Tata begins, "was the daughter of a poor man and her father was the son of a poor man whose father was even poorer, if that is possible. For so long as there has existed peasants and kings, my family has owned nothing but the rich pride of poverty. But for my mother, this was not enough. My mother did what is seldom done in a poor family, and never by a woman; she fell in love. Love is a luxury that even the rich can ill afford, being far more costly than rubies or spikenard or gold. Having none of these, my mother paid in the coin of her own life. And with mine. When she was fifteen, she fell in love with a Roman soldier, and that is all that need be said of him, that he was a soldier, that he made good use of my mother's love, that he moved on. All that can be said of my mother was that once having birthed her babe, she sold it for money to send to her family, and then, I am reliably told, she died of a broken heart. Or shame. Or both. She did not see her sixteenth year."

Tata pauses here. I glance over at Addai for his reaction, but there is none. He sits quietly, his beard splayed out over his barrel of a chest; his clever hands idle in his lap. I glance back at Tata. There is nothing about Tata that I usually see, no quick pride or fierce humor. There is only a simple seriousness.

"I was sold to a woman named Euodia who was a sacred harlot, a Temple prostitute, a divine whore, which to the Jews is called a *zonah*. From the moment I could walk and talk, Euodia set about teaching me all she knew. And though women like my mistress were no longer allowed publicly in the Temple, I grew up secretly servicing men in the name of a god, the very men who barred us from that god's house. In all else save this and the art of healing, Euodia was ignorant. Those who shared this life with us were as ignorant as she, all but Theodora, a woman of Cyprus, who taught me everything I have taught you, and one other, a woman from far to the east, who taught me all I have never taught you, and will never teach you, for you have no need of such skills."

Tata tosses her head. Salome and I live for what she might now say.

"I should have lived an honored life for mine is an ancient and honorable profession. But not now, not here in Judaea where the female has fallen so far, where the goddess is driven from her place. Here, what I did until the day I came to your house was done in secret, but it was done and is done by many. There is much in and about the Temple that is not freely spoken of, and some things that are not spoken of at all."

Tata pauses again. This time I see she struggles. She is coming to something it will be hard for her to say. I suddenly wonder how hard it is going to be for me to hear.

"And now I shall tell you how I came to be in your father's house."

Suddenly, Salome inhales so sharply and so loudly we all start. Her eyes have grown round with understanding. Tata smiles at her, but there is no humor in the smile.

"Salome with her quick fox mind sees what I am about to say. I came because Josephus bought me from Euodia."

I blurt out, "Father bought you for us?" I say it in order not to hear the truth, because of course Father did not buy Tata for us.

"For himself."

Oh yes, it is very hard to hear this. How much more will Father hurt me?

"The visits of Josephus became so frequent, Euodia offered me to him for a great price, an impossible price, and he paid it. I came to your house as your father's bedmate and I remained so until the day I left. If you had chosen to obey Josephus, Mariamne, and live with his brother-in-law, I confess that I should have stayed until I thought you settled, for I love you as my own child—you and Salome *are* my own children—but I should then have found my way here no matter the cost. I am, after all, the daughter of an unusual woman."

I understand now why Father did not punish Tata the day he drove Salome from his house.

Tata has more to say. Can I hear more?

"I think it time I also tell you that I am now the companion of Addai of Shechem and, if he wishes, I shall stay his companion for all that remains of my life."

"Wish it?" Addai breathes in Tata as he would breathe in a priceless scent. "You are my other half, the half I lost at birth."

Salome sends me a quick sign—the Love of Plato! That we should see it!

It is settled. Neither Tata nor Addai will go to Egypt. Instead

Salome and I go with Seth and with the actor Dositheus. It is now we learn who the last of us shall be: black Helena, not from the south, but from the northern city of Tyre.

∝

We are going to the land where life began, where the gods and goddesses were born, where history was first written and the stars first studied, or so claims Salome. We go to Alexandria! The first thing I shall do will be to see the museum where they say the great Alexander is embalmed in honey, and where I know there is a library more wonderful than any in the world. And oh, we have never seen Seth as he is now. He smiles, he talks, he must take all his books, his astrolabe and his maps, his inks and his desk and his reeds. He must take so much, Addai lends him Eio to carry it all.

The sun burns red. In moments it will sink into the Great Sea. In an hour it will be full dark and by then we are to meet up with Ananias who waits for us in a hidden place arranged by John of the River. John himself, as well as Queen Helen and her son, Izates, are already away, gone with the caravan the night before.

Addai and Tata have packed our things on the donkey that travels along with Eio, have whispered with Dositheus and with the woman Helena and with Seth. There is nothing left to do but to go. At the last moment, I throw my arms around Tata's waist and cling there. Tata gives me a small leather purse, gives one also to Salome. "Tie them to your belts," she says, "and whenever you have need of them, think of me." Addai looks on us as a father whose child has died, and I rush to him, take his beloved face in my hands and kiss him full on the lips. "I shall see you again," I whisper into his mouth. "You will know me again, and I you."

And that is the last I see of them for seven years.

Straightaway, Seth sets off at a brisk pace. And straightaway we find the merchant Ananias and his caravan hidden in a deep defile. Ananias has been waiting to leave at first sight of us, and leave he does, with an astonishing speed and silence for beast and man.

That first night, and for three nights afterward, we travel only by the light of the stars and a growing splinter of a moon. On these first three nights, we are more silent than not. It is when we pass the Fortress of Herodian seated atop its man-made mountain that Salome reveals to me her feelings for John of the River. Salome whispers that just as Addai is Tata's Platonic other half, John is hers. "I shall never know a man," she quietly declares, "never marry, never birth children, for I have decided to dedicate my life to John. It is done and it shall not be undone."

When she tells me this I am consumed by a terrible envy of Salome. Where is the man created from the other half of me, as we waited in the treasury of souls to be born?

After these three silent nights, Salome and I fairly burst into chatter. Allowed finally to talk, we live with our heads in the stars. There are times when my neck aches from staring up at the worlds of light. Cicero said, "If anyone cannot feel the power of God when he looks upon the stars, he cannot feel at all . . . if anyone thinks it mindless, then he himself must be out of his mind." Metrodorus of Chios said, "To consider the Earth as the only populated world in infinite space is as absurd as to assert that in an entire field of millet, only one grain will grow."

As for the two who travel with us, we think Dositheus could play nothing but tragedy, for his every movement speaks of studied woe. The hills ring with his doleful voice reciting poetry and declaiming the great speeches of the great characters written not only by Greek playwrights, but by brutal and bloody Roman playwrights, and even a few by Jewish playwrights. And as for Helena, she has about her such a curious air, I have carefully stepped into her mind, and as carefully stepped out for the sorrow and the pain. Salome imagines that Helena allows the doleful Dositheus to "lie in her lap." Dositheus calls her Ennoia, which he says means First Thought, saying also, "Surely God's first thought was female." But Helena gently rebukes Salome. Before coming away with Dositheus, she had been a common prostitute; now she suffers from something she does not name, a thing that sites itself in her female parts.

Ah, think I, this is the darkness within her; this is her pain. Both Salome and I are now fascinated by God's First Thought—and slightly repelled.

Somewhere after we leave the limestone hills to the west of Idumaea and are traveling south along the shore of the Great Sea on the old Nabataean spice and perfume caravan route, Seth begins speaking of the inner Nazorean. Salome and I exchange looks. Shall we learn the secret teaching now? Will I understand it?

Seth strides along as he speaks and I run behind him, almost tripping him up, Salome close on my heels. "Outwardly, the inner Nazorean, which are the Few, appear as other sects, seem to cleave as close to the Law as other sects, but inwardly this is far from true. If others should know what is really believed and truly taught, we would be seen as deceitful apostates, as spiritually wicked. For what would the priests of the Temple who take in coin and spill blood daily, or the righteous men of the Law who shun other men as unclean, or the fervid Sicarii who shout for death to those God 'hates' make of a teaching that placed no blame, nursed no guilt, sought no redress, harbored no hatred, followed no Law, suffered no priests, and looked not to an angry arrogant god, or to a savior king, a messiah, but looked *within* for knowledge of Source?"

This is almost Greek! It seems finer than Greek. But no messiah? I thought the Nazorean believed John to be the Messiah?

Salome is shaking her head. "I have heard what men say John teaches, and it is not this."

"For all that the Baptizer seems a wild man of rage and repentance," replies Seth, "he hides from all but the inner Nazorean that which he knows."

"What does he know?" I ask. I have tripped over four rocks in succession.

"That in all men there lives the divine spark, but that gnosis, or 'knowledge of the divine,' comes only to the few, for only the Few are bold enough to look within. For all others, those many who look without, who would be told, who would follow rules set by others, *especially* if that other is called a god or a king or a priest, these are as sheep who seek a shepherd. These must be led. Or driven. This is

John's calling, to be that shepherd. And to offer himself freely. If they would call him a messiah, a messiah he would be."

I glance at Salome who has chosen John. Her face shines.

A day or so later, Ananias leaves his camels and beckons me aside. He does not beckon Salome, who is well caught up in a discussion with Seth and Dositheus on what Dositheus calls the "threefold nature of God." Ananias tells me this: In the Jericho market buying up the Galilean oil for Egypt, he has heard word of me. Father has let it be known far and wide that I am no longer his daughter, Salome is no longer his ward, and that we have been entered by demons. It is said that these demons number three for me and four for Salome, but this number rises each new time Ananias hears the tale. Father has also let it be known that he would not transgress the First Noachite Law; therefore, our fortunes, hers from her father, Coron of Memphis, mine from my mother, Hokhmah, are deposited in our names with the Temple priests, and there they shall remain until we are proven dead or until we come for them, demon ridden or not demon ridden. Ananias says Josephus has called me whore, a cruel word men use to brand females not in the care of a brother or a husband or a father or an uncle or a son.

By the stars, even our very sons have precedence over us.

Ananias's news is like a blow to my heart. My father calling me whore is more terrible than John the Baptizer calling me unworthy of life. But I will not tell Salome. I will not tell Salome because I would not see her hurt more for my very soul. And I will not have Ananias tell Salome.

By and by, with much talk and little adventure, save the miles under our feet and the dust in our throats, we come out of a world of heat and sand into a world of heat and wet. Here, in the confusion of the seven waters, Ananias dismisses his camel drivers and his camels, off-loads his jars of oils and aromatics onto a large slow barge. From the fortress city of Pelusium on, where the lakes are bitter with salt and the sea is a sea of reeds, it is much too marshy to walk farther. It seems we shall come to Alexandria by way of the fabled Nile!

Therefore, in this manner we reach the westernmost branch of the green-watered Canopic Nile and from there sail into a reeded canal cut through the flat and endless delta. And all along, there have been waterwheels, and boats of many styles and many purposes, and houses made of mud-brick, and sloe-eyed people born out of Egypt's bounty. There have been great, flat, fearsome-toothed water lizards hiding in the rushes, and there have been great, fat hippopotami lurking under our keel. I have hung my head over the side as keenly as has Salome, for what amazing things they are! They are like enormous gray pigs with huge fatty yellow mouths that could swallow Goliath whole. Their teeth are like the stubby legs of Father's best table. Their ears turn full round in their great fat heads like pegs in holes. They could turn us over, barge and all, with one watery grunt.

From the canal we enter an enormous lake edged with reeds and scattered with islands. We float in and out of a jungle of bean plants that hold up their huge leaves like cups to be filled with the light of the sun. The islands are out where the water is clear, and on the islands are temples, but on the banks of this lake, and spreading out as far as we can see, are vast vineyards lying green under the Egyptian sun.

Tacking against a wind from the north, we slowly move across the lake of islands and wine. Upright in the prow, Salome and I strain for our first sight of Alexandria. We see nothing but more islands, nothing but water birds rising above us, nothing but the blue flash of a kingfisher in the reeds beside us, nothing but strange fish gliding below us, and around us nothing but other boats laden with wine from the rich estates on the lakeshore. Where is Alexandria? *Where is Alexandria?* We shall fall in a faint if it does not show itself in all these reeds and all this water. But there is nothing, nothing, nothing, and then—a dark line between the blue of the sky and the blue of the lake. And then—tiny boats, tiny docks, tiny buildings.

Salome seizes my hand. We are almost there, almost at Alexander's great city set at the edge of the sea. A moment later, there is movement in the distant streets. A moment after that, and the whole city lies clear before us. It is almost more than our hearts can bear.

As we said we would, Salome and I have come to Egypt.

Alexandria

I walk under a golden gate in a golden wall of golden towers and stand awestruck. How to speak of what is entirely flat and entirely wonderful? Everywhere is the yellow of sand in the sun. Or the blue of the great green sea. Between sky above and salted sea ahead and the vast southern lake of sweet water behind me, there stretches an arm of land from east to west, no more than twenty stadia wide, but on it sprawls such a stupendous display of temples and theaters and baths and palaces and shops, that it stops the breath. It is all of it so large, so tall, so wide, so spacious, so imposing, so grand, so ordered, so many, so *much*.

Already our barge is off-loaded at a customs checkpoint. (What Ananias had to say at the hefty fee I will not repeat.) Already he's sent off the bearers along with the cargo of oils. These were followed by the three criers Ananias hired at the docks who shouted to one and all of the olive oil newly arrived from Palestine. They extolled its Galilean quality, pulling along a growing crowd eager to buy, at the sight of which, I saw Ananias put aside thoughts of his hefty fee only to gather in thoughts of his hefty profit.

And now we push through utter chaos along the wide and bustling street running from the fresh water harbor of Lake Mareia to the saltwater harbors of the Egyptian Sea, until we come on a synagogue so large Ananias says someone must signal with a flag so that those in the back can know where the ceremony has come to for those in the front. Further, says he, here there is no sacrifice and no ritual; here there is only prayer.

But out in the streets, how all the people shout! Our eyes and our ears and our noses are assaulted by the entire world in one city. There are not only Jews and Egyptians, but there are Greeks and Romans and Syrians, Libyans, Cilicians and yet others from farther countries: Ethiopians, Arabs, as well as Bactrians, Scythians, Persians, even Indians! Here, Helena of Tyre's color is no more than all other colors, one color among every color. Ananias announces there are a million souls around us and as many more below us in the City of the Dead. I stare at Salome and she stares at me—the dead have their own city? Ananias, catching our wonder, explains that if we were to walk into the shadow of the Gate of the West, then summon nerve to pass through that gate, we would find ourselves outside the city walls and in the Necropolis, the vast city of Hathor, she who guards the newly dead. The embalmers are there, shop after shop of them, for although the Greeks would cremate and the Jews entomb and then bury, the Egyptians still think to take their bodies with them wherever they go. Our merchant of sponges and oil tells us that more than one sorry soul has lost himself in the labyrinth of tombs or fallen into holes meant to light the maze of underground catacombs, and was never seen again. Salome and I shiver with delicious fright.

Striding along, pushing people out of the way, Ananias has inflated with the pride of the informative and with the need to make himself heard over the din. I do not hear all that he says, but this I already know: Alexander the Macedonian's greatest city is everywhere Greek or it is Egyptian or it is Roman or it is all of these. Both the Greek religion and the Egyptian religion thrive here and often in the hearts of the same people. This too I know: out into the Egyptian sea there is an island called Pharos, and between it and the city are two harbors divided by the Heptastadion dike seven stadia long— to think that men have built a bridge across the salt waters! To think that on Pharos, there is a lighthouse as high as forty giants and its beam of mirror and of fire can be seen far out into the Great Green Sea! I am made silly by giddy delight. Jerusalem is a city huddled round a jealous and vengeful god. Its people live in houses built like ovens or beehives or dove cots, each house squeezed tight against its neighbor. In Jerusalem, only the rich and the Romans have room to breathe. But here, though some might say the only god worshipped is money, there are open spaces of comforting green for the pleasure even of the poor. There are wide streets, each lined from end to end with colonnades, wide enough for a dozen chariots abreast. There are sphinxes on pedestals and obelisks standing against the Egyptian sky, and there are statues and pink granite pharaohs and pink granite gods and pink granite goddesses. There is one who makes me pull on Salome's traveling cloak. "Look at that! Does it not seem as someone we know?"

Salome squints up at the massive face of pharaoh high above her, a face of smooth and perfect beauty. "Yes," she replies, "if someone like Izates were to break its nose, it would look just like Seth."

We hurry on after Ananias. There are temples everywhere, to Isis, to Horus, to Poseidon, to Serapis. Dositheus remarks to Seth that in Herod's Temple in Jerusalem, only Yahweh can live; all others are called demons. But here Osiris, Zeus, Pluto, Apis, and many others live in harmony. I think of Tata's goddesses and I smile.

With a showman's flourish, Ananias says more awaits us.

Dodging beggars and vendors and chariots and a mob of assorted people going about their day, we have come to the center of the city, stand now in the vast open space where the Canopic Way crosses the steaming Street of the Soma—by the gods, Egypt is hot! Not the dry heat of the wilderness, but thick wet heat. There is almost a drowning to breathing. Ananias points to our left; we all look left. There stands the Gymnasium, the four porticos of which measure more than a stadion in length. There, Mark Antony once divided up the world among each of the children he had had by Cleopatra. Salome and I look at each other. What could it be like to think one owned the world, that one could apportion it at will? Ananias points to our right. There is Cleopatra's temple built for the worship of Mark Antony, save that it is now the Caesarium, for as soon as the lovers were dead, Augustus Caesar had thrown out their statues and replaced them with his own. This tells us at least one thing it means to think one owns the world; both the thought and the world are fleeting.

Farther along, there is a small green park, and in the middle of the garden in the middle of the park is Alexander's tomb, a pretty thing of pink alabaster that leads deep down into the earth where the body of Alexander forever lies. But we spend no more than a moment looking, for rising up before us is the Palace of the Ptolemies, a magnificent palace so enormous, I wonder there is room left for a city at all. But it is not the palace itself that makes my heart now beat as it does; it is knowing what is in the palace. Somewhere behind its walls lies the museum and, in the museum, Ptolemy the Savior's library!

Holding Eio by her halter, an *eio* carrying his own library, Seth looks up at the golden walls. The man of dignity we knew in our wilderness fell away the night he learned he would travel here, replaced by an eager boy. Now there is yet a new Seth. This Seth is full of wonder and full of awe. "They say," he says softly, "that the books number more than five hundred thousand and that agents are sent throughout the world to acquire more. They say there is no manuscript in any library anywhere that is not in Alexandria. Archimedes lived and invented here. Here, Euclid wrote his *Elements* and his *Optics,* and here Herophilus of Chalcedon came to understand anatomy by dissection and vivisection. In this place, Aristarchus of Samos explained how the Earth and the planets revolve around the Sun."

The Earth revolves around the Sun? How Father and his friends would laugh at that. But that the human body is dissected here? At that, they should not laugh. Oh, but more than five hundred thousand books! *Yea Balaam!*

And now we learn that Ananias goes immediately back to the

wilderness, taking with him his profits, as well as Eio who must be returned to Addai. We learn also that the actor Dositheus and his companion, Helena of Tyre, are to stay, by choice, near the Eunostos Harbor amid the bars and the brothels. But as for Seth and Salome and me, we three are to live in the royal district of Brucheion, in the very palace. Our rooms shall be those in the white marble museum given over to scholars, directly off the covered walkways along which are the very books themselves! And this will be so because we are believed to be kin to Seth, who is a Maccabee, as well as a son of the Queen of Adiabene.

The room I have been given as mine, is more than any room in Father's fine house. It is more than any room in Herod's grand Temple of Jerusalem, and yet it is nothing more than a scholar's room. Not only have I a whole room to myself, but so too has Salome. Hers is across a great hall of brightly painted pillars, but I can call out to her any time I wish, and I do. Our happy childish voices echo from end to end of the great hall and are immediately returned by a chorus of an unseen scholarly *sssssshhhh*! We laugh to hear this displeasure, but we shush.

Seth seems to have been given a small palace within the palace, where he has eagerly taken himself with all he has unloaded from the back of Eio. For this he required the help of two slaves, who seem also to have been given him.

And now I am left on my own. This means I run from place to place, exclaiming at the marble, at the ebony, at the gold, at the ivory, at the rich Arab carpets underfoot. I throw myself on the bed, an enormous thing, larger than any I have ever seen, even in the house of the high priest Caiaphus, and fear I shall sink into it. I jump up again and examine the walls, one whole section of which is my own library. Or will be when I acquire one. But the gleaming shelves and buckets await and my heart soars as I imagine what I shall place there. Scrolls of my own choosing. Scrolls of my own devising! By the horn-ed moon, if there could be such a thing as the complete opposite of our tent in the wilderness, this is that thing.

I remember something, and turn to dig in my bag. It is the book

Heli gave me as we left his house that night on our way to the wilderness. Heli's book shall be the first to find a home in my library.

With so little to put away, I am back out in the tiled hall, rushing into Salome's room. I know she too must have run from place to place, have jumped on her bed, run her hands over the tapestries and the counterpanes and the cushions, but now she stands at a window overlooking a fabulous park extending all the way to the Egyptian sea. Saying nothing, I come to stand beside her. I take her hand and she mine; together weep great fat tears of happiness.

We are home. At last, we are home.

And then we see the library. Ten huge marble halls filled from floor to ceiling with books, every book that has ever been written. And everywhere scholars come from all the corners of the world, reading and writing and discussing and teaching. Oh! There is no describing the joy of this for such as Salome and myself. It is a great feast, a feast of the gods, and we are favored guests. I cannot imagine choosing another life.

There follow months of learning and then years of learning; our heads are crammed full of learning. We live in the world as males; we live in our wonderful rooms in the greatest library on earth and we eat in the library and we sleep under our mosquito netting snuggled deep into beds that would suit any queen, and we read and we read and we study what we read and, of course, we argue. There is no shortage of teachers to argue with; thousands from every nation under the sun come here to study or to teach or to invent or to write. If no teacher, we argue with each other as we have ever done. Our lives are a quest for *ataraxia*—philosophical peace of mind. Outside these walls, life and all it contains is thought of as governed by blind chance. And if life is not seen in this way, then it is said to be ruled by *pistis*, blind faith in the gods, or *a* god. But here in the Great Library are gathered men and women in common community hoping for tranquillity from such dark depressions of the spirit by seeking philosophical truths for the mind.

This is the course of our days.

Salome is instructed in medicine by Sabaz, who was born far to the west in a nomadic desert kingdom ruled by women. Sabaz is so old and so venerated she can barely walk from one end of her rooms to the other. Therefore, she is carried wherever she wishes to go by her slaves, two of whom seem as aged as she, and one of whom is the biggest man we have ever seen, John of Delos, who must duck to pass through doors. We have heard that Sabaz was physician to Cleopatra herself, and to her children. All during the first year, Salome learns the fine art of potions and narcotics and poisons. By our second year, Emperor Tiberius's truly terrible mother, Livia, widow of Augustus and connoisseur of poisons, had nothing on Salome.

From Theano, born in Alexandria of Jews who fled the Law, we are instructed in *harmonia*, or the fitting together of all things that *are:* music, geometry, astronomy, and the sacred numbers—she tells us Pythagoras of Samos said, "Number is the *within* of all things." Theano wears nothing but white; her head is shaven, she is severely economical of movement and emotion, and so hideous, she is compelling. As a Therapeutae, an ascetic, she lives secluded with others of her sect somewhere outside Alexandria. We are very soon dazzled by Theano, and she is dazzled by Pythagoras, and by my Salome, who becomes cleverer by the hour.

Within a month, Salome is full of nothing but the love of Pythagoras. She talks of him endlessly, saying he understood the code of number and of shape on which all reality relies. That he lived for twenty-two years in the temples of Egypt drinking deep of the ancient Egyptian Mysteries, and when he returned home to Greece, he wandered from place to place preaching all he had learned. He divined the future, he performed miracles, he raised the dead—meaning he awakened to wisdom many so unthinking they might as well be dead. He gave the Greeks the dying and resurrecting godman, Osiris, who is here a god of the most blessed ecstasy and the most enraptured love. But to Salome, this above all: Pythagoras loved women, thought them equal to men in all ways. If she had been blessed to follow Pythagoras, says she, she should not now be known as Simon, but could stand forth as who and what she is, Semne the Magus.

I learn the art of poetry from Julia, born near Rome but who boasts Etruscan blood. With Julia I have decided to add poet to my list of intended accomplishments, though it is here that Seth, not Salome, outshines me. It is he who shows a true gift.

Day after day, when we are not one of us with Sabaz or Theano or Julia, we scribble away on our tablets of wax, as the historians Valerius Laertius and Zopyrus of Rhodes read us much of the prolific Roman Livy, and talk of the doings of Greece and Persia, while the Alexandrian historian, Apion, extols the history of Egypt. Apion has no taste for Jews, saying we worship an ass, and when I hear this I think of Eio and I laugh. But as he has such an appetite for teaching, and as he is moved to his marrow by the appetite and erudition of Seth who is also his student, he forgives us our heritage.

When I am with none of these, I read Homer. Oh Homer! If he is not a god himself, he is like unto. That is, if Homer were ever a man at all and not a name to signal the talents of many. It is Seth who tells me Homer might be the work of many men, just as the Jewish Torah is the work of many men. I am shocked at first to hear this, but soon enough realize it makes no difference. The work is the thing. And then there is Ovid. *Metamorphoses* becomes my secret delight.

Each day, Ammianus the Younger unrolls a large papyrus scroll on which there is a copy of Strabo of Amaseia's map of the world. And each day I fall into Strabo's map as if it was water and I were a fish. There is India, where Indian noblewomen are trained in the ways of war and ride into battle with their husbands and their sons. There is Britain, about which Plutarch wrote: "The fight had been no less fierce with the women than with the men themselves." Oh, I dream of traveling the world as Strabo did! Or as the historian Herodotus once did. Herodotus set himself the task of discovering everything there was to discover about all things. Now this is surely a purpose. Nor did he shrink from telling the truth. To think that the oracle at Delphi took bribes. That in Libya it was once the woman with the most lovers who was honored. I love Herodotus.

Yet if Salome or I attend three lectures a day, Seth attends four. If we walk out into the city to hear this lecturer or that, he walks farther. He would travel to Sais or to Naucratis, or journey a week to hear someone speak in Memphis, the city of the birth of Salome, now Simon. It is as if Seth were starving, and Egypt a great banquet. He cannot fill himself enough. He does not seem to sleep. He does not seem to eat. He does not seem to be as other men and have need of a woman.

In public we have taken to calling Salome "Simon the Magician" to distinguish her from all other Simons, just as I am now called "John the Less" to distinguish me from all other Johns, though mostly to distinguish me from John of Delos, the very large slave of Sabaz. Where once she learned lower magic, tricks and illusions, as did I, from Addai, now she learns the art of transcendent magic from the famous Joor, son of Sipa of Thebes. As do I. But once again, the greater gift is Salome's, who has become, as said, Simon Magus.

∝

The sea curls white over the seawalls. The rain falls as a shifting silver curtain. It rains so hard on the library roof, we barely hear Joor, though he shouts out our lesson as John the Baptizer would shout out over the Jordan. "What have your people taught you of Adam and Eve, John?"

Hearing my name over the pounding rain and the crashing sea, I blurt out, "That the serpent was Satan who causes all suffering."

"By this," shrieks Joor, "since the serpent represents Wisdom, you are told that wisdom is bad and therefore ignorance is good. But good for whom? Only priests and politicians benefit from a people's ignorance. Could it not be that the God of the Jews did not wish men to have recollection of Ultimate Source, that which we call 'All That Is,' not wanting them to know that he himself was nothing more than they were, writ large? But as the serpent brought the man and the woman *knowing,* which means full gnosis of the mysteries within, is it any wonder that your god would be full of fury at the betrayal of the snake?"

I listen to such things stunned by revelation.

On another day, Simon Magus and I are seated on the wide palace wall. Below us is the royal harbor in which floats the island sanctuary of the "New Isis" who was Cleopatra herself, where the walls were once white with ivory and the doors once green with emeralds. Before us, the light of the Pharos shines out like a small sun over the Great Sea. Behind us, we hear the murmur of scholars in the ninth reading room, busy taking scrolls out of their wooden chests or buckets or baskets, busy slipping them out of their niches along the marble walls, or busy putting them back. Above us, glitter the stars of Egypt. I am given up trying to read Artapanus's *History of the Jews* and am now enthralled by a great poem of the philosopher Parmenides in which he descends into the Underworld to be instructed by the Goddess. For jest, or perhaps in boredom, Simon Magus leaps from our wall and begins striding up and down before me. "Who is greater than a magician?" she asks of all the scholars within hearing. "A magician can call down the rain, a magician can heal the sick, a magician can cast away sins. Even Jews call forth magicians. The rainmakers, Elijah and his disciple Elisha, were they not magicians? John the Baptizer's grandfather Honi the Circle-Maker also brought the rain. Was Honi the Circle-Maker not a magician? Hanina ben Dosa heals the ill at a distance. Is he not a magician?"

Hearing this, our teacher Joor, who is also head librarian, appointed by Gaius Julius Caesar Octavianus himself, also busy with a scroll, gazes fondly on my friend, then tells all who would listen a story. It seems that far away in Hanina ben Dosa's native Galilee, a lizard has been poisoning people. Hanina came when the villagers bid him to, and he asked them to show him the lizard's hole, which they did, and eagerly. As soon as Hanina saw the hole, he put his naked heel over it. Oh! sighed all the villagers, amazed and awed. And ah! they all wailed when immediately the lizard rushed out and bit Hanina's foot. But nothing could compare to the sound they made when immediately the lizard died.

Simon Magus, my Salome, dances a small dance on the flowers made of tiny colored tiles on the library floor.

Joor explains that Hanina did what he did by being a power unto himself. A magician, male or female, controls what is outside by controlling what is inside. "And what does this mean?" he asks, only to answer before Simon can. "The *outside*, the stuff of matter, is no more than a reflection of the *inside*, meaning *nous*, or mind. The mind controls matter in its own perception, and in the case of a magician, in the perception of others. Is this not exceedingly simple!"

Yes, I think, it is simple, though it is also terribly hard, as many simple things are.

Continues Joor, "A man who gains control over the rain can surely gain control over sin, which is merely a word for error."

"Eloi," say I, "but this would infuriate the Jewish priests, who claim through God only *they* can heal, only *they* can forgive sins, only they can bring rain, at a price."

Joor shakes his head. "A great magician gives these things freely."

I know whom Salome thinks of when he says this, for I too think of John the Baptizer on his river healing all who come to him for the mere asking.

And by sitting for hours under the black dome of the Egyptian night in the exact middle of the largest palace courtyard, Joor also instructs us in the science of the heavenly bodies and their orderly array, which he himself learned from a pure line of Sethians, those who claim descent from Seth, the third son of Adam and Eve, but who is also Set or Seth of the Egyptians. Listening, I ask myself, is our Seth named for the third son of Eve, or is he named for the Egyptian Seth who as the night sky is the twin and beloved enemy of the sun, Osiris? Is there a difference, since all these names, Hebrew and Egyptian, name principles of being?

It is now we learn that the stars do not cause what occurs but instead indicate or sign events to come. We learn also that much myth and much symbol comes from observing the heavenly vault of the stars. That Isis or Issa is truly the Moon. That Ra is truly the Sun. That El means all the stars.

Does this not then signify that Issa-ra-el is the land of heaven?

And did not the Loud Voice say this: Children of Issa-ra-el?

I run to Seth with what I have learned. I tell him all in a rush that we are Children of the Heavens, barely noting his stricken face before

I run off again. Only later did I think what it must have meant to him, to hear it said that Issa, the great prophet of the Nazorean, was already known in Egypt as Isis, the Moon Goddess.

On a day of wind, so fine a thing in Alexandria, Salome and I race to be in, I learn that I am more than my *eidolon* which is merely my waking self. I learn that I am my *Daemon* which is my true self who is immortal and does not die and cannot be harmed. I learn I am my own eternal witness and that I live forever. Death is only more Life. I learn we are eternally safe in Consciousness.

Seth taught us this as we stood on the highest place on the library wall so that the wind might blow the heat from our bodies. And even then, as the wind blew and Salome hallooed out over the Royal Harbor and the seabirds were swept from the sky and the waves foamed over the seawalls, Seth talked of Socrates.

He said all men experience themselves first as the *eidolon*, which is the mortal self, the personality, becoming lost in the belief that their *eidolon* is all there is of self, and when this died, they died. Blinded by the *eidolon*, small and suffering, they could not do otherwise than perceive God as "other" and separate: that which is enormous and unknowable. Anything that is enormous and unknowable is also a thing to be feared. As this small self, they would see their higher self, which Socrates called the *Daemon*, as also separate; they would think it an independent thing, call it a guardian angel. But to those who blessed themselves by seeking gnosis, or complete self-knowledge, the *Daemon* would be discovered to be the Divine I, the One Soul of the Universe, the Consciousness in all men and in all things. To know this, all men could say: I am God. To know this would be to know what is meant by I AM.

Over the wind, I hear him say this of "men" and that of "men" and all things of "men," and I call out, "Seth! I am not John the Less, but Mariamne. Salome is not Simon Magus. How does a man teach women?"

And this is how he answers me. "Do you not know Socrates was taught through the use of reason by a woman, the wise Diotima of

Mantinea! Do you not know that he taught women! Am I less than Socrates that I should do less?"

Salome begins to laugh so hard and so long that she tumbles backward off the library wall and into the garden below, there to lie struggling with her robe. If the wind had not blown all the scholars inside, everyone in Alexandria would have known within the hour that Seth teaches women.

×

In the early spring of our second year, I am almost killed. It happens in a most suitable place: the City of the Dead. Julia, thinking to have us each write an ode on death itself, takes Simon Magus and John the Less and Helena of Tyre out through the Gate of the West, and thence into the goddess Hathor's city called by all Alexandrian's the Necropolis.

We pass the shops of the embalmers, so many of them, and so eager for custom, they crook their long brown fingers: come here, come here! These we veer away from in great horror. We pass the small gardens for mourners to sit and weep in. As for these, we try not to stare at the grief so publicly expressed. We pass the stonecutter's huts and I am reminded of Addai and by this am saddened, but not for long, because by now, filled with a kind of curious gloom, we come on the labyrinth of tombs cut into the solid rock, so many we stand awestruck. As well as dismayed. Or I, at least, am. How long have they been here? How many have died to fill these holes in the ground, one layered on the other, down and down to some unutterable depth? As well as on and on for as far as I can see in all directions. I peer over the edge of one among the uncountable many. Stone steps descend down to small stone rooms and in the stone walls of each room are holes like honeycombs. But there is no honey here. Some of these are newly filled with what seems a cocoon of rags; some are so old those who once lived but now are long dead are no more than a carpet of dust on the stone shelving. How deep does it all go?

Far below there is movement, perhaps three, perhaps four levels down, and I see this by the light of a small lamp held by someone who has business there.

I am leaning forward; I am exclaiming, "Oh, what a place this is . . ." when I lose my balance, tip forward, clutching out for something to stop me. But there is nothing near, and no one close. All have been moving farther into the City of the Dead, making their way toward a large and recent cave-in.

I tumble headfirst into the tomb.

I know nothing else for I do not know how long. And when I awake, I awake in the rooms of Sabaz who hums over me with a pot of one of her vile ointments in her ancient hands. I also awake with a headache the like of which I could never have imagined having. I see that my left arm is bound and the broken ache of it makes me set my teeth and my eyes water. Sabaz has shaven my head. She must have, else how does she smooth on her ointment on my skull? But there is Simon Magus, white of face, and there is Julia, who cannot sit still for nerves, and there is Seth. Seth is not white of face, nor does he move from place to place. He is as still as the stone of the tombs.

"Until your true time comes, John, I bid you stay far from the dead."

And then he smiles. And I try to smile. But when I try, I cry out for it hurts my head. And then I cry out because crying out has hurt my arm.

I did not write a poem about death. But Salome did. In it she compared me to Thales of Miletus, but where he fell into a deep dark well from looking up at the stars, I (disguised as a fallen *neter*) fell in from looking down.

Soon after my arm is fully healed, as is my head, though my hair is as short as a dog's, Simon Magus discovers a Brahmin from India inspecting scrolls in the seventh hall of the library and drags me from my books to meet him. Sudheer is a follower of a prince of India known to him as the Buddha. I have heard of this Buddha. The Buddha taught that life is filled with suffering, and that suffering is caused not by a thing *outside* the self like a demonic serpent, but *by* the self in the form of desire. Sudheer explains that if we would cease our desire for things, we would not suffer. By this, I am reminded of something I have read in Plato's work, "Each pleasure and pain is a sort of nail which nails the soul to the body." This so pleases Sudheer he grins ear to ear. "Indeed, indeed," says he in perfect, oddly accented, Greek, "and if we would pry out these nails, we would be wise to follow the Eightfold Path."

This path turns out to be much as the commandments of Moses, but being only eight in number seems more understanding of a human heart. I like best, "to intend to resist evil." I am charmed by the word *intend*. Does Joor not talk of intention in his magical teaching of mind controlling matter? Does not Seth talk of intention? But we both like best of all what Sudheer has us read. The Vedas of his people are so old and so beautiful, I touch the words on the silk paper as I would touch a lover.

Today Apion is pleased to tell me thousands of Jews have recently been driven out of Rome. He says that Tiberius, who once banished all magicians, now tires of so many Jews shouting so loudly that Rome is soon to fall before an avenging Jewish god and his messiah. Worse, people everywhere are weary of Jews who go about inciting them to revolt against tyranny, while at the same time shunning and scorning them for being unclean.

I ask Seth, "I am a Jew. Father is a Jew. What am I to think of all this hatred of Jews?"

He replies, "The Children of Israel are not more beloved of the gods than the Children of Greece or Rome or Egypt, yet ours is a noble race. Did we not create the Sabbath which brought leisure to the people? With leisure, the mind had time enough to play. And from this, did we not come to value the mind? And did we not also create justice for the powerless and charity for the orphan and widow?"

I nod, yes, though I remember the Sabbath on which Salome said, "You Jews are not so much allowed to rest, as *commanded* to rest. You make a law of it." Since we were, by Law, shut away in our rooms at the time, Father fortunately never heard that.

"Best of all," continues Seth, "is that we argue with God. If one can argue with a god, surely this means that one's own thoughts count, however humble the source. In the Jew, humanity is elevated, for while other gods and goddesses bestow gifts on their people, the god of the Jews requires us to gift ourselves." Seth touches my hand. "Was Moses not a Jew? Is Hillel not a Jew? Is John of the River not a Jew or, in any case, a Nazorean? Are you not a Jew and the Magdal-eder? Are these not great things?"

Listening, I think I am pleased to be a Jew. But I also think I shall be even more pleased when I am an inner Nazorean and understand what he means by Magdal-eder.

This is a day I share with no other. On this day, I have been walking in the park, a thing I would never have done had I not come to Egypt. To walk on grasses, to sit by fountains, to smell flowers of rare beauty and startling color, I am transported. I have found a small bench under a tamarisk tree and I hold no scroll to read, nor tablet upon which to write. I do nothing but sit and stare about me.

After a time, a woman draped in cloth of many colors sits beside me. I have not invited her. Nor have I signaled she not do so. She says nothing. Nor do I. Moments pass during which I am beguiled by her color and her scent.

It is she who speaks first. "You must forgive my impertinence, sir, but I have overheard you conversing with great scholars in the library, and I have longed to speak to you."

I am surprised. "With me?"

"Oh yes. You have said many things with which I wholly agree and there is something about you which makes me think speaking with a woman would not distress you."

I look at her now. A woman of beauty, I have not seen her like. Her hair is so black it is blue, her nose is small and flat, her brown eyes are long and tilt up at their outer edges. I have never looked into eyes like these.

I spend an hour, two hours, on my bench with this woman and this is what I learn. The questions she asks me, the answers I give, the way she listens to me, and I to her—I know now what I would be. I would be a teacher.

I do not tell Salome of this day. I do not tell Seth. It is my secret and I hold it close.

Glory

Theano comes in time to believe her favorite pupil, Simon
Magus, should benefit by meeting the Master of the Therapeutae, he who she calls a hierophant of Jewish Mysteries. She believes even I, John the Less, might be worthy of such a meeting. I
think, a priest of sacred mysteries? Jewish mysteries? Salome quivers
with what I call a lust to know more. As do I. But all we are told for
now is that her master has a brother, the very wealthy Alexander,
who is the *alabarch* of the Jews of Alexandria, and therefore the center of Jewish business and civic life, but that the man we are to meet
is nothing like this rich and important brother.

So, on a day of heat, Theano takes me and Salome to the Jewish
quarter. Seth would come as well for Theano, who has come to love
him, would not leave him behind.

The house we come to, entered into by nothing more than a
small blue door, is as no other. Within there is nothing of comfort
and everything that would excite curiosity. There are a hundred odd

things lying about to attract the attention, and I would run from one to the other exclaiming, What is this? What is that? And by Isis, whatever could *that* be for? But glancing once at Theano, she of the bald head and firm mouth, I behave myself. As does Salome.

But I see the glint in Salome's eye, as she sees mine.

I have been staring at a machine of some sort lying on a table of some sort, when suddenly, and without a slave to announce him, there he is, the hierophant of Jewish Mysteries, and I pinch myself not to cry out. It is said that after the death of Abel, Adam abstained from Eve for 130 years; but he did not go without. During this time, Adam knew the Dark Queen, she of the shadows, and from their union came a frog, one that taught the languages of men and of animals and of birds, but a frog nonetheless. Here is that frog, big headed and big eyed and so wide of mouth. Salome leans against me, holding back her laughter. I will myself to stare at his beard instead of his person, for by a philosopher's beard one can tell which his school of philosophy.

As his house, the beard of Philo Judaeus is like no other.

Is, then, his philosophy like no other?

No greeting, no offer of wine or grape or cake. Theano's frog master fixes first Salome and then myself with a large and intense eye, looks us over without the hindrance of self-consciousness. Under his gaze, I am back in the rounded room of sun and stars and fish under the wilderness settlement. I am back in the house of Heli and Dinah of the Many. Three times now, I and my beloved Salome stand before a man who judges us, who wonders if we are worthy. Twice we have passed such scrutiny. Will we pass a third time?

This Philo addresses us, "Which of you knows what philosophy means?"

I beat Salome to the satisfaction of answering. "It is a word coined by Pythagoras meaning lover of the goddess Sophia who in her person is the Holy Ghost, which is blessed Wisdom." And then I remember myself, especially noting how Theano stiffens beside me. I add, "It means lover of wisdom, Master."

"And wisdom is?"

"It is—"

"Wisdom is the seeking of gnosis through the goddess Sophia. And gnosis is?"

"I—"

"Direct experience of God. Very well then. I am assured you are born philosophers even though you are Jews of Jerusalem."

Salome winces at this, but as Simon, a Jew she is and a Jew she must remain, though hopefully, one day, she can be an Egyptian once again.

"Theano swears she has never met two more Greek than you." The master pauses to adjust something on the table nearest to hand, closing one eye to check that it now satisfies. "I tell you that philosophers are those who dwell in the cosmos as their city. I tell you that philosophers are an international brotherhood. They are the select of the earth and it is their duty and their joy to raise up those who are not philosophers. What do you think of this?"

Seth has come forward and now stands before Theano's master as we have been standing. I think him radiant in his beauty, in his natural pride in self. Without blush, he says, "This is what I think, Philo Judaeus of Alexandria. I think you have said a thing that sings with truth."

Immediately, Philo cranes his head forward so that his frog snout comes close to meeting the bent nose of Seth. "Who is this person who speaks so to me?"

Theano, whose ugliness has gone pale from fear of having insulted her master, rushes her answer, "Seth of Damascus, the last of the House of Hasmonaean, orphaned by the Herods, and raised in exile by the Queen of Adiabene, Helen of the Assyrians. He has studied with both the Carmelites and the Nazoreans."

"Indeed?" Philo raises an eyebrow. "An actual living Maccabee. Another Jew among Jews. He carries a great name, complex in its meaning. Tell me, is he a philosopher?"

"It could be that he will become in time one of the greatest philosophers," replies Theano, who is not immune to either the beauty of Seth, or his intellect.

"Good," declares Philo. "Shalom and welcome, philosopher. Welcome three philosophers! There cannot be too many such men, especially if they are Jews."

From this day forth, Seth and Philo Judaeus can barely leave the room in which the other is to be found. Not only are they bonded by the similar inclination of their character, but by blood and by natural privilege and by early teaching. In moments, they also discover they are bound by their love of the Greeks. As Seth lives and breathes Socrates, Philo lives and breathes Plato, whom he calls the Most Holy Plato.

In the soft blue etesian winds curling in from the sea, Philo reads from certain Egyptian papyri he calls the Book of Coming Forth by Day, but which he says some call the Book of the Dead. He says he would rather we did not use this name as it is sure to mislead the simple who take such things literally. "It is a book of life eternal, not the cessation of life." Listening as he reads, I have never, save in the Vedas, heard such beauty of thought, such beauty of language, such grace in the face of life and death. It seems my ear is sharper now, for this makes certain books of the Torah sound nothing more than howls of uncomprehending mortal terror. In the ancient papyri of ancient Egypt, there is no terror before the world, above or below, no righteous way else all is lost, no man exhorting other men to do as his god demands, no god willing to destroy those who would not obey. Some chapters are so old, there is no knowing who first spoke them, who first heard them. In this book is all of creation, all of being and becoming and living and dying, all that is finest in the mind of man and *neter*, as the Egyptians call a god, though they do not think of any god as my people think of their god. To an Egyptian, a *neter* is a spiritual essence or principle, and I come to understand that Egyptian gods and goddesses are in truth not many and many a god such as the Jews claim pagans have but instead are as the Jews claim Yahweh to be, One God. The seeming many are only aspects of the One.

As I listen, I wonder, could not the visible world be God speaking

to itself? I run with this thought to Seth, as a child runs to its mother
with something it has made.

∝

On the evening of a day that fire rages through most of the buildings
crowded round the Lake Mareia docks, and threatens not only the
bandit community that makes its home in the thick reeds of the
shoreline, but also Alexandria's second, younger, and lesser library,
the Serapeion in the Rhakotis district where the Egyptians live, we
are driven inside the house of Philo Judaeus for the ash that darkens
the air and chokes the lungs.

On a night of burning buildings, Philo lectures us, saying, "In the
Beginning there was Nothing, which can be thought of as 'dazzling
darkness' or Absolute Mystery. This is the singularity before all
thought and all things, which is called Temu. Temu came even before the shapeless void which the Greeks name Chaos and the
Egyptians call Nun. Temu cannot be Consciousness because Consciousness needs something to be conscious of. It cannot even be
said to exist because what exists does so within Consciousness.
Temu is unknowable. Temu is unthinkable. Temu is beyond being.
But by some way not even the most sublime of philosophers can yet
say, came from Temu the First Idea, named by some Logos, the unknowable knew itself by becoming both known and knower. And
thus was created duality, as in, the witness and the experience, the
God and the Goddess, Consciousness as the witnessing God and experience as the Goddess Sophia. The First Idea is that Temu is conscious of itself, being the One Soul of the Universe that is conscious
through all beings."

Seth asks, "God, then, is Consciousness itself?"

This idea transports me.

Evening after evening passes in this way, for we are now *mathetes,*
pupils of a philosopher. The Nazorean Seth and the Therapeutae
Philo come very close to the mind of the other but miss by the
breadth of a single idea, while the rest of us listen as if we were at a

theater and the play as enthralling as any written by the greatest of Greek playwrights.

This, for example: Philo teaches that a soul, which seeks to rid itself of evil and to preserve the divine within itself, will be born into this world again and again, until it is ready to reunite with divinity. "This," he says, "is what the Holy Plato called Orphism."

"And this," counters Seth, "is what Socrates would say was the ultimate benefit of doing good, for no man who values his own soul, and who therefore has no wish to return to this world over and over, would persist in doing wrong. Socrates taught that only ignorance is evil, for no man can knowingly do harm."

But Philo rebuts this: "You need only to look around you to see that many most definitely *do* choose to harm themselves as well as others."

"In this," Seth replies, "you are like Plato's pupil Aristotle, who mistook the meaning of Socrates. Socrates would say that if a man acts out of goodness, it benefits his soul, and if a man acts out of wickedness, he harms not only others, but his own soul. It stands to reason therefore, that any man, *knowing* this, would not do harm. It is also reasonable to say that a man who chooses harm does *not* know this, and is therefore ignorant. Thus it follows that ignorance is the only evil."

"The teacher is taught," says Philo, but only after swallowing a large bite of pride.

There are other nights when Seth must concede. Though never on nights when Philo discusses Moses. It is Philo's contention that Plato and Pythagoras borrowed the best of what they taught from Moses. Seth does not laugh at this, but we can see he does not accept it. Later, he quietly tells us that Jews who love Greek or Egyptian ideas often hope to defend themselves from criticism by claiming these ideas are originally Jewish. It is, he says, understandable in a conquered people, and something he has seen in many men and in many places. Salome and I sit near and listen for hours.

Seth changes as we change. Salome has become taller and I have become taller still. We are now boys on so deep a level that no one

would guess we were not. Hiding our breasts by binding is not difficult; hiding our menses by Tata's herbs and constant vigilance is also
not difficult. There are times I wonder if I could remember to act the
female. As we do no magic, we hear no voices. Most especially, the
Loud Voice is silent, for which I am grateful. As for Seth, he talks no
more of messiahs and Kittim and the Poor and their war of Dark
against Light. We can see he grows beyond these things, vital though
they are to most men he knows and, I presume, cherishes. In coming
with us to Egypt, Seth has discovered there is a peace and a beauty
not to be found in the world of men in their comings and goings and
plots and counterplots, in their rages and their desires and their fears.
Seth changes on so deep a level I think almost to see his bones grow.

And then comes the evening that changes us all: Philo Judaeus of
Alexandria allows Seth of Damascus and his nephews, John the Less
and Simon Magus, to see and to hear—even to *know* if we are ready—
the secret Passion of Father, Mother, and Child, Osiris and Isis and
Horus. And because Seth urges him to, he allows also Dositheus and
Helena of Tyre.

For a week before, we must meditate and fast and cleanse our
bodies in oil and scent. We are told little of what to expect, except
that we are to pay strict attention, for later, when we have returned
from all that we shall see and do, we will be asked to make sense of it.
If we cannot make sense of it, Philo assures us he will have wasted
his time with us, and he shall stop doing so on the instant—we will
no longer be his *mathetes*. He does not say this to Seth; he says it only
to Simon Magus and to John the Less. I do not think Salome will
forgive him for this, for all that she seems unconcerned. But for
me, hearing it, I can barely keep down the little we are allowed in
the way of food, which is nothing but a tasteless, watery, grayish . . .
something. Actually, I have no idea what it is, and I do not ask.

Salome and I have longed to know Mysteries, we have sought
them however we could, yet now that Theano has us dress in white
trousers and white tunics, and now that we come so close, I find I
would rather I could stay in my bed. We go barefoot and wear small

crowns of gold. Not one of us has ever worn trousers. How odd they feel between the legs. While it is yet deathly quiet and the city still sleeps, we meet with Joor far out on the flat Canopic Way. We walk for mile after mile, taking this featureless track or that, seeing others walking as we do, some alone, many in small groups, but making no greeting. Not once during this long day does anyone speak or slow, especially Helena of Tyre who knows only silence and pain. By and by, we find Sudheer and the poetess Julia waiting in a boat, a small thing of reeds with a curved prow. Taking our places in this, we move through the trackless reeds and rushes in complete silence.

The first shades of evening draw down so that above us stands the great constellation of Osiris. Joor points up at the starry sky to speak the first words we have heard this day. "There," says he, "see the three stars in his belt? Those are Mintaka, Anilam, and Alnitak, who are the three wise men." From the belt, Joor tracks a curve down to the bottom of the sky where shines in the east Sopdet, the brightest of all the stars, which the Greeks call Sothis, and the Israelites call Ephraim or the star of Jacob. "And that is who they seek, Isis, from whom Horus, the godchild, will be born this night."

With many others, silent as we are silent, we have come finally to the shores of a secret lake. Darkest night has fallen, and as we approach, there suddenly comes the wailing of flutes, but this is as nothing, for a moment later, our nerves are shaken and our ears shattered by the thunder of a mighty gong. Then comes the sudden flare of light from a thousand torches. Then darkness. We walk forward in utter gloom; then we are lit in our multitude by flaring torches, then plunged back into darkness, then blinded again by surprising light. The long line of initiates, each gold crowned and white gowned and without sandals, circles the lake, and some of us dance, no matter if there is fluted music or if there is not, and some of us do not dance but walk as solemn as Temple priests on the Day of Atonement. And I for one wake up as I have never been awake, and all the while the gong hammers on our senses, and the light flares up and dies, flares up and dies, and far out on the lake of black water there is a huge raft of reeds, and on the raft, the towering godman himself, Osiris.

It is now that we see that it is Philo himself who presides at this great and terrible rite and it is Philo who carries a wand. We are given three things: one to drink, one to eat, and one to hold. And it is now as thick incense infuses the air that the godman suffers and dies for us amid loud lamentation from the thousands around me. I grab Salome's hand, who would have grabbed mine if I had not done such a thing first. I am by turns terror stricken, then wracked with such pity I sob in my throat, and then comes joy, so exultant it is almost the joy of my secret time of illness. Osiris, born of God and a mortal virgin, is led before us in triumph seated on a donkey. But is then abused and is scorned and caused to die horribly, hung bleeding on a crooked tree. Just before I think I too would die from grief, he is taken down and placed in a tomb where three women attend his body. But oh! He rises on the third day! And how I weep as he ascends to heaven accompanied by such music as is made by the transported, and in the blaze of glorious celestial lights.

On all sides, there now comes a chanting. "Have we sacrificed thee?" the higher initiates around me cry. "Do we say that thou hast died for us? He is not dead! He lives forever! He is alive more than we, for he is the mystic one of sacrifice. He is our Lord, living and young forever!" And we all of us weep. And over some comes such a state it seems akin to transcendent vision, and they fall to their knees with upraised faces. But for a very few there is more than this. A man stands near, small and dark of skin, but shining out as a moon. This one does not merely feel, he *sees;* and he does not merely see, he *knows.*

I know this is so. I have felt into his mind.

This is what Philo calls a "sober intoxication," and what Plato names the "rapt" after observing Socrates standing spellbound for the whole of a day and a night. Sudheer, the Brahmin, calls it Moksha, which is God Union. But I am a Jew and I call it Glory.

I look to Seth when I see this; I wonder what it is he feels? And immediately I look away. I have trespassed against him, seen something in his face that was not for me to see, not without permission. As if the skin had been pared away, scraped down to the bone, I saw as if truly seeing, my first teacher, my beloved friend. I saw that, like Moses, though Seth could point the way to gnosis, he could not travel there himself.

On the third day following this night, when Salome and I are once again fed, once again clothed as Jews, and back once more at our studies, a messenger comes to take us to the Jewish section. Salome remembers, as do I, that when this day is over, we shall know whether the great philosopher Philo Judaeus will continue to honor us with his teaching, or whether he will not. Instantly, I am plunged into a fearful tangle of nerves, but Salome appears perfectly untroubled.

I am impressed. As well as annoyed.

As soon as we are within the walls of Philo's house, where we have not been for many days, Philo takes me to one room and Simon Magus to another. Thus separated, a servant sets ink and papyrus and brushes before me and, I presume, before Simon. Philo waits until all but my heart is quiet before saying, "I shall ask you, John the Less, three questions concerning what you saw by the lake, and you shall answer these questions in writing. When you are done writing, I will ask you to read your answers aloud. Since I am expected this night to attend a great dinner at my brother's house, and since I am the honored guest, we will not waste time. First, what is the meaning of Osiris riding a donkey? Second, why is Osiris the godman abused by the people as he walks to his death? Third, if man is a flawed creation of God and if the world is a lesser image of heaven as says the Holy Plato, why then were man and the world created? Now I will give Simon his three quite different questions. Start, please. I will be returning sooner than you can imagine."

With that, he is gone. And I am left quaking. I believe I know how to answer the first two questions. Osiris is our Higher Nature, that part of us which is akin to God. But being, as we are, in body, we are bound to our Lower Nature, seen symbolically as the ass. This is also why Osiris is said to be born of God and of a mortal. I think too that I can answer the second question: Osiris is treated as he is for the same reason the Jews treat the scapegoat on the Day of Atonement as they do, heaping it with all of our sins and then driving it and our sins out into the wilderness to die. But as for the third? I do not know the answer to the third question. *Eloi! Eloi!* I am lost. And so I sit and I stew and I make a mess of my papyrus.

Before I know it, Philo is back and he does not look at the mess I have made nor does he look at me. He looks at one of the many curious things he keeps in his house, and taking it up and fiddling with it with his long frog fingers, he tells me to read aloud what I have written. Having no choice, I read and he listens and he nods and he fiddles with his whatever-it-is and he seems satisfied, but when I come to what I have written in answer to the third question, there is nothing but silence for I have written nothing. Philo waits for what seems an eternity before saying, "Have you something caught in your throat?"

"No, Master."

"Then read, boy, I run out of time and patience."

I do not cry, and that is something. "I do not know the answer to the third question."

I wait to hear that Philo will no longer waste his time with me.

"Good." He sets down that which he plays with. "Neither do I. Though I am working on it. I wonder, do you agree that man is flawed? It could be that it is this postulate, and not man, that is flawed. But no, how else to explain wrongdoing? And if the world is not as Plato says, a lower copy of the higher, why then is it full of sorrow and suffering?"

I do not speak as he continues. "Yet what if suffering is only of the mind, thinking itself separate from Source? What if Seth is right when he surmises that the world is not a copy, but a *reflection* of Source, and that it is neither good nor is it evil, but instead endlessly creative? That would rather change things, would it not?" He shakes his head. "Plato would not have said such a thing, and Plato was as a god in his philosophizing. Yet I will tell you a thing, boy, and it is this, whether he is flawed or not, man suffers. For this, the Egyptian has the godman Osiris and the Greek has Dionysus and the Persian has Mithras, and others have their godmen, and they are all the same, but who does the Jew have as godman? Who is their envoy to the goddess Sophia, she who will bring them silent intoxication and lift them from suffering? They have Yahweh, but Yahweh will not do. Yahweh is for those who do not know the gnosis of Sophia, and do not know they do not know. Yahweh is the Law and the Law makes captives of our people. Therefore, I think to perform Midrash. I think to devise for the Jews a new myth, one crafted from old myth, but a uniquely Jewish myth of a godman. Would that I could call him Moses!"

I blurt out, "But it will not be true!"

Philo dismisses this with a wave of his hand. "Which of these godmen are true? What is truth? It does not matter whether a story is true or if it is not true. What matters is the eternal truth in the story. The goddess Truth does not come into the world naked; she has too bright a shine, so clothes herself in symbols, as all gods and goddesses are symbols. It is the height of foolishness to take their stories literally. Yet behind each shines a truth. The godman does not 'teach something' or 'think something' but rather inspires intense feeling unto rapture. The godman opens the self to God. This the Jews do not have, so I shall invent a new myth that will suit them. I will begin a passion here in his name, and I will see it spread. What? Are you still here? Run along. You may come again when Seth comes."

I run off as if I had sails and the wind were at my back.

If I have a hero, who is Seth, and if Salome has a hero, who was John of the River and is now Pythagoras, and if Philo has a hero who is Moses, Seth has a hero. Seth's hero is Socrates. Socrates said that one must question everything. Socrates said that the unexamined life is not worth living. Socrates said that what is important is not what other men think, but what the individual thinks. "Understand this," says Seth. "Know that as Socrates valued his own thought and taught each man to value his, so too the Nazorean values his own experience of god and would teach each man to value his."

Seth tells us that he hopes one day he will see his way to live as Socrates and die as a Nazorean. But his teaching of the inner

Nazoreans seems to change as he changes. Salome and I have talked it over and have decided that the Nazorean is a beginning and the inner Nazorean a continuation. We have decided that as Philo hopes to create a Jewish godman, pieced together from all other godmen, Seth is creating the inner Nazorean teaching as he teaches it. By this we come to see that religion, like philosophy, can be tended like one of Tata's roses.

Who knows when and how it will flower?

I have been sitting watching the sea. It is boundless and endless and timeless in its mystery. The vault of early morning sky is like an up-ended cup of blue glass. Tiny black ants labor in the soft brown earth near my hand. Nearby sits Seth, who works on a poem asked of him by Julia. After a good hour of this, my friend looks up and presents me with, to my mind, an odd question. "Is there anything," asks he, "that is not Life?"

I look about me and smile in all my wisdom, saying, "The stones are not alive. Nor is the Sea of Stink. If there is anything dead in this world, and surely there is, it is these things."

I shall not soon forget how he answers my answer. He picks up a rock that lies on the palace path, and he strikes it against the stone of the palace walls. Crack! Out jumps a spark from between rock and stone like the quick bright tongue of a snake. He says, "There is nothing that is not alive, John. What is death? What is dead? The Kingdom of God is the Life of life. Where is there not the Kingdom of God? Where can God not reach?"

Seth returns to his poem and I to my contemplation of the sea. But I no longer feel wise.

Over seven years, we attempt to read every book and every tome in every niche and every bucket in the ten halls of the Brucheion Library. And some of them we read over and over. We fill our minds with names and dates and potions and places. We fill our minds with the thinking of this one and of that one, of this school and that school, of poet and philosopher and mathematician and holy man, with the thoughts of women as well as men. But the names and the dates and the places and the gender are not the thing. Nor are the thoughts of others the thing, no matter how sublime, not even Seth's thoughts, or the thoughts of Philo Judaeus. What is meant by all this learning is that we might learn to have thoughts of our own.

Over these same years, Ananias the sponge merchant comes and goes, growing ever fatter. He has surprised us by marrying a woman of the wilderness who remains in the wilderness, a widow he tells us is called Sapphira. It is not surprising that within a year they have a son, and a year later another son and the following year a third son, and a fourth son the year after that. This does not make his comings any less frequent or his goings any less short. Ananias carries our letters to Addai and to Tata and delivers what they write to us. He brings us news. Father's brother-in-law, my uncle, Pinhas ben Yohai, lies near death with some strange corrupting illness that doctors cannot cure. Father has removed himself to Bethany to take charge of his brother-in-law's home and family. The Jerusalem house is closed down; Naomi and all Father's servants and slaves packed off to Bethany. I ask, "Is my aunt still mistress of her own home?" Shrugging, Ananias answers, "If Pinhas dies, perhaps Josephus will have two wives. There are rich men who have more than this." I shudder at the thought. But of course, this will not happen for it is forbidden by Torah for a man to take his brother's widow to wife if there are children, and Father is a man of the Law. When it suits him. But then, Pinhas is not Father's brother.

I put this away.

What means it to me who have no father but Addai?

∝

Seth and Simon Magus and Dositheus and Helena and I are coming away from a theater near the south harbor on Lake Mareia; we have just seen a very poor Roman play. Seth and Simon remain proper Nazoreans in white, as do I, but Helena has taken to wearing what the women of Alexandria wear, a thin almost transparent chiton, slashed to the thigh. In Judaea, she would be stoned for such wicked daring. Dositheus, more melancholic than ever, has taken up the Egyptian kilt and has curled his hair. Arrayed thus, we are passing by a bone carver's workshop and I am thinking of the actor I have just seen, a man with red hair. I find myself asking this question, "Seth, these many years in Egypt we have learned so much, and yet, we have still to hear the innermost teaching. When shall we know the deepest secret that lies at the heart of your Nazorean?"

Seth studies me for a long moment. I know this look. He is disappointed in me. "John, you have held the secret since that day on the Nabataean road."

Salome turns on a thought. From bemoaning the bloody Roman play to Dositheus, who has been bemoaning the bloody Roman acting, she asks, "What day?"

"The day I voiced our secret."

"Seth!" I wail as if I were a child once more and had not been in Alexandria all these years. "Do not tease. You told us the secret then? If you did, I did not hear it."

Seth looks at me, straight in the eye and then he fixes Salome with this same straight eye, and he says, "Then hear me now. The secret of the inner Nazorean is to place no blame, nurse no guilt, seek no redress, harbor no hatred, follow no Law, suffer no priest, and look not to an angry arrogant god, or to a messiah, but *within* for knowledge of Source." At my stricken face, he softens. "As I love you, John, do you not yet know the still, small voice that sounds within? That the secret is to listen and by listening to hear? You are the secret. Know yourself and you know the All."

Know myself. Again and again, this is what it comes down to.

As it is written over the sanctuary of Apollo at Delphi, *Gnothi Seauton,* this is where Seth's teaching begins and this is where it ends. Over and over, Seth tells us of gnosis. If we do not hear him one way, he tries another and another. Time after time he calls it this, or he calls it that, "raised from the Dead into Life," or "turning water into wine." He says that one who *knows* can say of themselves: I AM. But most often he calls it "knowing one's Name." And yet, and yet, I do not *know* in the way he means by knowing. And even though there is a thing I tell no one, that I have never told anyone, and even though both Theano and Philo take Salome and me to the Passion of Osiris each year and have passed through the sixth level of initiation into the Therapeutae, I fear we are as yet water, not wine; we are as yet Dead, not full of Life; we do *not* know our own names. I cannot answer for Salome, but I begin to think I shall never be other than this.

"I will tell you one more secret."

I am pulled away from myself. Seth will tell us one more secret?

"Five hundred years ago, the Greek philosopher Xenophanes wrote, 'There is one God, always still and at rest, who moves all things with the thoughts of His mind.' In this year, I, the philosopher Seth, *mathetes* of the philosopher Philo Judaeus, teaching my favorite students in Alexandria, would add, it is not that there is one God but that God is One, meaning All There Is. There is nothing that is not God. It follows then, that it is not *his* Mind that moves all things, for we are not separate, but 'our' Mind."

I walk the rest of the way home in perfect silence and perfect wonder.

I understand this! I do understand. I may not know my own name, but this I know in my sinew. God is not a separate being called Yahweh or even a godman called Osiris, or Dionysus, or Mithras, or Buddha. God is One, meaning God is All. Therefore, All is God. We are all in and of the Mind of God. We *are* the Mind of God.

Like myself, Salome walks home in silence. Does she think as I think? Is she too stunned by simplicity?

In the fifteenth year of Tiberius, Seth and Dositheus are summoned back to the wilderness. Salome and I are to go too for it is thought by all who concern themselves that we shall have been forgotten by now, and what could be safer than neglect?

My heart is broken, but Salome rejoices that she shall see John of the River again. How can she be so eager to see a man she has not seen for seven years, and then, only once? How can she be so eager to leave this place? Of all that she has gathered in these years, little will go back with her, and the most important seems to be a tiny vial Sabaz the physician gave her long ago. This she slips into Tata's leather bag, hanging, as ever, at her waist. She says her good-byes to all who have taught us for so long and so willingly, looks one last time out over the Royal Harbor, and is ready. Even her farewell to Theano is abrupt. The woman who first showed her the wonder of Pythagoras, who instructed her in the eternal truths of numbers and shapes, by the stars, even to Theano! As for Philo, a quick good-bye and that is all.

I stand aghast. The wind is blowing in from the Egyptian Sea, and with it comes a sea green spray that wets my face until no one could tell which is sea and which are tears. Seven years of a life such as is lived by few, and it does not break her heart to be going back? Oh, Isis and Osiris! Oh, Serapis and Harpocrates, his son by Isis! It is breaking mine. It is breaking mine even as I think of Addai and of Tata and of Eio, even as a small hope that I should once again see Father rises in my throat.

I swear that I will return one day.

I will come back to Alexandria and its library.

"Damascus"

No matter *where* I look the very air trembles with heat. To breathe it is like inhaling an open flame. It is Elul, the height of summer, the time of the date harvest. The flat blue sea below us sends up all the smells of Sheol. I am back in the wilderness.

I am John the Less. Beardless as his uncle Seth the Maccabee remains beardless, John the Less is a quiet young man, a contemplative, and much given to his own company or to that of his brother, Simon Magus. I am also very thin. Gone is the lovely fat of privilege that padded and softened me. I am thin and I am brown and by my daily work I am become very strong. The ache in my arm from falling into a tomb in the City of the Dead comes no longer now that I am stronger.

Since we returned from Alexandria, John the Less and Simon Magus have done little but toil in the sun.

There are moments still under the date palms of our *nahal*, but they are not many. Fat and furry hyraxes still sun themselves on the same rocks, though perhaps they are not the same hyraxes. Eagles still circle as motes in the blue eye of the sky. The unburning sun still rises each day over Moab. From time to time, and with my beloved Eio on guard, we allow ourselves to become Mariamne and Salome, for though there is much to be said for being the grave John the Less and the lofty Simon Magus, there is also much to be said for being Salome and Mariamne—though for the moment, I cannot think what.

Salome goes about with great content because John of the River visits the settlement. John is still much the taller, but Salome seems no longer so small. Behind her trails the black Phoenician, Helena, who once again dresses as befits the Land of Israel. She has attached herself to Salome, perhaps because though Salome is kind to no one, she is kind to Helena, though the poor thing goes about in almost Delphic trance. To ease her constant pain, she takes many times more *rosh* than Tata takes, and it makes of her a wraith in the land of the living.

I see that John more often chooses the company of Simon Magus than he does those he has favored for years. Does all this disturb the walking gloom that is now Dositheus? I do not know. John of the River might also walk with me, but I avoid him. This is not always possible, and in such moments I find him a wealth of odd information and odder opinions. I would so love to love him. Perhaps I blame him for our return from Egypt. Perhaps not. Perhaps I blame him for changing Salome. And perhaps not. I am too ill humored to know much of anything.

Tata is as fierce as ever, though thinner. She has also grown shorter in these seven years. Where once I looked up into her face, now she looks up into mine. But to smell her and to touch her brings me joy. She has learned to make pots; they encircle the women's tents, full to bursting with roses and poppies.

Addai is unchanged, even in face. Perhaps a line or two, a streak here and there of white in his beard, but that is all, and for this my heart, such as it is, is truly grateful. If there could be a thing that made a heaven of a place, it would be the presence of Addai of Samaria.

Yet, I think of nothing but Alexandria. Where is the sweet scent of books, the soft murmur of scholars, the blue secrets of the sea, the walks and talks in Philo's garden? Here there is nothing but work. Salome grows further and further away. I would read, but the only books are those in the domed and star painted room under the settlement, and I have read them all. It seems in seven years I have not learned *ataraxia*. For all my philosophizing, and all my writing of poems in the style of Theocritus, I have not achieved peace of mind.

I shall go mad.

Just as I am changed, so too is the wilderness. It is every bit as hot and dry and pale under the yellow cliffs and the yellow sun. The Sea of Pitch is every bit as salty; the thistles are just as brown, and the thorns as sharp. The same harvesters cut balsam with knives of bone or stone and the same hopeful faces come to be cured. Shipments of aromatics and medicines and black healing stones are, as ever, sent here and sent there, all bringing profit to the Poor. And Ananias is still a merchant here, though I see little of him since he is so often busy keeping far from his wife, the greedy Sapphira, and farther from the four greedy sons she has borne him.

But where before the wilderness was no more than a muttering and a railing half the night, now it is full of an ominous silence and a tension that buckles the very air. For everywhere the zealots grow more zealous, the righteous more righteous, the Lawful stricter, the prophets louder, and all grow more intolerant. The very land groans under their complaint. As for the expectation that comes the Messiah, the "warrior king" of zealotry, this has spread fast and as far as Jonah's gourd, which came up in one night. Salome cannot resist mentioning that Jonah's gourd also perished in one night. Nor can dour Dositheus help but say, "Who are kings but successful bandits? And what are bandits but would-be kings?"

So stern, her eyebrows seem a single brow, Tata says, "All this talk of End Times and Final Judgment, pah. The prophets are roosters startled by shadows. Their constant crowing of doom drives the people to madness. Comes here now those who need be healed of what the prophets have wrought!"

As for the daggermen, Rome crucifies the Sicarii in their thousands; crosses line the roads for miles. Yet there spring up more Sicarii.

And the Poor, who were once one sect, are now perhaps four sects, each new breakaway group becoming less and less peaceful until the latest is now more warlike than the Germans. Where once men came here to separate themselves from the children of the pit, they now come to plot more war.

To add to this roiling brew, Rome has sent Judaea a new governor, the fifth of such men appointed over the course of twenty years. He is called Pontius Pilate, and I have heard nothing but ill of him. Yet were he the best of men, as this Pilate is sent from Rome, still he should be loathed. Already men excoriate his name as they excoriated the name of the outgoing Valerius Gratus. I do not envy the Roman his new position. But I do at long last learn why the wilderness is called Damascus, and I learn that not only our camp, but all the camps are called this.

Damascus is code taken from the prophet Amos, the shepherd from Bethlehem who said that before the Day of Reckoning, the repentant would live exiled in the Land of Damascus until the Lord once more raised up the fallen tent of David. The repentant are the men who do not suffer the Romans in Jerusalem, nor do they suffer the Jews who do. The fallen tent of David is not only the Temple but also the House of David.

We have surely come home to a Damascus afire with blood and struggle. And in the midst of all this madness, Helen of Adiabene lives for the moment in Jerusalem. Her son, Izates, is now the King of the Assyrians, and she is building a palace in the city of David. Addai is become her master builder. The foundations of Helen's palace are already in place at the southern end of the Temple Mount near Herod's hippodrome and the city's east wall. I find it odd for a queen to build a palace in a city she is no queen of, but in truth it bores me. Why do things not interest me when once, and not so long ago, everything interested me? Here there are only Hylics, a word meaning "unconscious matter," as Philo calls the simple. Once again I am cast among people of the body; those who know nothing but do not know they know nothing. People who believe the body is all there is of self. People, as Socrates lamented, who live unexamined lives, and who do nothing but look for a king, or a prophet, or a messiah to rescue them. Oh, why could not Seth have left me behind in Alexandria? I am no use to anyone here, least of all to myself. Everything has changed, but it is I who seems changed most of all. I do not laugh, and I do not talk, and worst of all, I do not know my Salome.

On this day of tiresome heat more wild men have come to the wilderness. Scowling with irritation, I watch them from the shadowed door of a room near the tower. Salome is with me, though not in spirit, which only makes me the more irritable. Before we left for Alexandria this room was a storage room; now it contains a forge to make weapons. Someone has diverted water; someone has made a chimney. Even the fact my home has a place and a way to forge weapons barely stirs my blood.

Ananias has his fat hand on Salome's shoulder, which he grips in great excitement. Any moment she will pull away, but for the time being she is as excited as Ananias, and so is oblivious. In another doorway stand the women of the inner Nazorean: Tata, and Helena of Tyre, and a certain Joanna. These keep their faces covered with head cloths, all but their eager eyes. Joanna is short but sturdy; her eye is as shiny as obsidian, and I have seen a marking on her jaw the color of wine. She is wife to Chuza, the steward of Herod Antipas, who is son to the dead Herod the Great. Salome does not trust this one. If Herod Antipas wanted a spy, and he surely would for the followers of John the Baptizer grow daily more numerous and clutter Herod's east bank of the Jordan, who better than this one who professes such devotion to John she has left her rich husband and her fine home to follow a crazy old man? Does her husband not wish her back? Does he not begrudge the money she spends in abundance? Has she no children?

I know that Salome often seeks her out, listens carefully to what she says, but I cannot muster the interest, though Joanna of the court of Herod Antipas, King of Galilee and Peraea, would once have consumed me. Now I slip away in my mind, thinking other thoughts, thoughts of heat and escape from heat. On our return from Alexandria to the wilderness, we sailed on a cargo ship carrying vintage wine from the best Lake Mareia vintners all the way to the port of Joppa. How fine the wind felt. There is nowhere here that is cool save deep in the marl of the caves, or down in our underground chambers. There is nowhere here that is even tolerable. Why are we out in this leaden heat?

Addai and Dositheus wait by the sundial in the middle of the west courtyard. A group of men are gathered round the steps leading up to the largest settling basin. These are as excited as Ananias and Salome. But over and above these, there are men and women and children everywhere, on top of the tower, on the hot flat roofs two stories down from the tower roof, on every wall. Overhead, an eagle circles as if we might be prey. Eio, who stands behind Addai, snorts at the sight, laying back her ears.

I droop where I wait, but John asks us to greet more wild men. Why? There are always so many, they come, they go—entire caravans arrive with all their attendant confusion of color and noise and smell—how could these be different? Whole villages of the ill come to be cured, or to die. By now there are two cemeteries and plans for a third. There is John himself. Year after year, John makes his entrances and his exits, and never alone. Wherever he goes, a multitude of his raggle-taggle followers go with him. In this place, there is always a coming and a going, therefore, why does every human soul in the wilderness jostle for space to view *this* coming? And why has John of the River bid us greet these newcomers? More to the point, why *me*? Addai may know, certainly Dositheus does, even Salome may know, but I do *not* know. More than irritation, this has put me in a fine temper. So, like Simon Magus, John the Less wears a clean tunic of the purest white linen, his hair grows uncut as befits a Nazorean, he has rinsed his mouth three times. He is furious.

At last, through the north gate come now the latest arrivals to the wilderness.

By Isis, these have to be the worst of the lot! Their mantles of brown sackcloth are dirtier, their sandals more worn, their beards more matted, their skin more leathered by wind and by sun, their eyes deeper sunk in their heads. Each walks with greater purpose and a larger awareness of worth than any man come before them. I think how Queen Helen held herself, how Izates who is now a king held himself. To them, pride was as natural as flight to a bird. But with the men who stride up our path from the reeking Sea of Stink, it feels fought for, held on to, like a prize hard won, much valued, and jealously guarded.

There follows on the women. Comes with these the usual goats and chickens and children and dogs. And I would yawn and turn away, but—who is it that walks with this family? Who looks as this man looks, with legs like a bull and back like a bear? I am flooded with memory. The murderer and swaggering braggart Simon of Capharnaum had legs like this—and by Apis, he still does! For there he is, striding along, a great scowl over his familiar face. And next to him, his brother Andrew. Even after these seven years, my heart beats like the tail of a fish trapped in a net.

It is only now that I see what I should have seen before all else. I look to the other males who throw down bags and bundles, peering through all that dirt and hair and wildness, and my fish of a heart flops over. There comes the two of the wild red hair. By the heavens, Chaos has come to the wilderness!

John the Baptizer makes his entrance only now, as if he were a hero in a Greek play, as if the part were written for him by Aristophanes of Athens. I do not know where he has been while we have all waited for these homicidal Galileans to climb up from the Salted Sea, but I know where he is now. Beard as tangled as a stork's nest, he has appeared as if dropped from the cloudless sky. Striding across the sun-blasted courtyard on legs of stork, arms held out wide as if he would embrace the whole family and all their friends down to the goats, John shouts as he comes. "Yehoshua! Jude! Simon! Simeon! Hast thou finally come to share my wilderness?"

Simon the murderer and Simon's friends—plus their chattel and their livestock and what seems their entire village—come to a confused halt by the sundial. I see them through a shimmy of brutal heat. With a great whoop, John of the River has clasped one of the redheaded twins in his arms, is pummeling his broad back. Like Tata beating a rug, clouds of dust fume and gyre about their heads. "You are all here!" he shouts. "Welcome! Welcome! Shalom! You grace my home."

The Galilean he pounds manages to say, "Wilderness, John?"

John stops his pounding. He looks back at our settlement, noting how far it strays from the word *wilderness*. Goats and sheep there are in profusion. Courtyards and well-made walls and the tall stone tower and carob and fig trees and the plash of blue water running from bath to cistern to canal to settling basins. John turns back, laughing. "I see thou hast escaped Herod the Fox, Yehoshua. I hear it was well done."

In turn, the man Yehoshua now claps his brother-double on the back. More dust, more shouting. "To escape a fox, one must be a fox, eh Jude!" He says this as John would say this, in the slipshod accent of Galilee. The twin Jude does not speak, he growls, touching the knife that is thrust through a loop in his rope belt. And I am the child I once was in my horror of this Jude, of Simon of Capharnaum, of this Yehoshua. Once again, I feel blood, hot with life, flow over my feet.

And yet, Jude and Yehoshua are not as the man Simon.

There is a sight to them, or—what is it? In the midst of my wilderness, my half-loved and half-hated home of yellow dust and high rock and heat like a kiln, the brothers Yehoshua and Jude seem as thunderheads, seem like black clouds charged with lightning. They smell of great deeds. Father once said great deeds are the promise of bright beginnings and the truth of horrible endings. John asks them what I would ask them. "What did you do, Yeshu'a, to provoke Herod so?"

"Do?" He laughs. Of all these men, only this one seems a friend to laughter. "What did we *do*, Jude?"

Once more, Jude growls, and this time, Yehoshua translates. "Jude says he did nothing, but that I, his brother, vexed a priest in the city of Tiberius."

I think, is another priest dead for God?

"Jude says that Herod Antipas would say I preached sedition and full merited his jail."

It eases me so to learn this one talks, and does not kill.

"But if that is so, my brother should like to know why John the Baptizer is here and not rotting away in a similar cell at this very moment?"

Salome's eyes widen at this. Her nostrils flare. If this Yeshu'a is not careful, he will have an enemy before even he has settled in. If such a thing should befall John, Salome would dig him out with her nails if need be, or bleed to death trying.

John the Baptizer laughs like Eio. Or at least as loudly. "He would not dare. I am more popular than he is. Do not the Pharisee and the Sadducee visit me more and more often, demanding to know my business?"

Yehoshua does not laugh like Eio; he laughs as Father used to laugh, big round sounds. He is not the only one who laughs. Addai laughs. Salome laughs in delight at her favorite. The men and women laugh. Even I almost laugh. The children laugh because we laugh. We are all fools for laughter. John can do this; often he makes us lose ourselves in joy. Or fear. John can do either with equal skill.

Through his laughter, Yehoshua says, "Perhaps we were jailed so that there would be people in his new city, Tiberius. Having built on a Jewish graveyard, Herod must now drag them in by the scruff of their necks. Not that they stay. Have you been there, John? It stinks as this place, steam and sulfur. Now, where do we eat? Where do we sleep? Where do the children play? Have you work for us?"

John sucks in air so that he might shout out his answers, but another has stepped forward. This one has never known a smile, inside or out, there is no room on his face, black bearded to the cheekbone, for other than rage and gloom. In a land of serious men, I have seen none grimmer. Even John, who towers over him, thinks to take a step back, but does not. "Ah," says John of the River, "Jacob."

Jacob has thoughts as dark as pitch in his head, thoughts as hard as stone. His mouth when it opens is like a cave. And now he yells as a prophet would yell, as if he too were an immerser on the banks of the Jordan and his accent is as thick as the mud of its banks. "The Righteous will taste more than jails; the Righteous will die by their thousands. Open your nose! Smell the war in the wind? These are the Last Days. These are the End Times! Are you prepared?"

As Jacob yells, I feel Salome's hand on my arm and am pleased. It has been so long since she touched me. She allows me into her thoughts. This one, she says, has made himself stupid in his righteousness. There is a power in this kind of stupidity that can drain the very sea.

But John is John the Baptizer, famed from one end of the Jordan to the other. None will be allowed to yell louder than he. He opens his mouth and lets out a mighty bellow, "Prepare yourself, Jacob! If every man cares for himself, all will be cared for." With that he turns back to the brothers, which stops Jacob's flow as a farmer stops water by closing a sluice gate. Jacob steps back, but his silence is as loud as his voice has been loud. There is more anger in this one man than in any man I have known, and by now, I have known enough angry men to whip the Great Sea to frenzy. John ignores him, therefore all ignore him. John flings out an arm. "Here, we are far from Galilee. Here, neither Herod nor Herod's men will find you. Nor yet Herodias, the woman he makes his wife, though she be his half brother's wife as well as his niece. Here, you will make your home, you and all your family. And here you will find many others who flee the law, and none, so far, are snared by it. Not so long as they keep to the wilderness. My home is your home, cousins."

Cousins? This, then, is why we are bid to witness their arrival; these are John's kin! But I am wondering, by law, does he mean the Roman law, which is also Herod's law, or does he mean the Law, which is the Law of Moses—which, among all else it does, forbids Herod to take his brother's wife to wife? But in truth, I do not care. I have done what was asked of me; I have waited in the sun to witness the coming of his kin. I have felt fear of Simon. I have felt a certain wonder at Yehoshua. Some for Jude. And none for Jacob. Now I should like to go back to my *nahal* and my sulking. Those who have waited for John move forward now to greet those who have arrived. There is much confusion. I see all this, and I could not be more vexed. It is hot. I am bored. There is a hairy brown spider on the wall near my ankle. I know it is harmless, and yet, in spite of myself, I lean away from it. By this, I push Salome who, not understanding, pushes me back. I am so irritated I kick her. She cannot believe I have done this and stares at me as if I were a hairy brown spider.

I wish with all my heart that I were again in my Egyptian bed under its Egyptian netting. How I long for the voices of the Egyptian night: the murmur of a last few scholars too engrossed to go to bed, distant flutes from the rich district of the Brucheion, the heated song of the streets, the call of night watch to night watch on the ships out in the harbors, salt harbor or sweet—but no. I am in the wilderness and all around me everyone is engrossed with coarse Galileans. If I cannot be in Egypt, I would rather be talking to Eio, scratching the hard hairy bone between her eyes. I would rather be in the cool of a cave reading a book. Lately I reread the book given me so long ago by Heli, the philosophy of Epicurus of Athens. Oh, that I should have my own *eudaemonia,* that "good guardian spirit" Epicurus speaks of, that I should know freedom from bodily and mental pain, and attain *ataraxia*! I imagine myself an Epicure. Like the followers of Pythagoras did, Epicureans admit women as well as men, slaves as well as the free, the poor as well as the rich. How far this from the ideas of the Poor or the Essene! All they wish for is a mind free from disturbance, a body free of pain, and a simple personal happiness that can only be found by loving the world on which Epicurus placed such high value. I find the Epicurean idea of everything being made of invisible indestructible moving particles, and there being more worlds like this world, wonderful. As wonderful as Metrodorus of Clios saying the stars are surely peopled. But as for Epicurus denying immortality, this I know to be false, for long ago, when I was ill at Father's—

"And this," I suddenly hear John say no more than a pace away from my ear, "is our young magician and this our young prophet."

My eyes do not snap open for they have not been closed. But no part of my mind has been looking through them. It does now, all that I know of it, and with a suddenness that is almost like falling off the top of the tower. As so long ago, once again I am staring into the face of the man Yehoshua—but now he stares also into mine.

I know John is very near me; I know here too is Salome. I know all the others, even Sapphira and her brood of red-faced brats, have moved into the courtyard. I can hear John say, "Simon. John. I would have you meet my favored cousin, Yeshu'a." And I can hear that the Baptizer does not shout; that instead he almost whispers. But what I know more than I know anything is that I do not know what I *feel*. It is not irritation. It is not anger. It is certainly not the weariness of the spirit that lately plagues me. What is it? It feels as if a small tooth nibbles on my heart. This man cannot remember me. It was so long ago. I was a child. A female child. Who would remember such a one? But I, I remember this man, and I cannot look away.

I am grieved to see that Yehoshua *can* look away, and does so when John points to Salome. "This is Simon Magus whom Seth says already confounds the mathematicians and the magicians." He points to me, "And this is John the Less."

Once more, Yehoshua looks my way. "I have heard of these youths."

He would say more, but the moment Yehoshua turns his face from mine, I say, "I have not heard of you."

Yehoshua laughs. He laughs! I love him for his laughter. I hate him for laughing at me. My petulant self would say more, but suddenly another face pushes into mine. This face comes as a shock.

"Who is this?" asks the face. "John? Yeshu'a? Come away. The sons of Judas would have a word."

In his eyes I see all I saw the first time; Simon Peter of Capharnaum is as he was. Does he remember me? He had demanded my name so that he might remember me. But no, there is no memory there. I was a child then, and as nothing to him. I am as nothing to him now. With no more than a glance, he dismisses John the Less.

John and Yeshu'a move away, Simon Peter eagerly leading. Why do I grieve? Why do I *grieve*?

Salome nudges my foot with hers. By Isis, I have all but forgotten my Salome! "What do you see, Mariamne?" Salome asks this of me, using my name, my own name, under her breath. "I see John who lights up my heart. I see the Simon who darkens the air I breathe. But what do you see?"

I do not know what I will say until I say it. "I see that the One has finally come."

The dark that falls over her face is darker than any Simon of Capharnaum could draw down. For Salome, John is the One. And from this day forward, for Simon Magus and John the Less, nothing is ever again the same.

Two days later, and Salome is pretending to hoe, but it takes only a glance to see she works out something from Pythagoras, a problem in geometry Theano once set her at lessons that results in a twelve-rayed star. I am actually hoeing. I have found I like to grow things, to tend them. There are rounds of salted dirt on my knees. There is salted sweat on the back of my neck. The sun does not burn my skin, but it heats my blood. All this morning, we have been down by the river far below the settlement, and now that it is the month of Tishrei, I have prepared a new bed for sowing more *rosh* poppies. I have washed salt from the stony earth through a sluice I myself have made, for the poppy does better when the soil is sweeter.

Eio is nibbling at the wild grasses that grow on the riverbank at the end of my unfinished row of poppies; one long shaggy ear bent forward and one long ear twisted back. I imagine myself Eio. I imagine myself Eio because it will be a change from imagining the brothers Yehoshua and Jude. It is Yeshu'a who does not leave my mind. I feel also the first stirrings of the Loud Voice since I cannot recall when, and I am afraid. I cannot ask help of Salome; neither of us has made further mention of voices, or much of anything else. I slip into Eio's hide, curl like smoke through her nostrils, move through her blood—and the first thing I feel are the flies that torment her. The buzzing, the crawling. I toss my shaggy head and they come back. I toss them away again; they come back. How maddening not to have hands to swat them! I am tormented by flies. I stamp. I snort. I gather myself to bray—

"John!"

Yea Balaam! I must leap a cubit. I find I have not been working at all. I have been a fly-crazed donkey and all the while I am a donkey, Mariamne's body has been leaning on a hoe. But I am back now. Who shouts at me?

"A word," says Tata, who has come all the way down from the settlement, across the entirety of the poppy field, and now appears before me without my notice, but not without Eio's. Which of us has truly brayed? I find I do not know.

Salome glances up from her star in the dirt, wondering if a word is wanted with her as well, or if something is happening she would be interested in. If it concerns John of the River, Salome is always interested.

"I come for this one," offers Tata, removing me from my hoe. "Addai has need of Eio." She pushes at me, urges me away from our field on the banks of the Jordan. "Eio works for no one but John the Less and Addai."

At the word *works*, Salome goes back to her dots and her dirt. In all this heat, I am hardly more interested in work than Salome, but, it is true, Tata could not make Eio walk a step. I call to Eio who trots over at once; gone for seven years and still Eio is mine. And so we walk away, Tata and Eio and I, out of the poppy field and up the steep path leading back to the settlement.

We are walking into the moment I will remember forever.

Addai awaits us in a drying room near the pottery workshops. From its door I can see the great kiln. This is where Tata now spends her days, for by now she has become more than a passable potter. Waiting as well are Seth, and the man Yehoshua, and Yehoshua's twin, Jude.

I am put off balance. Not only is it clear that Addai has no interest in Eio, but this is the first I have seen of Seth since he left many weeks ago for Jerusalem on some business of Queen Helen's. I smile at Seth; I stare at Yehoshua, at Jude. So alike outside, yet the man inside each is not the same and it shows in the eyes and the mouth. Addai comes forward, touches my shoulder. I am startled. So intent on the brothers, I have lost myself. He bids me sit. There are no benches, no chairs, in this room. There are only shelves of drying clay: pots of all shapes and sizes, cups and bowls and jugs. So we sit on the dirt of the floor, which makes no difference to me, as I am already dirty. It makes no difference to the brothers who seem as baked as the pots. Why am I here?

Now that we are all seated in a circle, Seth says an odd thing, "You know who I am, John?"

"Of course. You are my uncle, Seth of Damascus, the last of the Maccabees."

"And you know who Addai is? And Tata?"

"I do."

"Do you love us?"

"With the whole of my heart."

"Then you will not question what we ask of you." This last is not a question. I keep my eyes on his eyes. I keep my back straight and my hands folded. "I would have you tell us of your illness. I would have you tell us what you heard and what you saw, even if it sounds as the Book of Enoch."

I look from face to face. My illness? Sounding as the Book of Enoch? Enoch is full of fantastic visions and terrible secrets. It is full of a Jew's Seven Heavens and of a Jew's hell. Enoch teaches of fallen angels and an avenging messiah. For a moment I do not understand, and then I do. My eyes come to rest on Tata and I see why I am called here. She has told them how it was with me at Father's in the month before Ananias came to supper that night.

She has told them that eight years ago I died.

And that I rose from the dead.

In all this time I have told no one what I experienced, not even Salome. I do not know why I have not shared it with the friend with whom I share everything, but I do know—and have known all along—that the Loud Voice was born of my dying. Only Tata, who never left my side in those days and nights, could have even the smallest idea of what it might have been like, and Tata has no idea at all. And yet she *does* know, for it was she who saw the skin of my face shine with a light like unto Moses on the mountain, and she who told me this is what she saw.

I sit in silence. Seth asks me a terrible thing. I do not want to tell them. And if I did, I would share with only Addai and Tata and Seth. Why would I tell these brothers something I have not told Salome? And there is this: I do not have the courage. Having told no one, I have no oft-told tale to tell. From that time to this, I have thought of it seldom, and when I have, it seems more a fabulous dream than a doing. But I know it was not a dream. It was not a dream and it was not delirium, though delirium was the door through which I walked. But to explain where I went? To describe what I saw? To offer what I brought back into this world? Would they understand my answers? I went nowhere for there is nowhere to go. I saw nothing but what is always here. I brought nothing back but what I took with me. But I think of Addai and Tata and how I love them. I think of Seth and all we have been to each other and all he has taught me. Suddenly I feel ashamed. Seth has given me freely of his life and his skill and his mind, vast as the green Egyptian Sea, and I keep such as this to myself?

I will tell them. Or I will try.

But from the very first word, my telling is confused, disjointed. In the space of no more than a moment or two, I think it futile. My words hold no color, no scent, no music, they are pale things, as pale and as eyeless as worms. But even as I stumble in the telling, awe sings in my veins, for nothing else in the whole of my life has compared to my journey out of the body of self and into the body of Glory. Not even the Passion of Osiris, which is a journey like no other.

I have read Enoch. I have read Jubilees and Ezekiel and Daniel. I have read of Jacob's ladder that reached to heaven. I know whoever wrote these things stood in the first Great Hall of the House of Glory. Just as John the Baptizer did, which is something I think I shall never say aloud, and why I know he is not the One. I know though their visions were terrifying and though they were beautiful and though they yearned for God with a torment of longing, all these stood apart; they did not go *in*. They did not learn they are as much *in* Glory and *of* Glory as Glory *is*. They did not see that they themselves *are* Glory. They did not learn they were not "caught up" by something apart and distinct from themselves, but rather they flew up on the wings of their own splendid Being. If they had learned such a wonderful thing, I know they would have said so. It would be in the books they wrote or that were written in their names. But it is not so written. To a Jew, the Invisible God is always above and apart. But I have seen with my own eyes that God is not above and apart. God is within and without. There is nothing that is not God.

As Seth once said, "It is not that there is one God. It is that God is One."

At this, I feel a sudden heat, like sheet lightning in the veins. In this instant, I know why I have not spoken of it—*this* is why. I have thought no one would hear me. Or if they were to hear me, they should scorn the listening. But more, I did not want to know I *knew* and that I have known all along. I have tasted gnosis.

I tell them that the Kingdom of God is a book, they might go there by the unrolling of a scroll. I tell them that the Kingdom of God is a mirror, they might go there by the refocusing of the eye. Even now, they stand in the Garden of Eden, and the only leaving they have ever done is a forgetting. I tell them that I have walked in the true home of the inner Nazorean and that it is more a home than any home they have ever known, full of such tenderness as to melt an obsidian heart. I prowl through my mind, seeking more ways to tell them the simple thing I know, but it is hopeless. Unless a man jumps in the sea, how shall he know to swim? And I suddenly see that of them all, even Seth who knows with the mind and yearns with the heart, it is the brother called Yehoshua who hears me. I see it by his skin, by the bones in his hands, the way his head fits on his neck, by the radiance that escapes his eyes. This is why I think of nothing but him. He too has looked upon Glory. I cannot express my relief. But I can cry. Even now that I am John the Less and am learned beyond most men, I am still a wonder at crying.

I weep aloud to know I have not gone alone.

Without a word, Yehoshua leans forward.

He touches my forehead with the tip of one finger, and it is as if a mother has come to sing me to sleep. He traces the tear that rolls down my cheek, and it is as if a father has encircled me with his protective arm. I look into the brown of his eye. I smell the sun and the dust in his hair. I feel his touch though he has taken his hand away. I am helpless with the need to ask. So I *do* ask. "Are you the One?"

His face is a wash of surprise. Then comes a flood of bewilderment, and then fear. He shuts his eyes, and with no movement other than this, he leaves me. But I have asked and I must know, I must know; and I do as I do with Eio, I follow him. I slip under his skin, curl like smoke through his nostrils, move through his blood, and the first thing I feel is pain. I am infused with such pain as I have never known, more than black Helena knows. It lies behind the ball of his eye and in the bone of his skull. It is unbearable. It is unutterable. I open my mouth to cry out, and all the while the Loud Voice rolls down on us as a great stone would roll from the top of a mountain. "AS I AM THE ANGEL SPEAKING TRUTH—THE ONE HAS COME AMONG YOU."

The room has gone still as stone. Yehoshua opens his eyes wide. There is nothing in his face, there seems no breath in his body, yet he looks at me as if it were I who had spoken, as if these words were mine. They are not mine! It is not me! I am not an angel! I do not speak as an angel! I know nothing! Are the others as surprised as I that the Voice comes now? Do they wonder it comes to the brothers, or are they stunned that I, Mariamne, would ask this Yehoshua of Galilee if he were the One? I look at Seth, but his mind is closed to me. Seth looks at Yehoshua. Jude does not smile nor does he move. In this moment I understand that Jude would do nothing other than his twin would wish him to do. In this moment if Yehoshua were to want me solaced or silenced, so it should be.

It is now that all begin to hold me apart. The change is as delicate as the brush of a pale shadow on a pale wall, but Salome misses nothing. Already grown distant, from this time on, I rarely see her from day to day.

∞

It is as if I were missing a hand; I do not know what to do with myself. It is as if I were missing an eye; nothing looks as it did. I do not know what to feel. I have lost the friend of my youth. No one knows me. I no longer know myself. I am alone in the wilderness.

Eio grunts when I come near, nudges my hand to see if I have brought her anything. Today I have brought her only me, but that is enough if I scratch her hide hard enough. Not knowing what to do, I wander off, and Eio follows, and by and by we find ourselves hidden among the date palms far up our *nahal* west of the settlement. For a time, how much time it is hard to say, I lie flat out on the sand in the shade of the largest tree, a smooth stone for a pillow, and stare up at the cliffs and the sky. I lie so still, a baby hyrax tests my sandals for taste. Another, negotiating a rock, falls off with a soft plop onto the sand and then waddles away. Eio stands over me, flapping her lips and nodding her head. I would laugh if there were laughter in me. Instead, I rise only to seat myself in my curved bowl of a rock. I get up. I wander from date palm to date palm, absently picking at bark. I unwrap Salome's copy of the Book of Issa and look at it. I look at our game of green stone. I unwrap the three small figures we long ago found, Salome and I, and I smile to see what had once shocked me so. After so long in Alexandria, such natural things as breasts and delicate triangles of flesh no longer move me to embarrassed horror. I set them aside and pick up an unripened date fallen from a tree. I absently consider its design. If I were a god, would I have thought to create a date? I think to practice my tricks of magic. As it has been some while since I have done so, I am sure to fumble, so I begin with what I do best. In the purse at my side, Tata's gift of long ago, I have, besides my word stones, a handful of olives. I will change an olive into a date and the date into a large stone and the large stone into whatever occurs to me when I get that far.

But first, the olive.

It goes well. The olive has become a date and the date become a stone and the stone become a clay pot! Two clay pots! Three! I would defy anyone to know how I do this—even I am impressed. I juggle the three pots. I am sure that Eio cannot believe her eyes. "You, donkey," say I, "tell me, are you not confounded!"

"Prophets always confound me, even more than magicians," says a voice behind my back.

One of my pots remains a pot in my hand, one falls like a pot onto the soft yellow sand, but the third smashes like a pot on a rock. Too late, a hyrax barks warning. I whirl in place. Standing beside Eio, who unlike the hyraxes has not uttered a single warning bray, is one of the redheaded brothers. Even without his words, I know immediately which this is. Yehoshua is alone. I am alone. We are both alone with Eio. I am disquieted, if for no other reason than some find such magic as I have displayed an offense against Yahweh. But there is more reason than this. In all my life I have seldom been alone with a strange male, and it helps but little that he knows me as John the Less.

Yehoshua speaks again. "I have seen Addai do something like this. I think you do it better."

I would thank him if I had use of my tongue. As it is I scramble to remember myself. I am a Maccabee, and I am a scholar. I have lived in the palace at Alexandria. I have been taught by the famous philosopher, Philo Judaeus, and the famous astronomer and magician, Joor, son of Sipa of Thebes. Also by the famous Apion. I can read and I can write, which is without doubt something this one cannot do since virtually no one in the entirety of Palestine can do either. I can speak a dozen languages well and this one speaks Aramaic with a Galilean accent. I wear white linen. He wears rough cloth, mended and patched. He has no sandals, no wallet, no cloak. Against Jewish Law, his dark red hair is long. His dark red beard is tangled. I have asked him if he is the One, and he has answered by a startled silence.

Here, in my own hidden world with Eio, it suddenly seems a great foolishness to think I ever thought him anything of the sort.

I do not reach into him for I have not forgotten what it felt to do so. Could a perfected man feel as dark as this? I think not. But one thing that helps me now is that I sense he has a small fear of me. I am used to the fear of others. But this one's fear is unlike any I have ever felt. It seems not so much a fear of my being unlike, as it is fear of my being too like.

By thinking all this, I recover my wit. I will repel him with foreign erudition. He will then go away and leave me to my sorrowful self. "As for prophets," I say to him in my loftiest voice, "remember what the Greek Aeschylus wrote: 'And, truly, what of good ever have prophets brought to men? Craft of many words, only through evil your message speaks. Seers bring terror, so to keep men afraid.'"

Yehoshua is looking at my sanctuary of sand and palm and rock, and seeing this, I see also that the three unchaste figures lie where I have left them. Quickly, I pop them into the pot I still hold in my hand. But instead of retreating, he seats himself in my bowl of stone. Seated he says, "Do you believe that?" And when I say nothing, he asks again, more firmly this time. "Do you believe that prophecy is an evil craft meant to keep men afraid?"

I look at him and find I have no idea. Do I believe it? I have not listened to what I have said. I have only quoted the playwright Aeschylus because his were the first words that came to mind about prophets. But has this Zealot really asked such a thing of me? Men such as this man do not question prophecy. They live by it. Therefore, as this could not be a question, it must be a challenge. I am alone here. He is a stranger. He stands between me and the path down to the settlement. I answer, "I do not know."

To which the Galilean then says, "But if what this Greek says is true and this is all there is of prophecy, is God then mute?"

Again, I answer that I do not know. It is a difficult thing, measuring dismissal against civility. But it is as if I had said nothing. This one persists.

"If God is mute, can we still assume he concerns himself with us? And if God remains mute, how do we know he exists? And what then of prophets? If God is mute, are they charlatans?"

By now, I barely look at him, but I admit I do listen. How could I not? This kind of thing is to me as rain to the grasses.

"Is my cousin John what some say he is, a deceiver? Even with such a death as you once died, are you?"

This is interesting. More, it is surprising. What kind of a man is this to pose such knotty questions? He sounds a lawyer, yet I know he is no scribe. I see I have made a mistake. He is not repelled by erudition, not even the erudition of a Greek. He is not repelled by incivility. Not only is he not repelled; his being here is no accident. He has not stumbled on me in this isolated place—he has sought me out.

"Are you afraid of me, John?"

Yes! I hiss to myself. Yes, I am afraid of you. What is it about you that makes me afraid? How would you harm me? I know there is a confusion in you, a whirlwind of contrary feeling that blows you every which way as a blizzard blows sand. You are not an Addai with the most settled of hearts. You are not a Seth with the most composed of minds. You are not a Simon Magus with her talent and her comforting conceit. Or even a Tata with her strength and her pride. Who *are* you? "No. Why should I be afraid of you?"

In answer, he leaps from his place on the curved stone, saying, "Because I am afraid of you. Men who fear each other are a danger to each other."

Even though by his leaping he has startled me through and through, I hold my ground. Is this honesty? In the world as it is, a dark place where the mind of man is hobbled by fear and awed by unquestioned and dreadful Powers and therefore ruled by priests, where a place like the Great Library at Alexandria is as a small lamp in a cave of utter blackness, I do not have the freedom to be honest—many would do more than shun or banish me, I should be stoned. Other than with Salome, I have never been truly honest, and even with Salome, lately I have kept my own counsel. With Father, I hid my interests and my opinions. With Tata and Addai and Seth, I do not hide my opinions, but I hide my feelings. With all others, I hide my sex as well as my origins and opinions and feelings. I am not what I seem and I envy this man his honesty. And I admire it. Or is he clever? Do I walk into a trap? Once more I lie, saying, "I am no danger to you."

His reply is as swift as his leap. "I have never met a man more dangerous, even as you are a youth. Would you know where the danger lies?"

Here, I must respond honestly because I must know his answer. "Yes, I would know this."

"The danger lies in being known. I think you might know me."

"I do not know you."

"I think you do. As I know you."

He is right. This is a danger to me. It must be, else why am I now more afraid of him than ever? He turns away, walking toward the small seeping spring where Eio is sucking in water and making a tremendous racket as she does so. He clucks his tongue. On the instant she follows him. Eio, who obeys no one but me and Addai, obeys him. They are now both at the head of the path that twists and turns down through the rocks of the *nahal* toward the settlement below. Over his shoulder, Yehoshua calls, "As you know me and I you, come meet my sisters and my brothers."

I put down the pot and come away.

The Fourth Man

I *hear the women* before I see them.

There is a great commotion near a small grove of thorn acacias, much louder than the busy assembly of collared doves and babbler birds who live among these thorns. Eio's ears flicker at such tumult, her stump of a tail twitches.

In this blistering heat, the family of Yehoshua has set up its tents on stony ground between the yellow cliffs and the wilderness gardens. As we come closer, the women change from colorful mirage to colorful Galileans.

"This, John, is my aunt Martha," says Yehoshua. Martha, who makes much of this noise, has a goiter, a great bag hanging under her chin. Small children and chickens underfoot, she shrieks at a tall red-faced girl who chases a small red-faced boy, and the bag swings on her neck as a full udder swings on a trotting goat. "And that is my sister Maacah," says Yehoshua of the tall girl.

Maacah reminds me of Salome when we were young, and I am

instantly charmed, though as a youth of substance, I do no more than glance her way. Yehoshua has now come to the acacia trees. Seated on a shaded mat of woven reeds is a woman spinning wool; she seems frail in all her parts. Around her, gather all others that are female. These do not spin, but prepare food.

Yehoshua points from one to another. "These are Babata, wife of my brother Joses; Bernice, wife of my cousin Simeon; Veronica, wife of my brother Jude; and Miryam, also my sister."

I acknowledge the wives of Simeon and Joses and Jude, as well as this second sister, though they, of course, cannot look me, an unrelated male, full in the face. I take note that the wife of Jude holds a suckling babe. I note also there is a last woman seated alone, far under the deepest shade of the bristling trees, and that Yehoshua, seeing her, merely nods in her direction, saying only, "Salome, daughter of Zebedee, the mother of Jacob and Simon." The mother of Simon and Jacob must hear him, but she does not look up. It is as deliberate a thing as I have ever seen.

It is only now that he comes to the frail woman who spins, and at whom he also nods, though he does not smile. "And this is Mary."

And so I meet his mother.

Mary seems a bloodless thing, too tired to do other than briefly lift her eyes to mine. The eyes are as faded by the years as her mantle is faded by the sun, but I see she was once comely. Under her head cloth, her hair, though shot with gray, is black. The red hair in two of her sons does not come from the mother, and it does not come from his cousin John. All those I have seen of his family are dark of hair and eye. I wonder, Where is the father? And why is this mother of so many mentioned last among women?

"Mother, this is John the Less, the young man I have taken as a friend."

Swiftly working fibers through her hands, Mary inclines her head, and while I am acknowledging her with great courtesy, as befits a youth meeting the mother of a friend, I catch the eye of the youngest sister, Miryam. I am not more than five years above her age. I am well bred and well spoken. I am unmarried. Miryam flushes from

round forehead to round bosom, and so do I. Before she can lower
her glance, I suddenly understand what it is to be thought a man.

To my horror, Yehoshua notices. "Come, John. We are done with
the women. Now you will meet my brothers and my cousins and my
friends."

Eio and I following, Yehoshua pushes his way through a confusion of goats. Lifting a sharply divided hoof from off my foot, I walk
toward these brothers and friends alone. Beyond the goats and the
tents and the women and children and chickens under the acacia
trees, the sheer yellow cliff rises into the thin blue sky. Here at the
foot of the cliff there is a shallow cave, wide enough and deep
enough to provide needed shade from the relentless sun. Yehoshua
walks toward this cave, and when we come near, I can make out the
shapes of those inside. It seems all within are seated, that they face
outward and watch us come. But not until we too are in the cave can
I see that it is the brother Jacob who leans forward, that it is he who
has quickly covered the ground before him with a cloth. Before the
cloth settles, I see the lines he has drawn in the dirt. It is not one
of Salome's problems in geometry, but what it is, I do not know. Is it
a map?

All I can do if I have walked into a trap is turn and run straight
into a herd of goats, for as Eio and I have followed Yehoshua, the
goats have followed us. I keep my face straight and my wits sharp. I
do not look at the cloth on the ground. I look at Jacob's head. By the
stars, he has shaved himself bald! Why? Meanwhile, all but one looks
up at me, and the one who does not look is Jude. Jude keeps his gaze
on his twin. I feel into him for only a moment. Jude thinks me an ef-
fete, a youth of no substance, no heat, no blood. For Yehoshua's sake,
Jude will allow me small room in this world, but grudgingly. Of the
thirteen we find in this cave, in one way or the other, I know six.
There are the two brothers from Capharnaum, Andrew and Simon
Peter. There are Yehoshua's four brothers, the newly shaven Jacob
(who is spoken of as Jacob the Just), Jude, Simon, and finally the
youngest brother, Joses. Of the remaining seven, there are two I have
never seen before, but know from an awed Tata that they are men of

fame, or ill fame to such as Father. I would not stare, but I am struck with the wonder of it. These are the sons of the woman under the tree, the sour Salome, sprung from the loins of Tata's champion, Judas the Galilean, the famous bandit who came out of the hills to lead a revolt against the taxes of Rome. These are Simon and Jacob bar Judas!

Simon and Jacob were with their father Judas on that day in Galilee; they were with their father's friend, Zadok the Righteous One. When the Roman general Varus caught the father and killed him, he did not catch the sons, nor did he catch the mysterious Zadok, who with Judas became heroes to a whole people.

As for the others who sit farther back, Yehoshua introduces these as the three sons of Jacob bar Judas: young James of Salome's age, the younger Jair, and the even younger Zoker, who could not be above ten years. The fourth is the son of Simon bar Judas, and named Menahem. I hear this one think John the Less should stay in his place. If he should say it aloud, I would not dispute him. The last of the five is a huge man, larger than Peter, with a nose as hooked as an Arab's; this one is Yehoshua's cousin, Simeon the Zealot.

Yehoshua puts his hand on my shoulder, urges me forward. "I have brought the young one who has taken my heart."

Jacob the Just keeps himself between the cloth he has placed on the ground, and me. Alone of them all, Simon of Capharnaum stands and walks toward me. For the third time in my life, he thrusts his face in my face. "Have I not seen you before?"

"Of course you have seen him before, Simon Peter, my rock," Yehoshua answers for me. "Do not bully. This is John the Less, kin to Seth of Damascus. It is my intention that he join us."

On the instant, all are as alert as a vixen with kits. "Join us?" snaps Peter. "How should he join us? He has no—"

Yehoshua places a hand on his arm. "Join us in conversation, Peter. What else could I mean?" His eyes are bright with mischief. "Simon bar Judas? Jacob bar Judas? Can my two Sons of Thunder think of nothing worthy to discuss?"

They stare up at him, anxious and eager to understand. The

mood of Yehoshua matters to them, that much is obvious. I can hear them trying to think of something worthy to discuss, by which I know that though they are men of violence, they are yet simple men, and sweet in nature.

"Or perhaps I interrupt something?"

Jacob the Just speaks now. "I have no stomach for this, Yeshu'a. We have waited for you. Where have you been? There is serious business up in Jerusalem."

"I know."

"You know? And yet—?"

"And yet I have time to talk of other things. We shall have a skinful of all this soon enough, for there is ever a surfeit of serious business."

Jacob half rises. "This is why we ourselves must be serious."

Yehoshua holds up his hand, which stops Jacob in his rising. "Do you think God is forever serious?"

"God? There is nothing more serious than God."

Yehoshua smiles on his brother. It is a tender smile. Even Jacob must feel it as tender. "There is nothing less serious than God. Consider the ass." He pulls on Eio's ear. "God could not have been serious when he devised the ass."

He has made them laugh. This man has the gift his cousin John has; he makes the way smooth with laughter. It is as if air is let out of a bladder, all laugh, even Jacob with his red lips and his bald blue head.

Yehoshua rubs Eio's cheek and she shuts her unfaithful eyes in bliss. "Take comfort, Jacob. What is to be done will be done. And as there may be some here we cannot trust, which means nothing can begin until the setting of the sun, it is useless to continue so serious while the sun yet shines. Jude?"

Jude reacts almost before he hears his name, his hand clasped to the hilt of his knife.

"Come with John and me. We will return to this serious business when we have eaten. And you!" Yehoshua means Eio. "You come too."

Eio moves as if I had bid her. And Jude is up off the ground and by Yehoshua's side while he still speaks. As for me, if I have walked into the lion's den, now I am about to walk out. It is good to be alive, though I should not have thought so earlier in this day when life felt nothing but pointless. As we four, the look-alike brothers and Eio and I, turn to walk away, I glance back just once. The others have returned to that which is drawn in the dirt, all except Simon Peter. He stares straight at me, and the look on his face could turn flesh to salt.

Yehoshua lies in the bowl of warm rock that is usually mine. From it he can see back down the path as far as the carob trees. Above the tops of the trees, there is the sky and the sea and the mountains. Under the simmering sun, they all seem as one. Jude has taken the soft sand under the largest date palm that would be Salome's if she were here. I sit, leaning back on Eio.

"This is a good place," says Yehoshua. "Do you remember where we would sit, Jude, when we were boys?"

Jude has closed his eyes. He lies on his back, his arms crooked under his head, and all the while the knife at his belt glints in the sun. He looks asleep, but he could not be for he nods, yes, he remembers.

I must listen carefully. Yehoshua's accent is so thick, he speaks so softly, and Eio's belly rumbles so loudly. "My brothers and sisters and I once lived on a hill and from our hill we could look down on the Plain of Jezreel where so many battles from scripture were fought. We would pretend it was we who had fought them, making swords of sticks and knives of shale, we fought valiantly and we died gallantly. Remember, Jude?"

With another nod, Jude remembers.

"From our hill we could see another far hill and on that hill stood Sepphoris, Herod's city of marble. At night, we would watch as the hundreds of palace lights were lit. I would imagine being the man who lit those lights. I would imagine being the man they were lit for. How endless the distance from our darkness to Herod's great palace of fire. When we were older and our sticks and our stones replaced by the tools of a trade, we still sat on our hill talking of the world in the shadow of Herod's lights. Did you do this, John?"

Caught out struggling to hear, I have no answer.

"Between you and your brother, Simon, what talk there must have been! Seth has told me of you. I think you were what I as a youth might have wished to be." I see that Jude opens his eyes at this. "What trade did your father follow?"

"My father was a maker and merchant of glass." Long ago it was decided that I would not change who my father was or what he did, all that should be changed is that he and my family were dead at Roman hands. "I was a merchant's son. Seth and Addai raised my brother and me, and though we have learned much, we learned no trade."

From his place in the sand, Jude grunts.

Yehoshua cocks an eye at his brother. "Pay no heed. Jude has always found it hard to know how a man might live without a trade."

Once again, Jude grunts.

"How he lives with himself, that is."

I watch this performance with much interest. All my life I have known the thoughts of others by hearing them, but this one knows his brother's words from grunts and shrugs and glares. Does Jude speak at all? Is he mute? I lie back against Eio and share her flies. The mood I awoke with is gone; the irritation I have lived with since Egypt is gone, which means I feel fit to argue. Live without a trade? I cannot imagine living *with* one. I am a philosopher; I am select of the earth. It is enough that I have learned to tend my trees and my poppies.

Because Jude is mute and perhaps also deaf, I say this, "Tell him I live easily with myself, for there is more to the world than a trade."

"Oh, I have often told him this, especially now that neither of us follows our own. We were once carpenters working for our uncle, the builder Cleopas. We worked on much in Sepphoris, the very theater itself. We built the stage building, and what a splendid stage building it was. The back wall alone had doors and openings enough to satisfy the busiest playwright. Is this not true, Jude?" Jude makes no sound, but Yehoshua seems satisfied that his brother agrees the stage building was splendid and the back wall satisfying. "Old Camel Knees demands we shun the ways of those he claims walk in the footsteps of Roman or Greek—"

"Old Camel Knees?"

"Our brother, the lately bald Jacob. Since childhood, Jacob has exceeded all others in zeal for the Law, his knees are a camel's knees for praying. Now he goes shaven until the Temple is once again God's. But I cannot shun the theater. Did Jude and I not provide the stage building?"

I know this theater in Sepphoris. Years ago, Father had business there, and how I begged to go along, and how surprised I was when he agreed to take Tata and me. Now I know that to take Tata was the entire point.

Yehoshua has gone silent. Jude seems asleep. I too am silent, but I know Yehoshua's mind teems with ideas and with questions, that his nerves thrill to them. There is something he wants to ask of me. This is why he found me this morning, why I have met his family, why he is here now. But he does not know how to ask, where to begin, and I cannot help him for I am as confused as he. It is as if I have known him all my life, yet I know him not at all. He does not know my real name. He wants to question me but is afraid of my answers. Yehoshua of Galilee does not know his way.

How could I have thought him the Perfected Man of the Nazorean? He is more than most men; he has wit and he has humor, but perfected? I smile into Eio's mane of soft brown bristles. I am almost drifting away to sleep, when Yehoshua's voice comes again, and I begin to hear the music in it.

"When we were young, my brothers and I, we were poor, without influence, and filled with anger. Being young and angry, we asked angry questions. Being Nazoreans, we asked *these* questions: if God is the King of the Israelites, how is it that we are answerable to an earthly king? If the Israelites must have an earthly king, why a son of the Arabian Herod who is not of us? We would stare at the towers and arches and porches of Herod's palace and ask how it was that a few men were rich beyond need and many men poor beyond pity?" Here Jude growls, and it is nothing if not unnerving, though it proves he is not deaf. "Simeon's father, our uncle Cleopas would ask the wisest question of all, why do ten priests or more stand between a man and God?" Yehoshua lowers his gaze. He has been looking out over the Sea of Salt as if he were looking out over Herod's palace. Now, he looks at me. "In time I discovered that all our questions had the same answer, these things were so because we allowed them to be so. Men of resignation had made all this. The fearful poor, resigned to their poverty, made this. The wealthy, who would not lose their wealth, made this. The priests, eager to keep their lucrative place at Temple, made this. All these have made evil run smoothly. But as I was young and not yet resigned, I had only one choice, only one path to follow—"

Listening, Jude becomes rigid in his place.

"And I have followed it ever since. I would not allow these things to be so. Even if men must die, they shall not be so."

I look at him; I do not lower my eyes. "You are Sicarii. You keep the company of Sicarii. Is your cousin John a daggerman?"

For a moment, I think Yehoshua will not answer, but I am wrong. "Though I did once, I no longer know John. Is he madman or priest or king?" Yehoshua turns his face from me, and from his twin. "But I have had such dreams." His hand clutches at his robe, twists the cloth. "Shall I tell you them? Will you hear me? You confuse me, John the Less. I am confused by you." I am silent. I can only listen, as Jude is doing. "But know that I have had such strange thoughts, and I have had such strange feelings, and once, just before coming here, I saw something. What I saw was beyond thought and beyond form and when it came, it spoke aloud as Job's Voice from the Whirlwind. My mind flew away at the sound of it. It terrifies me yet. Tell me, as I know you have walked with God, is it common, these thoughts? Is it common to see and to hear such things? They do not seem common. No other before you talks of them. No other knows them as you know them."

Is it common? Have others seen what I have seen, but do not speak? Have I walked with God? Or does every man hear his own god? For Jews, it seems one man's god has became the god of a tribe, and then he has become the god of a whole people, and now he thinks to become the God of gods—or his people think to make him so. I shudder. Yea Balaam! I have no answers, I have only questions. *This* is my trade. I am by trade a questioner!

Yehoshua's voice has risen from a whisper to almost a shout. "Not since Moses has a man seen him face to face. No one speaks as you do. Not even the prophets. For the prophets do not know God. They know only what they say are God's wrathful demands, and they are afraid. Are they all like Moses? Are they all like John? Have they been to the mountaintop, but not to the Promised Land?"

Yehoshua falters. Does he suddenly hear himself and, hearing, stumble at the sound? Has he been speaking blasphemy? I reach into him. He wonders if I am a spirit, an unclean thing? He wonders if he dallies with a demon. The cords in his neck work as if he would choke, and when comes at last his voice, it is a great half-strangled "Enough!" Though Yehoshua shouts at himself, I flinch. "All this can wait. The hour comes to be about my business."

He leaps up and once again I am startled. He has broken open the moment; it is smashed as my juggled pot.

Jude is also on his feet. Eio struggles up under me and I lose my balance, but Jude has caught at my arm and I do not fall. He is not gentle. There is in his eyes some of what I see in Simon Peter's eyes.

Just as he did hours ago, Yehoshua strides down the path.

"Stay here. Do not follow Yeshu." So saying, Jude strides off after him.

My mouth drops open. Jude speaks!

Of course I do not stay.

Before I am John the Less, I am Mariamne. What business do they speak of? I would discover this because it is my nature to do so.

I know another way into the settlement. Not by going back down the *nahal*, but by climbing farther up. In moments, I am back in the tunnels I have not seen since the night Seth and Salome, Helena of Tyre and Dositheus and I, set out for Egypt. I have no light, but all I need do is go down. Long ago, Addai instructed us to follow any tunnel that goes down.

How much can a day hold? Coming up by way of the steep and

narrow stairs from the circular room where first I met John the Baptizer, I stop in the shadow of the tower doorway. There is a confusion of shouting; I do not understand what I hear. It is all bathed in the hard white light of noon; I do not understand what I see. At the far end of the long room stands John of the River, and beside him Simon Magus, pale as the moon. Near Salome, cowers Helena, her face covered with her head cloth. Near an inner wall are Dositheus and several men of the Nazorean. The hem of Dositheus's clothing is stained red. Near John and Simon Magus there are women: Mary's daughters, and Joanna, wife of Chuza, among them. I see even Dinah of the Way, a woman I have not seen for many years. Why is she here? Why are there women in the meeting room claimed by the elders of the Poor? And why do they lean over something that does not move? What is it they look on? A bundle? Tumbled baskets? An animal, sick or dying, perhaps already dead? Looking on are Yehoshua's brothers and Yehoshua's friends and Yehoshua's cousins. What is happening?

Perhaps I can understand what occurs if I can understand the shouting.

"All will go!" shouts one in the center of the long room. "Suicide!" shouts another. "If all else are cowards, I will do what needs be done!" shouts a third, and this third man is Simon Peter of Capharnaum. He breaks from the crowd with two others, and then his brother Andrew appears among them with four more, and these eight run straight at the door I stand in. I clamp myself to the stone of the tower wall. All eyes follow their flight, meaning all eyes turn in my direction. In this single instant, my gaze locks with Salome's. There is horror in her eyes, and when she sees me, there is pity, a terrible pity. I understand her horror but not her pity.

At this moment, Seth steps forward. He fills the doorway these eight would use. If they would pass, they must run him down. He will be trampled and I will be trampled because I have already stepped out in front of him, but for the ringing voice of command that now sounds out over all else: "Stop!"

I expect to hear John of the River. It is always John who makes this much noise, and who presumes such obedience, but it is not. At a single word from Yeshu, the eight stop as if they were tied round the waist and had come to the end of their rope. And in this moment, though I understand nothing else, I understand now that it is Yeshu to whom they listen. It is this brother of all the brothers who leads these men. Yeshu is not only Sicarii; he commands Sicarii!

Yeshu walks forward, shadowed by Jude. The shouting men of the long room make way for him as he comes to stand with John the Baptizer. Yeshu's is not the face of a man confused by his thoughts or pained by his feelings; it is that of a man full in command of himself and of others. There is no hesitation, no indecision. "No one comes with me this night, but four of my choosing. One of these is my brother Jude, and another is my cousin Simeon." There is a muffled cry from Simeon's plump wife, Bernice, but a scornful Maacah shushes her. "I take another to guide us through the city streets, and into the Fortress of Antonia, but this one shall be neither of the sons of Judas of Galilee, for Simon and Jacob are too well known to the authorities in Jerusalem. Nor shall it be you, Peter, for you are needed here in my stead." Peter, standing very near me, has been grinding his teeth (surely how he broke his eyetooth), but at this his face brightens. He punches Andrew on the arm with the joy of pride. Yeshua finishes what he has been saying. "That one shall be Seth as no one knows Jerusalem better than he."

I look at Seth, though he does not look at me. A philosopher is needed to guide them into the Fortress of Antonia? Antonia not only billets the soldiers of Rome, it is the Roman jail. If a philosopher were caught nearby, he might be beaten. Having already escaped the jail of Herod Antipas in the new city of Tiberius, if Yeshu and Jude are caught, they might be killed, for Sicarii are crucified.

"Who is the fourth man, Yeshu'a?"

Jacob the Just asks this. Clearly, Camel Knees expects to be that fourth man.

"John the Less."

I do not gasp alone; there is surprise on every face, none more so than on Jacob's. Unless it be in Peter's. On the faces of some, there is dismay, on one or two, anger, on more than two, envy. I do not understand what I see in the eyes of Salome.

"We leave in the hour."

Yeshu steps through a side door into a private courtyard, followed by John, Simon Magus, Dositheus, and Jude. Helena hurries after them. At this, there is a sudden and silent turning back to what is at hand. The men disappear in a dozen directions; all seem to know why. The women struggle to lift something from the floor. I am left dazed, until Peter shoves his face in mine. His breath stinks as ever. As a serpent, he hisses, "You mistake much if you think Yeshu'a loves you better than he loves me!" He pushes me aside so he might rejoin his brother in the larger courtyard, and I stumble sideways into Seth. Seth! The one man who does not shout and does not push for place and does not think with his mouth before his mind. I would take his hand, but I remember myself. Instead, I content myself with a mere touch on his dusted sleeve. "What happens here? All save me seem to know."

Seth enfolds me in his arms; he embraces me—Seth does this! He means to comfort me, but instead I am frightened. He is covered with the dust and the dirt of the road; he smells of an animal. I know this smell. Only the wealthy have use of horses. He has been riding, hard. "What is it, Seth? What is it that causes all this?" And suddenly I realize a thing I have not allowed myself to see. "Where is Tata? Where is Addai?" Seth holds me all the harder. All the harder, I struggle to pull away. "Where are they?"

"If you would help them, John, you would act as a man."

Seth has brought his mouth close to my ear so that only I might hear him, but I am shaking my head. There is something in me that will not listen, mortally afraid of what it might hear. My mind babbles: I am not a man. I am Mariamne. What has happened to Addai and to Tata that they would need help of me? I look at the bundle the women of the Nazorean struggle to pick up. I think of the red on the clothing of Dositheus. I twist my body in Seth's arms as if he were a sworn enemy. "Let me go! *Let me go!*" The long room empties, but here and there a head turns our way. Seth holds me the harder, he whispers my true name in my ear, and what he says then is like the slap of a Roman sword. "Would you betray us, Mariamne? What you see is the body of Heli of the Nazorean."

I freeze in his arms. "Heli?"

"Heli is dead. Tata is wounded and hidden in a house near Heli's house."

I would empty my stomach with fear. I would fall to the ground and rub dirt in my face with fear. "And Addai? Where is Addai?"

"Addai is taken to the Fortress of Antonia. He will die on a cross tomorrow if we do not free him this night."

∞

The last of five cloaked figures, I hurry through the night, retracing my child's steps from the wilderness up to Jerusalem.

I think of nothing but Addai and Tata. Is Tata's wound fatal? Does she suffer? I cannot bear that she should suffer. But by the stars of Joor, *why* came she to Jerusalem? To set foot in Jerusalem was to risk becoming a slave again to Father, or worse. Addai is to be crucified? How could this be so? Why would the Romans take such a man? *Eloi!* Why crucify sweet Addai of Shechem who has done harm to no man? My heart hammers in my chest. I have no spit in my mouth. This *cannot* happen. To the west there is the bright star, Sopdet, blue as a northern eye, and I offer up a prayer. *Lamp of Isis, keep harm from Addai, the best of all good men. Lamp of Heaven, let him hear me and know we come for him.*

All my wonder at this god and that god, and all my scorn, yet the moment I know fear, I call on a goddess. I forget in a trice that I am more than my *eidolon*. I forget I am my *Daemon*, own immortal self who does not die and cannot be harmed. I deny my own eternal witness. Nor do I remember, as Seth taught, that the *Daemon* of Addai does not die and cannot be harmed. In my hurry and fear, I forget everything but love of Addai.

As we five race to Jerusalem, there is no moon, only stars to light our way. We follow no path. We climb and climb to the heights of the city that David made his own, and in which Solomon built his Temple, following the folds in the barren hills, some of which are as narrow as the streets of Jerusalem and some of which are as deep as tombs. But this time, I am not carried by the very man we go to save; I am myself a man on my own two feet, and though the pace is punishing and the climb long and hard, I have no trouble keeping up with the four ahead of me. I think if need be, I could be there before them. I could do this for Addai if it were twice the distance and twice the height. No one talks, no one does anything but stride through the night. We disturb a group of ibex, mothers and kids, who bleat in surprise to see us, then scramble away. But other than these, there seems no life here but ours.

Away from sight of the others, Simeon with the hooked nose has given me a curved knife. He tucked it in my belt and clapped me on the shoulder. "In times like these," said he, "no man should be without a weapon." Since then, I have kept my hand on its hilt, making sure of it, feeling the weight of it. I try to imagine myself the Indian queen Masaga, riding a war elephant, a lance in one hand and a sword in the other. But such foolishness does not last long; I remember what Seth has told me, that John the Baptizer had gone up to Jerusalem from Jericho by the treacherous road running through the steep-walled Nahal Perat, for it had suddenly entered his head to preach on the very steps of Herod's Temple. He caused an immediate sensation. Great crowds massed to see such a man. From the inner walls to the outer walls, they gathered from all over Jerusalem. They flocked in from the surrounding countryside: priest and merchant, beggar and farmer and vendor and peasant and scribe, all manner of men and women, and not all of them there to admire him. The great crowds caused the swift appearance of great numbers of Temple police and Roman soldiers. As John had chosen to speak in the Court of Gentiles, this meant Roman soldiers were positioned from the heights of the Royal Basilica to the tops of the colonnades, both to the east and to the west. But there were more even than this, there were some who stood armed among the crowd.

And when all had come and when there was a sea of faces looking up at him as he stood at the top of the steps leading to the inner precincts of the very Temple itself, John the Baptizer began to speak. He spoke for so long and he spoke so well, there were some who swooned, and some who surged forward to touch him, and some who merely stood where they were, spellbound. There were some who muttered among them and some who shook their fists. And finally there were some who called him king.

A voice here and a voice there rose up out of the silent mass, calling out, "John is King of the Jews!" Like a wave in the sea, an excitement flowed over the crowd, and with it came more voices, and more, all calling, "John is King of the Jews!"

In the midst of all, there stood one man, Stephen, a moneychanger who heard more than John. He heard a voice saying, "Stephen, disciple of John! Smite the oppressor!" Pushing through the crowd, Stephen came upon a soldier at his post and seized that which hung at the soldier's hip, a short thrusting sword. And the soldier, who had not heard a voice saying, "Beware the disciples of John!" went down to his knees at the first blow to the neck and died at the second.

This Stephen, the moneychanger, lies beaten and bloody in a wretched cell deep under the Fortress of Antonia. And with him lies Addai.

Addai is there because at the death of a Roman soldier, the crowd panicked. Addai had been near John, had seen the swaying of the crowd near the bottom step, had seen it pull back as one, opening up a small space where there was then only Stephen and the dead soldier. Addai understood at once what he saw, that the new governor of Judaea, Pontius Pilate, would call this "inciting a riot." He saw that even though the Romans had always hesitated to touch John for fear of the wrath of the people, this time the new governor had been handed a key to John's downfall. With the killing of a Roman soldier and citizen, Rome could now act. And when Rome is angry, Rome kills with great passion and it kills at random.

Immediately, Addai pushed John through the double gate into the Court of Women, the few others with John following on. These included Seth, who had come away with Addai from the building of Queen Helen's palace when they had heard John was in Jerusalem. It had also included Heli and Dinah. All in all, they were a handful of men, and three women, one of whom was Dinah, the other of whom was Joanna, wife of Chuza, and the last of whom was Tata, her face hidden by a head cloth. Shielding John's body with their own and following Addai's unerring lead—for as master stone carver, Addai has intimate knowledge of Herod's Temple—these made their way quickly into the Chamber of the Nazirites, and from there through a hidden door down into a series of enormous domed halls of unending arches under the platform of the Temple Mount. Avoiding the public Hulda Tunnel, they went deeper, entering into a maze of subterranean passageways. By secret tunnels, each torturous and sly, and most made by order of the great Herod himself, they made their way toward the west wall, and then out into the Valley of the Cheesemakers by a second hidden door that exists in the shadow of the Upper City Bridge. This bridge, and its aqueduct—one long leap from the platform high above them to the streets of Zion, the Upper City to the west—sheltered them as they ducked among the stalls of the nearby Xystus market. From there, it became a matter of moments to seek safety in the house of Heli bar Nehushtan.

But someone must have seen them emerge from under the Upper City Bridge. Someone must have noted their course. And that someone must have reported it to the authorities, for in no more than an hour from the soldier's murder, the Romans were at Heli's door, loudly demanding entrance. By then, John, along with Dositheus and Joanna, had already been hidden in a safe house that stands near the Pool Tower, and there it was intended John wait for the rest to join him so that at the fall of night, all might hurry away from Jerusalem, disappearing into the wilderness as so many had done before. But Addai and Tata, Heli and his wife, Dinah, had remained behind in the house of Heli to gather up certain scrolls of the Nazorean and to take away certain treasured possessions.

It was Tata who first barred Heli's door to the Romans, and it was Tata who was first to receive a single hard blow from the hilt of a Roman sword. At this, my beloved Addai did what would spell his doom; as Tata fell, he wrested the sword from the soldier who held it, and raising it up, prepared to bring it down on the next Roman head he saw. Instead, three soldiers at once seized him from behind, bound and gagged him, and led him away in chains. This was not done without a terrible struggle; in the end, the Romans had overrun the fine house of Heli and of his wife, Dinah, destroying what they did not take, setting fire to the library, and leaving Tata for dead. As for Heli, he had been pushed from his own roof into the steep street below, and the fall had broken his neck. And Dinah, rushing away in grief, sought shelter in the house where John hid.

It was then that Seth, taking horses from his mother's new stable, delivered John, as well as the body of Heli, from Jerusalem.

I have known little of death in my life. Too young to feel my mother's death, I do not even recall it. A priest dying at my feet was a hideous shock, yet no more. But I feel *this* death; I will remember *this* death. Heli made me welcome in his home; he opened his library as well as his heart to Salome and to me. To think that he is gone, that it took but a moment of brute rage and a man such as Heli the Nazorean no longer breathes, that a heart such as his no longer beats. That Dinah is a widow . . . a terrible thing for a woman without issue.

John the Baptizer is now a hunted man. In the search for John, more than John will die. It is not only Rome that will seek him; so too will the Herodians as a gift to the emperor who gives them their power. So too will the priests of the Temple and the Sanhedrin. These last are the ruling body of the Jews, and to remain in their place, they must answer to Rome. They will do this because they will think it better to kill one Jew than to endanger many Jews. Father is a member of the Sanhedrin.

I do not cry. Yeshu has given me purpose. Though it is too late for Heli, and perhaps it is too late for Tata, Addai shall not die at Roman hands. Nor shall he die at the hands of my father.

We have come over the crest of the last hill and stand now looking down into the Kidron Valley. On the far side of the Kidron rises another hill very like this hill and on the crest of that western hill lies Jerusalem. It is only moments past the sixth hour, and the dark fills up the night as water fills a sinking ship. I feel drowned in darkness. Exposed on the top of the eastern hill, which is the Mount of Olives, we scrabble down to a place where we can hide ourselves better. Here, though I can barely see them, I know new tombs and old, dug into the rubbled earth, surround us. I know some are sealed with stones and some are open and waiting. By the faint light of summer stars, it seems an ominous place.

I grip the hilt of my knife—but what good should a *sica* do me here?

Above us shines Sopdet, who is Isis, who is the Virgin, who is Inanna in Heaven, who is the Queen of Sheba, the Queen of the South, "She who is black but beautiful," and is forever chased by the great red dragon, yet never caught. I take heart from this. Limned against the starry sky, Jerusalem lies as a lion lies, as the Great Sphinx lies, sloping up from tail to head, shadowed and silent and still. The city is sited at the crossing of no major road, is watered by no river, boasts no markets of distinction. Yet it is here; it seems as if it has always been here. This is the first I have seen of my home since I was yet Mariamne, daughter of Josephus, privileged and, I now know, isolated in my happy ignorance. To see it this night with the eyes of John the Less, a scholar taught by scholars in the Great Brucheion Library, is wondrous. I had not known I missed it or what it should feel like to see it again, but something within me keens at the sight.

Straight ahead is the Gihon Spring Gate flanked by its two massive towers through which passes the Kidron Road, and under which flows the Gihon Spring through Hezekiah's Tunnel. Behind this towered and gated wall is the lower city where lies Tata, but we do not go there. We are trusting that Rhoda, the servant of Dinah, will nurse Tata as lovingly as Salome and I would. Rising up behind the massed and steeply terraced houses of the poor is a second wall inside the city, and behind this wall is the Valley of the Cheesemakers. Rising up again behind the markets, are the mansions of the rich, which includes Father's house. To the north, near the Upper City Bridge, is the palace of the Hasmonaeans from whose line Seth is come, and finally, behind all these, stands the palace of Herod the Great with its three tall towers. To our left, the city wall curves round toward the Pool of Siloam and the Rose Gardens where Megas of Ephesus lives, and to our right, the Bridge of the Red Heifer leads from the Roman road to Jericho to the great wall above which is the Temple of Herod, so splendid it astonishes. The Temple is built atop a vast platform of tremendous stone blocks laid over the highest point of land in the city, the holy Mount Moriah, and somehow made absolutely flat. Heron of Alexandria would know how this was done, and so would Salome to whom he taught his applied mechanics, but I do not know. All around the edge of this platform are Corinthian colonnades that look from here exactly like those running the length of the Canopic Way. The eastern colonnade, the very one we stare into, is Solomon's Portico. Behind this portico is the expanse of the Court of Gentiles, and in the middle of the Court of Gentiles stands the Temple itself, with all its attendant offices. Even in the moonless dark it is as white and as shimmering and as fine as milk. Deep inside this hallowed place is the Holy of Holies where no one is allowed ever to go save the high priest once every year on the Day of Atonement. There lives Yahweh, who is surely the loneliest of all the gods.

On the southern end of the platform stands the Royal Basilica above the Hulda Gates, and on the northwestern end looms the Fortress of Antonia.

The fortress does not shimmer like milk. It is like a table set over on its back, the four unequal legs thick and stubby, the table itself a simple rectangle of massive and impervious stone. There is only one way in, and one way out, for other than a Roman citizen, and that way is on the far side of the fortress, a long climb toward the Mount of Olives to the north of us, then down and to the west past the Sheep Market in full sight of the fortress guards.

As I have been standing in the midst of the dark tumble of tombs, so too has Yeshu. He holds his arms at his sides. He keeps perfectly still. There is no breeze to stir his robes, or to ruffle his red beard, or to lift the leaves of the olive trees. There is no sound from night bird or beast. There is only the night and the quiet city before us. In Jerusalem, most must sleep. I see no lamps on the porches, no fires in the hearths. What does he see?

"Come closer, John," he says, and as ever his voice is low, and it does not seem to travel, yet I hear him clearly. I move closer, make a place for myself near him, and I listen.

"Here before me is all my mind rails against, and here sleeps all my heart longs for, and yet I must come as a thief in the night." There is so much of sweet Addai in his face that I am as hard struck by fresh grief for my old friend, as I am struck by a tender green love for this new friend. I begin to see that Yeshu might be a friend, though I do not yet see what kind of a friend. But even as I feel this, I see the Sicarii who stood by Peter as Peter killed another.

Jude moves up behind us. "It is time, Yeshu. Tell us what we do now."

Yeshu tells us. I look from face to face. Is no one as horrified as I? Oh, Salome, each day I learn what it is to be a man. If I were the Mariamne of long ago, I should live now in comfort in Bethany, likely a rich man's wife and the mother of children. If I were the Mariamne of only hours ago, in this very moment I should lie in my tent, safe and bored and fretful with discontent. How easy a thing is discontent. How undemanding. But I am John the Less. I am seen as a man, and I will do what must be done. I will prepare myself for what I have chosen to do by what I have chosen to be; though I do it in quiet fear.

As one, we move down the hillside, following Seth who takes us away from the tombs and into a field of flax and thence into the first of the olive groves. Not I, but the others do this as a great beast of the night would do this, with grace and assurance and a calm acceptance that once begun, a thing must continue to its appointed end—there will be no turning back. I would be like this. I would be as a leopard by night, and to this end, I begin by pretending I am like this. Swiftly and silently, we drop down to the Kidron Road, and then, as if we are no more than travelers late on our weary way, we openly enter the city by the Gihon Spring Gate. The customs station is unmanned.

There are no guards, either Roman soldiers or Temple police. Perhaps this is so because no one would expect that having made his escape, neither John, nor any of John's people, would return.

We are now inside the first of the city walls. Before us, and to our left, is the northernmost Pool Tower where the sweet waters of the Gihon Spring are stored against drought or siege. Following Seth, it is to the foot of this tower we now quickly climb. We disturb nothing, wake no one. No dog rises up to growl warning, no roosting hen flaps away in loud alarm. At the tower, we pause as Seth pauses, waiting here for one long breathless moment. Then Seth is moving again. As before, he walks as one who has nothing to fear from those who frown on those out and about at night. We cross over side streets, always keeping in full view of any who might see us. We turn up this narrow passageway or that, and it is not long before I have no idea where we are. All I know is that we do not go toward Father's closed house and that we have passed through the second inner wall of the city. I know the ground under us rises, that we must be near the hippodrome, and that we climb north toward Herod's Temple. By and by, we come to a new wall, one unfamiliar to me. It is not tall enough to be the south wall of the Temple platform, yet it is a very fine wall indeed. Seth makes his way directly to a door in this wall, takes a large key from his bag, and unlocks it; as the door swings open into gloom, he slips inside. After him go I, then Simeon, then Yeshu, then Jude. Yeshu would go last, but this Jude would never allow.

Seth lights a small golden lamp set in a carved niche in the inner wall, and now all around us appears, shadowed and silent and huge, a great hall of finest ashlar stone. "Welcome," says he, and the word echoes throughout the vastness, "to the palace of the Queen of Adiabene, Helen of the Assyrians."

I would stand and I would stare, but we spend no more time in this unfinished palace than we did among the tombs overlooking the city. Enough to get our bearings, enough to know Helen herself is not here, enough to know that Seth is at home between these new walls as he is in the wilderness, as he was in the Great Library at Alexandria, enough to wonder at this or at that shining hall or courtyard or bath or private chamber as we hurry past it. And certainly enough to know that there is yet no roof; above us shine the stars that map our hope and our wonder.

Throughout the night, there are men in Helen's employ who guard her palace, and as we pass them, all nod at Seth, the second son of Helen. In a matter of moments we come to the north wall of the palace of Queen Helen, a wall that is entirely completed. Seth tells us this wall abuts on the very wall that encloses the courtyard below the Temple's southern Huldah Gates. Here we find one last door. Once again Seth retrieves a key from his bag and once again a door opens into deepest gloom.

"It is now," he says, "that we go under the courtyard. This tunnel system was ordered by Helen and built by Addai, and I know it well. But once it joins the old tunnels under the Temple Mount itself, it must be a matter of trust that I will find a way through."

"You will lead and we will follow," says Yeshu. "This night is our night."

With that, Seth shines his lamp into the first tunnel. And then he is gone, swallowed by the gloom on the other side of the door. Before he goes too far, we follow.

Again and again it seems he loses his way; this is more than the tunnels under the settlement, more than the tunnels that rise up into the settlement cliffs. The hills upon which Jerusalem sleeps are as shot through with tunnels as the surface is shot through with streets. Like the wilderness, there is a world under Jerusalem, and it is dim and chill and secret—whose world is this? I lose myself in thoughts of Alexandria, for just as under the Temple there is another temple, so too under Alexandria there is another Alexandria. Beneath her streets and temples and palaces and parks and gymnasia and quarters of this people or that, is a city of vaulted cisterns and canals and columned halls stretching away endlessly, story upon story of them. Under Alexandria flow the floodwaters of the Nile, forever whispering and chuckling in the dark. Here, there is also the sound of running water—we have come to the Pool of the Lark, the black water brought out of the hills around Jerusalem. We go deeper and deeper, only to rise again, and then for a time we climb, only to plunge down once more. There is a timeless moment we pass through a tunnel so narrow we must walk in single file, and there is a time we pass through one in which we must bend to half our height. More than once we seem in no tunnel at all, but in a vast cave of shifting echoes. Some of the tunnels are arched, and some are no more than cuttings in the stone, and then, once more, we climb, and we continue to climb until, finally, Seth hesitates, pauses, walks back a pace or two, and then stops to shine his lamp on a wall of stone. "Blessed be," I hear him whisper in infinite relief. In this wall there is a door I can but faintly make out. To this door, Seth has no key, but then the door has no lock. It is no more than a thick slab of wood.

At a gesture from Yeshu, Simeon and Jude, being the largest of us, push at it until it swings back with a terrible protest of ancient wood against even more ancient stone.

"When we go through this door," says Seth, "we will be under the Fortress of Antonia itself." Taking the lamp from his hand, Yeshu steps forward into the opening as Seth finishes what he would say, "From here on, I do not know the way."

"Be at peace," says Yeshu, "we will do what we have come to do."

I think, We must be gone from Jerusalem while it is yet dark, and not one of us knows the way from here? I look at Jude and at Simeon. In neither face—lit from below by lamplight, their beards are enormous, like flaming trees—is there anything but undaunted resolution. I look at Seth; he waits for Yeshu to do whatever it is we will do next. I look at Yeshu. His eyes shine; he claps Jude on his broad back. "Come, Jude, if we do not know the way, any way we choose could be the right way." Then he is off into the last of the tunnels, which seem older by far than those through which we have come. We must run to keep up with him.

Our tunnel branches into three tunnels, each dug through bedrock: two lead down, one leads up. Without hesitation, Yeshu chooses that which leads up. In time, we come to a chamber, dank and cold, in which there are stone steps carved into the stone wall. These steps lead up to a door in the chamber's ceiling. From the state of the steps, scattered with grit and the debris of ages, no one has been here for a long time. But perhaps there is an armed guard standing beyond the door even now, waiting for anyone foolish enough to push himself through? Or perhaps, long ago, a weight has been placed against it, a stone as big as the wilderness kiln? Or perhaps this door is long forgotten. For without doubt, these tunnels and these steps have been here much longer than Rome herself.

Staring at the door, Seth says, "It was only a stonecutter's rumor, a rumor of rumors."

If Yeshu or the others wonder at their entire plan being based on rumor, no one mentions it. It has been a gamble to come here, and it will be a bigger gamble to climb the steps. We climb the steps. Jude goes first, for Jude will always go first, or go last, whatever is needed to protect Yeshu. Then Yeshu, then me, and then Seth, and finally Simeon. All have drawn their knives, so I draw my knife, which feels heavy and strange in my hand. If I had to, could I use it? I do not know. Seth has left the lighted lamp on the floor of the chamber below us, so that as we climb the light grows dimmer and dimmer. Up here, the dark tastes of rust and mold and fear. I hear the sound the door makes as Jude presses his shoulder against it. I am sure everyone in the entire Fortress of Antonia hears this sound; more than a protest of wood and stone and the dead weight of years, it is a shrill drawn-out complaint. And then Yeshu is moving up, which must mean that Jude is moving up, so that I climb the next step as well, and the next, and here we are, through the door and crouched in what must be the lowest, and most terrible dungeon in the most terrible place I can imagine. There is a faint light far ahead of us, and by it I see there is nothing here but stone and filth. I crouch because a man cannot stand here. The stone ceiling brushes the top of my head. And if I crouch, how must the others contort themselves? There are no arches or vaults or ornaments of any kind, and the floor is nothing but the scraped stone of the mountain itself littered with rubble. The air is old and unmoving and cold, and it will never be other than cold. Holding up the low ceiling, which is, no doubt, the floor of the story above us, whatever grim place that might be, are crudely chiseled pillars, so many they make a thick and dreadful forest of stone.

Stooped and silent, Yeshu starts toward the light.

We leap over a rivulet of vile-smelling filth running along the floor. Everywhere we avoid middens of broken pottery and refuse, twice become confused by the trees of stone, but finally Yeshu and Jude come to the source of the light. It turns out to be no more than a torch fixed to a pillar and, below the pillar and the torch, a rough wooden stool. Someone has recently sat on this stool, and judging by the wooden platter of bread and olives they could return any moment.

We have come also to a low wall of large, fitted stones, and in this wall there are doors to a dozen cells that are as much like the tombs in the City of the Dead of Alexandria as they are like cells. My stomach roils to see them; the ache in my arm returns. Each small door is bound with straps of iron, and in each is a barred opening. All have heavy locks, though I see no key.

Holding the torch he has taken from its place on the pillar, Yeshu is at the first of them, peering into the opening. He moves to the second. Then to the third. At this, there comes a faint cry, and before Seth can stop me, I rush to this third cell, press my face against the bars, gagging from the stink. Against the far wall, Addai lies among refuse. He is thrown on the stones as the carcass of a dog or a murderer would be thrown. His hair and his beard are matted with blood and with vomit. What have they done to his face? What have they done to his hands? How could any man hurt such a one as Addai?

No matter that he is broken and bloodied, no matter that he soils himself, this is Addai, and I call to him, and would touch him, and give him what is mine to give, and I will not be stopped.

He hears me! And hearing me, tries to pull himself up from the floor of his cell, and I can see how painful this is, and I can see how hard it is, for Addai is a strong man, and he does not show effort, but he cannot seem to rise. He lifts his bloodied head and there! He sees me! He smiles! Addai's is a smile that can warm even here, even here, and I smile back, demented with love. But still, he seems unable to rise.

"We are come, Addai," I call to him, my voice low and frantic. "We are come."

Why is it he cannot rise up? And then I see. *Eloi!* They have broken his arms. They have broken his fingers. A master stone carver, an artist, and his hands are destroyed. Oh Isis! I turn to cry out that Addai of Shechem, who harms no one, has been cruelly used, but behind me, I hear Jude hiss us all to silence. The guard is returning. On the instant, I drop away from the barred window, move more quickly than I have ever moved into the shadow of a pillar. As does Seth and Jude and the cousin from Galilee. Before he too slips into shadow, Yeshu has only the space of a breath to replace the torch.

A moment later comes the guard, only one, for who would need more for cells that are deep in the earth under Jerusalem? One is enough for such a lost and hopeless place. It is Jude who is closest to the man, nothing more than a thin-faced, long-nosed Roman soldier, young and obviously ill tempered, as who would not be to find himself stuck on a stool in a place like this? And it is Jude who reaches round from behind the man to clasp him in a fierce and silent embrace. Stiff with shock, I watch as Jude cuts off the soldier's wind, and when the youth goes limp in his arms, Simeon is also upon him, binding him with cord, stuffing his mouth with cloth. This is all done so quietly and so quickly, I am half appalled and half thrilled. Jude has done this before; Simeon has done this before—have they not been Sicarii for a very long time? Immediately, Yeshu kneels over the tightly bound soldier to find the key, and I put away my horror at such efficiency as he unlocks the cell in which Addai is caged, and I am inside and I am holding him so soon as I possibly can.

I croon to him, tenderly wipe the hateful mess from his face with the hem of my mantle. Seth, who has once more taken the torch from its place, stands over as Yeshu slips his own mantle from his shoulders and his knife from his belt and begins slashing the cloth into strips. On the instant I understand. With my own knife, I take a large piece and cut it into smaller strips. We bind Addai's poor hands, make slings for his arms. With that, Simeon heaves him over his shoulder, and with such movement, Addai passes out from the pain. It is merciful.

A moment later, we would be gone, save for Seth who calls out, "Yeshu'a, there is another."

Simeon and Jude and I are only a breath away from rushing bent backed into the dark, which this time we will do without a light to guide us, for we leave the soldier's torch where we found it in the hopes that our method of entrance and exit will elude our certain pursuers, at least for a time. But at word from Seth, we turn back. Seth holds the spluttering light over the huddled form of a second shapeless heap. Using the tip of his sandal, Jude gingerly uncovers the face of this one. It is not so beaten and bloodied that Seth does not know him. "Stephen," he says, "the banker. This is the man who killed the soldier."

"Leave him," says Jude, turning away with Simeon who bears Addai.

Yeshu would stop his brother. "You leave a man to die, Jude?"

"A money exchanger? Who is he to us?"

"No one," replies Yeshu. "He is only a man."

So saying, Yeshu bends over this Stephen as Simeon bent over Addai, and gathers him up. He places the body of the banker over his shoulder. This one is not the man Addai is; his weight does not encumber Yeshu so much as Addai encumbers Simeon, but still it is not an easy thing to carry a full-grown man.

Jude grunts at the sight. I begin to understand him as Yeshu understands him. He means: suit yourself.

Once more, Seth returns the torch to its place in the pillar and the key to the unconscious soldier, and we leave this place. Stopping our noses to the thick and choking smells, moving by feel, we work our way back in the dark. Here is the door! Below us in the tunneled chamber our lamp is still lit. One by one, we drop down once more under the fortress, and all the while it is my sincere wish that I will never again see such a place, or know such misery, for so long as I might live.

A Terrible Truth

I *open my eyes* to full sun, and for the moment I do not know where I am—or when I am. As for who I am, even this escapes me. I am lying on a blanket of some soft woven stuff, my face pushed down into folds, and no farther away than the width of my palm I see fine grains of yellow sand as if they were as large as the rocks of my *nahal.* My own breath disturbs them.

How long have I slept? I ask this of the sand—I am alone—and my memory opens as a door opens. This is Seth's tent. Bearing away Addai and the man Stephen, as well as Tata with Rhoda who now nurses her, we came home to the wilderness on feet raw with the hurry and hurt of miles. Without sleep, I sat with Yeshu and the others as we talked of what we had done. And then, I fell here and I remained here.

I raise my head in wonder. We have done this thing. We have slipped in and out of a fortress, we have stolen Roman prey from beneath Roman paw. I did not know such a thing could be done. I did not know such a thing was ever done. I am a stranger to myself. I rest in my skin, but I do not know it. I see and I hear and I taste and I touch, but I cannot tell who does these things. Who is this new Mariamne?

Salome! I have not seen Salome since we left for Jerusalem. It is Salome who will remind me of who I am.

I find her in the small courtyard near the potteries.

Simon Magus sits on the broad yellow limestone steps that lead from the easternmost bath to the settling basin below it. Beneath that, the yellow ground drops away sharply to the yellow shore of the blue Salted Sea. Across this sea, Moab's mountains shimmer in the hot and weighted air. To his left and his right sits Maacah and Miryam, Veronica and Babata and Bernice. Veronica's now toddling babe lies asleep in her lap. Each of these women holds a stylus, each a waxen tablet.

At the feet of Simon Magus reclines, as ever, Helena of Tyre. With the help of Helena, Simon Magus teaches the women to write and to read.

Simon turns to me and I see Salome shine in his eye. There is love there. There is love for me, and my heart soars. Simon rises. "John! You are awake. Come away. I have a great desire to speak with my brother."

We do not hide in our *nahal*. Yeshu has been there. Jude has been there. There is no surety they would not come again if it should suit them. We do not descend to the underground chambers, where Dositheus is writing what must surely be a great work—why else does the parchment mount around him? We cannot go to Tata's roomy tent; there Dinah and Rhoda will be tenderly caring for Tata as well as Addai, my beloved Addai, whose jaw is broken, as well as his arms and his hands. Therefore, and without a word between us, it is decided Salome and I will go to our sleeping tents. My tent is as if a battle has been fought within it; hers is as tidy as a triangle. We choose hers. Her tent and mine, our manner of choosing between, is as wine to me. It is as we were. And might be again?

But now I am suddenly shy. I have so much to say to her I can think of nothing at all to say. Wordlessly, I arrange myself on her rug, compose my hands and my face. But my heart beats as a drum. Salome sinks onto her bedding, smiles at me as if it has been only hours since last we were girls together. And to begin, she uses my name, saying, "Mariamne, people are so taken up with Tata and with Addai, and with what John shall do now, no one has time to tell me truly what you have done. I know certain of it, but not the all. I must know the all."

This is my Salome. Forever curious and forever demanding. With such a beginning, I talk of what was done for hours, leaving nothing out, every moment of horror and tedium and thrill. I tell her that in the Jerusalem we have left behind, Romans search the city, house by house. I tell her how all that happened changes me, how I am become lost to myself. I tell her that sitting as we are sitting and speaking as we are speaking, brings me peace. And Salome listens as I am used to her listening, as a child to one of Tata's stories.

"And John?" she asks when I am finished, when I have brought us all back again, and Addai and Tata are safe and cared for. "Tell me what was said of John on that day in Jerusalem."

"I have told you," I begin. "Because of John, a Temple banker was moved to kill a Roman soldier."

Salome waves that away. "No. Not that. Tell me what the people listening said of him. Oh, that I had been there that day! Did they *hear* him? Did they *know* who they heard?"

"Do you mean did they know it was the Prophet of the River? Of course they knew it was the Baptizer! Because they knew this, a very great crowd had gathered. So many, the Romans had come out in force."

"A great crowd," sighs Salome, "a very great crowd. And tell me again, as John spoke, how did this great crowd listen?"

"Dositheus said that it was as if Moses had come among them once more. There were those who pushed forward merely to touch his robe."

Salome shuts her eyes with the pleasure of it, and my thought that we are as girls again dims. Though she has listened to talk of tunnels and secret ways and the death of our old friend Heli, of trussing a Roman guard as one would truss a sheep meant for slaughter, of Addai's terrible pain and how Tata's poor fierce head has been split like a gourd, now I think her listening is only to hear of John. At this, I feel a sudden flare of anger. I look directly at Salome in the hope that I might force her to look directly at me. I do not speak my sorrow, but I show it in my eyes. And though I have never known a time when Salome could miss such a thing, she misses it now. Or ignores it.

"Was anything said? Did the people call to him?"

My voice has gone flat, but Salome seems not to notice this either. I say, "As I have told you, there were those who called out, 'John is King of the Jews.'" I watch her eyes, which now shine with something I find in them more and more often: the lift and the light that shines in John's.

"Then I am right. It *is* time."

I say nothing even though I do not know what she means. I am too unhappy to speak. But Salome is too excited to be silent. "As you are one of us, you must feel it too. Of course you do, my friend, my oldest and dearest friend."

Hope leaps up again at this.

"You know Yehoshua's mind and the thoughts of Seth. I speak only with John, and John concerns himself only with the coming day. As Yehoshua is and always was the first behind John, it is Yehoshua he looks to for the how and the when. And as Yehoshua follows John, the others follow the planning of Yehoshua. Therefore, I ask you, how long now before we move?"

I have no idea what she is talking about, though I begin to have a horrid suspicion. But move? How can John move when he is now a hunted man? He would be seized by the soldiers of Pontius Pilate should he leave the wilderness, perhaps should he leave it ever again.

"Does Yehoshua say when we go to make John king?"

Somehow, I manage not to flinch. Nor to gasp. Make John king? And how would *we* make a king of John? The Romans make a man a king. Does she see the emperor Tiberius giving the throne to John of

Kefar Imi? Or does she mean we shall wrest it from him? I search her face for signs of jest, but there is none.

"The timing is crucial! The people must rise with us. Does it seem to you enough would rise at his word? There must be enough!"

I sit, as I have been sitting, hands in my lap, the fingers slightly curled, my eyes downcast as if I were deep in serious contemplation of all that she asks. In truth, I cannot believe what I am hearing.

"But if they come forth in their thousands, how can we doubt the outcome? It would make us a people again! As in the time of the Maccabees, it would mean the return of David!"

The throne of David! She means to remake a time when Jews ruled Jews? Salome is not a Jew. She has never been a Jew, nor wanted to be. And now she would raise up a king of the Jews? Is this a game to her as our word stones were once a game? I use a voice I would not use if I were easy in my mind, though it sounds calm enough. "But is it not your belief that John is the Nazorean Messiah, not a king, but a perfected man to provide example?"

Salome shakes her head, impatient with me. "Then he would also be king. The times speak to us. We must hearken to the times. Mariamne, how can you not understand such a thing? Have you not been listening?"

I remember what Seth said, "Those who are yet Nazorean look for the coming perfection of man. We await the Lord of Salvation, who will call forth a Transformation of Being the like of which has never been seen on this earth." Salome has forgotten this. Has John? Does Seth forget as well? I ask, "Seth knows of this?"

"How could he not? It is the will of the Nazorean. It will be the will of the Few. It is the will of Queen Helen and of King Izates. Has she not already come to build John a palace? You do not think the anointed one could abide a palace of Herod's?"

I am staggered in my lack of understanding, but of this I am certain: If I would regain lost Salome, I must follow where she goes. Is this a thing I can do? Is this a thing I *want* to do? I tremble where I sit. Hold myself still by pure will. But Salome, who once knew me better than I knew me, knows me not. On she goes in full flow, "It is the will of the first families of the Nazorean, it is the will of John. By the Voice within you, it is also God's will."

And now I know what I have not known. Though I went with Yeshu up to Jerusalem, and though I sat all the following day listening to talk of John and of Addai and of Rome, I know that I am not told the secrets each share with each. But Salome is told. This is why she knew what had befallen Addai and Tata in Jerusalem before I did. This is what she and John must talk of as they stroll about the settlement, their heads and their hearts so close entwined. Salome knows all this, and I do not. And I have thought it was I who was closest to the Nazorean. And I have thought I was Mariamne Magdaleder, meaning "She of the Temple Tower," a name Seth calls me, taken from the tower of a sacred temple hidden on Mount Carmel where once he studied.

I am such a fool. Nothing is as it was. Nothing will be as it was ever again.

A pat of my hand and Salome is gone. I shall not forget the look she could not hide as she left. She thinks that great things occur around me, but I cannot see the truth for my willful blindness. She thinks I am in danger of being left behind. I think she is right. But I cannot help but also think she is wrong.

John of the River is not the One.

He may speak and the people call him king. But I do not think he is the Perfected Man. Would my friends forgive me if they knew my mind? I suddenly think: Perhaps they *do* know my mind. Perhaps this is why I am told nothing . . . Yet there is still this truth: we cannot *make* John king! We cannot overcome the will and the might of Rome! Even should all of Jerusalem rise, such a thing cannot be done—it has been tried before. People in their thousands have died in such efforts. Is Rome gone from our land? Are the Herodians any less powerful? Do the priests in the Temple cower before us? Are men like Father a coin less rich? By the moon and all the stars, I now understand that this is what Salome expects shall happen! I see with horrid clarity the truth, a terrible truth that John the Baptizer asked me to see so long ago. I am not worthy of Life. I am an intruder in the tent of Simon Magus and Salome is not known to me. I am an intruder in the wilderness that is not home to me. I am friend to no one. I am nothing to myself. I serve no father, no husband, no child, no messiah, no god. In truth, I serve nothing. I am vastly learned, and yet I remain entirely a fool. I have neither use nor purpose.

This is what has become of me.

I stand as abruptly as if I am burnt. I push aside the covering of the ordered tent of Simon Magus and I rush away. I do not know where to go. I have nowhere to go. I merely run from the tents and the stone of the settlement walls toward that which is surely farthest from man and from woman and from the pain of knowing either, down the path leading to the salted Sea of Stink. The path is steep. It is littered with stray stones. But I leap down it without error. Without thought, I run as I have never run, as an athlete in the games, as an ibex, as a hare. It seems if I run fast enough, I might fly.

I reach the shore of the sea. It is flat and stinking and crusted with salt. I do not run north. North will take me to the sweet-water Jordan and to strangers in their fields of wheat and barley and medicines. It will take me to my poppy field. I run south. South there is nothing.

I do not know how long I run, but I know that I run past all endurance. I would run past life if I could. I would throw myself into the Sea of Salt, there to slip under its waters and find oblivion, but nothing sinks in our sea, not even an entire bullock. As I run I am sure that I will not stop, I will never stop, for where will I be if I stop but with myself, and I do not want to be with myself. Yet I do stop. I stop by falling headlong, and I lie where I fall, and my whole world is pain. My whole body is pain. I hold it close, I embrace it. I do this because I can bear the pain. What I cannot bear is what has become of me. I cannot bear who I am. And then there is nothing because I will it. I will myself to leave myself, to become as black as the back of a cave, as empty as the castoff skin of a scorpion, as unfeeling and as unthinking as a hung and butchered corpse.

When I open my eyes, it is evening.

Not yet night, there are long shadows on the cliffs above the sea, shadows the color of wine. Roses and saffron shift on the cliffs to the east, the last touch of the sinking god of the sun. The stench of brimstone fills my nose; its taste fills my mouth, burns my tongue. I am alive. I would wish this was not so. If I do not move, if I never move again, will my wish come to pass? I close my eyes in the hopes of this . . . breathe in, breathe out. How long must I lie before breath stops?

I do not mean to, but I listen to the sounds of the coming night. By a sea in which life cannot live, on a shore that feeds nothing, there is little to hear. But by and by I note that though it seems utterly silent, the world is never silenced, that it talks and laughs and sighs, and that it fills the ear: the distant short bark of a waking fox, the more distant trailing scream of an eagle, doves in the acacias far to my right. A slight whisper, a second breathing, behind me, to my right. What is that? Does something await my death as eagerly as do I? With this wretched thought, I raise my head, turn it slightly to the side, and there sits Yeshu of the magician red hair, a color burned deeper red by the setting sun. What is it he does here? Nothing more, it seems, than I am doing. Facing east, his eyes are closed and he breathes as I do, in and out, and in. I lower my head once more onto the salted pebbles and the bitumen, onto the black and salted mud. I close my eyes. Death will come eventually.

When I open my eyes it is full dark. I still live and the sound of breathing is still behind me. Once more, I close my eyes.

I am awakened by a beetle. I have no fear of beetles, but neither can I remain still as one scurries past the corner of my mouth, hurries into my hair. I lift my chin on the instant, shaking my head back and forth, and lay it back down again. I have found patience in loss and despair. Yeshu is still here, just as he was. If he is asleep, he has slept sitting. His back is unbent, his head on his neck uplifted toward the rising sun. Where last night his face glowed in the light of its setting, now it glows in its rising. I look east into the return of the light. Where has the sun been all this while? Men have answered this question in so many ways, but where has it *truly* been? And what if it should never return? Is it foolish for men to see it as the face of God? Or to see God as Light? Oh, but by Isis! Is there no way to stop the voice in my head? Mariamne is nothing but questions. She will never be other than questions.

Though I have not eaten and I have not drunk, I feel no hunger, no thirst. Though I have run until I dropped, and though I have scraped the skin from my elbows and knees, abraded my cheek against the gritted crusts of salt, and then lay in this way for many hours now on the cold shore of a lifeless sea, I am empty of feeling. "Yeshu?" I say.

His answer is almost a whisper. "Yes, John?"

"John the Baptist will not be king."

Yeshu says nothing but I know he is listening. I say, "He will die and those with him will be scattered." Yeshu remains silent, but I am not discouraged. I am beyond discouragement. "John is not the One the Voice within me prophesies."

"Who has told you this? Was this you or was it your Voice?" Yeshu's voice is soft and sure, but in it is something I have not heard before.

"I have told me this. I do not need prophecy to see what there is to see."

We are both silent again. I am no longer sure that I can lie here until I die. There are things that will not allow this. I have an itch on my inner thigh that becomes maddening. There is something that pokes into my stomach, a sharp stone or a stick. I reach under myself. The muscles of my back endure a strange sensation. I must move, or shout with irritation.

Now both Yeshu and I sit in the saline mudded sand, sand and mud and bitumen stuck to our feet and to our legs, and look at the coming sun. Vast flat cakes of ice-bright salt float on the surface of the briny sea, forming even as we watch. Across the salted waters, the tops of the mountains of Moab burn as they did on the day I first saw the settlement from Addai's shoulder. Addai! Could I die and leave Addai? With the memory of Addai, feeling floods back into my heart. So much so a sound escapes me, and I look to Yeshu in hopes he has not heard me, and by so doing, catch such pain on his face that my own flees at the sight of it. His hands grip his knees. The morning is still cool, yet he is drenched in sweat. His skin is pale. His lips chapped and dry. It is as if he has been drained of blood. "Yeshu?"

"It is nothing, John. I have known it since my youth."

"Known what? What do you know?"

"The pain inside my head. My eyes become full of broken light so that I cannot see as a man should see. When it comes, I can do nothing but wait until it leaves me. It always leaves me."

I touch his wrist. The skin feels as cold as the scales of a fish. "How often does this come?"

Yeshu takes his time in answer, but he answers. "Often."

I look at this man in surprise. He can live with this? I think of silent Helena who endures a pain that never leaves her, a pain that makes her shrink and creep and cleave close to Salome. I think of Addai and his broken arms, his broken hands, his jaw. I think of Seth who grieves that though his life is a search for gnosis, gnosis eludes him. I think of my own pain. Though not of the body as the day I fell into the city of the dead, it is surely pain. Do I endure as they? "You do not take *rosh*?"

Across the face of Yeshu there moves the ghost of a smile. "I have learned that once begun, there is no end to the taking of *rosh*."

I think of Helena, even of Tata. Perhaps in this he is right.

Yeshu turns to me. Even the turning causes him agony. "You speak of John the Baptizer. You awaken from dreams of death and the first thing you speak of is John. Who else but you, new friend, could I tell that all this night I have thought of nothing but John? A man was killed hearing John. How shall things go that begin with death? Another man is killed by Rome for failing in his duty, because you and I went up to Jerusalem. Did you know? I know his very name, Acilius Marius. He gave no more offense to me or to you than to be at his post when we came for Addai."

"No offense!" Yeshu has made me angry. "He is a Roman, a soldier. Perhaps he hurt Addai. Perhaps he broke his hands! Perhaps he deserved his death."

"Even so. Even so." Yeshu would take my hand, and I would pull

away for fear he would feel its softness, but I do not. He raises his
broken eyes to mine. "I am in danger, John the Less. Once I believed
God would kill or have killed. How did I believe such a thing?"

I do not think Yeshu expects an answer. I could not answer if
he did.

"All my life I have known my cousin as head of the Nazorean. In
my youth, I thought him almost a god. Think of it, to walk as a youth
with John of Kefar Imi, who was at that time called Zadok the Righteous One, who walked with Judas the Galilean. What boy would not
worship him?"

So John of the River was the mysterious priest who did not die
when the Romans caught and killed Judas of Galilee! And young as
he was at the time, younger than I am now, Yeshu was one of those
who rose against Rome. No doubt his twin rose with him, as did all
his brothers and cousins and friends. These men know what it is to
strike out at the Romans. These men know what it will be to walk
into Jerusalem proclaiming John as king. And I understand yet again
that there is Nazorean and there is the inner Nazorean. The inner
Nazorean, the Few, are fewer than even Seth thinks. The Few are
Seth of Damascus and now perhaps only myself. I have learned the
teachings of one who stands alone. All the rest, even Salome, believe
in war. They believe in being chosen. They believe in the coming
of kings.

Yeshu yet holds my hand. His grip grows tighter and tighter. "I
have never questioned John and I do not question him now. But I
question the way of things, the how of things. I question what is done
and what will be done in the name of God. I sicken myself with my
questioning. I grow ill with my doubts."

I understand this as I understand cold and hunger. I too sicken
myself with questions. Socrates taught that one should question
everything, but Socrates was condemned to die for his questions!
And now my questions become as hemlock to me. My hand aching
in his, I listen to Yeshu. I watch the sweat ooze from his skin, run in
rivulets into his beard. I think of the pain in his head. I wonder what
he sees through broken light but cannot imagine it.

"I do not welcome the doubt. I would banish the questions. I would be the man I was before the dreams. John! How do you live with the things you see?"

But I do not see things. I do not dream as he dreams. For all that I have walked in Glory, I do not walk there now. For all that I have seen the Passion of Osiris, I do not see it now. The voices come, the voices go. Once it was that I died and while dead flew up in splendid unspeakable *urtom*. This is all. Being witness to Glory does not change the whole person, for I am as foolish as I have always been. I am as reckless and as thoughtless. I have no answers for him and I tell him so. I loose my hand before it would break, and I tell him that I cannot help, I cannot even understand what it is he dreams or what he sees. What does he see?

Yeshu is looking toward the mountains. In this instant, the sun blazes forth, and Yeshu turns full toward me, "Why is it that I speak with you as I speak with no man, not even Jude who is my truly beloved brother. Why do I tell you such things?"

I quail inside. I tell Yeshu nothing. He knows little of me, and what he knows is not truly so. It suddenly occurs that I cheat him of his trust, that he offers me what I do not give him, what I *cannot* give him. For how can I give that which would drive him away? But if I cannot give him the gift of who I truly am, perhaps I can give him the gift of what I truly think. "Perhaps you come to me because I am as you in this way. I have nothing but questions. And all the answers I learn, pose me more."

I see hope of a smile in Yeshu's shattered eyes, though it is gone before it forms. He says, "Then I will tell you a further thing. I have sat all this night to know that you do not harm yourself, and now that I am assured you will not, I must leave you."

I thought I could not be surprised. But I am surprised. "Leave me? Where do you go?"

"That I can only know when I get there. But you will do this for me, John, you will go back to the settlement, and you will live until I return."

"When? When will you return?"

"Tell no one, not even Jude, for I would not have them search for me."

And with that he stands. He stands as if he felt no pain, as if his sight were as mine. I stand with him, but I cannot do as he does. My legs are shot through with aches and creaks and weaknesses. I reach for him to keep from falling, and when I am firm and standing, he walks away. Not back from whence we came the day before, but farther south, the way I would have gone because there is nothing there.

It is only now that I realize that Yeshu carries no wallet, no water skin, no head cloth, no sandals; his bare feet crunch in the crusted salt and salted rock. I have the sense to say nothing. I stand and I watch him for so long as he remains in sight. A stadion away, he passes a small pillar of salt, and then another shaped like a crouching figure that Salome once called Lot's wife, then three grouped together which she named the Three Sages, and I note that after a time, shimmering in mirage, he turns toward the west. There is a way up the cliffs somewhere near where he turns, a track made by wild things, and it leads to the top of the cliffs where there begins more of nothing, miles and miles of nothing. But on the way toward nothing, the track passes close by a series of caves, and in one of these caves we had found our little women; our limestone and reeded women with staring white and black eyes, and uplifted breasts, and tiny black vulvas exposed without shame.

When I can see him no longer, I turn north and begin the long walk back.

All around is fret over Yeshu—where is he, what does he do? Jude calms them all, saying even as a boy his brother was wont to disappear from time to time.

All now growl and mutter that John the Baptizer would be King of the Israelites. But as usual, none can agree on how to make him king. None can think what best to do; especially now that John is in mortal danger from Rome.

I am no part of this; though none of it passes me by. I sit by Addai, I read to him, I perform the magic he taught me, as well as a few tricks I devise on my own. I talk with Tata, watch her make pots. I notice that Stephen, the man Yeshu would not leave behind, finds a place for himself in the wilderness keeping accounts for the Poor. I collect the thick white blood of my poppy seedpods. I tend my balsam and my carob trees. I care for Eio. I wait for Yeshu to return. And I watch as all the others wait as well. On this all agree: when Yeshu comes back, he will know what to do, and then it will be done.

∝

John goes often to the very northernmost point of the Salted Sea, there to stand on the banks of the Jordan as it empties sweet into salt, and to shout at those who, in their search for the Baptizer, have found him. There is much danger in this, for any of the people who come seeking his teaching could be sent by the Temple priests, any could be agents of Rome. But just as there is no stopping the people, there is no stopping John. Though there is a curtailing him; with much maneuvering by the Nazoreans he now strays no farther from the settlement than this.

As for me, I avoid listening to John. I have heard enough of his teaching, which cannot also be said of Salome, who seems never to get enough. It is an accepted thing for people to see Simon Magus, John's favored disciple, wherever they see John. And whenever they see John, the excitement grows, for these days he speaks of the Climax of the Ages, howls that it is upon the whole of the earth, that his people are the Holy Nation and that they must lead the way or be destroyed by the fury of a betrayed God. He tells them there is yet hope, there is salvation. He tells them that if they follow their divine destiny there comes final deliverance for the faithful.

Hearing this I think a madness comes over him, more than any madness he has known before. I know a madness has come over Salome. By the times and by the stars, she claims that these, and others like them, would rise up, and by rising, God will make of John a king. This is not what Seth taught us of John. This is not what John taught

us of himself in the quiet times. What is it that John does now? Of
what god does he speak? I know the people who hear him assume it
is Yahweh, but is it?

On this day, Tata would have me wash Eio who smells of camel
dung. This is not surprising, as she has rolled in camel dung. So I too
am on the banks of the Jordan, though Eio and I stand away from the
dozens or so gathered around John and Simon Magus and Helena
of Tyre. I pour river water over Eio's back from one of Tata's water
jugs, scrub her reeking hide with salty mud and rough barley stems.
Within the space of no time we are soaked to the skin, she loudly
complaining, me wringing out the sleeves of my tunic. John, who has
been shouting, now shouts louder to be heard over Eio.

"Near at hand is the end of the world! And the Last Days! And
the judgment of immortal God for such as are both called and chosen! First inexorable wrath shall fall on Rome—"

I am not listening, but I am looking. Not at John and not at Eio
but out over the stinking sea. And there comes a something, a very
dot of a something, up from the south. I squint but still I cannot
make it out. Is it an animal, one so fierce it would show itself before
men in the heat of the day? Or one so ill it does not care? Is it a man?
I am curious, a bit puzzled. No one walks the shores of the dead waters, and never as this one seems to, coming up out of the wastes that
lie to the south of us. For a month, there have been no Roman patrol
boats, and only a few small ships bearing Arabian spices. What or
who could this be?

I stand straight and shade my eyes. Eio, no longer watered and
scrubbed, no longer brays, but walks off to sample muck and river
reeds. To my left, John yells about himself as "a voice of he who cries
in the wilderness," and with that part of my mind that hears him, I
think this last a thrilling thing to say—Isaiah is a book of many
thrilling things—but with the rest of my mind, I am intent on the
speck. And of a sudden, I know; of a sudden I see—it is Yehoshua! By
the goddess, Yeshu has come back!

Dripping with watered camel dung, I would run toward him, but
somehow I know I must not. I would shout out that he has come, but
somehow I do not. There is that within me that sees Yeshu is

changed, that he comes as he would come, without fuss. And there is more than this. Whatever it is he brings, goes before him as clouds before a storm, as heat before a fire. Even if I would look away, I could not look away.

It is now that John, in search of his next flight of winged words glances beyond his flock. He too sees who comes. He starts. He steps forward. He points. "Behold!" he shouts as he points, "Behold the Lamb of God!"

Each man and each woman turn as one, every eye seeking this lamb, and no eye faster than Simon the Magician's. I cannot stop myself, I touch the mind of Salome. How does she bear to hear her beloved greet Yehoshua in this way? What can it mean? She does not know what it means, and not knowing cuts her down to the bone.

Yeshu is by now less than a stadion away, his face shining as the morning sun over Jerusalem, shining as Tata told me my face shone when I awoke from Glory. If I did not know better, I should think him somehow larger. We all stand in perfect silence as Yeshu walks toward us. We all of us watch every move he makes, even Eio who has lifted her head from the river reeds. She has turned where she stands so that she faces him, silently dripping, silently chewing.

He is closer now, and closer, and as he comes, the light that shines forth from his face is more than the sun. It is the light of all the stars that Joor of Thebes has taught me are also suns, also worlds. Yeshu looks at me—at *me*! There is no movement of his mouth, no movement of his eyes, yet I know that he smiles in his heart to see me. As for my heart, it beats as the heart of a bird, so fast I might fly away. I do not question how this has come to be, this feeling for Yeshu, this joy. It is enough to feel it.

Yeshu turns his attention from me to John of the River. "Come, cousin," he says, and for once his voice rings from riverbank to riverbank, and from cliff to cliff. "Bathe with me in your river. We will wash away the dust of the wilderness." And with that, Yeshu walks past John and past Simon Magus and past the astonished people, and straight into the water. He does not stop until it reaches his chin. A moment later, John laughs, throws up his arms, and plunges in.

I have never seen a more surprised people than those who have come to hear John. I do not think a single one of them has ever heard a prophet laugh, nor wishes to. But oh, he laughs now! He and his cousin Yeshu'a laugh in the water as if they were yet boys, and I stand on the bank of the river and I am as one with Salome. Her envy is every bit as green as mine.

John is louder than ever in his enthusiasm. Up to his chin in the water of the river, his gray beard floating before him as a child's feeding cloth would float, his loincloth coming loose under the water, he holds on to his small bit of goatskin, and he shouts, "Where have you been, Yeshu'a, son of my mother's sister? What have you done with yourself, Yehoshua of the Nazorean? You come as one who has had his fill of strange foods, as one whose eyes have been opened with strange sights. What have you eaten? What have you seen?"

Yeshu is splashing near John and the dust of his wandering comes free from his person, coats the skin of the water. I see him swallow river water, but it only makes him laugh. Yeshu is full of laughter; there seems nothing else in him but laughter, laughter loud as John's laugh, as loud as thunder. "You would hear, John? You would know? I shall tell you! I saw the Spirit descend like the whitest of doves with wings as white as linen, wings as white as clouds! I felt it land full on my head! On my head, John! And in that moment I ate of the Spirit as I would eat fistfuls of honey. I feasted on meaning. You would behold? You would see the Lamb of God?" Yeshu spins in the water, and shining drops of the Jordan shoot from his red hair and from his red beard as stars shoot in the sky. "We are all the Lamb of God!"

Shouting as John shouts, and all the while spitting out water, Yeshu in his great joyous laughter looks toward the shore where the people stand aghast and agape, each one listening to the ravings of this second wild man. But this one they think spouts nonsense. Yeshu knows they think this, and it makes him laugh all the louder. "Hear me, Lambs of God! There is not one of you to whom God would not say you are my beloved sons and my beloved daughters and I am well pleased with you!"

Simon Magus gapes with the rest. Does he hear nonsense? I do not know. All I know is that I do not hear Yeshu spout nonsense. I have heard such words before. I hear it when the Voice speaks, when Glory rang in my head like a great bell. I look at Yeshu in his splashing and his shouting and his stars of bright water and his delightful foolishness, and if I could stretch my skin to smile wider, I would.

Yeshu waves his arms, he kicks his legs; sheets of bright water spray those who stand too near. As John pointed at him, he points at me. "And there stands a true Lamb of God. There is my friend whom all call John the Less! Come, friend! Be baptized by the Baptizer. As you seem already half drowned, come! Drown yourself further!"

All stare now at John the Less, at Eio washed clean of dung—at *me*. My smile turns down into horror. Bathe with them? Jump into the river with them? My eye catches the eye of John. He knows my horror. I catch the eye of Salome. She and Helena know my horror more than John. If I should become wet as John, as Yeshu, all should see what I am. If John's loincloth threatens to drift away from his maleness, my tunic would cling to me, would show the female body it forever hides. Mariamne would be exposed. Yeshu is splashing water over his head. His hair and his beard run with the Jordan. His laughing mouth is full of the Jordan. Still he calls, "What keeps you, John? Jump in!"

At that, I simply spin on my naked heel and run. Not as I ran weeks before, but it is fast enough and close to blind enough. I run for the safety of Tata's tent. And then I remember Eio. By the moon, I cannot leave Eio behind! So I turn back, grab her by her halter lead, and once again run away. Eio is more than good to me; for once she trots along as fast as I need her to.

The laughter as we leave is as the buzzing of bees.

It makes me run all the faster.

Tata fusses from place to place, and I watch Addai as he watches her. How should it feel to have a man gaze on me as Addai gazes on Tata? I have told them what has happened at the river, that Yeshu has come back a changed man. Tata says she will wait and see this for herself. Rhoda, who knows who I am and knows my true name, offers me food as if I were male. I take it as if I were male. By now, this has simply become what is. I sit with Addai until the sun goes down, until Tata is forced to shoo me away, and then I am off to my own tent, moving carefully so that I might not be seen. I would not be seen by anyone, anyone at all.

I lie in my bed and I am quiet, but I am not asleep. Outside the night sings and things of the dark I know to be far away seem close. Through the skins of my tent and of hers, I hear Salome's breathing and know that she dreams and that she is restless in her dreaming. I do not know what troubles her, but I know what troubles me. I am uneasy because of Yeshu. I am uneasy because I do not yet understand what it is I feel, or if I will come to understand it. I have not loved Salome's love for John of the River, nor have I been best pleased to see her change for him. Is this then what will happen to me? Is this the nature of women? If such a thing can come over Salome, it can come over me who am not half so willful or half as clever.

Out of the hearing of Addai, I earlier had asked Tata if what I feel is what any woman feels? In this thing, I asked her, am I more Mariamne than John the Less?

Asking, I could already hear her answer. She would say that men and women cannot help themselves; there is nothing they do that is not, at bottom, sexual. Tata will remind me that any *zonah* with a cup of sense knows this.

But Tata surprised me. Turning from her work, which was mixing up a hideous potage of medicines and aromatics, she stopped stirring and stared at me. "Are you more Mariamne than John, you ask me this?" The smell of whatever she stirred was strong enough to water my eyes, her glare strong enough to water my knees, yet I nodded, yes, I ask it.

This was her answer: "Just as Salome is not more Salome than Simon, you are not more Mariamne than John. You are both as singular as the moon. As John of the River said, you are as men, for there are not many women who can rise above their sex."

"I have a man's mind, Tata," I said half in hope and half in despair, "but is my body weak and foolish and vain and driven by the lusts of the flesh?"

Tata put down her spoon. She flicked a speck of muck from her hand. Her eyes slid to the left, then to the right. "There is no man to hear me, so I can say to you, Mariamne, in whose throat lives the Loud Voice, rare as riches in my mother's house, rare as pity in the house of my father, do you not *know* who you are? Have you not understood? You are free of your sex. Though you might feel the sexual desire of the female, yet you are free. This is a great thing! This is a miraculous thing! Rejoice in this, Mariamne. Treasure your freedom." Tata took up her spoon once more, once more began stirring. "Not by my will was this done, but by yours. In Salome, it has been an effort of will that astounds me. In you, it seems a suppleness of mind. This too astounds me. Now go away before I make a mess of this. As you would be a philosopher, on the life of the rarest Addai, I would be a contriver of medicines."

I lie here now and think of what Tata has said. I ask myself, is Yeshu as most men? Does he think as most men think? He too is as singular as the moon. But in this one thing on which all other things rest, is he as multiple as the ant? I recall the treatment of his mother, the pallid Mary. By this I would answer yes. I recall his treatment of his sisters. By this, I would answer no. If I should ever show him the truth of who I am . . . But he knows Torah. In Deuteronomy it says, "A woman shall not wear any garment that pertains to a man, neither shall a man put on a woman's garment: for whosoever does these things is an abomination in the sight of the Lord your God." I am an abomination in the sight of his God. I would not be an abomination in his eyes.

There is movement outside my tent. I cease in my unspoken chatter, and listen. It comes again. *Yea Balaam!* Is it a wolf? I reach for my knife. I sit up, fling aside the flap of my tent, and there, looming out of the black of the night, is Yeshu. I am too dumbstruck to think of a single word. Not so Yeshu. He would laugh right out, but I see him check his laughter for fear of waking other than me.

He glances over at Salome's tent. "He is asleep," he says. "Put down your knife and come away before we wake him. I have need to talk with you."

On the instant, I drop my tent flap. I struggle out of my sleeping clothes and into the usual robe of John the Less. I find John's toga and his head cloth, and when I am thoroughly clothed in all these things, I come away.

The moon seems to me a coin. It sits like a coin in a purse of stars, and on it is stamped the face of a man. King or emperor or god or even messiah, I cannot tell. But the face has eyes, and the eyes look down on Yeshu and on me, who have arrived by their curious light at my secret place. I see Yeshu has already busied himself in the sand and the rock of my *nahal*. He has made a small fire. He has made a place to rest himself during the night.

I sit with my knees tucked against my chest and my chin on my knees. My hands are clasped round my ankles. I am alight with expectation. What does he think to share with me?

Yeshu reclines in the sand across the fire from me. His left leg is stretched out before him, his right leg drawn up. With a casualness I have seen before, he scratches. By Horus, we are certainly males here. We are equals in gender. I find I would not change this. Not for all the lusts of the male, or the female. But as I look at him, lit from below by fire and from above by the face on the coin of the moon, I see a whole man lit with more than these feeble things. I see Glory come from the inside.

Yeshu stops his scratching, sits up. "John, I must speak with someone. And I know that someone is you."

I say nothing. I am not here to say anything. I am here to listen.

"I have been tormented with anger and with bitter tears, made frantic with calamity and desperate with injustice. Everywhere I looked, everything I saw, seemed full of rage and of fear. And I was moved to pity by all I saw, and to terror, and my terrible pity moved me to rail against what I thought was unjust and to raise a hand against those who oppressed what I deemed the piteous. In truth, the world has seemed a bitter place; its taste has been the taste of gall. I have also pitied me grievously, John, wept tears and ground my teeth for the helpless, hopeless, thing that I am. I rent my clothes and tore at my hair at the death of my father. As for my mother, my grief for that most worthy of women broke my heart."

Caught up as I am, still I think, Mary, how is she lost?

"It was this man to whom dreams came, dreams of such confusion I would shout myself awake, strike out at shadows, soak my bed with sweat. I tell you this so that you might know the man who walked out into the desert. I was as Moses in my walking, but I was as a fool in my understanding. And there on the high place, I stood as this fool, and I raged as a fool rages, and I shook my fist at the God of my people." Yeshu shudders as he sits, then leans closer in his need to be heard. "If I am to speak more, new friend, I am to speak blasphemy. Do I trust you to hear me?"

I do hear him. His blasphemy will not trouble me. But I see that it will trouble him, down to the nerve and down to the bone.

"Is there any wonder that the man I was, craven with fear and in-flated with pride, would make a god like Yahweh? This is the way of men, afraid before life, tormented by pain they cannot escape, and desires they cannot appease. Would the god of these not also be a god of rage and fear and jealousy and desires he cannot appease?" Yeshu opens his palms to me. I do not look away. "What can I say that you do not know beforehand? Knowing it shall never leave me as it has never left you. What is there to tell *you* of it?"

I writhe inside. He thinks so much more of me than I think of myself.

"I walked deep into the desert until I could walk no more. When I could no longer walk, I crawled. And when I could no longer crawl, I lay on my back under the sun and stared deep into its terrible eye until I was gone blind. Until I was tormented by hunger, and worse, by thirst. Until I was sure I would go entirely mad and cry out as David cried out: 'My God, my God, why hast thou forsaken me? Why art thou so far from helping me, and from the words of my roaring? I am poured out like water, and all my bones are out of joint. My heart is like wax; it is melted within me.'"

I am staring at his face now, captivated by its changing shape.

"These things I did. These things happened to me. Or perhaps I happened to them. There came a time I could not have told the dif-ference, and I have not relearned it. And there I lay under the burning sun and the freezing night as a woman might lie to give birth. I was as a woman in the agony of my labor. In that time and in that place, I knew what it was to be woman and I pitied her for it, and I loved her for it, and I labored mightily as a woman labors."

I thrill to these words. But I do not move.

"But I did not die. Nor more than you died. Or is it that I have died to myself and have been reborn? It does not matter. Death does not matter. It is nothing. It is illusion. I know. I *know* because a moment came like no other, a moment that was of no time and no place. But it did not come as Ezekial by the river. No four-faced monsters or Great Wheel of the stars, or great swords. A voice did not shout out revilements. To me, when I had been laid on the ground, when I had been drowned and buffeted and burnt, only then it came, as a perfect white dove."

Yeshu reaches out once. He touches the back of my hand with the tip of his forefinger. Once, no more than once, and for only the briefest of moments. If I had not had my eyes open, I should not have known the truth of it.

"I say to you, John, it came as the deep soft sweetness that comes over a man when he looks into the eyes of his beloved. In that moment, the jealous and vengeful Yahweh left me. And in that same endless boundless moment, the Father entered."

Now it is I who lean forward. Now it is I who listen to a man tell of Glory. I am certain he will tell it so much better than I. Joor would say that Yeshu was like Pharaoh, the divine cobra springs from his brow. If Seth or Philo could only hear, they would say Yeshu has gnosis.

"I became unbusied with myself, unbusied with that which has so concerned me. I came to rest in he who is at rest. There, on a high place, I know that the covenants made by men are worthless. I know there is nothing demanded of us. I have looked into the eternal eye of All That Is and know there is nothing to be done but to walk in the Father's Sight. From that moment to this, I have not ceased looking into his Eye."

This last surprises me—more, it touches the fear that lives within me. It frightens me for I do know whereof he speaks, all save the very last. When my life came back to me, I came back to myself. I was my mortal self, my *eidolon* again, somehow more, yet still Mariamne, daughter of the Jew Josephus. I put away the Large and became small once more. Who has Yeshu come back to? Or has Yeshu come back at all? Does he remain in his *Daemon;* see as his *Daemon* sees?

But *eidolon* or *Daemon*, agony now replaces his joy.

"He set his Eye on me, John; he wrote truths in my heart. He ended my wandering so I might stand unshaken in the glow of perfect light, forever, where no darkness is, forever, where peace is, forever. He showed me that I am this as much as he is this. That I am God as he is God. He showed me that I AM. He told me my name and my name is Man and my name is Woman and I am All That Is. And so are we each of us, every man, woman, child, every Jew and Gentile. I have learned that I and my Father are One. There is no man and no woman who are not this, and who cannot know this."

I do not move and I make no sound, but I cry with the unutterable truth of it, the bliss of it. There is no one who is alone and no one who is not beloved! And yet there is no one here save Salome and Seth who can understand this, and even they do not yet *know*. When I tried to speak of it, they heard nothing, though they listened with the whole of their hearing. Though Socrates and Pythagoras and Philo and Buddha speak in the clearest of ways, who hears them?

Yeshu smiles at me, and his smile is sad. "And yet my people are afraid. As I was. And what they fear most is the god they have made. As I did. The prophets of my people fear the god of their hearts, and shout their fear into the ears of all who can be made to listen. As John of the River does. Fear and anger is our god."

Yeshu grips my wrist. I do not move.

"I would have them know that not fear, but love, is god. I would have them see that all their hate and their fear is ignorance. If all should *know*, the world would be as the Kingdom of God! It *is* the Kingdom of God if they would but look! There are none God loves more than he loves the all! There are no people chosen, for all are chosen! I would have them see they are not different than God, or separate from God, or need to placate God, or please him or fear him, that they are God, and of God, and in God. I would show them the Kingdom of God does not come; it *is*."

Yeshu looks at me, and his face is as ashes. My wrist burns under his hand.

"How do I tell other men this? What I can tell you so easily, knowing that you hear me, how shall I tell those who *cannot* hear me?"

Who is this man? No one has taught him these things. He knows nothing of the Egyptians, nothing of Pythagoras, nothing of Socrates who taught that there is no evil save ignorance. He knows nothing of Philo, perhaps not even of Seth. His life has been nothing but loss and the Law, nothing but toil and knives. Yet he has seen these things for himself; he names them himself. He amazes me. For Father and Father's friends, what is Law but the hope that Yahweh be pleased by a man's action and reward him with a good life? Or at least not punish him with a bad one. But if what Yeshu has seen is true, of what use the Law?

It is as if Yeshu has heard me. "What need we of Law when we are full of grace, and being full of grace would do no harm?" He lets loose of my wrist. And still I do not move. "As the Father sends me forth, how do I teach this?"

It is only now that I speak. "To find the Father and Maker of all is hard, and having found him, it is impossible to utter him. This was said by the god of Seth, who was Socrates." Yeshu laughs. It is good to hear him laugh. "Seth teaches that all men and all women are angels of light clothed in the cloth of self but do not know it. Not knowing is the dark in the center of the soul. Seth says it is the heart of gnosis to know it, that merely to know this one simple truth is to be set free. Ignorance is all there is of Evil."

Yeshu's eyes glow with pleasure at this. "Seth is a great teacher. I would be such a teacher."

I think of Diogenes, who owned nothing and lived in a great jar at the gate of a temple, and who wrote that teaching such mysteries "is a hard road to follow, filled with darkness and gloom, but if an initiate leads you on the way, it becomes brighter than the radiance of the sun." Who would be the initiate to lead Yeshu who has walked with God? Could he think it would be me?

Yeshu sees all this in my face. He must, for he says, "You once asked if I were the One. Do you know your asking caused me to walk out into the desert, to live or to die? Am I the One? I would answer now: we are all the One. How do I keep what I have seen and what I am to myself? How would I not help those who stumble and those who cry out? How could I not hope to raise their sight so they too might walk in the sight of the Father? Therefore, tell me John, how shall I do what I must now do? Who shall walk with me?"

I cannot avoid looking into his eyes. And there I find my answer. Yes. He thinks it will be me. In a heartbeat, there comes a trembling in all my limbs. There comes a heat, which rises up from the base of my spine and spreads out into my blood as floodwaters fill the lotus delta of Egypt. I hold on to my senses as I would hold Eio on her rope, for fear they might plunge away from me, run where I would not go. More than a memory comes, more than a reliving. I could once again know Glory—or would if I would allow it. But I do not allow it. I am not Yeshu. I cannot hold God in my hand as he does; I cannot be God in my mind, and still breathe and stand and continue in my being. But I can remember Glory and know that Yeshu now lives in the Kingdom of God, which is *Daemon,* with the Father who is the Mother who is All That Is. This man appears as a shepherd among lambs, and this man stands forth as a lion, and I know him by his word. Yeshu is the One who comes.

My own voice rings forth as the Loud Voice: "I will walk with you, Yehoshua the Nazorean."

Hearing this, sorrow comes down over Yeshu's face as the shadow of a blade might come down over a neck. "This thing we will do will break our hearts."

"I know," I say.

I am not a fool. I do know.

Separate Paths

The *days pass,* one on the other, and still Yeshu hides himself away in my *nahal.* I hear much complaint of this as I go about the settlement, contentedly doing one thing and another and knowing what I know. It is not John of the River who complains. John walks and talks with Simon Magus and with Helena of Tyre and with the sons and the grandsons of Judas of Galilee. He preaches at the southernmost point of his beloved Jordan, waiting out Yeshu as patiently as my poppy field awaits the changing of the seasons. Nor does Simeon complain. Simeon keeps to his wife, for it seems he loves the sour Bernice more than a man is wise to love a wife. Jude also does not complain for he has settled himself at the foot of the path up to the *nahal,* and seems likely to stay there until Yeshu once more appears, or until he, Jude, starves to death. Not that he will. Miryam and Maacah daily bring Yeshu and Jude their meals. Jude allows his sisters to pass and he allows me to pass, but we are all he allows to pass.

If I am not about Yeshu's business, I sit with Addai as he suns himself near the potteries, while Tata fashions *bilbil* after *bilbil*, curious little jugs to fill with *rosh*. Dositheus sits often with us, elaborating by the hour on all he has seen and heard in Egypt. He tells Tata that there are scribes and such who take *rosh* so that they might ride Ezekial's chariot and see what Ezekial saw; he says the Greeks call it *opion* and the ancients of Sumer called it *hul gil*, which means "joy plant." At this, Addai would have raised his hands if he could. If he could, he would have laughed. But he can only whisper, "I would that my daughter had known joy, and if not joy, then *rosh*."

These few are those who know peace as they wait for Yeshu.

But the many, led by Old Camel Knees, Jacob the bald brother of Yeshu, stomp about the settlement with iron in their eyes and bile on their lips. It is the month of *Tishrei*. The fast of Yom Kippur, the Sabbath of Sabbaths, is only days away. Up in Jerusalem, the high priest of the Temple will soon plead with YHVH to reconcile himself with his Holy Nation. These grumblers are saying it has been the month of *Tishrei* for many days now and where is Yeshu? As leader, when shall he command them to make John king?

I do all I can to avoid them.

It is not always possible.

On this day, Jacob and Simon Peter and Andrew and a handful of others, among them Essene from En-geddi, stand in the courtyard of the small sundial that I must cross if I am to feed Eio. They all shave their heads, and swear to continue to do so until the rightful king is on his throne. The blue of their skulls shines under the sun like a row of Tata's glazed pots.

As I pass, keeping myself small, Menahem, the son of Simon, stands with these men, trying to appear as they do: righteous and fearsome. He succeeds in appearing an anxious, overgrown, bearded child. As kin to Seth who keeps his chin clean, John the Less also keeps his chin clean. As does Simon Magus. Or so, thank the stars, it is assumed by all these bearded men. For the fifth or so time, I hear Simon Peter saying as if it were the first time, "If John would cause the people to rise, Succoth is surely the time to appear before them. Why does Yeshu keep us waiting?"

As Peter has spoken, now Jacob speaks. "Does Yeshu forget that Succoth comes on the heels of Yom Kippur? If John does not show himself soon, Yeshu will have waited too long. Is it not timely for the King to appear in Jerusalem on such a feast day as Succoth, the joyous Festival of Tabernacles? Everyone will crowd into Jerusalem, who would know there was one more?" Jacob so moves himself, he shakes his fist in the direction of my *nahal*. He so inspires himself, white spit sticks to his red lips.

Not wishing them to notice me, I keep my eye averted as if I do not notice them. But Menahem is ever eager to single me out. He pushes at Andrew who pushes at Simon Peter, which causes Simon Peter to turn and face me full on.

Simon Peter's eyes are full of envy and hatred. He knows I am free to see Yeshu and that he is not. It takes him no time at all to step between me and the gate from the courtyard. This gate leads out onto the hot flats under the western cliffs where Eio wanders about searching for something to eat. She will bray when she smells my poppy seeds. The tuft on the end of her tail will quiver. I am eager to see this. I am more eager to avoid Peter.

"You," he says. "You, John the Less."

Simon Peter means for me to stop.

I stop on the spot. But where I have stopped requires the rest to come to me. It is not far, but it satisfies my foolishness. I keep my eyes down as suits a youth before his elders. I keep my hands folded in front of me. The bag of poppy seed I would share with Eio dangles from my belt. There is nothing to fault my deference.

It is Jacob who speaks to the intruder who has by some wickedness bound his brother Yehoshua. "Tell me, John," he begins, holding on to his temper as I hold on to my nerve, "what does Yeshu'a do?"

I do not raise my eyes to his. I am humbleness itself. "He is thinking."

"Ah! This must mean he plans our actions!"

I know he wants me to assure him this is so, but I do not. I hold myself steady in a ring of men who lean toward me. I breathe them. I smell them. I feel the heat of their bodies and the ardor of their passions. They would walk with John to Jerusalem. They would follow prophecy. All the men of the settlement, Jew, Nazorean, Yahad, the Issa-ene, the Many and the Poor and so on, now all believe it prophesied that John is the Messiah. I stand silent before Jacob who would turn on his heel and run to Jerusalem at a word from Yeshu.

"When will he be finished thinking?"

This I can honestly answer. "I cannot say."

"Will it be before Yom Kippur?"

"I cannot say."

"Does he agree we should go in time for Succoth?"

"I cannot say."

Simon Peter, at my elbow, cannot contain himself. He leans into my face and he shouts, "What *can* you say!"

Jacob restrains him with a glance. I answer Simon Peter. "I cannot speak for Yeshu."

Jacob moves closer, and I reach into him, feel for his heart. He may be, as Salome once said, made stupid by his righteousness, but he is cunning. He is not Simon Peter of Capharnaum; he knows his own mind. Jacob the Just has no thought of Glory or gnosis, has never desired to ride Ezekial's chariot. He is a "son of man," rooted deep and steady in his need for restraint and control and for Law. And his sublime conviction, fed by an aching passion for what he calls justice, is that what is right for him is right for all. What Jacob does not know is a single moment of doubt.

I would say that Nicodemus knows what it is he knows, but were Nicodemus to stand against Jacob in his certainty, he would be as fine sand before a great wind.

I am more fortunate than sand. I have come to see that I know nothing at all. In this I am no more than the grass. Before the mighty wind of Old Camel Knees, I bend.

Jacob the Just leans toward me as I lean back; he comes so close, his breath flows into mine.

"I would ask that you grant me a boon."

Please Isis and all the gods, make this something I might grant! "If it is in my power."

"I would have you go to my brother. This I am sure you can do."
I nod. I can do this.

"I ask you to say that his brothers and his friends wish a word."
Once again, I nod.

"I ask that you do this now."
I nod one last time and I walk away.

From the corner of my eye, I see that Eio turns her great hairy head my way, that she lifts her soft upper lip and waggles her long tender ears in astonishment. Where do I go? I walk away from her? At this, she lets out such a bray of surprise and dismay, I am almost compelled to turn away from Jacob's task.

✂

All who have gathered find Yeshu in my bowl of warm rock. It is the middle of the day, yet he seems to doze. But I know he does not. He does as Socrates once did who was often discovered to be staring at "nothing" for hours. Seth calls the nothing of Socrates a state of rapture.

Not knowing rapture, most who crowd into my *nahal* glower amongst themselves.

They ask themselves how it is he sleeps when all around there is much to discuss and much to determine and much to do? As a youth among men, I do not sit, but I stand near Yeshu. I would wriggle with curiosity if I would allow myself. What shall Yeshu say to these men who hear him as second only to John?

Salome's and my secret place has never seen so many. I am surprised they find room. There is Jacob the Just, as close as he can come to Yeshu without climbing up onto my rock. There is Simon Peter, and there is the ever-bald Andrew; these two sit farther back but are still too close. Seated in the sand, the Sons of Thunder, brothers Simon bar Judas and Jacob bar Judas, have come, though they have brought with them only one of their sons. This is the eldest son of Jacob bar Judas, who is called James. James, whose face is roseate with perhaps a rash, stands and keeps silent as suits his place. He seems as solemn as I must seem. I wonder if his solemnity is as much a fraud as mine? As for the absence of Simon's son, the bearded, preening, tall and irritating Menahem, I find this a blessed relief.

Simeon is here. From his place near the head of the path, he shows me his wonderful teeth in his wonderful smile, and my heart smiles back at him for this. The youngest brother, Joses, is also come. He kneels near the seated Simeon, and for the first time I get a good look at him. His ugliness is not a thing of birth. Joses has once had a great slice taken from his face. Where it is scarred, his beard will not grow. Seeing this, I look away. I would not shame him. But I do not doubt his scar is because he is Sicarii.

Because there is so much zealotry here, no woman is allowed. Without Tata to lean on, Addai must be helped by Dositheus and by John of the River. He sits where he has always sat, in his place under his date tree. Near him, John unfolds himself on a soft floor of sand. It pleases me to note that he has not taken a place of prominence for all that he would be a king. As Yeshu does, John closes his eyes. Near John stands Simon Magus. I do not look at him. He does not look at me. But I know, and I know he knows; we look at each other through and through.

Right beside me, crouching down by the bowl of rock, is Jude. He has not been asked to do so; Jude simply does what he does. Just as he would sit at the bottom of the path stopping all who might pass, now he chooses to sit by his brother Yeshu and to glare out in silence at the men who have come for answers.

Among these there are none who call themselves Poor or Essene or Yahad or Friends or the Meek or the Little Ones or the First or the Many. But there are nine who call themselves Zealot, and all nine carry knives. It is Seth who is missing here, Seth who is needed, yet he remains in Jerusalem, overseeing Queen Helen's palace. I would have him to talk to when I do not understand a thing. I would have him to listen to when I would know a thing better. If Addai is my heart, then Seth is my mind, and suddenly I am struck with such a longing for him, and for what is past, I think of Salome who thinks of me, and I quickly look up.

She stands by her beloved John, but she looks at me. From where

I stand near Yeshu, I look back as openly as she. Without speaking, I say, *Is this what we meant to do, you and I?* From the moment our voices began, we waited for the One. And now it seems we have found him, one for each. I say also this: *I miss your laughter and your briar tongue. I miss your sightedness and your true-speaking.*

It is a thing of blessedness to hear in return, *As I miss you, Mariamne, friend of my youth, and she who is my heart.*

In this moment, Yeshu stirs, and whatever else we might say to each other fades as a drop of rain on burning sand. On the instant, those who have come to confront Yeshu strain forward, eager to hear his thoughts so that they might know their own. All, that is, save John. John does not open his eyes. I hear John of the River. John knows his own thoughts. He will walk to Jerusalem. He will be made king. He will be king because the people would have it so.

Glory plays about the head of Yeshu as lightning might play in the distant hills. I wonder, does anyone see this but me? Do I see what is truly there, or is this as my voices are, a thing of strangeness peculiar to me?

Yeshu speaks. In tones as clear and as beautiful as the lute, he says, "Now you are come, what is it you would have me say?"

At such a question, it is Jacob who looks most askance, causing him to blurt out, "You ask this? As you have ever been the right hand of John, and as it is time to be about a king's business, we would know how you see this thing done."

Reclined in the bowl of stone, Yeshu answers, "How do *you* see it done, Jacob?"

Jacob would seize this chance to say how he would see it done, but Jacob is a cunning man. He thinks that now is not the time to stand forth. He knows the men around him have come to listen to Yeshu, not to Jacob. "I, Yeshu'a? I would see it done as you think it wise. What is it you think wise?"

Yeshu sits up as a desert Arab would sit, cross-legged, with his elbows on his knees. In my sight, Glory now rises from his whole body as steam rises from boiling water. "As you have come to hear me, then I shall tell you, and when I have told you, you may do as you wish."

There are puzzled looks, mouths that turn down, beards that stiffen as the chins beneath them stiffen. No one knows what he means by this, and they are made apprehensive in their not knowing. Of all, John looks neither puzzled nor apprehensive. Yeshu looks from each to each. "I tell you, of those born of woman, none is greater than John." Hearing this, Simon Magus could not be better pleased than if the emperor Tiberius himself had said this thing. But Yeshu has more to say. "I ask you, who is our true king?"

There is much mumbling and a host of sidelong glances, Salome's chief among all. Does Yeshu test them? John is rising from his nest of sand so that he stands before all as the very king they would make him, but it is Jacob who answers. "As Issa, the first Nazorean, taught, God is our true king."

To which Simon bar Judas eagerly adds, "It was the battle-cry of my father, 'No ruler but God!'"

Jacob bar Judas flushes that his brother would speak. But Yeshu smiles and as he smiles, he says, "Then it is God who would rule us."

There is much looking around at this, each man checking to see what the other man thinks.

"True, Yeshu'a," replies Jacob when all is again still, "God is our king. But as men have need of God, God has need of *one* man, so that he might rule through him."

There is much approval at this.

Yeshu replies, "Each man rules himself."

There is more than confusion now; there is dismay, and Jacob's is spoken: "How so, Yeshu'a? You know and I know that men cannot and do not rule themselves. Have we not spent our young manhood taking the part of those who cannot, or will not, take it for themselves?"

"Yes, we have spent our youth in this way. Tell me now, what has come of it?"

"What has come of it!" Jacob cannot believe he hears this. "It has brought us to this moment! It has made the people ready for their rightful king!"

All eyes turn to John, who does nothing more than listen, nothing

more than stand as tall and as thin as an obelisk. He seems a very
Caesar, yet to me, this is as nothing compared to Yeshu. Yeshu is the
perfection of man, not coming, but *here*. Can these men not see this?
Can they not see that though he walked away from them one man, as
small as most men believe themselves to be small, he has come back
another: a man as large as man *is*? Jude is looking up at Yeshu, and I
know the hair rises on his head. He does not know what Yeshu has
done or what he has seen, but he knows there is a change in his twin.
All his life, Jude has been as a shadow to this one. And though he has
done as is expected of all the men of Palestine: married and fathered
a child, still, the path Yeshu walked was Jude's path. Jude is who Jude
is: the one quiet as the other talks, the one somber as the other
laughs, the one who remains earthbound as the other soars into
flights of fancy or wit or passion. As Sicarii, he fought at his brother's
side for the weak and for the fearful and for those who could not
fight for themselves. Or thought they could not. Jude knows well
what it is that his other brother, the righteous Jacob, means by saying, "Men cannot and do not rule themselves."

But it is I who finish this thought, though I finish it only to myself:
For if they could, they would. Father would say, and I would say it a
truth, that the strong rule the weak.

"These things are so because we allow them to be so," I hear
Yeshu say again, as on the day he and Jude together first visited my
secret place. "The men of resignation have made all this."

I hear Jude prepare himself to grieve. I feel him full of fear that
he does not know his brother and if he does not know Yeshu, there is
nothing to know at all. My heart goes out to him. He is a great heart
and has great pity. I think of Salome, and by this I know what it is
Jude faces. I would reach out and touch him if I thought he would
not scorn me. But the truth is, he would shake off my hand. He does
not loathe me as do the others, but he does not love me.

"I would do more than make the people ready for their rightful
king, Jacob. I would show them what I have seen."

I see how all listening, yearn to understand him.

"For I have seen the Kingdom of God."

How do they hear this? What is it they think he says to them? Quickly, I reach from one to another. There is one who is made eager; this one wonders if Yeshu returns from a place he himself might be shown? There is one made anxious; he imagines Yeshu become poetic, by which he means weak. But among the rest, only a few have the least idea what might be meant. Jacob, who understands least of all, has the wisdom to remain silent.

But there is one who knows what is meant. "There have been others who would do this, cousin," says John of the River, "and among these others, I count myself. None have succeeded."

Yeshu does not lower his gaze. "I must try."

"Then our paths diverge, as I knew they must."

"Yes," replies Yeshu.

I find I understand John. He knows he has tried and he has failed to bring people to gnosis, to know directly the God in themselves. Once he cajoled, he urged, he did not threaten. But the people could not hear him. Now he rages at them, pleads for their very souls. And this, at last, they hear. The noise he makes, the lamentations, brings them to the river in their thousands. Yet even now he fails. For instead of knowing themselves, they look to him to save them from themselves. Only the Few seek within; the many seek without, and the many are counted as legion. So that now he seeks a third way to teach. He will allow the many to make him king. If he is king, then perhaps he can teach as a king. Perhaps they will hear a king.

Yeshu must also try. He is suffused with the need to show others what he has seen, to have others know what it is he knows. By this, he believes their suffering will end; for, by this, they will see themselves free. And not merely from the yoke of the Romans, or the despair of their secret hearts, but from Yahweh and his Laws.

By all the stars, if Jacob or Simon Peter knew Yeshu's heart, like caged lions they would roar in their rage! Yehoshua the Nazorean will not lead them to Jerusalem to make John king. Yeshu will walk among the people to make them all kings in the Kingdom of Heaven.

John is right. The path of the cousins diverges.

As he would speak with Yeshu as an inner Nazorean, John sends all others away, save Addai and Simon Magus and Dositheus. Yeshu motions for Jude and me to stay. All others go quietly, but they each go with deep misgiving; they now know that Yeshu will not be leading them as they walk with John to Jerusalem. And if there is no Yeshu, there will be no Jude. Jude is the rock that Simon Peter would be. Who else might abandon them? Simeon? The Sons of Thunder who are devoted to Yeshu?

Tonight, there will be much grinding of teeth in the wilderness.

High above us, the sun is hung from the white roof of the sky, and there seem no shadows. John and Yeshu are still; Yeshu lost to *makarismos,* which is the blessed nature of one who has seen the Mysteries. John and Addai seem simply to wait. Jude has not moved from his chosen spot. Salome and Dositheus use stubby bits of palm leaf to write each to each in the dirt. I am watching tiny brown ants pulling and pushing the great bulk of a bright green beetle toward the door to their underworld home, such a single-minded struggle.

It is John who pulls me from my ants. "Soon I will leave this place, Yeshu'a."

Yeshu does not open his eyes. "I know."

John sighs at this. "As I know that you will not travel with me."

Yeshu says nothing, and I watch John quietly accept what is not said. He lifts his hand in small supplication. "But tell me, cousin, as I have depended on your advice, I ask that you advise me now, and perhaps for the last time. If I should go up to Jerusalem, if I should do what is asked of me, what is it you see coming to pass?"

Yeshu looks now at his cousin, a man it has been his duty and his pleasure to follow all of his life, and his eyes are full of what he sees coming to pass: he sees a man who will die for pity. Yeshu has no need to reply, for over the face of John comes an acceptance of what Yeshu would not say aloud, and by this I see at last how worthy John is of Salome's love.

John too knows he will die for love and for pity. He turns to Salome with a fond and impish smile. "Tell them what it is you have heard your voice say."

Salome darts a glance my way. Does she too see her favorite die? All her life, Salome has seen further and faster than I—does she still?

"I heard a voice," says Simon Magus, whose own voice sounds out firm and confident, though I know the truth of it, and the ring of it causes the birds to cease their babble, "and the voice came to me not at night from out of the darkness but at the height of the day, and the voice said that the name of John the Baptizer would ring through the ages with a mighty sound." And there he stops.

"And?" urges John.

By the moon, Salome fears to speak. Is it because I hear her?

"And?" John urges once more.

Simon Magus is left without choice; he must continue. "And the voice said that where John led, a people would follow."

John slaps a hand on his knee. He turns back to Yeshu and smiles a child's smile. "You see! How could I not go when everyone will be following?"

This is what Salome fears, to be responsible for what is to come.

John is still playing the innocent fool. "But as I must follow my own advice and chart my own course, I think I will not go up to Jerusalem." At this, not only Yeshu lifts his head, we all of us do—not go to Jerusalem? John sees this, and laughs. "Oh, I will go. Have you not heard Simon Magus? It is my fate to go." Only I know the cost of the smile that stays fixed on Salome's face. "But first I will make my way up the Jordan, keeping always on the bank of the river ruled by Herod Antipas, for Herod has fewer teeth than this ferocious Pilate." John shows his teeth, snaps them. "Though Joanna, who serves as my eyes and ears in Herod's court, assures me Herod's false wife, the proud Herodias who hates me more than she hates all others, has more teeth."

I have never warmed to Joanna. Perhaps she will serve also as Herod's eyes and ears in the court of King John? I look at Salome. Does she still hold a similar thought?

"And the people will hear that I do this, and they will come, and when it is right and when it is proper and when it is time, I shall turn my face south again. And then, we shall all walk up to Jerusalem."

"And there," exclaims Dositheus, sitting up straighter and straighter as he listens to John, "a miracle will occur!" We each cock an ear to hear how he will finish what is begun. "For what is the history of the Israelites if not a history of miracles, and the promise of greater miracles to come? Is scripture not a record of God's intervention in the affairs of his people? That being so, it follows that a people who are steeped in the miraculous expect no less than the miraculous. Expecting this, they will simply assume what is said will be so, *will* be so, and by their very numbers and by their very faith, they will have their miracle."

Now I too sit up. The people *will* flock to hear him; they always do. How will the priests and the rich stand against them if they come in such numbers? I shiver; am I as deluded as all those who clamor to make John of the River king, or has Dositheus caused me finally to see a thing?

Brushing sand from his hands, John says, "It is settled then. We leave at first light." And rising, adds, "Know you, Yehoshua, that a free state of Jews newly exists on the banks of the far Euphrates? Know you that this town of Nehardea is subject neither to Romans nor to the Babylonians nor to the Parthians?"

"I have heard this."

"If all goes unwell with me, the brothers who have founded it would welcome you."

Yeshu laughs out loud. "I will remember that, John."

⋉

This night, Jude will speak to me, and I am made anxious for I cannot imagine what he would say. We are met in the shallow cave at the foot of the cliffs, and for light there are only stars. So soon as I sit, Jude begins. He talks as I have never heard him talk, it is all I can do to keep up with his flow of words.

"Even as we were young," says this *didymus*, this twin, "Yeshu was not as I was, nor was he as any other boy. I would watch my brother at play, or at work, or as he slept and I did not, or as he discoursed with learned men as I could not, and I saw that in body I was as alike to him as an egg to an egg, yet as unlike in mind as a peasant to a king. You see how unlike?"

I nod, yes, I see how unlike.

"Yet I knew that those things I could call Jude, and not Yeshu, were the very things he lacked, and by the lack thereof, was in need of them. By this, I knew I was sent to keep watch over him. Was it not a sign to be born so alike and yet so unlike?"

He watches me carefully. Once again, I nod, yes, and this pleases him.

"Even I could not miss a sign such as this. I cannot remember a time I did not know who I was. I was Jude, he who shadowed his brother to shield him from harm. I cannot remember a time I did not rejoice in what I was. Therefore, if you are in my brother's heart, you must be also in mine."

I am touched. But I see how hard it is for him to place me anywhere near his heart. As for me, I warm to Jude, the Sicarii. I warm to his rough ways and his silences. I warm to his fierce loyalty and his single-minded devotion. If once again I were out on a dark night and in a dangerous place, with me I would once again want Jude, and I find I hope there will come a time when this brother of Yeshu shall think this of me. But I would not place a wager on it.

"There are things you must know of Yeshu."

For a third time I nod.

On this night, Jude talks longer than he will ever talk, at least to me. And for a man of few and grudging words, what he says is said well.

In green Galilee, there was in the time of the first Herod a small hill among many small hills overlooking the Plain of Jezreel, and on this hill there was a small town called Japhia, a place of twenty families or so, each family knowing the other. The family of the brothers Joseph and Cleopas of Japhia were builders, not rich, but very far from poor. Every house in Japhia and many in the nearby countryside were built by Joseph and Cleopas. The brothers married young as was expected, and in no time Cleopas fathered on his wife, Martha, a fine assortment of children, both male and female. But year after year Anna, the wife of Joseph, continued barren, which became more and more a source of great unhappiness to Joseph, as he loved Anna, who was as lovely as a field of flax and as wise as she was kind. In the town of Japhia, Anna was well beloved by all. But no matter how loved, the Lord did not intervene. Years passed, and he sent no angel to quicken her womb. In time, like Sarah, the wife of Abraham, Anna agreed that Joseph should take a second wife. Joseph left the choosing of this wife to Anna, and she looked over every likely girl from Japhia to the slopes of Mount Tabor. In the end, it was in the village of Kefar Imi, only a few miles from her very doorstep, that Anna found what she was looking for. Serving in the family of her much older sister, Elisheba, the sister who had married a priest, one Zechariah of Kefar Imi, from the priestly course of Abijah and the Nazorean, Anna found a maiden not yet fifteen years. This girl's name was Mary. Just as her name was common, there was nothing in her character to distinguish this Mary from others of her type and class, save a remarkably passive nature, and this more than anything besides health was what Anna was looking for.

Neither Anna nor Joseph were disappointed in the girl Mary. But if Mary could not disappoint, she could surprise. When the contracts were signed and all the traditions upheld, Anna found Mary had arrived already with child. Though she was yet a virgin, having not begun to menstruate, she had conceived. And though a virgin conceiving was a thing not unknown, it was still unusual. Anna heard this with grace and with forbearance. Having made her arrangements, and knowing how eager Joseph was to bring forth their children, she decided to accept what she could not change. A child was a child, and for a woman who had no child, any child was a blessing.

But she did not tell Joseph.

It was this fatherless child who was born first, though he was not born alone. The firstborn child was named Yehoshua and his twin, born moments later, was named Jude. Of all their acquaintance, only Anna and Mary knew that Yehoshua and Jude were not the sons of Joseph, though much was made of the red hair. No one in Joseph's family had ever had red hair. Nor had red hair appeared in the eternally humble family of Mary, those who had sold her to Zechariah the Nazorean priest. Anna, being not only wise but also prudent, looked quietly into the family of Zechariah, the husband of her aged sister Elisheba. There was no red hair in the priestly lineage of Zechariah. Having nowhere else to look save among a cohort of Roman soldiers lately billeted in the area, Anna wisely let the matter rest. Shortly thereafter, the soldiers, made up of men of many races and many lands, and of these there were those with red hair, moved on, and with them went all hope of an answer.

But no matter, for Anna came eventually to see that of all the seven children of Mary, whoever the father might be, it was Yeshu'a who had brought great gifts to herself and to Joseph. In Yeshu'a, her years of barrenness and worry were finally fulfilled. By the child Yehoshua, red of hair and laughing, she had made the right choice in the mother, Mary, for Yeshu'a was Anna's own true son, and she lavished on both him and the quiet Jude all the love of her great and generous heart.

I am surprised that Jude tells me that he and Yeshu are born in this way, but I do not show it, nor does he speak of it with shame. He is ashamed of nothing about Yeshu. As for himself, he thinks so little of Jude that shame cannot enter.

The life of Anna and Joseph and Mary and their children continued to be peaceful and productive until the conception of the last child, a daughter who would be named Miryam. In that year, with Miryam a mere month in the womb of Mary, Anna and Joseph, along with Cleopas and Martha, traveled to the town of Asochis to attend the wedding feast of the son of a friend, and on the way home again, Joseph and Anna and Cleopas fell ill with a fish they had eaten there. Though Cleopas recovered, Joseph and his beloved wife Anna died that day, and many another wedding guest as well. It was a terrible day for the small towns of Asochis and Japhia, but for Mary it was an unequaled disaster. Being possessed of no beauty and no wit, a widow left with seven children, one still in the womb, being also a second wife and with no claim to the property of Joseph, Mary was thrown on the mercy of Joseph's brother, Cleopas the Builder, and on Anna's brother-in-law, the priest Zechariah, and both of these already had large families of their own. From that time on, the life of Mary and the children of her body was hard indeed, even though John of Kefar Imi, the eldest son of Zechariah and Elisheba, and much older than any of the children of his uncle Joseph, did all he could to ease it.

And from that time on, it was Yeshu who was head of his family. If there was thought of his becoming learned—and there was, Anna had nurtured fond hopes for his future—or of his marrying well (here Anna had already a bride in mind), these thoughts were set aside. From now on, it was Yeshu, as well as Jude, who would provide for the family of Joseph and Anna.

In the year of his parents' death, Yeshu was as old as Mary had been when she birthed him. In that year first came the pain in Yeshu's head and, with it, his broken sight. For if Anna had loved Yeshu, Yeshu had returned her love fourfold.

"I, Jude, have watched Yeshu since coming here. I have seen him listen to you. And I have worried that some illness is come upon him in the wilderness. But I have thought and I have thought, and I have remembered that he has been this way before. Yeshu was born as he is become again."

He confuses me. "Forgive me, Jude, but what do you mean?"

"I mean that Yeshu was born with Sight. Have I not said he would wander off as a boy? Did you think I meant he was idle and useless? When his Sight would come over him, he would walk forth to talk with God. Of this, he spoke only with our mother, Anna. And even, at times, with me."

As ever, I am Mariamne. "With God, Jude? Which god?"

Jude looks at me as I say this, and I am sure he thinks to strike me, even if only in irritation at being questioned when it is hardly the point. But he contents himself with saying, "You speak as Yeshu speaks. I have known no man who speaks as Yeshu speaks or asks the questions he asks. This is why, on my mother's head, I swear I shall try to love you."

Oh—how he does not love me! I would laugh with delight, for it is sweet to see him try and, by trying, to expose his own loving heart. But for his need to finish, I know he would run from me.

"The things you say, some of which is gibberish, and some of which is blasphemy, and some of which could come from the mouth of Yeshu himself, I am sure this is why he loves you. As he confuses and confounds me, so too do you."

I hasten to make my peace with him. I would not have him leave me. I have so many questions. There are those who say not fathering children is alike to murder: therefore why is Yeshu not married? Jude is married. Joses and Simeon are married. I do not count Jacob; Jacob is as single as he is single-minded. For Jacob, there will be no wife and there will be no meat, and no hair, until the Temple is cleansed. But what reason has Yeshu? I would know too of the years he has spent as Sicarii. Where has he traveled? What has he seen?

But Jude has said what he has come to say. He makes his first gesture of rising, a matter of putting out his hand to push himself up, and then does not. "I have almost forgot."

"Yes, Jude?"

"I came to know your mind." He sees that I do not understand. "I am a blunt man; I do not have your wit. As a blunt man, I ask you bluntly, Yeshu turns from John, he turns from the Sicarii . . . has a demon entered Yeshu?" Before I can answer, Jude hastens to make clearer what he means. "If a demon has entered him, I must fight a demon. I ask only to know what I must prepare for."

I make of my face and my eyes a window into my mind. I say, "There is no demon in Yeshu."

Jude thinks for no more than a moment, then smiles. His smile is wonderful for it being so rare. "I thought not. But I would know what you thought. I shall speak no more of it."

It is night. I do not know the hour.

Salome stands alone on the very edge of the farthest cliff looking out over the Sea of Salt. Above her shines Osiris, the Shepherd of the White Stars, he whose starry purse hangs at his belt. What is it, I wonder, he keeps there? This night I think he keeps more worlds as this world, a purse full of worlds, each one complete and perfect unto itself. Below him, Sopdet, who is Isis, the brightest of all the stars, stares down like the eye of Horus. I have been taught that beyond these lies the realm of the Pleroma, the fullness, and that in that unutterable place there are more worlds, but who can truly know such things?

I come up behind the friend of my youth, and I barely disturb the ground. I cannot hear my own footfall. All I can hear is the far-off cry of some small frightened thing, dying in sudden violence. I am not the small child who followed her wherever she went, but I am still the Mariamne who loves her and would stand beside her, quiet and awed beneath the fields of heaven.

She hears me as I do not hear myself, and her voice comes now as a whisper in the dark, saying, "I am afraid, Mariamne."

Salome, afraid? No one farther away than I am could have heard her, but do I truly hear, or is it a trick of the night and the starry worlds above us? Salome turns to me. I see her face by the light of the White Shepherd, and I see it is *that* face, the one she wears so often now. Like John's, it is the face of a man who is called. I have yet to say a word, and there is nothing I can think to make me break silence.

"You see John will die. I know you see that. I know the man Yehoshua sees it. But do you see more? Do you remember how it was in Egypt? Do you remember how it was at the Passion?" Suddenly I am become rigid with what it is Salome says to me, what it is she thinks John walks forth to do. Her eyes shining with a light come from the inside, she reaches for my hand and her touch is hot with what I think fever. "No matter whether John is made king or he is not made king, he is already king, and he goes forth to claim his kingdom. Mariamne! He is Osiris! Do you see this?"

I see that what I held most dear is lost to me.

I see that Mariamne and Salome have taken separate paths and there is no going back. I cannot summon even what was lately mine, the fine fret of my irritation, the long moments I savored of boredom, the fitful longing for Alexandria; all these seem now as paradise to me. What I would give to have them all mine again! Nothing is as it was. Everything is edged with a hard and brittle light. Everything stands forth in my sight as if I am seeing it for the first time. As if thoughts were blows, I reel.

"No, Mariamne, hear me!" I feel Salome's hands on my hands. "Please! Is this such a terrible thing? To die as Osiris dies? Is it so terrible if by John's dying, a whole people will be saved?"

I see her dear face, so close to me now, so lit with the madness of fervor. I find my voice; it comes in a rush, and I loathe the very sound of it. "Saved? No Jew thinks his Messiah will come to die for them. They think he comes to do battle for them."

"But John will not die! He shall rise and live again!"

I look straight into her eyes but she does not flinch.

"All others have their godman," she cries. "Why not the Jews? Remember what Philo thought to do? He thought to create a Jewish godman. In Egypt, he is Osiris. To the Greeks, he is Dionysus. Mithras lives and dies for Persia, Attis for Asia Minor, Adonis for Syria, Bacchus for the Italians. But no matter his name, he is the *same* godman! The Jews call out to be saved!"

I say, "Philo would create a myth as these are *myths* and in this myth, he would hide the great truth of gnosis. You know this Salome! But as John truly lives, he shall surely die."

Salome speaks over me. "They wait for their Messiah. Like Pythagoras who brought him as Dionysus to the Greeks, could the Jews wait for other than such as Osiris? And now the Baptizer walks among them, and they cry out for John. You have heard their cries! The people say he is their Messiah. What other is the Messiah but the godman?"

Salome clasps her hands before me. It seems almost a supplication. "Remember what is sung at the Passion? Remember, Mariamne? 'Have they sacrificed thee? Do they say that thou hast died for them? He is not dead! He lives forever! He is alive more than they, for he is the mystic one of sacrifice. He is their Lord, living and young forever!'"

Has my skin paled to white? Isis, Queen of Heaven, do I hear what I hear? Salome would be as her hero Pythagoras. She thinks to bring salvation to an entire people. I howl out in my grief, "Salome! Are you mad?"

The face of Salome is replaced on the instant by the face of

Simon Magus. For the space of one eternal moment, he stares at me, his features hardened to stone, and when finally he speaks, what he says is said quietly, but there is more power to it, more finality, than a mighty shout. "Leave me now. And do not return."

Eloi! Eloi! Beyond all hope of forgiveness, I have mortally offended my friend. But I cannot leave her. I cannot walk away from Salome. I must try one last time. I begin, "On my life, Salome—"

"My name is Simon. Leave me."

Silver in the Hand

We *will walk* to Galilee, Yeshu and Jude, Eio and I, and we will go as the Cynics of Diogenes do, and as Pythagoras did, taking nothing but the clothing on our backs, our staffs, and our wallets. Jude goes because Yeshu goes. I go because I said I would go. I go also because I am sure my heart is broken. I cannot remain unoccupied now that Salome is lost to me. Eio goes because Addai thinks her a protection for me, as well as a diversion. Yeshu goes because he would teach in Galilee.

On the third day after John and Simon Magus set forth, followed by a great company, we four also set forth, climbing down before the coming of the sun to the shores of the Sea of Pitch, and then north along the Jordan, its waters brown with the first of the rains, intending to pass through the city of Jericho. As we go, Yeshu asks that I talk of philosophy.

By the moon, what a task teaching turns out to be! I, who have always been a student, and who has had such dreams of teaching, had no idea. Salome has done it. I have seen how the women hang on her every word. I have assumed if she could, I could. More fool, I. I wish to tell him of Pythagoras, thinking this a good place to start, and I make a point that cannot hold if I do not make another point, so I run back to find what I have missed, and in no time at all, I am thoroughly muddled.

Yeshu smiles at me. He nods his head. With the patience of Job, he encourages me. And by and by, I say a thing and he understands a thing, and we make progress. All of it seems as water to Yeshu; he drinks as he would from a well. I range from the Greeks to the Egyptians to the Persians to the ancient Vedas written when the Hebrew was as yet unknown to life, and of each of these, especially the life-loving Epicurians, Yeshu questions me closely. And even more closely when I come to what Sudheer has said of the Buddha, whom he called the Light of the World, and who is said to have lived when the greatest of the Greeks lived. And more closely still when I talk of the *Tao-te Ching,* written by an ancient master of China called Lao-tzu, another who lived when the greatest of the Greeks lived. I quote from memory, amazed I do not stumble: "The Tao that can be told is not the eternal Tao; the name that can be named is not the eternal Name. The Nameless is the Source of Heaven and Earth; the named is the Mother of the Ten Thousand Things. Desireless, one may behold the mystery; desiring, one may see the manifestations. Though one in origin, they emerge with distinct names. Both are mysteries, depth within depth, the threshold of all secrets."

Hearing this, Yeshu says, "And this was also when Socrates drew breath? It seems the Father bent close in those years, to send so great a company among us."

As we go, Jude follows along; I can see that though he says nothing, he listens.

And as we go, the sun climbs in the sky, and under it Eio finds much to eat, and most delights the palate of an ass. She becomes a spring lamb. She lowers her head, humps her back, and kicks out her back legs, braying and bounding about in the dust of the road.

By and by, we come away from the river and walk across a flat plain toward sharp toothed mountains rising to the west and then through the gates of not the old Jericho, but the new Herodian Jericho. It has taken us all of this day, but here we are now, dusted and weary with the miles. We are also without food and without shelter for the coming night. All around is the clamor of a great marketplace, a thing I once went to in fevered excitement, my purse full, fierce Tata hovering near. But for the first time in my life, I cannot buy a single thing for I have not a coin to my name.

I shift my gaze from stall to stall, from the goods of this one to the goods of that one. But I have no thought for the oddities, the trinkets, no thought even for the sellers of books—it is the smell that intoxicates! Fruits of all kinds. Wines and breads and sweetmeats, delicacies sizzling over fires. I turn this way and that, sniffing the air. My mouth floods with spit, my heart with self-pity. Fasting before the Passion, I have known hunger; but since I fasted then by choice, this I endured. And now that I would eat by choice and cannot? Eloi, and by Isis, how hunger hurts.

I look at Yeshu with all this in my watering eyes. I look at Jude. How can they smell these heavenly odors and not fall upon a loaf on the instant? I enter their minds without second thought. Jude is waiting only for what Yeshu will do. Yeshu is thinking, How to begin, by which he means not eating, but teaching. He is thinking that it is one thing to be on fire with Divine Insight and very much another to find oneself jostled by uncomprehending strangers in the middle of a great market square in the new Jericho. We could be any three men with an ass. He and Jude have red hair and beards of red, but red hair has been seen before. They are as alike as alike, but twins can be found in any land. We are not rich, nor are we rabbis or scribes or the Pharisee. We are not famous, not John the Baptizer or the young man we have lately heard tell of, a certain Apollonius of Tyana who travels about claiming to be Pythagoras come again. Apollonius is said to be gifted with beauty as well as wealth, performing miracles and healing whomsoever asks him, even if they be at a distance, but all magicians can do such things. All that sets us apart is that we are wanderers and perhaps not so beset with the constant troubles of this life: how to feed our children, how to pay our taxes, how to avoid the lambastings of yet another prophet.

People push by us; a man shoves Eio out of his way, which earns him a lowering glare from Jude that makes him move off as fast as he can. But Yeshu stands still as a rock in a tide pool. I know the Glory in him as I know the blood in my veins, but who else shall know? Why should any listen to Yehoshua the Nazorean who is lately Sicarii? And how shall he begin?

I know he will not teach that these are the last of the days. He has asked me how can there be a last day when the world is as it has always been and always will be, as endless as a circle? He will not teach that the Father would judge his world. How should a creator judge the Lion more worthy than the Lamb, value the sky over the sea, prefer a beetle to a bee? Does he curse the night? Nor can he teach that some will prove worthy of the Kingdom of God, and some will prove unworthy, and that those judged unworthy will be cast out into Darkness forever. He will not teach that any need saving, since none are lost.

How Yeshu will teach what he has learned and not be stoned, I do not know.

Holding Eio's head halter, I look about me. I hear these people. They are filled from birth with "truths" they are too tired or too preoccupied to question. They are whipped to madness by prophets and doomsayers. They are battered on all sides by taxes and Law and prophecies of doom. And if not by these, then by poverty and ill health and endless misfortune. And if not by these, then by ignorance or hatred or guile or some other nameless misery. These are those he would teach. To these he would show his heart. I shudder in my skin. I glance at Jude. Knowing Jude stands near, balanced for anything that might happen, gives me strength. I notice there is a sudden eager jostling on the far side of the square. A crowd gathers under a great sycamore tree, and I strain to see what attracts them. A storyteller! As a child in Jerusalem, I would do as these people now do, eagerly push forward when a teller of tales comes weaving his spell. The man sits on a low wall that encircles the tree, and around him now stand the women with their water jugs, and the young males who for the moment have nothing better to do, and the farmers in for the market. Among these, there is also a gaggle of assorted beggars and bumpkins. And under the feet of all, there are chickens and children. Yeshu has begun to move. He too would hear the man's tales. Jude and Eio follow on by rote, but I go happily.

Already, the storyteller has made the people laugh, and for the pleasure of laughter they press closer around him. As he tells his tale of jackals and broken pots and a wife whom a dozen children and a lazy husband plague, he mops the fetid sweat from his face. He smells. He is unwashed. But there is not one here who cares, so long as he makes them laugh. In moments, I too no longer care. Even my hunger leaves me as I lean forward, following the story of the poor woman whose every move causes more calamities. Comes a moment when even Jude laughs aloud! But Yeshu has laughed from the beginning.

And when the tale is told, immediately there is a woman, still weeping from laughter, who presses upon the teller a coin, and another who gifts him a cake—a cake! Even a child holds out a bit of something, a date or a fig. Closer than I leaned to listen, I now lean in to watch the storyteller slip the coin into his purse, but more, I lean in to watch him eat the fruits of his labor. Oh, but how the pain of my hunger washes over me.

"Yeshu, we—" I stop when I notice that Yeshu is no longer beside me. Nor is Jude. Not even Eio remains. I spin on my heel. All three are halfway across the marketplace. I scramble after them.

As I catch up, I hear Yeshu explaining to Jude that he has still much to learn, that there is a way to teach and a way to tell a tale, and that he is sure that people will listen to a thing if it is told as a story. "John! Would you not agree laughter is life's greatest gift?"

I might answer this if I was capable of thinking of else but my stomach.

Yeshu answers for me, "Did not Abraham's Sarah say, 'God hath made me to laugh, so that all that hear will laugh with me.'" And then he falls quiet as he continues across the square, past all the heaped and odorous food, and down a narrow alley. We three follow along and all the while I mourn my hunger.

It is only when we emerge once more into a smaller market, quite as crowded as the one we have left behind, that he speaks again, saying, "I think, my friends, that we must be about the business of an evening meal." Yes! I offer up a moment of thanks be to whichever god might chance to listen. "And as it is too late to hammer and nail for our supper, and as I have not yet learned all I need, we shall have to depend on young John here, and on his magical skills."

At this they both turn to me, smiling smiles of complete confidence. I am left gaping.

⌒⋉

Yeshu means to travel to Galilee not by way of the Jordan River, which is where John and his followers walk, but by the difficult way of mountainous Samaria, the land of Addai and Dositheus. In this way, and by the time we arrive in a poor village called Kefar Neba, I am become quite the street magician. I speak Chaldee, the language of magicians taught me by Joor, the very tongue that Tata and Dositheus knew before me, and that Addai once astounded me with long ago in the house of Heli and Dinah. And Yeshu has become quite the storyteller. Some are the reworkings of folk stories all children are told, and some are the stories told by rabbis and sages, but some are his very own, and these last are by far the best. But no matter the intent in the tale, to instruct or to delight, he has labored over each and every one of them. If we are not careful, we shall make a reputation for ourselves.

Along the way, we have heard how goes John of the River. Word travels from village to village that John baptizes again and that greater crowds than ever before flock to see him. I am sure this is so, for in some of the villages we have come through, there is scarcely a soul left to notice us. But if we hear all this, what does Herod Antipas hear, he who is now at war with the Arab king, Aretas, his former father-in-law? And what of the new Roman governor, Pontius Pilate? Shall these sit back and do nothing, while a man they would jail if not kill walks among them? I try not to think of John. I try not to think of Salome. It is hopeless. My mind, as ever, knows nothing else but runaway thought.

As a village well is where one can always find people, even in a land made rapt by John the Baptizer, we pause by a well on the day that, yet again, all things change. It is on this day that Yeshu does more than tell a tale.

This is another small village, so small we have not learned its name, and it sits on the high road to Shechem. We are not hungry, nor are we thirsty or tired, though the way is rocky and steep; we mean merely to pass through. But here Eio brays out her thirst, so here we stop by the well. To wait her out, Yeshu seats himself on a nearby wall, and I seat myself at his side. His knife prominent in his belt, his hand on its hilt, Jude strolls a bit farther into the village. Once a Sicarii, always a Sicarii—Jude would know what is in a place before Yeshu would come there. Besides, this is Samaria, and despite his loving Addai, as all must love Addai, and despite his knowing Dositheus, Jude has the Galilean's and the Jew's lifelong distrust of Samaritans. Just as the Samaritans distrust Jews and Galileans. There are those here who might harm us for being either.

Yeshu and I fall to talking. I speak again of my old teacher, Philo Judaeus of Alexandria, and of his hope of the Jewish Mysteries. By now, Yeshu knows much of what I know about the Passion of Osiris, that Philo and his Therapeuts name as Moses. Yeshu has come to understand that Philo and others like him, those Seth calls men of maturity, meaning those with understanding, seek to do as Pythagoras once did in Greece; they would establish a godman among the Jewish people in order to free them from the shackles of the Law. But knowing how this would outrage the Sadducee and the men of the Sanhedrin, as well as the Pharisee and the priests of the Temple, all of whom live fat on the fear of others, knowing how it would drive to murderous frenzy those who call themselves zealous for the Law, Philo would do as Pythagoras once did. Pythagoras made the godman seem a Greek idea by transforming a minor Greek deity called

Dionysus into Osiris. Philo thinks to slip Osiris past the Jews—who have no gods save Yahweh—as the One Who Comes, their promised Messiah. In Greek, the word for Messiah, or the Anointed One, is Christ.

Understanding this, Yeshu is very quick. Before I need tell him how my brother, Simon Magus, he who was also taught by Philo, sees John of the River, he has surmised it; he sees suddenly and clearly that Simon Magus would also create the Jewish Mysteries, and would use a living man to effect it.

This is what we speak of in a nameless Samaritan village, when two men fast approach us, talking each to each. Their voices so carry, we cease trying to hear our own. When they are but a pace or two away, one of the two puts back his head and howls. I find this so surprising, I clutch at Yeshu's mantle, and Eio pulls her head out of the trough, lips spraying water, yellow teeth bared, eyes rolling back in alarm. But the companion of the howling man, a fellow whose hair, both head and beard, is entirely white, is not a bit surprised, rather, he flushes with impatience. "Hush, Ismael. You do him no good."

But the man, Ismael, howls all the louder, loud enough for Jude to hear, and to cause him to come running back from halfway through the small village. "*I* can do him no good, Gadia? You tell me this, who have done him nothing but harm!"

At this, the second man stops still, his mouth an *O* of indignation. "Nothing but harm? If not for me, he would be already dead."

"He *is* already dead!" shrieks Ismael, who stumbles on, tearing at his beard.

Yeshu stands away from the wall. He slips his head cloth from his head so that his face might be seen and puts himself before the man Ismael, who seems not to see him and so continues blindly walking forward. Yeshu must stop him by reaching out his hand and laying it on the man's shoulder. It is only now that Ismael looks out of his eyes and at Yeshu before him. What does he see? I know for a certainty that where before a man such as Ismael, a poor Samaritan living in a small village on the barren spine of Palestine, would see a warrior, a Zealot—for the bearing of a true Sicarii is not to be missed—and seeing this, would take fright as naturally as sighting an asp, now I swear it seems he *sees*. Perhaps because he suffers so, perhaps his very suffering would allow him sight; whatever it is—and while the man Gadia continues another few steps on his way—Ismael stops his howling and stands quietly staring into the face of my friend, Yehoshua the Nazorean.

"How may I help you?" asks Yeshu of the man Ismael.

"No one can help me. My son is dead."

Yeshu speaks quietly, asking, "Where is your son?"

Tears coursing down his cheeks and into his beard, lips bit and bleeding from grief, Ismael points at the village before us, in particular to the first small house on the road, the one with an open door, the very house that Jude now trots by on his way back to Yeshu.

Yeshu touches the man again, this time low on his forearm. The man Ismael shudders in his limbs; his eyes roll back in their sockets. Yeshu says, "Take me to him."

I stare at Yeshu. What good will this do the man or his child?

Gadia has walked back to us. Seeing only his own anger, he does not see what Ismael sees. By now, Jude is with us as well. Jude has not heard what has passed between Gadia and Ismael, nor between Yeshu and Ismael, but it does not matter. Yeshu follows Ismael to the small house with the open door; therefore Jude follows Ismael. So here am I, following Jude. The man Gadia is left behind, but not for long. Cursing under his breath, he has caught up with us by the time we stand on the threshold.

Though it is brightest day, inside this house there is little light, no more than that given by a small lamp at the far end of the one room. Inside, there is no air, yet there is a stink to make me gag. Yeshu seems not to notice, nor does Jude. As for Ismael, slipping off his sandals, he walks forward until he comes to stand by a mat near the back wall. Barefoot, Yeshu comes to stand beside him. I go in as far as I dare, allowing room to rush out again if I should heave.

And here is the howling man's son, his dead face as perfect in the lamplight as an almond blossom, his body as perfect as an almond. No more than four, he will reach no higher age. Ismael howls again and rends his clothes. Comes now a whimper from the corner, and I turn my eye to see what must be the wife of Ismael and the children of Ismael. Her arms held tight at her sides, her fists balled, the mother weeps quiet tears of quiet sorrow. Her young, three little ones but each older than the dead boy and, most tellingly, all girls, huddle behind her skirts. This is a dark dead place, and it reeks of excrement and sick. I would be out sooner than I would leave a tomb.

But Yeshu drops to his knees and leans his head over the child's chest, his red hair falling on the dead face. We watch this, even the indignant Gadia, in perfect silence. Yeshu touches the child's cheek. At this, I hiss in shock and surprise—Father would never touch the dead. But Yeshu is touching the poor cold cheek, the still temple, then the dead boy's neck up under one ear. Here, he holds still, keeping his first two fingers pressed against the tender blue skin. Now he leans his ear against the child's chest. We watch as Yeshu raises his head, looks down into the unbreathing face, as he himself breathes out and in, in and out. And then, worse than his gentle touching, his odd probing, he begins to rub the child's unmoving chest.

I am barely breathing myself, have almost forgotten to breathe. I have seen dead things; the dead are everywhere among us. I have seen dead children, younger than this sweet boy, even babies lately at their mother's breast, but I have never seen a dead body touched, never. This is for those who do such things, lowly people Father and his friends scarcely know exist. It is unclean; it is forbidden by Noachite Law. Yea, Balaam! Father and his friends would be expected to go to the Temple. They would be required to ritually cleanse themselves with lustral water.

Yeshu takes the body in his arms, he raises it from the mat, and then he raises himself from the dirt of the floor. Carrying Ismael's dead son, Yeshu walks out into the sunlight, and—perfectly transfixed— so do we all. Yeshu does not stop until he comes to the trough Eio has drunk from, the trough Eio still stands by, switching her tasseled tail against the tormenting flies. Leaning down, he places the boy on the ground by the trough, and then he takes the end of his mantle and plunges it into the water. With this, he begins cleaning the body, beginning with the face. By now we—the mother, the father, Jude and Gadia, the little girls, and John the Less—all stand in a disbelieving circle around them, each of us peering down at this amazing thing. Yeshu pays us no mind but goes on wiping the sick from the body, rubbing its hands, its legs. And then there comes something I think I might swallow my tongue to see. The tender eyelids flicker; lids blue with death move.

All back away in fear. Except Jude, who moves not at all.

The eyelids flicker again, a corner of the small mouth moves. Yeshu is once more dipping his mantle in the trough, and I see he means to daub more cold water on the child's brow, but before he can do so, the wife of Ismael throws herself between him and her son. "Ahhheeeiii," she screams. "Matti! Matti!" I am sure she would push Yeshu away if he had not already quietly removed himself.

He stands beside me, the end of his mantle dripping, and I look at his face as he looks down at the child and its mother. To me, his face grows more beautiful by the day.

Ismael has slipped to his knees and holds the mother who holds the child. The child, Matti, who has opened his eyes, looks about him in immense surprise, and who should not be surprised, finding himself alive when he was dead?

Gadia, he who no doubt tried curing the boy in some way or another, has been standing over all three, his face a picture of ill temper mixed with superstitious awe, when suddenly he twists his head to look directly at Yeshu, more white in his eye than iris. "Who are you to have brought back the dead?"

Yeshu's voice is as low as Gadia's is high. "The boy was not dead."

"He was dead!" Ismael, it seems, is not done with howling. "Matti was dead! But now, he is alive!"

And the whole family sets to sobbing and wailing and exclaiming that the man come among them is a magician! That he is surely a famous healer! That he must be a great this! And without doubt a wondrous that! While the man Gadia has decided to call out to Adonai in a tremendous voice, yelling would he please take notice of what

miraculous thing has happened here! And then it occurs to all of
them at once to demand to know Yeshu's name. This terrible clamor
calls others out of their houses, and in moments I see we will be
swallowed up by all who live in this village.

Jude looks at Yeshu and Yeshu at Jude: they mean to be away as
fast as they can. With a cluck of my tongue for Eio, we are off up the
road before another moment passes.

Later, the town safely behind us, I say, "Yeshu, you are sure the
boy still lived?"

He smiles the smile I so love. "Would you have the dead called
back from the Kingdom?"

I do not know how to answer this.

Two days later, we are in Shechem. The most wondrous thing
about Shechem is that it is the city of my beloved Addai's birth. Because of this, I look about me with much interest.

Shechem sits high on the back of a mountain. But unlike Jerusalem, there stands nearby a taller mountain, Mount Gerizim, and it is
this mountain the Samaritans call sacred. Walking through the main
gate in the city wall, I stare up at this farther mountain trying to
mark the ruins I know must be there. If Father has shouted once
about the abomination on this high place, he has shouted a dozen
times, for there was once a temple on Mount Gerizim. To the people
of Samaria—loathed men, women, and children by Father and his
friends for not loving Father's Sanhedrin, which means they refuse
to recognize its authority, and for not believing as the Jews believe
that God expresses himself through history but believing instead
God expresses himself through the person—this Temple was the
most important in all the world; for the Samaritan it was the *true*
Temple, which must explain why the Jews in the form of the Maccabees took it in mind to destroy it. Yet Addai says his fellow Samaritans still go to their mountain as the Jews to their Temple.

Standing now in Shechem's main market square, I see there is not
much to tell a Samaritan city from one that is Jewish. The houses are
jumbled one against the other. The streets are narrow. There are no

parks or public buildings or museums or ways wide enough for a chariot. There are no chariots. There is sound, a constant hubbub rising up from whatever it is people are doing in a given moment. There are Greeks here, as there are Greeks everywhere. The Greek tongue is spoken around me, as I hear it spoken everywhere. Here, as everywhere, there are Roman soldiers, and catching sight of my first example, a splendid fellow with long strong legs, and on each leg a kneecap the size of Tata's best pottery bowl, I try not to flinch, but I do shrink back behind Jude. As for the brothers, two noticeable "once Sicarii," the sight of a Roman soldier seems not to stir a single red hair on their heads. In turn, the soldier pays them no mind, merely strides along on his wonderful legs with their wonderful knees and right out the gate we have just come in, shoving all out of his splendid way. No doubt to a Roman, all Jews look alike.

There are groups of travelers just like us. There are caravans great and small coming, and there are caravans great and small going. There are dense flocks of goats and of sheep, stirring up clouds of grit and dust, each flock raucous with stink. Pushing through the usual melee, there are a few wealthy townspeople such as I once was. Pushing against the rich are the sellers of everything under the sun. And, of course, there are thieves. But what is truly here, as they are truly everywhere, are the poor, whose numbers are as the ants in the dirt. These are as disregarded by soldiers, as by merchants, as by thieves. For once, I do not disregard them. Remembering how I first thought of Addai, poorly robed and without sandals, I stand regarding them intensely until I am pulled away by Jude. Looking back, I say, "The poor have at least the neglect of thieves."

To which Yeshu says, "If all had, would any steal?"

I take this in as I can, as a farmer stores grain, against the day I might understand it. Of all those whose voice has rung on my interested ear, Yeshu's is by far the most surprising, and a surprise is the most interesting thing of all. For where Seth and Philo asked questions of philosophy that I still struggle to answer, Yeshu now asks questions of moral right and wrong I also have no answers for. Perhaps because I am the daughter of Josephus, or perhaps because I am a Jew, or perhaps because I am simply human, I have taken such things for granted—but now? The most surprising thing of all turns out to be how hard it is to look at old things as if I have not seen them before.

Poor or rich, old or young, a speaker of Greek or a misser of an eye or a limb, a man or a woman or a child, even a thief, the people of Shechem go about in the same clothes, they wear their hair and their beards the same, there is the same smell to them; in short, there is nothing but a thought between themselves and the Jews, and an old thought at that. Yet Jude walks among them as if they might, at any moment, sprout horns from their foreheads. And he does this merely because they are Samaritans. But Yeshu goes among them as he would among flowers in a field, with a tender look for each. Some smile back, some do not. Some shy away from the pleasure he takes in them. It makes no difference. Yeshu seems content that we do what we do. Leading Eio, I am content to be doing anything, and not back in the settlement alone and without Salome. Though I admit that with all that we see and all we do, my grief lessens.

It is gone the sixth hour. Above us, the sky is as gray as ash and seems closer by the hour, for this is the season of the rain. All morning it has filled itself with water, and any moment now it will let its water go—how it rumbles from end to end with discontent.

So soon as we see Shechem's well, Yeshu stops as we are become accustomed to stopping, puts back his head cloth so that his hair and his beard and his alikeness to Jude is easily seen, and when enough are gathered round us, more than a dozen this day, curious to hear him, as all are curious to hear a storyteller, he tells them one of his newest about a rich man and his two sons. One son was dutiful, but the other was a wastrel who willfully left his father's care. Yet when the wastrel came home again, hoping for welcome, the father lavished as much wealth and as much love on the wastrel as on the dutiful. Jude and I have heard this now several times, and I marvel how each time Yeshu tells it, I find more in it to hear. Or, perhaps, Yeshu puts more in its telling. He does not tell the people who the rich man is, or who his faithful son might be, nor does he tell them the true name of the prodigal son. He hopes they will see what is meant for themselves. I see that the people hear what they will. Do they know the rich man is gnosis, which is the Kingdom of God? That the faithful son is he who is always with the Father in the Kingdom, and all that the Kingdom has is his? But the prodigal son is the man who has turned away his face; he who is "Dead" and does not "know" the Kingdom. By prodigal son Yeshu means every man and every woman we meet. By prodigal son, Yeshu means also himself as he was, before he awoke and turned his face once more to the Father and by so doing, came again to the Kingdom. Yeshu means, like the prodigal son, he was Dead and now he Lives, that he was lost but now he is found. He means that they too are prodigal sons, lost not in sin or unrighteousness as the Poor and the prophets would have it but in ignorance of who they are and where they are. By his story, Yeshu means that we can all go home where the Father awaits us.

I do not think they hear this. But how could they hear, when they do not know the Kingdom of God? Nor do they know what is meant by such a thing as "home." Still, whether they hear or they do not hear, oftentimes there are those who linger for more. People gather and, having gathered, would engage this man who tells them stories, he who travels with a twin of himself, and with a female donkey who carries nothing. There is almost as much wonder that a beast does nothing but nibble at whatever she can reach, and bray when she feels called to, and roll in the dust whenever it suits her, as over my magic. Though, as the days have gone by, I become less and less a market magician and more and more a silent youth listening intently to every word anyone says, for as Yeshu talks more, I need do less.

This day in Shechem, of those at the well, one woman stands alone. There is something about her of Tata. Like Tata, there seems an understanding that leads to pity. There is also something about her of Theano, the Pythagorean Therapeutae. She is prideful, but it is not overweening. There seems also a certain scorn for those around her. The others shun her, turn away their faces so that she might not catch their eye, yet she is as a queen among them. Watching, I am somewhat ashamed I hide my sex, that I am not such a woman, that I must act as a man to be a woman such as this.

When Yeshu's story ends, some leave, some do not, but the woman has come only for water. As others stay to question Yeshu and as an older man touches him for attention, she dips her cup in the basin. It is to this woman that Yeshu chooses to speak, softly saying, "Give me to drink."

There is a moment of shock all around. The people are scandalized that this man, a Galilean by his accent, would speak to this woman. The woman is startled anyone speaks to her at all. Yet she is quick to recover. She looks at Yeshu, at Jude, at myself. She does not look at a single one of her fellow townspeople. She says, "How is it you ask drink of me, a woman of Samaria? For the Jews have no dealings with Samaritans."

Yeshu smiles at her, and it is so loving I hurt for it being hers. "If you knew God's gift, and who it is that says to you, 'Give me to drink,' you would have asked for, and I would have given you, living water."

Because there is something in her proud eyes as she hears this, because there is a quickening of her breath and a tremor in her lips, I am compelled to reach into her. I find it is as easy as slipping under the skin of Eio, as easy as turning toward myself, as easy as—by the stars! What I find alarms me. She *hears* Yehoshua of the Nazorean! Her hearing quickens my own breath. Have we not come out from over the Sea of Stink to have people hear? Have I not promised Yeshu this should be my delight as it is his? Why then do I not open my heart to this one—a woman!—who is the first to hear? I know my answer before I have finished asking myself. I am jealous. There. I have said it. I will say it again. I am jealous. *Eloi, Eloi!* I shall put this away from me.

The woman with the cup looks upon Yeshu, "Sir, you have nothing to draw with and the well is deep. Where shall you get this living water? Are you greater than our father Jacob who gave us this well? Are you more than the John who baptizes and who is called the Messiah?"

It seems almost without thought that Yeshu has an answer. He says, "Whoever drinks from this well will surely thirst again. Does it not seem there is no end to hunger and thirst and the desires of the heart, no end to the sorrows of woman and man?"

"Yes," replies this Samaritan, "and a prudent man would say that what seems to be so, *is* so."

Yeshu laughs. "Woman, that is well said! But as I am what I am, I say to you, whoever drinks of the water I can give will never thirst, for I offer living water from the well of everlasting life."

I shift uneasily, as do the people hearing these words. Yeshu has said nothing like this before. Before, he has only told a story, answered a few questions, has been careful in what he might say and how he might say it. But here in the city of Addai, something about this woman has made him say more.

The woman of Samaria dips her cup in the water and hands the cup to the storyteller. Yeshu takes it from her and from it deeply drinks, and as he does, she says, "Sir, give me this water so that I would not thirst." Then, lifting her fine dark eyes to those around who listen with open mouths, and looking at them one after the other, she says, "And so I need not come here again to draw water."

Yeshu looks at none but the woman. "Go," he says. "Call your husband, and return here."

All around I feel the movement of people drawing nearer. They would not leave this well for their very lives. I know why I am interested, but what so interests them? As firmly as she has said all else, the woman answers, "I have no husband."

Behind me, comes a clucking of tongues, a sly snickering. There begins a faint hissing. But Yeshu smiles a smile of warmest love. "Again, how well you answer. You who have had five husbands."

Five husbands! This woman has had five husbands? I have never heard a woman have so many, nor any who would wish to. Though I do remember Herodotus writing that in Libya it was once the woman with the most lovers who was honored, but he also wrote that a mare once gave birth to a rabbit, and I have assumed that in some things Herodotus was perhaps a bit credulous. But no wonder the people remain to hear. Salome would laugh with delight to know this woman lived. I struggle mightily with myself not to hate her.

"And the man you live with now is not your husband."

Comes such a murmuring of the people around us. Tongues that clucked now wag, and by this, and by the look on the woman's face, I understand that what Yeshu has said is true. And that this is why the woman is shunned. The woman's eyes have grown round and rounder. "Sir!" she says, "Even as you are a Galilean, yet you are a prophet."

Yet again, Yeshu laughs. He is delighted with this woman. "Even were I what you say I am, I tell you an hour comes; I say to you that the hour is already here, when no mountain is needed to know the Father. Nor any temple be it Jewish or Samaritan, or yet Nazorean." Yeshu turns to the others now, all of whom listen closely, though who knows what they hear? "You worship you know not what, and you abase yourself yet you know not why, but I would give you what is in me to give. I would give you what is in you to *know*. Not only do you seek the Father, but the Father seeks you, and yet you are not apart."

At this, the woman regards Yeshu as she might regard a new husband. She has heard him; I *know* she has heard him. Now I think she hears more. "I know the Messiah is coming. Have we all not heard that John the Baptizer is he? I know when this Messiah comes he will tell us all things."

Yeshu touches her brow as he once touched mine. "I am one who can tell you things of the All."

I begin to think Yeshu's way of saying a thing numinous. By the hour, his words move closer to the poetry of Julia of Alexandria. Just to hear Yeshu's words from Yeshu's mouth is worth every step I take, no matter where it leads.

But now, from out a narrow side street, one of three leading into and out of this place of the well, comes a group of men, and such a sorry group of men as I have ever seen. Even at a distance their sorrow is plain on their persons, as plain as the dust of the road on their clothes. And as these draw near us, there sounds a shout from out among them, then another. "Yehoshua! Jude!"

On the instant, Jude is off, moving quickly, and I am confused as I watch him do this. Yeshu too has turned away from the woman at the well, and he too moves toward these men. Eio brays in alarm as they leave her, and the people gape in surprise. The brothers have broken into a run, and now, finally, I too see whom they run toward. It is Simeon, the son of Cleopas. It is Joses, the youngest brother with his poor scarred face. It is Jacob bar Judas and it is Simon bar Judas, who are the Sons of Thunder. Behind these, I see the fearsome brothers from Capharnaum. And behind these, there are more.

Is Dositheus among them? Is John? Is Salome!

I too break into a run.

The house of Thecla, the woman at the well, and the house of the man who is not her husband, is small and it is humble, and I would take comfort here if I could, but I cannot. My mind will go on and on, speaking not in Aramaic or in Greek, but in Egyptian, and I wish that it would stop no matter what the tongue. I would that I had no thoughts at all for I am numb as stone, as cold as the rain. But this I wish above all: that I did not know that John is taken. Zadok the Righteous One, who walked with Judas of Galilee and who was not taken then, is taken now.

But Simeon has told us of it, and there is no untelling.

John and his followers were sleeping when the soldiers of Herod Antipas appeared, for they had come for John in the darkest part of the night. And there followed such a terrible confusion, such a loudness of lamentation, that none can tell what truly happened, save only to themselves. The tents were torn open. The animals slaughtered or scattered. Dositheus is missing. Helena of Tyre is missing. As is Jair, the second son of Jacob bar Judas. As is Joanna, the wife of Chuza. Even Jacob the Just is lost. I am stunned. Even Old Camel Knees? None can say where these are now. There is no one who knows if they remain well. Or if they do not remain well.

We all of us sit in the house of the woman at the well, huddled here and huddled there, each a miserable lump of sodden clothing, and we listen to the din of the rain on Thecla's flat roof. The woman moves among us offering food and wine that Menahem eats from the greed of youth and Yeshu eats out of compassion, for no one else takes Thecla's food. I cannot eat, nor can I drink. I do not know where Thecla's man is, and I do not care. I do nothing but watch the rain. Moments ago the sky opened as a great mouth would open, and it rains now as if all the rain at once would fall. Water rushes off the limestone of the walls outside Thecla's door and over the stones of the street before her stoop, forming quick and sudden rills that could grow into rushing rivers that might wash away the whole of Shechem. I too would wash away in the rain.

All this is as the bitterest bile. All this is felt with the deepest sorrow. The heart of the father Jacob bleeds as he sits by the hearth, bent over and rocking, back and forth, his face in his hands. Anyone could know his thoughts. Where is his son? Is Jair locked away with John in the Fortress of Machaerus, a place of hopeless horror in Herod's Peraea, which is the Land of Moab? Is he dead?

I know his grief as I know my own. I am broken with it. Simon Magus is also taken. Simeon tells us he watched, helpless to do other, being held down on all sides by Herod's men, as young Simon would shield John with his own body. By this, the soldiers who bound John the Baptizer were forced to bind also Simon Magus. Simeon says that John offered no resistance, nor did Simon, but that all this changed when one among the men of Herod struck John. It was then that the youth Simon had turned and fought for John of the River as the wildest Sicarii, until both were chained into a high-wheeled, high-sided, ironbound wagon brought along in the dead of night for just this purpose.

I do not weep and I do not gnash my teeth. I do not rock where I sit in Thecla's doorway. As I did on the shores of the Sea of Salt where no thing can live—except me, except me—I long again for death. I long again for anything that will take me away from where I am now, even if it would place me in the darkest cell, just such a one that must now enclose Salome. By this thought, I have thoroughly surprised myself. Salome must be in a cell! We could go to her as we did to Addai! Surely if Yeshu could rescue Addai from the Fortress of Antonia, he could rescue John, and, of course, Salome, from the Fortress of Machaerus?

I raise my head. I look for Yeshu. He is seated by his brothers Jude and Joses. Just as he did on the salted shore of the Sea of Salt, he clasps his knees. In this same moment, he looks for me. His eyes are not shattered. Not once since he saw the Father, has the pain revisited him. Has he heard my brilliant thought? I would rise. I would go and ask to speak to him. But in the very next moment Simon Peter of Capharnaum shouts out, and by his very first word, all is swept away in what it is he demands of us. "How was it known where John slept?" He leaps to his feet. He shakes his fist at the rain. "How was it known which tent of all tents, when all tents were the same! How was it known which bed of the hundreds of beds? I would know these things!"

By way of answer, a more terrible question by far is asked by Simon bar Judas, who does not raise his head from his knees. "By this act, will the tribes rise from Ituraea to Judaea? If they do, there will be no stopping a single man without John to calm us."

Peter slaps his thigh so hard, the sound cracks on the ear. "By all that is Holy! By the hair of all the prophets! How you have spoken!" He stares around him. He pulls back his upper lip, showing his stump of a tooth. He pounds on the shoulder of his brother, Andrew. "Have you all heard him? Do you all hear what it is he says? I tell you now that the words of this Son of Thunder contain a great and wonderful truth! I tell you now that this is how it will be!"

This proclamation, given at the top of his voice, raises heads. Even Jacob bar Judas ceases his rocking. Immediately, all save Yeshu become alert as foxes. Yeshu has closed his eyes but I know he listens to every word.

Peter stares at us, turning from each to each. He turns even to me, to me. "Think!" says he. "The Poor, the Essene, the Yahad, the Many, even the Pharisee, all of them! None will resist the Sicarii now. All will join. By this act, there can be no more argument among us. If we should see John's arrest as good? If we should see what Herod Antipas has caused to be done as the will of God? Has not John all along told us that the Lord would act when the time came— well then! Who are we to decide *how* he will act? Was I alone when I heard Simon Magus prophesy? We all heard that the name of John the Baptizer would ring through the ages with a mighty sound. We all heard the voice in Simon Magus say that where John led, a people would follow. Jude, of us all, I know you hear me now."

Jude hears him. How could he not, when such words must be sweet on his warrior ear? Peter knows this, and knowing it, is satisfied. He turns to Simeon. "Is this not a thing? Could not greater things come of it!" Simeon must also hear him; is he not Zealot? He turns to Yeshu, for now that John is arrested, it is Yeshu who heads the Nazorean. This is why such as Peter have come for him; this is why they are here in the House of Thecla.

Yeshu has known this might happen. But he had hoped, even against his own Sight and mine, that John the Immerser would not fall. He must still hope that John is not fallen, but merely pauses on his way. After all, he is only so far arrested, not killed. I terrify myself with thought. If John were dead, should we hear of it? Herod could have him killed at any moment, for any reason. Who would tell us? So much happens in courts and courtyards, in private chambers, with few as witness. Have I forgotten the tunnels under the Temple, the bent-backed room under the Fortress of Antonia? John and Herod are many miles away. John the Baptizer could be dead, and we have yet to hear.

Jacob, the sorrowing father, speaks. I strain to hear him over the drum of the rain. "Yehoshua? Tell us what it is we now do."

As he did on the day all came upon him lying in my bowl of rock, Yeshu opens his eyes, and out of them shines not the storyteller and the teacher, come out among the people to talk of the Father and the Mother and the Kingdom of God, a man these men do not understand and do not wish to, but Yehoshua the Sicarii. I hear Jude's hope that all might be as it was, that he should once more be the warrior he was meant to be.

"Go out," Yeshu commands them. "Go each of you to a different place. Gather the tribes. Bring them to where it is we meet near the Sea of Galilee. A week from now, I will speak with them."

∝

Leaving behind Pilate's Samaria, we find ourselves looking out over Herod's Galilee. Westward lies Phoenicia and the Great Sea. North the enormity of Syria. To the east is the heathen Decapolis and

Gaulanitis, meaning they are thoroughly Greek if they are not Roman. South is, of course, Samaria. All these are hostile each to each. Galilee seems an island, for here Father's Judaean Sanhedrin has no say, here a Herod still rules, and here Rome treads but lightly. I would think it enchanted if my heart did not bleed within me.

With us walks Thecla. I do not remember her asking if Yeshu would allow this, nor do I remember Jude protesting. Thecla gathered up some few of her belongings, bid a fond farewell to the man she did not call husband, as surprised a mild fellow as I have ever, briefly, met, and came away with us.

All morning we make our way down from the Samaritan mountains into the plain of Jezreel, and all morning I admire the land I see spread out below me.

While Samaria is more favored of water than Judaea, and is therefore greener and more fertile, Galilee is much the greener and wetter and more fertile still. In Galilee, the soil is dark and rich. I cannot help but stare at the fields on either side of the road we travel. So much grows here. Here there is wheat, and there barley. To one side an orchard of walnut trees, to the other side a tidy vineyard. And everywhere, there are orange groves. Where I would scratch in the hard dry dirt for my *rosh* poppies, sea salted and desert stoned, and where I would carry water to each and every one until they flowered, here whatever is sown will come up in a shout.

Galilee is a land of orchards and meadows and roads. Just as Seth said, there are so many roads leading to so many Galilean villages, and farther. Here a fine wide way leading to the Great Sea and then to Phoenicia and to Tyre and to Sidon, and there a road winding away to Ituraea and to Syria, coming on Damascus, even unto Palmyra.

Yeshu and Jude set their feet on a road that crosses the valley and then seems to vanish into the high land that rises to the north. Above us, the sky remains fat and gray with rain and Eio holds her nose to the ground when the water pours down so that she might more readily breathe. But I hold my face up to the rain. It is as if somehow I am in the delta of Egypt again, wet and rich and fine.

✂

We are leaving the village of Harobah when a man we do not know comes running toward us, shouting out, "It is the Holy Man! Look, it is he!" In a rush, he is on us, eager hands held out to touch Yeshu, eager mouth ready to kiss Yeshu's face, his hands, the hem of his soiled robe. Yeshu would gift him with a smile, and then would gently turn away, but he cannot, it is too late. The man falls on his knees, beats his head on the muddy ground, letting up such a cry that no one but the deaf could fail to hear, "Here is he, who raises the dead!" Out from their houses come those who are in no way deaf. Seeing them, the man calls out, "It is he! I saw it. I saw it in Samaria with my own two eyes. And there have been others, also dead who now live!"

And no matter that Yeshu hushes him, or that Jude kicks at his backside, stuck up as it is in the air, still the man shouts and weeps and bangs his head in the mud. In the end we must flee from the uproarious fellow and the gaping people he has called forth, each now standing and wondering and marveling at Yeshu. We leave them nodding and whispering among themselves. They point at us. "There is the man, there is the man!" they seem to be saying, though I am sure they do not know *what* man.

I see the face of the woman Thecla as she flees with us. She too marvels.

When we are well past Harobah, Yeshu laughs at such foolishness.

We pass through Kefar Imi where John the Baptizer was born, and then through Gath-Hepher where the prophet Jonah was born and is now entombed, and then a few miles farther on, we are in Japhia.

✂

Last night, I dreamed of my mother.

Hokhmah seemed soft as water in a pool and her hair hung free as water over a fall. Beneath the black fall of her hair, her face shone white as milk and her eyes shone like the moon on still water. On her body she wore a pure white *pellae,* as pure as the white of her girdle, and her neck collar was as red as blood, while over the whole of her person floated a veil like a net of stars. I stood before her as she turned me this way and that, saying, "How you have grown, Mariamne."

Waking, I cry for the Mariamne that my mother so loved, and for the mother I would have loved if only I could. I would be that Mariamne again.

◇

I am in Yeshu's village.

These are his neighbors; this is where he was born and where he spent his boyhood. Here it is that Anna lived, and here it is that Anna died. It is the village to which the very young Mary came, quickened with secret seed, and where she was left widowed and burdened by seven children. Somewhere near is the hillside where Yeshu and his brothers and his cousins played, and when they were older, where they lay and discussed the way of their world. That same hillside looks out over the Jezreel Valley we have this day crossed, and from it one can surely still see the city of Sepphoris and the palace of Herod. I have it in mind to find this place.

Out from Japhia, no farther than I would climb to reach my *nahal*, I have come to a place of grasses, green and fragrant under the hard white sky. Here there are smooth rocks and the slope beneath is gentle, while all those nearby would tumble a body clear to the valley floor. Below lies the Valley of Jezreel where Saul once consulted the witch of Ein Dor, only to have the shade of Samuel foretell his doom. Somewhere below, King Saul fell upon his sword rather than risk capture by the Philistines. Gideon attacked the Midianites. The judge and prophet Deborah led the Israelites to victory over the Canaanites. Even Jezebel, the wife of King Ahab, who loved not Yahweh once walked this valley—that same Queen Jezebel whose daughter Athaliah became ruler of Jerusalem when her son was killed by the rebel Jehu of the House of David. Crazed with grief, Athaliah swore to avenge Ahaziah by destroying every descendant of David's house. She very nearly succeeded. For the daughter of Jezebel, Salome and Tata and I have nothing but fierce admiration, for no woman but Athaliah was ever sole ruler in Judah or in Israel.

I pluck one blade of grass to weave through my fingers. Though the sky remains full with rain to come, still, I can plainly see what the brothers and the cousins saw each night. To the east Mount Tabor, to the west Mount Carmel, behind me and toward the north Herod's splendid palace on its high hill in the city of Sepphoris. It seems splendid still, though it is no longer what it was. Sometime during our first years in Alexandria, Herod Antipas removed himself to a new palace in his new city, Tiberius by the Sea of Galilee.

"I thought I would find you here."

I do not start. I answer, "I am here."

Yehoshua seats himself beside me, looks out as I do across the Jezreel. And though his nearness warms me, still my mind is burdened with thoughts of Salome, with thoughts of John, with Yeshu's teaching turned aside by what he must do because he is who he is, with the remembrance of my mother, who stays long after my dream, and whose face, so long unremembered, is now fully the face of the dreaming mother. So too am I burdened with feelings of the flesh that I will not acknowledge, and a yearning for Mariamne as she was. But Yeshu is beside me. We are alone. We have not been alone since we left the wilderness. I can ask Yeshu if we go to rescue John as we rescued Addai. I can ask him anything, tell him anything—but one thing. I cannot tell him my name.

We sit in silence, broken at last by Yeshu. "I once came here to imagine myself David, the sweet singer of Israel who was much loved. As David, I knew that King Saul would kill me for fear that his own people would grant me his kingdom, so I would run and I would hide. But I did not run alone. Behind me ran a hundred men of my imagination, each as ferocious as I, though not one as cunning or willful or half as ambitious; for if the truth be known, I *would* be king! And we would hide, my men and I. We would live in caves; we would raid the towns we found. We were outlaws, we were Hapiru, kings of the desert." There comes a faint color in his cheek. "What do you think, John? Now that I need it beyond ever I have needed it, do I have the cunning of David?"

On impulse, I lay my hand on his hand, and though he flinches, I do not take my hand away, nor does he. And with this, words I do not expect to say come from my mouth. I ask him, not in Aramaic, but in the language of the most divine poets and the most sublime philosophers, "How wouldst thou know God?"

And the man who had been Sicarii turns to me, and answers me in as perfect a Greek as mine, "Knowing God is as rain falling on the sea. What then is rain and what is sea? All are One."

And I laugh like silver in the hand and I say, "Thou hast surely died and been born anew." My laughter rings out over the valley so many have fought for, and in fighting, have died. But my laughter does not die, it echoes back and back and back to me. I have not taken my hand from the hand of Yeshu. I say, "You cannot abandon what your heart will do. You cannot return to who you were now that you know your name."

Yeshu lifts my hand to his mouth. He kisses my palm.

As I am a man, perhaps I should wonder at this. Or fall into confusion and dismay. I might even start to my feet, red with insult. As I am a woman, I would do these things and more, for this could be thought to be *yetzer ha-ra,* an evil impulse of the flesh. But as I am Mariamne—in this moment, I am Mariamne!—I look down into the palm of my hand and there I fancy I see it shine. I *do* see it shine, as Yeshu shines. I lift my palm to my own mouth and I kiss his kiss.

It is Yeshu who falls into confusion and dismay.

It is Yeshu who leaps to his feet.

I give him his privacy; I do not spy within. If he will tell me, he will tell me, though he cannot tell me yet. But I can feel his disquiet, know that his very blood is hot with a conflict so profound that he is inwardly speechless, and still he does not flee. At length, he quietly says, "Come. Seth of Damascus has just this hour arrived in Japhia. He travels with Izates of Adiabene and with the merchant named Ananias. Seth has asked to see you."

I am joyous until I note the broken light in Yeshu's eye.

A Fool Beyond Any Fool

How good to see the face of Seth again! Rising from the table of Cleopas of Japhia at first sight of me, my friend is as beautiful as Egypt. His mouth is a golden basket from which all good things come. His eyes are like the scrolls of the Indian Vedas. It is good to be clasped to his chest in manly welcome. It is good to inhale of him, to sink into his skin, to feel the scratch of his shaven cheek, to have my mouth so near his ear I am free to whisper, "I am afraid."

Seth whispers back, "Speak when we are alone."

I step back, only to find myself crushed against the fat bulky chest of the sweat-soiled and scent-oiled merchant Ananias, who has caused all this. Which is, of course, not in the least true—I caused all this by allowing him to hear the Voice. But to reach back and reach back and then further back to know causes is to look backward forever. If Father had not allowed Salome and me to dinner? If the merchant Ananias had never come calling. If the Temple priest, Ben Azar of the House of Boethus, had not been stabbed that morning—is it nine years ago now? If I had not fallen ill unto death the month before, which had softened Father's heart toward females at his table? How far back is planted the seed that grows into a thing? And which the seed and which the flower? Or are all seeds flowers and all flowers seeds?

Ananias knows I am female, but I know, as he has ever done, he will treat me as John the Less. It is in the nature of Ananias to wish to please, and by this he pleases the inner Nazorean. There is also this: he does not forget I might curse him. I might curse also his wife and his sons and every one of his camels. But in truth, he is not a cruel man and would do me no deliberate harm.

But there is another here who knows who I am. Is he a cruel man?

Izates, the son of Queen Helen and the stepbrother of Seth, does not rise from his place at table to slap my back or press my hand. Once I too am seated, I lift my eyes to his, and what I see there touches my heart with frost, as I am sure he means it to. Like Jacob the Just, Izates has no time for women, even though now that he is king he marries, and he marries again and again. But in his coolness toward me, there is more than this. Izates is repelled by my being John the Less; that I pass myself off as male boils his blood. And that others allow this stiffens his already stiff neck. I see him glance at Yeshu and at Jude and at Cleopas, and I see the contempt on his Assyrian face. He thinks them utter fools for being duped by me, a female, a being that ought to be and *is* less to a man than his horse. Or, if the man is poor, his donkey. He is offended that I sit at table, when I should instead be serving. What stays his tongue?

Seth has taken hold of the bare upper arm of Izates; he squeezes the warrior's muscle there, just below the golden band he wears as a king. I have my answer. It is Seth who keeps the tongue of King Izates in his mouth. There is only his loyalty to Seth that stands between disaster and Mariamne, the wayward daughter of Josephus of the Sanhedrin.

Yeshu and I take our place at table. Mine is with Ananias, down near the foot where the wife of Cleopas would have us. Yeshu's is at the head, placed before her husband and the King of the Assyrians, though few here know Izates is a king for he would not have them know. Cleopas faces Yeshu from the bottom of his table, as is only right.

As the Babylonian astrologers teach of seven "lights": the sun and the moon and the five planets, which the Jews have made their Menorah, and which Joor taught were more truly the Seven Sisters who are the Pleiades, so there are seven of us here this day.

Cleopas, who looks very like his son, Simeon, has half a loaf of bread speared on the end of his knife and he is waving this at Yeshu. "Word has reached even here that you go about teaching, nephew, that you tell long stories in village squares. Are you now a rabbi? Is this how you fool Herod's men? And the healing? Is it true? Have you raised a child from the dead? Nothing else has been spoken of in Japhia for two interminable days before your coming! Everywhere I go, my neighbors are saying, but it is Yehoshua these things are said of, how could it be merely Yeshu'a, he who once fetched my wood? Or he who once stole a cooling cake from my wall? Or he who had his bottom smacked by his mother, the virtuous Anna, right there in front of my door not so very long ago? Who is this Yehoshua to go pulling people out of their graves?"

Already, I warm to this talkative uncle of Yeshu and Jude.

Uncle Cleopas is pulling on his lip, which makes his speech less than easy to follow. "Does it matter how long they are dead? I mean to say, could it be weeks? Even years? What a terrible idea, Yeshu'a, what a terrible *Egyptian* idea! As it is, I expect my neighbors to open their tombs and bring decaying bodies to my door any moment now. Will they take up embalming in the hopes one such as you will pass by?"

Though I know Yeshu now struggles with pain come again in his head, he has listened to all this as he listens to most things, easily. Cleopas means no offense and none is taken, and should he mean offense, even then, there should be none taken. But as I sit, and watch, I am an offense to myself. I blame myself for Yeshu's pain. I blame myself for my evil impulse. I would cut off a finger, slice off my whole hand at the wrist, if it would stop his pain.

Yeshu manages his smile. Knowing what it costs him, I shudder with my own pain. "Do not believe everything you hear, uncle."

"Pity." Cleopas bites into his hunk of bread. All else he says is said between chewing. "One hears so many interesting things. Perhaps you will tell me what else I should not believe."

Izates now speaks, though not in answer to Cleopas. His speech seems urgent, as if more than he need hear the answer. "Tell me, Yehoshua, as you would not allow Addai of Shechem to die at the hands of Rome, I know you will not allow John to suffer at the hands of Herod or to languish in Herod's prison. Nor will you wait for Herod to deliver him up to Rome."

It is as if I have been touched with a heated blade. I am alert on the instant. As are all others at the table of Cleopas, who wait for what Izates would say next.

Izates does not disappoint. "Knowing what you will *not* do, would you speak now of what you *will* do?"

Yeshu raises his broken eyes to Izates. But as he cannot see, still he can think and he can speak. "I will do nothing."

Nothing! Have I heard aright?

"Not before speaking to all who are concerned with this business. In two days time, I shall meet with men from all persuasions who but yet hold one thought steady, the fate of John the Baptizer."

Izates flushes to his hairline with thought of honor and of valor; Jude, who sits at the left hand of Yeshu, does not flush but I know he too is alive to the ends of his red, raging hair. As for Ananias, he keeps his silence for Ananias has the mouth but not the gut for such as this. And Cleopas is too old. But as for me, I am also alive. If I had a beard, I should pull on it. Something shall be done about John! And if something is done for John, could the fate of Simon Magus not be entwined?

Says Izates, "I will go with you. Where is this meeting?"

I know that the pain in Yeshu's head grows. I know it is all he can do to hear the son of the Queen of Adiabene. But still he says, "You are welcome, Izates. All who love John are welcome."

I do not know if Izates loves John, but I do know he loves what his mother loves; Queen Helen looks for a messiah as eagerly as the lowliest peasant in the rockiest field. If Yeshu should signal me, I

would be up on my feet. I would take him away from this clamorous
room, for even this little gathering is clamorous when the pain is
upon him. I would find a place for him where there is dark and there
is quiet. But he makes no such signal. Instead he speaks again, and all
must lean forward to hear. "The tribes gather near the town of Bethsaida, which is in the Tetrarchy of Herod Philip and not in that of
Herod Antipas. Jude?"

Yeshu's twin is on his feet.

"Would you come with me? I have need of you."

Jude is by his brother's side before Yeshu has finished asking.

<hr/>

I wander the village of Japhia; Eio trots behind me, her small hooves
tapping out a din on the dried clay and stones of the steep and narrow streets. She causes much merriment to all who see her, for few
have a friend in an ass. Both she and I ignore them. As ever, I am lost
to thought and my thoughts fly hither and thither like chaff in the
wind. We could be bandits now, Salome and I, caring nothing for
philosophy, or for Glory, or for Osiris the Messiah. If we were bandits, or rich wives, our lives would never have come to this. I could
claim the fortune of my mother Hokhmah from the Temple priests.
I could be rich. But could my riches buy John or Salome's freedom?
Could it heal the blessed Addai or banish the pain in Yeshu's head? If
it could, I should spend all that I have.

How long have I been silently weeping before I notice my tears?
No wonder the sudden blushes and attempts to look away from
those who buy and those who sell and those who see me pass before
their door. They see a youth in white climbing aimlessly up and
down their streets, followed by an equally aimless ass. What an utter
fool I feel. I am as Proteus in my crying. If there is a kind or a type of
weeping to be done, I, Mariamne, daughter of wet and salty shame,
have done it.

I turn onto a path near one of the larger houses, three crooked
streets beyond the large shop of Cleopas, and there stands Seth.
When I would be seen by no one, I am seen by the one person in all
the world I would be seen by the least.

But as he is also the one person in all the world I would see the most, I run to him. I throw my arms around him. I weep into his shoulder until his white tunic is sodden with my grief. Seth does not push me away; he makes no attempt to silence me, but stands quietly in my arms, his own arms strong about me, and allows me this moment of Mariamne as she was. And, beneath all things, is still. And when I have cried myself out, and when I stand catching my breath, and when most of my wits return to me, he says, "Now we shall talk. Unless you have said all it is you wish to say?" In answer, I hold him all the tighter. "Come away then, and you shall tell me what you will tell me."

And I do, leaving nothing out, not even my *yetzer ha-ra*.

Being still a youth, I thought nothing of Seth's heart.

∝

We are on our way before first light, Yeshu and Jude, Ananias, Izates and Seth and I. Still unburdened, Eio walks behind me. Thecla, carrying her few possessions, follows on behind Eio.

From Japhia we take the road north to Cana and there find another road eastward toward the Sea of Galilee across the Plain of Azotis, and then through the narrow Valley of the Doves, which Yeshu tells Izates is also called the Valley of Robbers for the thieves who daily prey here, though not normally on such as us. Before this pass, the land remains rich and richly carpeted with prosperous villages; after this pass, we walk nearer each to each.

As I go, I read what Seth has brought me, a copy of Philo Judaeus's latest masterly effort explaining the entire world and all it contains. This copy, on Augustan Royal in a cedar box with red tabs and red wrappers, is inscribed to Simon Magus and to me! It is not easy to walk and to read philosophy at the same time, but I manage it.

In time, we come on to the Great Highway, and I stamp my feet in its crusted dust. This is the Via Maris, the ancient way of the ancient Egyptians, set into the land long before there were Israelites and Jews and Samaritans and Galileans. On it walked the armies of Egypt when Egypt's glory was beyond a simple man's dreaming, and on it too walked men and women of the wondrous and ever-changing

kingdoms between the two rivers, people so long past, they become
the stuff of legends. I try to think myself the historian Herodotus; as
in reading the latest work of Philo, trying to be a historian almost
keeps me from thinking of Salome. Or of Yeshu.

For a time, the Via Maris runs along the western shore of what
the Romans are pleased to call the Lake of Tiberius but is in truth
the Lake of Gennesaret, or Sea of Galilee, and when it does, there,
under the sheer and tremendous face of Mount Arbel, from whose
caves the great Herod once flushed with grappling hooks those hidden men who opposed him, forcing them to their deaths on the rocks
below, we find the bustling city of Taricheae, which stinks of fish. As
I am named Mariamne Magdal-eder by Seth, meaning "She of the
Temple Tower," this place has a tower, ruined now, that stands looking out over the harbor, alive with what must be at least three hundred
long-bodied fishing boats. In the shadow of Taricheae's stone tower,
taller by far than our tower in the wilderness, I look out at the busy
work of man, and suddenly I feel as ruined as this tumble of stone.

In all this time, from Japhia to Cana to the Via Maris to the salt-
fish city on the Sea of Galilee, I have kept my distance from Izates.
From time to time, he casts upon me black and hateful looks. From
time to time, I think him tempted to expose me for the sweet pleasure it would give his kingly stomach. But what is worse is that in all
this time I have also kept my distance from Yeshu. When he would
be in one place, I would be in another. When he would speak to me,
I would have found something important I need say to Seth. And when
we would bed down for the night, I would feign sleepiness rather
than sit and talk with Yeshu as the stars faded one by one. I do this so
that I might not cause pain. He does not force my hand.

It is like to break my heart.

But Seth is with me, and I shelter in him as a sun-struck creature
would seek shade in a world of shifting sands.

A boat awaits us, bobbing at anchor a short distance offshore, as it
has done these past few days. In it, we are to cross over the whole of
the width of this Galilean sea, west to northeast, from Taricheae in
Herod Antipas's Galilee to the city of Bethsaida in Herod Philip's

Gaulanitis. Once there, it is no more than an hour's walk to the place where the tribes await Yeshu. This sea is fresh where my wilderness sea is salt; it is also less than half the size. The journey across should go swiftly.

Eio must be brought along, for neither Yeshu nor I would leave her. But to bring her, Yeshu must pull, and Jude must push, and Ananias must aim a good hard kick at her backside. Struggling, Yeshu laughs, "An ass is wiser than a seer for was it not Balaam's female ass who saw the Lord—Eio, will you move!—and not the sage Balaam himself?"

To which Izates replies, looking straight at me, "Better to bring the she-ass than a woman, for a woman speaking is like the Lord opening the mouth of a donkey."

Both Thecla and I flush, she with fury at the insult, and me with the fear of exposure, though I would be insulted if I had the luxury of it. But Yeshu, still pulling Eio, looks only at Thecla when Izates says this thing, thinking her his only target, and says, "Could it be as Addai once said, that woman was God's First Thought, and that man is an afterthought?"

Thecla gifts him for this with her rare and handsome smile, and I would as well, and I do, but Ananias bursts into noisy back-slapping laughter at such an idea. I hear him thinking how Yeshu can say the most outlandish things and bring light where there was only dark. Izates laughs as well and as heartily, but he never takes his eyes from me, and his eyes do not laugh at all. Moments later we set sail in the boat of the fisherman Joazar who is brother-in-law to Simon Peter and to Andrew. Izates and Jude keep a tense and watchful eye on the receding western shore, the one governed by Antipas, for if so many await us in Gaulanitis, surely news of this has reached more than one important ear? Herod Antipas must know how many eyes and hearts turn east and south toward the Fortress of Machaerus where at this very moment he stands embattled against his mortal enemy, King Aretas—and where in this same moment John lies chained. No doubt Herod has doubled his military wherever he senses trouble, or at least as many as can be spared from his defense against the Arab king.

But nothing more happens than Eio trying to jump overboard—
once as we leave land, the second time as we approach it.

And by and by, we come on Bethsaida in the land of Herod Philip,
whose wife Herodias is now the wife of his half brother, Herod Antipas, a thing that incensed John the Baptizer—who denounced the
"fornication" of Herodias and Herod Antipas from one end of the
Jordan to the other. This place is much of a piece with Taricheae,
hidden now over the sea, save for Taricheae's distinct and distinctly
ruined tower, and for it being two cities: a citadel on a high rock and
a humbler village by far on the shore of the lake. The land itself is
greener yet, fed by the fresh water sea and by the Jordan and by its
many springs that have formed deep and quiet pools, around which
stand trees that would die of thirst in Judaea. Bethsaida also smells
like fish. There are people here who note our passing, and some
point and some stare. We hurry by them for the hour grows late. If
we linger, the Sabbath will be upon us while we yet travel, and
though Yeshu cares little for the Law, there are those waiting to
whom the Law is above all other things.

But as we leave behind the last house of the lower city of Bethsaida where the poor live, a woman quickly steps out to bar our way;
Jude has barely time to draw his knife. But she is unarmed and can
mean no harm, save that we would hurry and she delays us. Jude
keeps his knife in his hand but puts his hand behind him.

"Master," the woman says, and by this she means Yeshu, not King
Izates, "I have heard, and I believe, that you can raise the dead, but
can you also cause the blind to see?"

Before Yeshu can answer, she points to the side of the road, and
there under a tree, and as ragged as its bark, sits a blind man. At the
man's feet there is a begging bowl, and on the man's body, a bit of
shabby cloth no more than would cover a suckling child, and around
the man's head, flies. His mouth is encrusted with ancient spittle, the
folds of his body are embedded with ancient scum, and his sightless
eyes, oozing with yellow matter, are the flat and lifeless white of bird
dirt. I shudder, for I have never seen a filthier thing, and I would step
back but remember that Yeshu would not. Instead, like Yeshu, I move

closer to the blind beggar. The man hears us. He pushes his bowl forward with a hopeful toe and smiles where he determines we should be. The tooth that is left him is as broken and black as his toe.

The woman pulls at Yeshu's mantle. Both Jude and Izates bridle at this, would push her away, but Yeshu stops them with the smallest gesture. She is saying, "He is blind from birth, Master, and cast out. Now I would know the truth of it, who did sin? This man, or his parents, that he was born blind?"

"Neither," answers Yeshu, "for God would not punish that which is loved."

The woman's eyes widen, her thoughts plain on her face. This man has said that God would not punish that which is loved? What, then, does God love? For it seems all are punished in one way or in another way. Her way of saying this is, "But he cannot see, Master!"

Yeshu leans down to scoop up a handful of dirt, saying, "There are some things that cannot be undone, being intended for one purpose or another, but there is this thing that can be done, and it is greater than eyes that see. I can give him the sight that is within him." Spitting into his hand, he makes a paste of dirt and spittle. I have seen Tata do this. I have seen Yeshu watch Tata do this. With the paste he has made, Yeshu anoints the old man, first tenderly rubbing the lid of one poor eye and then of the other. "If you would *truly* see, old man, go, wash in a pool of Bethsaida."

And then, once more, we are on our way, moving quickly before the setting of the sun. But as I am quite the last, and as I do not concern myself with whether we break the law of the Sabbath by our movement, I think I am the only one to hear the woman answer the blind man when he asks who has touched him. "Yehoshua of the Nazoreans, old man. It is said he can raise the dead."

At this, the blind man cries, "Is he a prophet? Is he a magician? Is he a *gazer*? He must be one of these! Help me up, woman, for I would wash my eyes!"

The last I see of him, he is struggling up from his place in the dirt and stumbling away. I am sure he makes his way to a pool; Bethsaida has no lack of pools. But such a thing holds less interest for me than

what it is Yeshu has said, which has long been said in one way or another by Seth: "There are some things that cannot be undone, being
intended for one purpose or another." Again, the word *intend*. I know
Yeshu does not mean "intended by God," nor does he mean "intended by the Fates." He means "intended by the Self," which is the
Daemon. But who will believe they would intend themselves blind or
crippled or poor? Who could knowingly shoulder such a responsibility? Yehoshua would ask a man to know he is entirely free, that he
is not beset with demons, nor is he a victim of circumstance, nor
even of the gods. He would ask a man to know that his life and all it
consists of is a thing of his own making.

Who can face such freedom?

Soon enough, as the fiery boat of the sun sets sail toward the sea
of night, we are climbing a wooded rise, passing through a stand of
fig and walnut trees, and then, coming at last to the top, we see
spread out below us in the last of the light a wondrous sight. There
are not hundreds here but thousands. Thousands upon thousands,
perhaps as many as five thousand in all. The whole of the valley floor
is tented and cameled and peopled, and the stream that runs
through these runs brown with their presence. The sight and the
smell and the sound of them come up as the din of approaching
thunder. It is a daunting sight.

As we stand looking down on this, I find I am between Ananias
and Seth. Yeshu is halted a distance away with Jude and Izates and
Thecla. Perhaps they too are struck with wonder, for I would swear
they have come to a sudden halt at the sight of so many gathered
below. But we three, who have known each other in other times and
in other guises, stand apart. And as those with Yeshu talk of the astonishing number below, how he shall manage to be heard by them
all, and of what the more fiercely lawful will make of his speaking on
a Sabbath, and how so many are surely proof of the strange and dan-
gerously volatile mood that has come over every kingdom in Palestine, Seth and Ananias and I fall into talk as easily as we once did. For
did we not travel to Egypt together, and did we not together set eyes
on the fabulous city of Alexandria, and did we not, after many and
many an adventure there, travel back to Judaea together?

Looking away from the great spectacle below, I note that Ananias has grown more chins, two more of them, and I tell him how I admire them.

Says he, "A man needs bulk as a buffer between the world and himself, the more bulk the better. How else to defend against a wife and her litter? By the spit of my camels, how they increase! They spring up overnight like weeds in a poppy field, like evil spirits in the footsteps of Agrath, the Queen of Demons . . . like customs officials! Not to mention a man's wife's brothers and her sisters and her aunts and her uncles and on and on as far as a man's purse and a man's mind can stretch. In this, you are wiser than I, Seth."

"How so?" asks my friend the philosopher, who is so much wiser than Ananias, I almost find cause to smile.

"Is it not obvious? You have never married."

I think Seth will laugh at this. I think I know full well he will brush away the teasing of Ananias, as he would brush away a troublesome fly. For of course Seth has never married. What need he of such things? Though both Shammai and Hillel, the very greatest of the Jewish teachers, insist that marriage is a sacred act from which no one shall abstain, and though it is true an unwed man cannot be a rabbi, such an uncommon man as Seth is not made for such a common thing as marriage. Therefore, when he replies in all seriousness that he would marry, I am more surprised than I was at the sight of the thousands below us. I snap my head toward him.

Seth holds his beardless and beautiful face as impassively as I have tried to hold mine in these last difficult days. "I would marry," he continues, "if the woman I would wed would wed me."

By the ancient stars of Sumer! Who could this woman be? Has she been wooed and lost, far away and long ago, but is yet unforgotten? Is she a daughter of Jerusalem? Or of Adiabene? Is she rich or is she poor, beauteous or plain? As clever as he? She must be as clever as he; I cannot imagine he could bear a feeble or a foolish woman. But how could a woman, any woman, not return the love of my beloved friend? Or not wish to wed him? More remarkable still, how could any father of such a woman not take it upon himself to see her wed to Seth, having once seen she is too foolish to see to it herself?

I look up at Seth with all this alight in my eyes, my indignation and surprise and disbelief and wonder, not to mention my quiver full of questions dying to be fired from my bow of a tongue, and I find he looks down at me with such a look I think my eyes might turn back in my head; I think I might swoon. I know on the instant who the woman is. I know on the instant what I should have known all along. Not because of a thing said, and not because of a thing done, but because I am a prophet and a toucher of minds. *Eloi! Eloi! Eloi!* Isis, Queen of Heaven, how you must laugh at such a one as I. It is all I can do not to fall on the ground and beat my head bloody on stones. I am not a prophet. I am a fool beyond any fool. He means *me.* Seth of the Maccabees, who once ruled Israel, would take Mariamne, daughter of Josephus, to wife!

If ever a thing took away my very breath, it is this thing, and I am not sure, but it seems the body of John the Less stands witless and voiceless and helpless and hopeless, while the mind of Mariamne shies away, shies away, her heart beating as the heart of a poor bird caught stunned in the fine tangles of a fowler's net. But if I have seen who it is Seth would wed, so too has Ananias. Wily Ananias is not left witless, and he is not left voiceless. For some unfathomable reason, in this astonishing and terrible and long-lived moment, he is delighted. He pats his fat hands together. He licks his fat lips. He wobbles his chins. He winks at Seth. He says, "Hear me, my old friend. Would you have me put in a good word with her father?"

Though I am graceless as an overturned tortoise, though I am as mute in my unbalance, Seth has the grace to smile. He has even the equanimity to answer. "I would rather you put in a good word with the woman herself."

Ananias opens his hands in mock supplication. "Can you hear this, fair maiden, and not be moved?"

Indeed, Ananias, I am moved. I am moved so that I cannot move and I cannot speak, and I turn my heated face away to hide all that I cannot think I think, and in hopes as well of gathering up whatever it is I might feel, so that I might more fully feel it, and turning, I hear Ananias say, "As you were born a woman, would you not live as a

woman? Surely, Mariamne, daughter of Josephus of the very Sanhedrin, even for you must come a time to be wed?" And still I turn
away, and as I turn I see what I would hope never to see. The blood
in my face flushes red as a poppy petal. The blood in my head roars
as the sounding sea. The blood in my heart drains away. For I find
myself staring directly at Yeshu who is staring directly at me. I
thought Yeshu still engaged in talk of John and of Zealots, of kings
and Romans and messiahs, and of a mood on the land that is like
unto a great plague, but I was mistaken. My Yeshu moved away from
this talk, away from those who still speak of such things, and has
come closer and closer to Seth and to Ananias and to me. Has he
come close enough to hear what passes between my friends and myself? I cannot take my eyes from his eyes. In them, I seek his mind.
Has he heard us? Does he know what it is Seth has said? Has he
heard what it is Ananias has said? Does he now know who—and
what—I am?

He knows.

He has heard the words of Ananias. He has heard the name Mariamne. His skin made ashen by his discovery, his eyes made bleak, he
opens his mouth to speak, and I would join his mind to save myself,
but I am pushed away. Yeshu pushes me away! He takes an awkward
step toward us; I take an awkward step back. I do not know what Seth
does, or what Ananias does, but at this very same moment, a moment
that spans the eternal and in which I see that the look-alike Jude has
heard as well, a name is called: "Yehoshua!" Someone among those
below has seen him. And when this one has called out his name, it
causes others to look up, and then others, and looking up, the tribes
massed below us find him, see that he who they await is come. As
one, they see Yeshu, head of the Nazorean, cousin of John, and son of
Joseph of Japhia, he who has called them here, and whose call they
have heeded, and there begins a murmur which grows into a singing,
which becomes louder and louder, until the valley below is filled
with his name: "YEHOSHUA!"

It is Simon Peter who reaches us first. It is Simon Peter who races
up the hillside, massive legs leaping up through the rocks and the

shrubs like a marathon runner, massive arms pumping for balance and for speed, black hair and black beard and brown robe streaming out behind him. Behind Peter runs Andrew, bald as last I saw him. Behind Andrew come more and more, and more. First the Sons of Thunder and then Simeon and the sons of the Sons of Thunder. Then comes Old Camel Knees; Jacob the Just walks up the hill, he does not run, and the skin of his blue head is freshly shaven. I should be astonished to see him, for when John was taken, Jacob was one of those who went missing. Yet here he is now, and he is merely a beginning. If not stopped, would the whole of the five thousand leap up the hill after Peter?

Yeshu steps back at the sight. So too does Jude. I think they might have mind to flee.

But now sounds three sharp blasts on a ram's horn. Even though Bethsaida sits a mile away, the *hazzan* blows clear and insistent. The Sabbath has finally come, and the coming of the Sabbath stops the rush for Yeshu in its tracks. All save the front-runners. Nothing would turn Simon Peter from Yeshu, unless it be John. But John is not here; only Yehoshua is here. I know what Peter now thinks; he thinks that if not John as king, then perhaps Yeshu'a?

And I know what it is I think. There has finally come a thought into my roaring head, the first to visit since all thought fled. Get away! Get away from these men and from this life, Mariamne; hide yourself, make yourself small. No! Not small. Make yourself over. Reclaim yourself. You will not grieve and you will not weep. You will be as the women you have known. Brilliant Theano the Therapeutae, lover of Pythagoras and friend of Philo Judaeus. The long-lived Sabaz, doctor to the last of the Ptolemies, who died in the arms of the slave who adored her. Julia, the exquisite and poet, who loved Seth but made no show of it, rather fusing her love into art. Fierce Tata, *zonah* and storyteller and runaway slave. Beautiful Helena of Tyre, silently suffering, as innocent as a lamb, as strong as a lioness. Even the handsome headstrong Thecla of Shechem, who boasts five husbands and has come away from the last of these to follow she knows not what.

While all the world seems centered on Yehoshua, while there is such a confusion of voices and of faces, I turn. I take one step, two. Now I am quickly walking, and now I walk even faster, and here it is that I run. As I have run before, I run now, and as before, I do not know where I go. But this time I know who I am.

Or will be again.

I run straight into Tata.

✂

For those who consider such things, and there are many, Yeshu waits throughout the whole of the Sabbath before addressing the multitude who have gathered to hear him. Great hairy men with curved knives under their cloaks, men with fierce looks and fierce words, men whose blood burns hot enough now to march against Rome itself at his bidding. They have come from barren Judaea and from forested Ituraea, from the low coastal plains of the Great Sea to the farthest high deserts of eastern Peraea. With Jude, Yeshu secludes himself in the tent of his brothers, Joses and Jacob. There is much coming and going, but not once until the Sabbath ends, and it is a long Sabbath, gray and cold and wet, does Yeshu appear openly among the tribes.

As he secludes himself this entire time, so too do I.

I hide in the tent of Addai.

I rejoice to see that Addai thinks himself well enough to come here, though I see his doing so distresses Tata terribly, just as it does Dinah and Rhoda, who hover near him, Dinah almost without sleep. He is careful of his arms, careful of his jaw, cannot use his hands, his voice is still no more than a whisper, and he eats *rosh* as he would eat bread, but he lives.

In every way I know, I have shown them how beloved they are of me, how it moves me to see them again. Though I am numb of heart, still I fuss and chatter of where I have been and what I have seen. They are amused at the idea that people talk of Yeshu raising up a dead child. They are interested in Thecla and her many husbands, especially Tata, and they wonder as I do, at the blind man in Bethsaida. Has he bathed in every pool yet? If so, does he see? And Addai, who has not come near the city of his birth for many long years, listens to what I know of Shechem as I would listen to someone newly come from Alexandria. I have told them of Yeshu's discovery of me, and I have told them of my discovery of Seth.

All this I do as a sleepwalker. From the moment when Yeshu saw me, I have acted as I would require myself to be, as Mariamne, a woman of maturity and learning. This *will* be the truth of things. This woman will be born no matter how hard and how long I suffer her birth.

Already, I dress in some of Tata's clothes, putting away the clothing of John the Less in her traveling basket. I shall keep with Tata and with Addai as befits my unmarried state, but I will not become quiet in the presence of men. Nor shall I act as if I know nothing, feel nothing, am nothing unless as a reflection of my use as a woman: mother, wife, daughter, mistress. I will be as Tata and Thecla and I will do as I please, and if I am shunned, then I am shunned. I will go to the Temple in Jerusalem and there I will ask for the ear of the high priest Caiaphas. From him, who has always feared me, and who will be happy to get rid of me as quickly as he can, I will claim my mother's inheritance so that I am better protected by my wealth from men, and from their terrible hurtful beliefs. And finally, I will not place myself in the way of any of the brothers, the sons of Anna and of Joseph; I will not further shame them, and I will not further shame me. As for Salome . . . by all that breathes, I do not know what I shall do about Salome.

But even as Mariamne, I swear I shall think of something.

Late on the day of this interminable Sabbath, Seth joins us. I am heartened that he does, though his beloved presence brings the blood to my skin, and I flush yet again from top to toe. Seth is quiet and composed. He makes no mention of what was said before. As ever, I am impressed by my friend's dignity and self-possession. And as I sit quietly, talking with those I love who love me, these three who know who I am, I now know I will return to Alexandria. It is decided. I tell them when next Ananias has business there, I shall go with him. Perhaps I will begin a school.

The Sabbath is over. Outside, there are people stirring, speaking in louder voices. Great numbers pass close by our tent as they make their way to where Yeshu will speak. We hear the dull clatter of metal bells hung round the necks of sheep and of goats, we hear the bright chatter of children, for this is not only a gathering of fierce Sicarii come to show their knives and call down curses on all who are unrighteous, this is a gathering of whole families. The arrest of John of the River and the scattering of his followers have caused distress to entire villages. They come here to hear what it is that will now be done. They would hear prophecy.

I look at Seth, at Addai, at Tata. Shall we go hear Yehoshua? I look into one after the other of their beloved faces, faces I have known full half my life, and I settle at last on Seth's. Now that I have babbled of my intention to return to Egypt, and now that I no doubt wound him again, I must finish the deed. It takes courage to hurt one you love and who is fond of you, but if it must be done, it must be done quickly. I intend to say that if I would marry, there is no man I could better marry than he, but that I would not burden him with such a wife as I would now make. In all the usual ways of women, is it not true, I intend asking him, that what I have made of my life, has unmade me for a wife? I know he will hear me. Yet all this sticks in my throat, and I can say none of it. Seth sits and he looks upon me, his face composed, his body still. I open my mouth in the hopes that something will come from it that will soothe him, or solace me for my cruelty. This is what I finally say, "Please. Go. Hear him speak. I will stay here, as suits me."

Tata would laugh. I snap, "Why is this cause for merriment, Tata?"

"Oh, my daughter," says she, rising to help Rhoda with Addai. "You are as the moon or the sun. There is no other."

I take no comfort in this. The moon and the sun are alone.

I sit unmoving as they take their leave. I hear them join with others who greet them. I hear the assembling of thousands on the hillside near the valley floored with tents. The clamor of this competes with the meeting of the Street of the Soma and the Canopic Way for noise, or for standing on the steps of Temple at Passover. As laughter would spring up from the belly of Tata, grief would rise as bile from mine. Mariamne, who cries, will not cry. I know Yeshu stands now at the top of the hill, and with him stands Jude and all the others. I see it in my mind, the tribes of all Palestine sitting in ranks, fifty of these, a hundred of those. They talk among themselves, ask each of each what it is Yeshu might say as they finger their curved Persian knives, hush others for making such noise, nibble on the barley bread and the salted fish they have brought with them.

And I should be John the Less and have taken my place at Yehoshua's side. As John, I would take precedence over Peter and over the brothers of Yeshu and over the Sons of Thunder. Even Addai and Seth and a king of the Assyrians would stand behind me. And this, by the wish of Yeshu.

But all has changed and can never be again.

I try to banish Yeshu from my mind, as I am certain he has already banished me. He cannot do other. What is, is. What I am, I am. Better he should know it now than to know it later. Better he alone should discover my name and my true sex than for all others to discover it with him. Jude will say nothing. Those who know me will say nothing. There has been no true harm done. Surely, I have harmed none but myself. And Seth. In certain ways, I have harmed my friend Seth.

The tears fall from my eyes and wet the cloth of Tata's plain brown robe. I cannot stop them falling.

Comes a great noise from the hillside. Yeshu must be speaking. By the sound of those who call out to him, he has surely said something that heartens them, makes them roar their approval. I cannot hear him, but I can hear those who can hear him.

I cannot bear it. I must see Yeshu again. As I breathe, I must see him once more. And then I will leave him as I must leave him. I swear to Isis and to Osiris, I swear even to Yahweh who so loves the blood of a woman's heart, that it shall not be my doing if I should see him again in this world, just as I know, and how this knowing tears at my flesh, it will not be his doing should he see me.

Picking my way through the righteous of all Palestine grouped by family and by tribe on the grass of Gaulanitis, stepping over baskets and mats and feet, and around the tumbling excited children, I work my way up the hillside. I am a young woman, one of a number of young women. No one takes note of me, other than to be briefly irritated by my passing. Dressed modestly, I move modestly, willing myself to walk as a maiden, to hold myself as a maiden would, to keep my eyes averted from the bold gaze of men, which was only yesterday *my* bold gaze. I make sure my person and my skirts touch no part of them. I am as yet so unused to Mariamne, I feel odd in my skin.

In this way, I come to within twenty cubits of Yeshu, and I quickly sit where I might, and where it is fitting, near a family of grandmother, mother, and three daughters. I hold my head cloth over my nose and my mouth. By this, my hair, unbound and uncomely as well as too short for a female, is hidden, as is most of my face. I cover my hands and my feet. By this, I think not even Tata would look my way.

Addai and Tata and Seth have taken their places behind Yeshu. Behind them, Dinah and Rhoda take humbler places. But who is near them? By the moon, Dositheus! Some part of me that still lives feels pleasure to see my old friend. Was he with Jacob the Just, and did they escape? Dositheus is no longer an Egyptian, nor is he an actor. Scent and curls and posturing are long put away. He looks thin and he looks tired; more, he looks possessed by pain. The pure melancholy of his nature seems deeper, darker, and I wonder at his adventures since John was taken, though I shall probably never learn them.

Who else is here? There is Menahem, the newly wedded son of Simon bar Judas, and there are James and Zoker, the sons of Jacob bar Judas, but of their brother Jair, the third son of Jacob bar Judas, there is nothing. And no matter that I look and look, I cannot see sweet Helena of Tyre.

But now I look away from these and gaze upon Yehoshua instead.

Has he too changed? Has the loss of his beloved friend and youngest disciple, the youth who would teach him what it was he could teach, grieve him? Does he pine and does he sigh? From this distance, it does not seem so. Yehoshua's face is alight with the regard of thousands. He stands on the highest point of the highest rise, and though full half of him, robed in purest white, is brilliant against the evening green of the grass, full half is limned against the dark roiling gray of the sky. By Isis, there is such a Glory in him as even I have not seen. The very hair on his head, the very hair of his beard, seems more than the red of Thrace, and they frame his face in the fire of the sun.

He speaks as he has been speaking, and it is only now, being distracted by Dositheus, that I begin to listen. For a moment I do not understand what it is he says. And then I do.

"I would give you drink," says Yehoshua to the Sicarii and to the *pagani* and to the varied sects, and to their women and to their children, his hands held out as if he offered wine, as if he offered bread, as if he would feed them all for the asking. "I would give you to eat. I say to you that five thousand times five thousand could be fed on the loaves and the fishes I offer, even if there be only five loaves and two fishes. Each man and each woman and each child could eat their fill of such food, and still there would be twelve baskets left."

I look about me. As ever, I wonder what is it they hear? These men and women of Palestine are gathered to hear news of John the Baptizer. They come for John the Messiah, and they would know what has been done and what will be done. They would know if these are the End Times. Therefore, what do they make of loaves and fishes and baskets, of fives and twos and starry twelves, when John is taken? But if they are troubled, it is not in their faces. There seems not a sound, not from man or woman or child, not from beast wild or beast tamed, or from the water that flows below us or the sky that threatens above us. Yeshu's voice, which so often I strained to hear, rings out over us as a great bell would ring.

"You come here to know how it is with John. And I say to you, that there are those among you who would rise against Herod. There are those who would rise against Rome itself. Among you are those who have ever been with us, and these shout out to all who would listen that only blood will pay for what has been done."

Comes a righteous murmur from this grouping, and that. Comes a scattering of raised fists and raised voices. Yeshu holds up his right hand, palm forward, and all this is silenced. Behind him, Jude and the others stand as silent as the grass, but many even of these have their hands near the hilts of their unhidden knives.

"You have heard it said, an eye for an eye, and a tooth for a tooth. I, Yehoshua of the Nazorean, have said this. I, Yehoshua of the Nazorean, have done this. This has long been my way, and the way of my brothers and of my cousins."

I see Jacob the Just nod his head at this. Yeshu's brother, who stands now in Yeshu's place as Yeshu stands in John's, looks out over this great gathering, his arms crossed, his face set with righteousness. Near him, I see that Jude grimly smiles. Yes, this has been the way of Jude, and it would be his way again, but only if it is also the way of Yeshu.

"But I, Yehoshua of the Nazorean, stand before you now, and I ask, what has been gained by all this blood? Is it not a truth that bloody soil reaps bloody fruit? I ask this also, what has been won by vengeance? Will the man you have revenged yourself on not then turn to revenge himself upon you, and if not you, then on your family? For I say that whatsoever you do in this world will be done to you. Therefore, resist not evil with evil. But whosoever would harm you, harm not in return, for what shall it gain you but a world of harm to all?"

There is much surprise at this. I have no need to see who is most surprised and most dismayed. I can hear Simon Peter's frustrated rage whistle through his broken tooth from here.

But if Yeshu knows this, he pays not a moment of heed. "If a man would see justice done, he would do justice. If a man would know the heart of another, he would first know his own. I ask you, is it in your hearts to kill and be killed?"

Simon Peter has been asked. He cannot resist answering, "But Yeshu'a! John is taken. Who among us knows if he shall be set free? Or be killed?"

Yeshu turns to his rock. He smiles into Simon Peter's face, a face blackened with thwarted ambition and thwarted grievances. "The Father knows, Peter. And John knows. Do you know better than these? Would you act for John? Do you know his heart?"

"John would have us come for him!"

"Has he said this to you?"

"No, but surely, we will go to him! I beseech you, Yehoshua!

Remember what has been prophesied by the Magus. Remember that in order for the people to follow, John must lead. By taking John, the Fox has caused the gathering of the tribes. More are here and more speak to the other than have ever been, and this is a great thing. But now John must come among us again, for how is he to lead from a prison cell? I cannot do *nothing*! Yeshu'a, as you lead us now, we must do what it is we can do."

Yeshu answers heat with warmth. "We can do no other thing than what is *in* us to do. What is in you, Peter?"

Not knowing the answer is anger, and not knowing that it is fear, but thinking that it is instead a righteous pride of cause, Simon Peter turns away, and I see that the skin of his averted face burns with shame for Yeshu.

"Yehoshua of the Nazorean!"

As all others, I too am startled. Who from this great crowd calls out to Yeshu in this imperious way?

But Yeshu is not startled, nor is he alarmed, nor yet is he even disturbed. Mildly, he looks down on one who now stands amid a group that sits close by me, saying, "Praise to you, Eleazar, son of Dinaeus."

In the mouth of Yeshu of Galilee, the name Eleazar sounds as Lazarus, but I do not mistake it. Eleazar, son of Dinaeus? The very name dries the spit in my mouth, just as it dries in the mouth of peasant and soldier from Idumaea to Trachonitis, for Eleazar is a lion among wolves, a bandit and a would-be king, and from under my head cloth, I squint my eyes to see him, only to find a very fly of a man, a man whose head works on his neck as a fly's head works. But looks can deceive.

Hands on his hips, he shouts up at Yeshu, "I will tell you what is in me, Yehoshua. I would drive the Romans before me as a storm drives a sail. I would sweep out the Temple as a woman sweeps away filth. I would do this before the passing of another day. I would do it in the name of John of the River. And I would not stop in my driving and my sweeping until there was neither a Roman nor an apostate priest left in all of Palestine. Only by this will we have peace!"

How the tribes love this! Eleazar is rewarded with a great roar, which he accepts as a very king accepts much deserved tribute. He does not turn to those who cheer him but in his triumph looks steadily up at Yeshu.

Once again, Yeshu looks out over the tribes. His eye is as mild now in the face of this roaring, as it was when he would lie in my bowl of rock gazing out over the Salted Sea. "I say unto you, Eleazar!" calls he down to Eleazar the Bandit, his voice carrying as easily across the noise as a bird on the air, "as I say to all of you who thirst for blood—"

It is wondrous how the roaring begins to die in every throat. It is as if the wind has dropped and the sails gone slack.

"If you would have peace, you must be peaceful. If you would know love, you must be loving. What it is you would see around you must first be *in* you. To return love with love, this is nothing, any innkeeper can do such a thing. But to return hatred with love, this is something. Who among us can do this? Show me this man or this woman and I will show you God's Light. For as the sun of the Father shines on the just and on the unjust, so too would you. I tell you now, evil is of this world and passes away, but goodness is of the Father's Kingdom, which is all kingdoms and all worlds, and is eternal. If you would know you live in the Kingdom of God, you would be therefore perfect in your goodness, even as your Father is perfect."

I sit and I hear this and my heart leaps up in joy. My eyes are pricked with joyful tears. I rejoice that Yeshu has become a speaker; and not only a speaker and not only a teacher and not only has he become a prophet, he has become a Voice. And his Voice is to mine as mine is to the voice of the mute. As he is bathed in Glory, as he emanates Glory from all his Being, the authority of his Voice holds them in thrall, and his words bind them to him with wisdom and with truth, and his numinous person awes them with beauty. And those who would wield their knives are listening as those without knives are listening, as are women and children. Eleazar, the son of Dinaeus, is listening. Those who are with Eleazar listen. Even Simon Peter has turned back from his black sulking; he too is listening. In this time and in this place, even Simon Peter hears him.

They have come to be told they are the Sons of Light, and their enemies are the Sons of Darkness. They have come to plot vengeance and have waited to hear they would do bold and bloody deeds. They have hungered to hear it said that John is Messiah, that the End Times have come, and that they and their God of Wrath would put the whole of the earth to the torch, but all this is struck from their hearts. I know this is so, I hear them. Better, I can *feel* them. Yeshu has filled their hearts with joy, and how can a man with a joyful heart do ill?

I cannot bear it. It breaks not only my joyful heart and cracks not only my woman's bones, but it threatens my mind. I have lost this; it is not mine. But by the moon, I would not lose myself. Mariamne is all that is left to me. Therefore, I must leave this place, and I must do it now. There is nothing here for me as I truly am.

I slowly rise. I slowly turn. I creep away as soundlessly as I am able. But as I go, still I hear Yeshu.

"As I say unto you, and as it is written, blessed are they whose spirit is open, for theirs is the Kingdom of God. Blessed are they who sorrow, for they shall seek comfort and be comforted. Blessed are they who trust, for the trustful shall have dominion over life. Blessed are they who hunger and thirst for grace, for they shall be filled with grace. Blessed are the merciful, for they shall know mercy. Blessed are the pure in heart, for they shall see God. Blessed are they who suffer for God's sake, for God shall raise them up. Blessed are they who are persecuted for the Kingdom, for by this they raise themselves up." Yeshu's voice, which I know grows steadily stronger, becomes stronger still. "Blessed are the peacemakers, for they shall be called the children of God."

I remove myself, carefully working back down the crowded hillside so that I might hide myself yet again in the tent of Addai and of Tata, and his words flow down after me, seeking me out, and it seems though they should, they do not grow fainter and fainter but louder and louder. It seems they follow me, curl round my body, find entry in the folds of my cloak. They insinuate themselves into my mouth and into my ears, trip up my hurrying feet. And the feeling comes that Yeshu sees me, that he has his eyes on me, that though he speaks out over all these thousands, yet he knows one among so many is John the Less, who is who she is, and knows too that John the Less is leaving.

The dark of the evening rolls down and as the fires leap up around me, I am yet a shadow among shadows. But the feeling grows, and it grows, and just at the last, as I reach the very bottom of the hillside and I would slip in among the city of tents and disappear from his sight forever, I turn once, as Lot's wife turned, and I look back. It is as if my heart has stopped. As if time itself has stopped.

From his place on the summit of the hill, Yeshu looks down at me.

⊂∘

The pampered daughter of Josephus of Arimathaea knew only to call for her slave. That very woman, Tata, now busies herself around me. Moment by moment I learn how much I must do if I would be a woman, and how so much of it chafes! From this day forth must I now mend my own clothing and grind my own meal and bake my own bread? Must I tend a goat so that I might have milk, spin wool so that I might have cloth? Comes into my mind the Book of Proverbs and the virtuous woman whose price is far above rubies. "She rises while it is yet night and provides food for her household . . . Her lamp does not go out at night. She does not eat the bread of idleness." *Pah!* I cannot spin and I cannot sew and I cannot bake bread. As for milking a goat? I have seen these things done, but I have never learned to do them myself.

I take solace in the thought of my mother's money. As Father has always done, I will buy the services of some other to do these things, though I shall not buy their persons. This much humanity, by now, is mine. For if I do not have a servant, as Dinah has Rhoda, how shall I ever find time to teach? Or to learn? Or to travel? Or to write as Philo Judaeus writes? I also take solace in my never marrying. If I have no husband, I shall have no child. If I have neither husband nor child, especially no male child, I will have no one who takes precedence over what it is I would do, and no one I would be required to be more precious than rubies to. This proves a small comfort.

Addai is returned, and when he is settled and when he is fed, a thing he does without obliging Tata to act as servant, he tells Tata and me what has been said among the inner Nazorean. Already there is complaint at what Yeshu will do, or will not do. The names of those who grumble come as no surprise. Simon Peter and Jacob are speaking openly to Yehoshua, as is Izates, who though he is king in another land, is here zealous. To hear Addai say that Dositheus too would act, even this name does not confound me. Just as Addai, Dositheus is an old friend of John's. Dositheus urged John to act and surely carries the guilt of his urging. I ask Addai if he too would free John?

"I have heard nothing," says he, "more wonderful than what Yeshu'a has said this night. And I know that freeing John will not end with the Baptizer preaching on the river once more. I know it will prove a darker beginning. John himself would say this if John were here, for John knows the wind blows as it will. And yet, I would free John for I love John as I love you. And I would see him king." Addai sits silently for a moment, and is as dark as the night is now dark. He who is the father of my heart cannot find his way. He tries spreading his hands to show the hopelessness of it all and by so doing wounds me. His precious fingers do not bend, nor do they straighten. "But if we go to make John king, would Pilate not set his soldiers on us as he does on all others at the slightest provocation? He would not hesitate to slaughter us in our thousands. And yet, I would free John."

I too would see John saved. Even more, I would see saved Simon Magus. There is nothing more to say, and there is little sleeping done this night.

∝

Three days have passed and no one leaves the valley near Bethsaida. I, now always Mariamne, would if I could, but neither Addai nor Tata nor Seth, not even Ananias, will leave until the very last word is said by the last and least of us. But if I do not leave this valley, I also do not leave this tent, not even to see to the small needs of Eio. Tata must do this, as she does all else I should do. So far, she has been patient with me, though I know her patience wears thin.

Seth comes only to tell us what is being said and what is being done. It seems that Yeshu is heard. Each day he speaks on the hillside and each day all gather to listen. So long as the tribes can see him and hear his words, the greater number of all here remains under his thrall. Seth, who is himself beguiled, tells us there are those who wonder at his teaching, saying Yehoshua of the Nazorean is become as a prophet from out of their midst, and these begin to listen with new ears.

But long into each night, some of the Nazorean, as well as others, argue. Yeshu sits among these, listening. Seth says that he seems to sleep and does not argue against them, but Seth knows he does not sleep. Jude sits as ever, near him, and he too listens. There is talk now not of an uprising—an uprising would surely spell doom, Rome is too strong, the Herods too devious—but of rescuing John. It is Jacob the Just who leads this talk, Jacob's voice that is listened to. Over and over, they ask each other the same questions. How is it with John? Does he yet live? If so, and if Herod does not kill him, when will Pontius Pilate order he be given over into Roman hands for the death of the soldier who was killed by Stephen the Banker? And what is it they should do to save him?

No word arrives for me from Yeshu, and though I expected none, still I sorrow. Seth never remains long and has yet to make mention of what has passed between us. He does not call me Queen Bee, nor does he call me Mariamne Magdal-eder. Ananias has come only once. He sat and talked with Addai for a moment. He did not look at the female Mariamne, save to demand wine and to wink.

Before dawn on the morning of the fourth day, it is finally determined that a band of rescuers will secretly set south for the land of Moab and the Fortress of Machaerus. Yehoshua joins them. I am not surprised. Even as he is no longer Sicarii and even though he would not be as Judas of Galilee who led his people to slaughter, yet Yehoshua the Nazorean would not see Herod kill John.

Jacob knows where John has been taken, having learned it in his own escape from the men of Herod Antipas, therefore knows where all must go, though no one knows how it fares within the walls of

Herod's prison, and no one has ever been inside. Still, no matter the how or what of things, these men must *do* something.

Rising from their beds, Addai and Tata have gone out to wish them well. As has Seth. But I have left Addai's tent on the pretense of fetching water from the small river that flows through this small valley and into the Sea of Galilee. The sun is yet to show first light, but I can see that farther along the riverbank Yeshu and Jude and Jacob and the others work in silence, and with speed. I creep as close as I dare, keeping to my bank of the river. Careful to keep my head cloth well forward on my face, I expect nothing more than to see them set forth. But in watching, I forget myself. I stand with my feet in the cold black stream, I hold Tata's water jug in my hand, but I am as one who is deaf and one who is dumb. I gather no water. Unmoving, and entranced, I hear myself whisper, "Pray Isis and Osiris, pray the Father and the Mother, pray Glory. Bless these men, and walk with them. Let them bring Salome out from the jaws of Herod."

Oh, that I were John the Less again and that I too set forth for Salome, and for John of the River!

They load what they would take on the backs of two donkeys, one of which is Eio. They do not speak and they do not look round, but are intent on what they do. Of the nine who ready themselves, it is plain they are led by Yehoshua. Yet for fierceness and steady purpose, Yeshu is well met by Jacob the Just and by Simon Peter, even by Andrew of Capharnaum. As for the two Sons of Thunder and the two men sent by the bandit chief, Eleazar, Timaeus and Saul of Ephraim, these four are cunning and bold. As for Jude there is none so resolute as he.

I remember to dip my jug in the stream, and as I have seen so many women do so many times, I try to balance the jug on my head, full now with water. How is this done? How is this done with comfort? I am not done with praying. "I cry out to you, Anat Jahu, wife of Yahweh, and to all the lost goddesses of Israel, and most of all to you, Zion, through these men, let Salome live. In return, I, Mariamne, shall find you and bring you home. I swear this." The eastern sky lightens by the moment as I struggle with my jug of water. There, it steadies . . . I straighten . . . look once more at those who—by Isis, what is it I see? There has come a disturbance among them. My uneasy jug on my uneasy head, I move closer.

Even though it is not yet the first hour of the morning, and the birds only now begin to awaken, some traveler has found us. Whoever he is, he causes Andrew to cry a short sharp bark of pain and outrage. He causes Jacob to curse the sky. Addai has limped forward. Yeshu is already at the stranger's side. The donkey that Simon bar Judas has been cinching up, kicks out and brays. What is it that dismays them so? Who is it that brings them bad news? For it *is* bad news, that much is plain. Simon Peter has a grip on the arm of the stranger; he pulls him close. Salome! The traveler is Salome!

The jar slips from my head. It smashes on the stones. Simon Magus has found us! From behind her there steps a second figure, Helena of Tyre. Though she is worn to the bone, Helena is still as lovely as the night sky. Helena does not desert my Salome. And now, as Simon Magus turns from Yehoshua to Jude to Peter, I hear a sound that comes from somewhere deep inside her. I cannot hear what it is she is trying to say; I do not want to hear. But I must hear it as she must speak it.

This is what she is saying, "They have killed John."

There is no body. There is no burial. But there is mourning; all of Israel weeps. All are *onens*, they who have lost a loved one.

Yeshu will go to the town of Capharnaum for shivah. And as Addai and Tata will mourn with him, so too must I, who am no more than Mariamne, an unmarried maiden in their care. As is, once again, Salome. With Seth's help, Salome has quietly put away Simon Magus as I have put away John the Less. So that none would remark on this, Simon Magus has been seen to depart for Adiabene. The arrival of a female named Salome is not remarked on at all.

Salome rides Eio. If she had not ridden Eio, Tata and I would have had to carry her every foot of the way, for Salome is as still as death itself. I would think her entranced, I would think her poisoned. But

in truth she grieves more than any here grieves. If by excess of grieving, Salome could call back John, she would grieve all the more.
With each step I assure myself that this too will pass, that when she
has ceased grieving she will surely be as she was again. I tell myself
that all I suffer shall also pass, and I too will be as I was again. But I
do not believe myself.

On the northern shore of the Lake of Galilee, Capharnaum is
large and it is prosperous and it sits on a small peninsula so that it is
almost entirely surrounded by the sweet water sea. The homes of
Andrew and of Peter, who are the sons of Jonah, are here. In this
town, they were fishermen before they were Sicarii, just as the sons
of Joseph of Japhia were builders before they were Sicarii.

When we all of us come to a stop before the house of Simon Peter
and the wife of Simon Peter, I at least know wonder. If ever I had
thought of Yeshu's righteous blood-thirsty rock as a man with a
home and a family, I should never have thought he would have this
home and this family. The house is large and white and has many
rooms and many courtyards. The wife, who is named Perpetua, is as
gracious as Dinah and almost as comely as Helena. Peter has a son,
Mark, of few years and as lovely as any girl child and as shy as a
desert mouse, and when the man who is his father walks through his
door, he becomes shyer still. He now lives tucked away in his
mother's skirts.

Salome and I have hidden ourselves in the smallest courtyard,
there to go unnoticed, and to wait out the time of mourning until we
might flee this place and these people. Or rather, I have hidden Salome, for if left to herself, I think it possible she might finally walk,
but only the short distance from the white house down to the blue
sea. And there she would keep walking until the water closed over
her head, and even then she would keep walking until she drowned.

Our small courtyard is behind the kitchen and is a distance away
from the much larger courtyard where Yeshu stays with those now
closest to him. Near us is a small and darkened room, and in this
room lies Sarah, the mother of Perpetua. No matter how tender her
daughter's care, Sarah daily comes closer to death. As others mourn

the killing of John of Kefar Imi in the largest courtyard, Tata minis-
ters either to Addai or to Sarah. This she does while grieving as
deeply as any in all of Palestine.

Tata believes neither *rosh* nor the oil of the balsam tree nor the
bitumen from the Salted Sea will help Sarah. Nor will any other potion or poultice or unguent Perpetua has to hand. But though she
does not know what ails her, having never seen its like, there is one
thing Tata says will help, and that is for the mother to be brought out
into the sun, though this causes the daughter to wring her hands
with worry and concern.

There are now six of us who make do in this courtyard . . . no,
seven. I have forgotten the boy Mark, whose eyes are the beautiful
black of Helena's skin and whose mouth is one of Tata's roses. This
is all we ever see of him, his eyes and his mouth and his tiny nose,
peering out from the clothes of his mother, Perpetua. And while
Sarah does not become well in the sun, she becomes better. Her
color improves. Tata thinks she will not die as soon as she might,
though a fever rages still in her blood, and she cannot raise her head
from her pillow.

The kitchens and a courtyard away, I know Yeshu'a mourns his
cousin, that he sits with Jude and with all the others, both men and
women, that even Addai is there, and that Perpetua and her servants,
with the help of Dinah and Rhoda, are hard-pressed to feed them
all, and to honor their presence in her house, and at the same time to
care for her mother and her son, as well as rejoice in the return of
her husband—though I suspect any rejoicing will be saved for his
yet again leaving. I know that Thecla and the other women do what
they can, and I also know the men do nothing but mourn and eat.

This last thought has roused me from my habits as John the Less,
and from those I knew as a person of privilege. If there are wonderful parts to being thought a man, there are parts that shame me. Why
would I sit when all mourn the death of John, women as well as men,
and expect only the grieving women to tend to me and to my needs?
I am Mariamne, and I will tend to myself and to those I love.

Though Helena would as well, I make myself solely responsible for Salome. I make sure of Eio's needs. I do whatever it is Tata would ask of me, and more if I notice a thing before Tata does. I sit by the hour near the side of the woman Sarah, and I bathe her hot skin with aromatics. I listen to her feverish mutterings. Plainly, having her son-in-law once again in her home and also the brother of her son-in-law, has done her no good. Sarah is frightened of them both, and I sympathize, poor woman. They are fearsome men, or they mean to be.

It happens that on the evening of our seventh day in Capharnaum, as the neighboring fishermen push their boats out into the sea so they might fish all night, and Salome is mercifully freed for a moment of the pain of John by sleep, and as Tata brews something over our fire, I am sitting by one side of Sarah and Perpetua sits on the other. Helena sits at her feet. We have been talking as we bathe her, Helena and I. We have been telling the wife of Simon Peter all that we can of Egypt, of Alexandria, of our time there. I have been saying that I mean to return, that I mean to found a school, and Perpetua has been listening, her dreams of far lands and exotic sights shining in her eyes. The child Mark too listens, and I am careful not to look his way, and by this, more and more of his eager wondering face appears, as he would not miss a single word. It is at this point that I notice that Tata starts and looks up. Therefore, I too start and look up.

Yeshu has joined us. As has Simon Peter and Seth.

My hand, in which there is a dripping sponge held over the bowl of Tata's aromatics, freezes. The scented water seeps down my arm, and the words I have intended to say rise no further in my throat. I am sure my eyes have grown as round as the eyes of the child Mark at the sight of Yehoshua, but I have no skirts to hide in.

Though Peter does not come close, Yeshu and Seth walk across the courtyard, Yeshu to seat himself at the head of Sarah's pallet, Seth to remain standing. Where he stands is directly behind me.

Yeshu does not look at me; he looks at Perpetua, saying, "How long has she suffered?"

Perpetua is too frightened to raise her eyes to this once Sicarii, perhaps even more than she is of her Sicarii husband himself, but still she finds the courage to answer. "Why, sir, for many weeks, and I tell you, I fear she dies."

Yeshu touches Sarah's weathered cheek, very softly and very tenderly. At his touch, the old woman's eyes fly open like the lid of a hinged box. They are red with fever and blurred with confusion. "Sarah," says Yeshu, "can you hear me?"

Though she seems to have heard no one else, it is obvious she hears Yeshu. "Yes," she answers, clutching her sheet to her breast, "I hear you. Are you a demon?"

Yeshu leans so close to her face his red hair brushes her heated skin. "Sarah," he whispers, "mother of Perpetua, as you can hear me, do you think there is a demon in you?"

At this, I come unstuck inside. All the things I have not allowed myself to feel, I feel now. To be so close to the friend of my heart and not to speak. To breathe the air my friend breathes and not to look into his eyes. All that we have said to each other, all that he has told me and no one else, and all that I know of his Glory, and he of mine, and here we sit in the house of Simon Peter of Capharnaum who did not love me when I was John the Less and who affects not to know me now that I am Mariamne, the castaway daughter of a rich Judaean. I have heard my friend ask a woman if she is possessed by a demon, and only I of all who know Yeshu know that he knows there are no demons. Yet he will act the role of *gazer*, he will be an exorcist. For as he has said, the people make a demon of their illnesses, and of their troubles, so that they might have a thing to blame. If they believe a thing, it is as magic. Which means if they think a thing is in them, then it is in them. And if they think a thing cast out, cast out it will be. Only I know this is what is in his mind.

Sarah, the mother-in-law of Simon Peter, struggles to sit up. So eager is she to know her demon so that it might be blamed for what she endures, she would sit up in her bed, not lie. I place a firm hand on her back to help her, as does her daughter. Together, we cradle Sarah until she can hold herself. "Oh, yes, Master," she cries as she struggles, "I am sure I am possessed of a demon. He tears at me." So saying, she points at her belly and at her heart.

"What is its name?"

"Its name?"

"By what name would it be called so that we may demand it go away?"

"Ah!" Sarah brightens so visibly, even Peter who is scowling in the doorway is astonished. "I do not know its name. Do you?"

Yeshu smiles down at her, places his left hand on the back of her head and his right hand on her brow. Sarah has closed her eyes. She has given herself over to his touch. I know what it is he thinks at this, for we have talked of it long into the night. The woman believes in her demon, and now she believes that Yeshu believes. And if he, as a proper magician, should also know its name? Surely by knowing its name, he has the power to send it away.

Yeshu now shouts so that all might hear, and so too that the demon might hear. "Its name is Dread. And I cast it out! Begone Dread! Leave this woman in peace."

At the moment Yeshu utters the word *peace* he releases his hands from her head, and in this same moment, Sarah rises from her bed, stumbles a step toward me, and then a step toward Helena, crying out, "It is gone! There is nothing left of it!"

Perpetua, who has watched all this in first fear and then awe, covers her mouth with both of her hands so that she might not scream, and by screaming cause the demon to flee back into her mother. As Sarah has done, Simon Peter has taken a step toward us, then another step, on his face a look of dawning wonder, and then of—what? Cunning? Ambition? I find I do not wish to know. Seth has not moved at all. And neither have I. But Tata comes forward to catch Sarah before she can fall on her knees and do as the man Ismael, father of Matti, had done, clasp Yeshu's legs and kiss his feet.

Yeshu, too, has risen. He looks at Perpetua. He looks at Simon Peter. He says, "Tell no one of this."

And with that, Yeshu leaves us. But not before glancing over at me, and not before I see that in looking at me, there is a light in his eyes of such strangeness I am almost alarmed. It is not broken, but then neither is it clear.

Yeshu had said, "Tell no one of this," and no one has, or so I think until the morning comes that we are finally to leave this place.

I support Salome, as Tata steadies Eio to take her weight. Rhoda packs the last of our provisions into the baskets Eio also carries. Eio grumbles throughout. We are traveling first to Jerusalem so that I might claim my mother's bequest. It is determined that I shall also claim Salome's from her father, Coron. Salome, who has been asked about this, has replied with silence. I have replied to her silence with chatter. I take both our parts, talking as we used to talk. If I could be heard, I am sure I would seem half mad. I *am* half mad.

Tata is turning Eio's head toward the door leading out from the yard where the animals are kept, when Seth steps from the shadows.

"I would travel with you," he says to Tata, and to Addai, "Izates, who is called back as king, returns to Adiabene. Ananias is already gone about his business. Dositheus thinks to remain here with Yeshu. But I must return to Jerusalem."

I do not smile. I barely look in his direction. My friend, who would wed me, looks as he always does, composed and collected. I think I shall always admire how removed he is from human cares, and I shall learn to emulate him. I have already begun by making no gesture for or against his traveling with us. But inwardly, how I re-joice to see him! My heated pain must surely cool in the shade of his tender regard.

Of course, Helena chooses to follow Salome and not go with Dositheus and Yeshu, so that by counting Eio we number nine as we move away from the house of Perpetua and Simon Peter. Coming from a side door onto the larger street that passes through the center of Capharnaum, I see there is a small knot of men waiting at Simon Peter's door. I recognize none of them, though they are surely the worthy of Capharnaum, by which I mean affluent in one way or an-other. Each of them wears something of mourning for the loss of the prophet John. Simon Peter is with them, and as we pass by, we all hear him say as clearly as if he were speaking to us: "I swear what I have said is true. He can make the blind to see. He can pluck back the body from the brink of death. I, Simon the son of Jonah, who has always lived among you, being born among you, saw it with my own eyes. He has cured Sarah. You all know how the mother of my wife suffered." Pulling on their beards, they all nod, yes, Sarah certainly suffered. "And you all know she was nigh unto death." Yes, they know this too. Simon Peter leans toward them as if what he said was for their ears only, then yells, "This morning I have asked that she serve me, and what do you think? She straightaway did. In this very time, I would not wonder to find she commands my wife and scolds my son."

He is rewarded by hoots of laughter, but these are short-lived, for Yeshu, followed closely by Jude, has just stepped out a main door. By now, we who travel to Jerusalem this day have moved away, shaking our heads as we go. If there is one man in all creation who cannot hold his tongue, that man is Simon Peter of Capharnaum.

As all have, Yeshu has heard every word, and his face is dark with anger. He shoots his rock a look that ought to shrivel his gizzard. But Simon Peter is rushing toward him, saying, "Yehoshua! Yehoshua! All these would bear witness to what you have done."

Addai and Seth and I exchange glances. What will Yeshu do about this? But before we can know, "Yehoshua the Healer" is swallowed in the midst of the men of Capharnaum, and then, as if by some signal, others, more men and now women and children, though they still mourn, come streaming out of their houses or away from their nets or their fish shops, and they each make their way toward Yeshu. And some of them carry their ill, and some of them are themselves afflicted in one way or another.

I watch this in horror. If Yeshu is thought a healer, if he is hailed as a magician, there will be no end to their coming. They will not push themselves forward to hear of the Kingdom; they will come instead to be healed in body. At the promise of a healer, there is nothing else in them, nothing, but the fervent need to be well. I look at Addai who must ride in a wagon, and whose precious hands are destroyed. I look at Salome who is slumped on Eio's back. Isis, Queen of

Heaven, if I thought Yeshu could heal Addai or Salome, I too would push forward, calling, Master! Master!

The last I see of him, Peter stands to the side of the clamoring and the calling, of the hands reaching out, and the piteous supplications, and on his face is nothing but prideful satisfaction. I close my eyes in sorrow. Simon Peter is a passionate man. Under all his foolishness, he means well. But does he not know what he has silenced in Yeshu by not silencing himself?

Mariamne Magdal-Eder

ow right Father was, and how wrong. He said I should not be a child when once again I saw him. This is true. He said also I should be a wife. I am no man's wife. Nor shall I ever be.

We are in Father's house in the town of Bethany, Salome and I. Bethany is sited no more than half an hour's walk east from Jerusalem on the road to Jericho, but to me it seems more remote than Gaulanitis. Each night since I have returned I have dined with Father. He does not ask Salome, but all here know he would not turn her away. Nor, as our traveling companion, would he turn away Helena. He allows, as few Jews do, women at his table.

Seth has accomplished our being here in Bethany. I do not know how and I do not ask.

Three months have passed since the death of John the Baptizer, and not once in all these terrible days and terrible nights has Salome smiled, nor has she willingly moved, nor does she seem to feel even to the extent of boredom. Semne the Egyptian does not speak, nor does she eat more than will keep breath in her body. Simon Magus believes he has killed John. And where before John died, Simon was sure the death he walked toward was Holy, now that John is truly dead, and he a witness to its horror, Simon is much surer still John's death is on his head. For who but Simon Magus taught John the meaning of the godman? Who filled him full of the thoughts and the dreams of men like Philo Judaeus? Who prophesied his great effect on the people, greater than he had already had? Who encouraged him to be not only a voice crying in the wilderness, but as Osiris? And who was it, when the soldiers came a second time, and again in the darkest part of the night, could not stop them from taking his life?

I tell Salome that John acted as he would. I tell her that John knew what he knew. I tell her that if she is guilty of these dire things, so too is Dositheus of Gitta. Perhaps also Seth of Damascus. But she does not listen. She does not even hear.

But no matter if she hears or if she does not hear, I will stay with her. I shall wait by her side as long as it takes, and when Salome lives again—and she will live again, she *must*—we will go home to Alexandria. When that time comes, we will do what we once meant to do, travel throughout Egypt, even unto Kush and the land of the Black Queens where we shall find the dark people of the shadows, the Ethiop. And we shall take with us Salome's shadow, Helena of Tyre, who, for all we know, may *be* an Ethiop.

But for now, we recline as Romans at Father's table, which was his brother-in-law's before him. It is nothing like as big or as finely made as the table in our house in Jerusalem, but it is grand enough, as are the rugs on the floor beneath me. I see Father has brought along his Persian rugs. By my right side, I have had one of Father's slaves place the listless Salome, and by hers is placed the faithful Helena. I speak only when spoken to. I do not flash my eyes as I would if I were John, but I do not keep them cast down as I might if I had never been John. Oh, but how cruel these years have been to Father. He does not stand so straight, nor does he recline so effortlessly. His eye is not as keen, his laugh as sure, his hand as capable. Over the whole of his body, down to his toes in their Greek slippers, he has gained a thick

layer of fat. But most startling of all, he is as clean shaven as Seth and
Izates are clean shaven; Father has cut off his beard. But then, the
Roman fashion has spread since I last sat with Father, and many of
his friends are also bare of chin. Not so Nicodemus. Nicodemus is
ever as he was, full bearded and craven before the Lord. But beardless or no, Father is as ever Josephus, and he is as ever a member of
the Sanhedrin, and he dominates his table as he is used to.

Looking upon his hairless face, his chin is like mine, his jaw softer,
I find myself as fond of him as ever I was, even though he once called
me whore and proclaimed me possessed of demons. By the last count
of Ananias, the number rose as high, I think, as seven. But then, as
Joor no doubt still teaches, because of the signs and the stars, if it is
not twelve, then seven is always the number of anything: worlds,
netherworlds, sins, sisters, wonders, spirits, and demons. But that he
remains fond of me at first unsettled me. On the instant I appeared
before him, clothed in the person of the maiden Mariamne and
doubting my welcome, we looked into each other, my father and I,
and as we did so, I knew Josephus rejoiced at the sight of me; for am
I not all that remains to him of his beloved Hokhmah—and am I not
the prodigal daughter?

He has asked me no questions. If I should stay here, I think he
never shall. I know Father. He will act as if I have never left, as if he
never demanded my leaving, as if these ten years never were. Because I will not stay here, and because I would not hurt him as he has
hurt me, I will allow him this.

Seth reclines on Father's right just as the omnipresent Nicodemus
of Bethphage, whose eyebrows have grown as tangled as brambles
since last I saw him, reclines on Father's left. The presence of a Maccabee both flatters Father and Nicodemus, as much as it alarms
them. Nicodemus, especially, is flustered. So far, he has spilled his
honeyed wine twice.

Rachel, my mother's sister and the widow of Pinhas ben Yohai, is
placed near the foot of the table with Father's wife, Naomi. Time
has done nothing to my aunt Rachel. She was never comely, and she
is not comely now. But she is as presentable as a man could wish of a

brother-in-law's widow. Or a wife. As yet, I do not know her status here. Time has not been half so kind to Naomi. The black antimony round her eye and the mulberry juice on her cheek is now more a mask than an adornment, and I think it meant not only to hide the marks of age but of discontent. It cannot be want that causes her sulks, for both she and Rachel are gowned in Coan silks, costly as gold, and they wear their hair as ornately as the richest Roman matron.

Salome and I are placed with Martha, my once cousin, and now perhaps also my sister. Martha, who is seventeen and betrothed for more than a year to a man older than Father, seems as discontent as Naomi. Staring at her plate of red clay—I see Father has also brought along his fine Italian plate—her tiny features are, just as I remember, drawn together into the middle of her broad face as a rope is drawn into a knot. Martha does not speak to me any more than my aunt or my stepmother speak to me.

Aside from Seth, there is only one here who has looked my way, and this is Eleazar, who might and might not be my brother. Eleazar, once as silent as the deep, is now as noisy as surf. Is this because his father is dead? Alive, Pinhas ben Yohai cast as dark a shadow over his household as a high priest casts over his treasury. Or Yahweh over his people.

I raise my eyes from my place at the bottom of the table. We who are women eat in silence, but those who are men, by which I mean Father, seem to talk louder than Eio can bray. At the moment, Josephus speaks to Seth of the Roman governor. He is saying that not only the Pharisee, but also the Sadducee themselves, fret under the rule of Pontius Pilate. If it is not one outrage, it is another. By now, his killings, if not his grievous insults to Jewish sensibilities, must number more than a thousand. There are secret meetings among the priests and the Sanhedrin. There is talk of a delegation of the most prominent men being sent to Rome to present a case to the emperor Tiberius. Father himself has been to see Pilate more than once. "Mark my words. There will come a day when he will kill one too many Jews, and on that day, when Tiberius finally tires of Jewish complaint—" Father draws his hand across his neck; I see the imagined blade so clearly, I wince, but of course I do not speak. Then Father laughs. "I begin to like the fellow, though his teeth are much too white and his Greek much too poor."

Nicodemus clears his throat to gain attention, not once but thrice, and when finally Seth dutifully attends, says, "I, myself, will be among these men who go to Rome. But I am more afraid of what Tiberius will do to us than eager to see what he might do to Pilate." Seth nods his head at this, and Nicodemus is encouraged. "Mark *these* words, more than any ten Pilates, it is our own people who endanger us. The Romans can only kill so many, but the Sicarii with all their crazed talk of righteousness and Holy Wars will kill us all. They are lunatics. Whatever brains they once had, dried up long ago in the sun of the wilderness they rave in. And they court disaster to every man who calls himself Jew, for though they preach that when they rise, God will rise with them, even a fool can see the truth of it. When they rise, Rome will rise higher, as high as a great wave in the sea, and when this wave falls, it will fall as the rain of God falls, alike on the unjust and the just. No day goes by that I do not expect the Poor to ignite the ignorant. Any day now, especially with the death of that fool, John the Baptizer, they will throw themselves against the swords of Rome."

I writhe with the desire to speak. There is a truth in what Nicodemus says, even if how he says it grates, but to call John fool is nothing less than the work of a fool.

It is Eleazar who now launches into the excited speech that I am denied. Where once I could say whatever it is I might say, now, as a woman, to men I would seem a hyena finding voice. Perhaps as Mariamne, and only as Mariamne, I might have been able to bear this, knowing nothing else, but as I have been John the Less close to half my life, it is slow poison in the veins. Each day that passes, I remind myself that no matter the beliefs of men, I shall make of Mariamne a great person. I shall be as the Delphic priestess, Themistoclea, she who proved to Pythagoras that the female is every bit as worthy as the male, if not more so. I shall be as Diotima, she who taught Socrates. Or as Korinna who bested Pindar at contests of poetry. I shall be as the glorious Sappho who was not silenced: "Although they are only breath, words which I command are immortal." I shall be as the seventh Cleopatra and use the men around me as they would use me.

Listening to the chatter of Eleazar, but not heeding it, I remember what Philo once said: "A man is like a house, and is therefore a thing of many parts." I tell myself that I am more than a house; I am a palace, and here, in the palace of myself, I am as much a queen as Helen is of Adiabene. I tell myself this, but it is hard to believe it when I look into the faces of men, and know I am nothing to them, but that I would be if I were John once again. There comes a cry of excitement from the men's end of the table and I am jerked from my fretful reverie. By the stars! Do I hear right? What is it that Eleazar says at the top of his voice?

"How I should have liked to have seen the death of John the Messiah! Think of it! Beheaded and his head on a platter!"

Not only has my cousin-brother said this, but he slices open a pomegranate as he speaks, holding up the fruit so that we all might see it bleed its rich red juice onto his hand. My absorption in self shatters as glass on tiles. Does Salome hear this? Does she see it? Helena has placed her hand on Salome's ankle. Yes, I think Salome is aware of Eleazar. And it does not end here. Now we are privileged to hear Nicodemus's indignant reply.

"All this talk of messiahs is the most perfect nonsense." Father's oldest friend pushes away his plate in a splendid show of exasperation. He rolls his eyes toward a heaven that as a Sadducee he does not believe exists, and then, addressing this heaven, he tolls, "How many times have I said that this John was not the Messiah but was surely the Deceiver? Have I not said this, Josephus? I have said it, and I say it still!"

His own face bright red with excitement, young Eleazar prattles on, and still he holds up the bleeding pomegranate. "Imagine! The wife of Herod Antipas asked for his head, and right in the middle of a great feast in the Fortress of Machaerus the head of John the Baptizer was carried in on a platter, dripping with blood!"

I am outraged, I am horrified. I cannot bear it. I am on the verge of standing up, of shouting at Eleazar, of saying something that will surely be a mistake, but Seth is there before me. "Eleazar!"

If I were Eleazar, I should go quiet on the spot. Certainly, everyone else does, even Naomi, who has been hissing at the slave who pours more wine into her cup of Father's finest glass. To his credit, my cousin or brother does at least become redder of face, and though his mouth continues to work, nothing comes from it.

"Who tells you such things, Eleazar?" demands Seth, who is angrier than I have ever seen him. "Where have you heard such a story?"

Because it is Seth, Eleazar answers with respect, though it is obvious he would squeak out his wounded indignation if he could. "Why, sir, I have heard it everywhere. Everyone is saying that because it was asked of him by his wife, Herodias, Herod Antipas had John the Messiah's head cut from his body and brought to him on a platter."

Again, I look to see how Salome fares. Her color is higher, her gaze fixed on a spot above the head of Eleazar. Should I be glad she hears at all?

When Seth speaks next his voice is low and flat with warning. "Herod has no stomach for feasting. What you have heard is not so."

Eleazar is not Simon Peter, nor is he the merchant Ananias. He senses his error, though he could not say where it lies. He counters, but he counters cautiously. "But if it is not so, then why is it said?"

And here it is that Father joins in, calling for a slave to take away the pomegranate whether Eleazar wishes to eat it or not. "If our guest says it is not so, young man, it is not so. We shall speak of other things."

If I did not pity Salome, and if I did not pity myself, perhaps I could pity poor thoughtless Eleazar for what he says next, and I imagine he thinks he is speaking of other things. "Well, then . . . what, sir, of *this* thing? Have you heard of the new messiah, the one some say is the prophet Elias?"

"Piffle," says Nicodemus, and contents himself that he said quite enough.

Father is engaged with Naomi, calling for a slave to mop her spilled wine. Seth peels an orange, which I think he does to calm himself. Eleazar therefore turns on his couch, seeking an interested eye, but the only eye he finds is that of his mother, Rachel. Poor Rachel stares at her son, unable to decide how best to act, encourage, or insistently hush him? "Have you heard of Yehoshua the Nazorean?" he asks her. "He who goes about making the blind to see and the dead to rise? I have heard that he drives out demons and that he calms storms and that he can feed thousands with a few fishes and a loaf of bread. He even heals ten lepers at a time. It is said that the mother-in-law of one of those who follow him was dead and already decaying, but that he laid his hand on her and her body was instantly as new and her spirit once again in it. On the spot, she jumped up and prepared food for a hundred men!" Eleazar pauses for breath, though not for thought. "It is said that Herod Antipas greatly fears he is the risen John, that Herod becomes as mad as his father, Herod the Great, was mad, and goes about ranting that he is beset by enemies. If not the King of Arabia, he is said to shout, then prophets returned from the grave, and he will kill this one—"

Eleazar pauses. I think he finally remembers who besides his mother listens to him, and how they listen. I think he thinks better of how he would end this, which is why he swallows the word *too*.

"It is also said," says Father, who has returned from glaring at Naomi and her spilled wine, only to glare at Rachel, she who brought forth this offending boy, "that 'a wise son maketh a glad father, but a foolish son is the heaviness of his mother.'"

If she could, Rachel would sink lifeless under the table.

But it is too late. Eleazar has finally said too much. Salome has risen; she stares at Eleazar, who has the wit to shrink from her as an Essene would have others shrink from his avenging god. Her voice rises against him as her voices once rose against the men of the Yahad and of the Poor and against all those who could not hear, nor even listen. Her voice is tremendous. If Father's red dishes do not tremble on his table, and his cups of thick glass shatter, I will be amazed. "Know you not of whom you speak? For shame! For shame, you dolt of a boy! Have you the power to judge angels!"

With that, she flees the room. Helena and I flee it after her.

Salome has talked for hours now. When at last the words come, they come until her throat burns dry with them, and still she talks.

I have turned away Rachel whose penance for birthing Eleazar was to be sent by Father to comfort us and to lure at least me back to his table. I have sent away the food he thinks we must have. I have sent all away save Helena, who would not go in any case, so that I might hear Salome speak once more, and by this, I have heard of the last days of John of the River, and it takes all that I have to listen.

This is what Salome tells of it.

As it was with Addai in the Fortress of Antonia, John was thrown into the deepest darkest hole in the Fortress of Machaerus in the mountains of Moab. Day after day, he was scourged and he was beaten by the soldiers of Herod Antipas, and he was given neither food nor drink. Nor was he freed from his chains. And if he was not kicked or slapped, or hit with the hilts of their swords, or cut with the blades, then he was dragged out before the other prisoners so that he could be taunted and could be laughed at for being he who said he could save his people yet could not save himself. And there came a time when they broke him, when John of the River, tall as a ladder and thin as a rung, and who was as full of joy as a child, wept as a child. There came a time when he cried out as a terrified child and clung to their legs, begging that they would stop, begging that if they would kill him, then pray God would they put an end to it and *kill* him.

I am put in mind of Osiris. I remember how it was each year in the delta of the Nile when exactly this was done to the godman, how he was reviled and spat upon, how he was humbled in spirit, and how he was killed, and how each time I wept as if all the tears in the world were mine, and through me they would find a way to fall. I weep in this way now. Over and over, I swear I will not cry again in this life, and over and over I find cause to weep.

And when the time came that John forgot himself and forgot all that he had taught and all that he believed, in this time, he clung to Simon Magus as they huddled in the cold and the dark and were covered in their own filth. John and Simon, and poor Helena, who had been jailed with them, her own pain dreadful to see, clung each to each, and John confessed to them, and to the dark, that he knew nothing, believed nothing, could save no one. He cried out that he was not the Messiah. That perhaps Yehoshua was he who was to come. Or perhaps it was some other. Or perhaps there was no messiah at all. He had always known there was no messiah; it was the hopeless dream of hopeless men. And though he had tried and he had tried, he could not make himself into the dream men dreamed. He cried out that life was nothing but madness. It was a hollow promise, a deceit, a trick of the mind. He clung to Simon and said that John of the River was no more than a fool before the one true God whose name was Suffering and whose name was Death.

But at this same time, Herod Antipas also suffered. There was no feasting and no dancing and no demanding heads on platters, for Aretas, the outraged father whose daughter Phasaelis had been the true wife of Herod, had come for him. Herod, putting away Phasaelis as if she were chaff, had taken not merely another wife, but Herodias, a woman who was wife to his own half brother, Herod Philip, and daughter to another half brother, Aristobulus. This had so infuriated Aretas and his tent people they had entombed the fortress of Machaerus as a storm of sand entombs a caravan. Trapped within, Herod was close to gibbering in his fear.

And so it was that while Herod cowered before the avenging Aretas, far below in his dungeons, John of the River fell, and in that hour of deepest falling, his god entered him and, by entering, took away fear. On the night they came for John—in his terror, Herod would put an end to at least one of his tormentors—he did not cower and he did not cling. In that time he stood straight before them, and the Glory in him blazed suddenly forth, and though the men who had come had swords, they were afraid.

Telling this, Salome's pride in John is fierce as fire. And I know that John. I know how it was when Herod's men saw him. They were each of them afraid to touch John the Baptizer, they were terrified before him, he who walked with Judas of Galilee, and they hung back, and they hung back, until one among them grew desperate in the face of what he had been sent to do. This man swung blindly out at the prophet in whose eyes it seemed God looked out at him. In this moment, all that John had ever believed, and all that he had ever taught, fused in the arm of this one man, and John's head was taken from his shoulders.

But Salome swears on her life and on mine that it was not carried away to be displayed on a platter. John is whole, secreted in a cave in the Land of Moab overlooking the Salted Sea, and within sight of his beloved wilderness. She swears there will come a day when she shall build him a great tomb, greater than Alexander's tomb, and there she will place his bones, every one.

With John's killing, Simon Magus himself was released as a person of no importance. So too was Helena of Tyre. As for the whole body of the Baptizer, it was tossed on a litter for Salome to do what she would with it.

There is something else. Joanna, wife of Chuza who was and is the chief steward of Herod Antipas, was taken with them. As John the Baptizer, shackled to Simon Magus and to Helena of Tyre, was being led down steps too dark to see, so too was Joanna, but though John and Simon and Helena were thrown together into one cell, Joanna was led to some other place, but what other place they could not tell. But this both Helena and Salome *could* tell: when they were brought up out of the dark and the cold, save for the body of John, they were brought up alone. There was no Joanna set free that day.

And now Salome weeps, crying out, "He did not rise, Mariamne! He was as Osiris and he was beaten and he was killed, but he did not rise!" She, who has not shed a tear in all this time, sheds them now.

As John of the River and Simon Magus held each other in Machaerus, the fortress of Herod, so Mariamne the Jew and Semne the Egyptian hold each other now, and I say, "John rises in *spirit*, Salome; he *is* risen."

But she does not hear me.

Helena watches as I cradle Salome's shuddering body, and as Salome is wracked with sobs deeper than any I have felt. I hold my friend and I rock with her as she weeps that John was killed as the Messiah who the people would make king. And I think, Oh, I have been blind. Salome straightaway saw there was a demon in John; there was a god in him. Was he not awkward and foolish? Was he not stern and forbidding? Could he not shout and cavort and terrify with his visions of wrath and righteousness? Could his face not wreathe itself in a smile as sweet and as warm as a mother's love? And then, from one awe-filled moment to the next, could he not blaze forth with *urtom,* an unclothed heavenly splendor like to singe? That was John. Small wonder if one could not easily know him or easily love him, for he was too terrible to love, too lovable to be so terrible.

I shall miss him now that too late I love him.

✄

Salome is alive again. She is changed, but she is alive. And for the moment I ask no more than this.

We live now in Father's house, taking our meals with Helena, and with Seth when he visits us. We talk of what it is we will do. I have collected the monies held by Caiaphas of the House of Ananus. Coming before him as I did, suddenly and unannounced, I have rarely seen such surprise on a human face and never seen such revulsion and fear. But I remember that for Father's good friend, the highest of all the Temple priests, I am not only a whore, and not only do seven demons live in me, I am the female Mariamne, who has never done other than cause him immense disquiet. Caiaphas, who sweats more than any man I have ever known—he is the very Jordan of sweat—has always shunned me. But he has given me my mother Hokhmah's money, and he has given me the money of Coron of Memphis meant for Semne. How could he not? Josephus is not dead, and Josephus keeps impeccable records.

Both Salome and I are now well-to-do young women, and should we wish it, Father could arrange to have us married. That is, if he could find a man who would overlook our past for the pleasure of his future with our wealth. But Salome is as a widow, and I will never marry at all. All that we wait for is the proper time, and the nerve, to set out alone for Alexandria. I have sent word of our intentions to Philo Judaeus, and to Theano the Therapeutae, and to the poetess Julia. We will take a small house near the house of Philo, we will paint its door green as I have a liking for green, and there we will make ourselves known as the Egyptian, Semne the daughter of Coron of Memphis, and the Jewess, Mariamne the daughter of Josephus of Arimathaea. I relish the day I will first stand before Philo Judaeus as Mariamne. Even more, how I long for that moment with Apion, haughty hater of women! As for Theano, I think she might swoon with welcome delight—to think her most brilliant student a female! And as for Julia, we shall surely cause her an anxious moment. If Simon Magus is female, and if John the Less is female, what then is the beauteous Seth?

From this house, there shall come no prophecy. If ever I was, I am not now a prophet. I do not portend that which will come, nor do I speak for a god. The Loud Voice is silenced forever, and I daily thank Isis for this large gift. I shall be a philosopher, for that is who I am. I will walk forth from time to time as did the learned women I once met in the house of Heli bar Nehushtan. I will teach and I will write and I will not give two figs for the opinions of men. And now that I am thinking about it, I will have a shell of stone in my garden and an almond tree and I will have doves in a dovecote. In this house, Salome means to seclude herself. In seclusion, she will set down in the best ink on the best vellum all that she remembers of John, all that he said to her, all that he taught, and all that he would have taught if he had lived. As John of the River was the most beloved teacher of Simon Magus, Simon Magus will be John's most faithful disciple. John may be dead in body, but so long as Salome lives, he shall not die in spirit, and should it take the rest of her life, he shall never die to the world.

In Simon Magus who is Salome, John is risen.

∝

Surprisingly, I have come to care for Eleazar. For all that he prattles, and for all that he primps, he is a sweet soul, and harmless. But

Eleazar is also ill, and I can do nothing. If only Tata were here, but she is gone with Addai to the wilderness. Or if Salome knew of other than poisons, odd mixtures of odd plants and odd animals that cause odd reactions for odd reasons, all the secret concoctions of Sabaz.

With no one looking, twice I did as Yeshu does: I lay hands on Eleazar. But to heal in this way, the person one heals must believe one *can* heal. Not only did I not believe, neither did Eleazar, though he was happy to have me try. We ended up laughing, or I did. Eleazar ended his laughter with a fit of coughing and a visit to the chamber of relief.

He worries me. In his sputum, there are bright red spots of blood. If I worry, Eleazar worries twice as much, staring in horror at his own blood. He staggers back to bed, throws himself on his pillows as if at any moment he might die. But whether he is dying or no, Salome says blood cannot be a good thing to find in one's mouth; it indicates ill humor in the lungs. I press my ear against the bony chest of my cousin-brother, and listen. It sounds as wind caught in a cave.

Meanwhile, I cannot keep Martha out of her brother's sick room. When first she came, I thought it a sister's tender regard. Now I know she comes from a strict sense of duty. I once believed the son of Pinhas ben Yohai broken to the Law, but Eleazar is too impetuous and excitable to be cowed by commandments. It is Martha who lives by the Law. Martha is twice the Law. My sister-cousin has rules even the rabbis or the Poor have yet to think to impose on their fellow man. Yeshu's brother, Jacob, old Camel Knees himself, would have trouble meeting this one's standards of correct behavior before a judgmental god. Martha begins to fascinate me. She teaches me that though I might fret at what it means to be female, there are those who take a terrible pride in it. She is still a virgin, not having had her first menses, yet she is a woman. And if God has decreed, as men claim, that a woman must cook and a woman must weave and a woman must bear all the burdens of a house, and none of its pleasures, then Martha will cook and she will weave and she will bear such burdens without pleasure as would make Eio bite. There is nothing of "woman's work" in which Martha does not excel. There is nothing expected of a woman that Martha does not do and then uphold as if a kingdom depended on it. Where then is the man who would wed her? I have seen no sign of him. Could it be that though men might demand a woman be more precious than rubies, they do not enjoy living with such a woman?

Seth has no answer for this. What does he know of women when the women he knows are girls who have lived half their lives as boys, a companion who was once a slave as well as a *zonah,* and a mother who is yet a queen, and who builds palaces for kings?

Where some months back I would sit on one side of the woman Sarah, while her daughter Perpetua sat on the other, now I sit by the head of Eleazar while Martha takes her place by his feet. He is slowed by his illness but not silenced. He babbles of a horse he hopes Father will buy him. He gabbles of how he shall make sure his slaves take care of this horse. Peeling an orange for Eleazar, whose fondness for oranges is as excessive as his sister's sense of duty, I idly reach out to Martha, idly enter her, and for a moment, there is . . . nothing. It is as if she were empty of sensation, of thought, even of self. How odd. I reach further and further, and then suddenly I pull back as if I were scorpion stung. What terrible black chaos is this? I cannot describe the hatred. How she loathes me. How she loathes Salome. Never in all my life, not with Caiaphas and not with Izates and not with Simon Peter himself, have I known such abhorrence of my person. I catch her eye, and there is nothing there. It is as empty of feeling, other than pious rectitude, as ever. Does she know how she hates me? It seems she allows herself only to know that she disdains me. But what have I done to cause such hatred? What has Salome done? And then, as clearly as dawn in the wilderness, I know. We left Father's house and his protection. We have not taken husbands, nor have we taken helpless refuge with brothers or uncles. What men would make of us seems not what we are. In short, we have not followed the Law. For this, my cousin cannot forgive us.

If I were Martha, the daughter of Pinhas ben Yohai, and she were me, perhaps I too could not forgive such things. Poor Martha. But if she detests me now, how much more if she knew my pity?

I write long letters to Philo Judaeus and to Addai and to Tata, knowing there is always someone who will deliver what it is I write, eventually. I wait for Salome's strength to return. I read to her from the new work of Philo, which was inscribed to us. In the afternoons, now that Nicodemus has gone back to his own home in Bethphage some four stadia from here, I spend an hour with Father as a loving daughter would with a loving father, albeit a learned daughter who therefore speaks to him of things that cause him wonder. I do not tell him of my time in the wilderness, or in Samaria, or in Galilee, or in Gaulanitis, but I do tell him of Egypt. He tells me how his glass factory fares, exceedingly well; how his ships sail, only three mishaps in eight years; how goes his position among his peers, he is risen not only in age but also in stature, being appointed to a small group who petition Tiberius personally. It startles me. My father's name is known to the emperor Tiberius.

Though times continue unsettled, and as Nicodemus has said, grow more unsettled so that here and there it amounts to hysteria, Josephus remains a fortunate man. He tells me of his life in Bethany. That Naomi continues empty-headed and empty of womb, that Rachel continues a widow and not a wife, and in neither does he find good company. He misses my mother, Hokhmah, as he would miss a limb. He longs to return to Jerusalem where he came as a young man from the town of Arimathaea to seek his fortune, but brigands become more menacing rather than less, and this in spite of Rome's increasing presence. He tells me without telling me that he fills with pride at what I have become, but that he would give half of all he owns to have me his son. I tell him without telling him that I understand. I see also there has come a certain darkness in Father, a certain aimlessness. Where once he would fill his days with business and with the importance of his position, now that he has business and importance to spare, it seems there is more time to fill and less that satisfies.

In the evenings I talk with Seth as I have always done, of philosophy and of poetry and of my dreams of a school in Alexandria. And he listens as he has always done. It is as if that terrible moment above the village of Bethsaida had never been. I tell him I shall teach what I have learned from him, what it is he has made of the inner Nazorean, and from which will bloom thoughts as sweet as Tata's roses. Is it too much to hope he might wish to teach as well?

Seth laughs, saying that Socrates would call my school a "Thinkery." Socrates would call me a Great Sausage bloated with Bamboozle. Seth tells me that when Aristophanes wrote a play about Socrates so that all might mock him, Socrates sat in the theater and laughed. The Holy Socrates laughed and laughed.

I do not laugh, but I have found a smile.

In this way, Mariamne grows into her new skin. And it seems that as Job once survived his grievous afflictions, I will survive mine.

⌒

I have spent the whole of the night in the room of Eleazar. Throughout this night, he has coughed. There is more blood in his sputum, more fever in his limbs. Now and again, Martha has entered the room, laid her hand on the brow of her brother, then left again. It is now the first hour of the morning. The servants and the slaves have been awake for hours, preparing Father's house for the day ahead. The large black guard dogs are already locked in their kennels from their night of patrolling the grounds, for these days the rich and the privileged cannot be too careful. I close my eyes, almost slip away into sleep, but again comes Martha. Fully dressed, fully awake—does she come or does she go? She leans yet again over a fretful Eleazar, fevered and sleepless, and she speaks to him.

By what she says, I learn that Yehoshua the Nazorean has come to Father's house.

I shake my sleepy head, rub my eyes. I do not understand. How can this be? Has Seth invited him? Does he look for me? I cannot think he looks for me.

My heart leaps from my makeshift bed before I do.

The new Mariamne, she who would be as Cleopatra, jumps after her heart, dresses hurriedly, and is now hiding behind a row of potted roses in Father's south garden. Before me is the gate leading out to the road to Bethany proper, behind me the large airy room where Eleazar lies, and behind that the hot rooms and the cold rooms and the bathing pools. Beyond the gate, lies the road, and from the road comes the sound of many people, their voices drawing near Father's south gate. My heart thrums as the strings of a lute thrum. My mind cannot grasp what it hears. My eyes cannot make sense of what they see.

It is true. Yehoshua comes—and he does not come alone.

As Jude and I once walked with Yeshu so that with Eio we were four, now Yeshu is followed as John the Baptizer was followed. A great crowd spreads out in his wake. I see not only Jude the Faithful, but Simon Peter and Andrew and Thecla. The Sons of Thunder and the sons of the Sons, all of these mingle with persons I have never before seen. My spirits rise at the sight of Dositheus who converses with Yeshu as they pass my place of hiding, and sink as I search for Addai and for Tata. Would Tata show her face here? By Law, Father could seize her on the instant. Among the women walks faint Mary, the mother of so many. And now there passes the men who lately followed Eleazar the Bandit, cunning Timaeus and bold Saul of Ephraim.

All this becomes more and more surprising, and all the more puzzling, and by the moment more terrifying.

There is a slight movement behind me, and I know without looking that Salome is come near. I know she too stands and stares. She places her hand on my arm, urges me away so we might not be caught out, perhaps not as spies, but worse, as afraid.

"Why is he come here?" I whisper as I turn away.

"Martha sought him. Martha heard he was near and went out from this house before first light to find him."

"But why?"

"So that he might save her brother."

"Save him?"

"From death. Martha fears Eleazar will die."

Once again I wrong another, for I had thought Martha heartless in her Law.

I crouch in the shadows of Eleazar's room so that I might not be

seen, and I tremble. But my cousin has raised himself from his bed in
febrile excitement at seeing the man second only to the dead Baptizer. Full lit in the morning sun, Eleazar stands wrapped in his own
rumpled bedding, his tousled hair every which way on his large
head. One could almost warm oneself in the heat given off by his
body. Outside his door, Father's entire household is in an uproar,
while the cause of this uproar, Martha, poses in inscrutable silence
near Eleazar, but I know her triumph. She has caused this new
prophet to come to us. She has called him, and he is here.

Yeshu steps into the room. Behind him, there is of course Jude,
and behind Jude—Addai! Addai is here. My heart melts with love at
the sight of him in his humble robe, more humble than any one follower of Yeshu, more humble than Yeshu himself. As ever his face is
as flat and as wide as the moon, and his feet are as bare as the feet of
Diogenes. Sandalless in Father's house, whatever shall Father do! But
my heart would escape from my chest at the sight of Yeshu. His face,
his red hair, his hands, his eyes, their light unbroken. I die with longing to know the friend of my heart once more.

Jude places himself in the doorway, meaning all others must remain in the south garden, which is barely big enough to contain
them all. Over Jude's shoulder, I see the look on Simon Peter's face.
He would push himself forward. But as he cannot, he makes do with
pushing away those as curious and eager as he, calling out, "As he is
dead, have pity for Lazarus!" Simon Peter, ever the rooster and always of Galilee, pronounces Eleazar as "Lazarus."

Yeshu comes up to Eleazar, stands quietly looking at him. But
Eleazar cannot be quiet, not for a moment. He looks from Jude to
Yeshu and back again. He is as I once was, amazed they are so alike.
Eleazar is not fooled. He knows which is which by the Glory in
Yeshu, and from my shadows, I revel in his cleverness. "I know you,"
he says to Yeshu. "I have heard of you. You are a magician. You are a
great magician. So great a magician, you can raise the dead."

Yeshu smiles at him, at Martha. "And I have heard of you,
Lazarus, son of Pinhas ben Yohai. I was told by now you yourself
might be dead."

The high color in the face of my cousin drains away, his jaw goes slack. "Me? Who says this? I am not dead!"

"So I see."

Eleazar sneaks a look at Martha, who does not flush, nor does she turn away. It would take more than this to rattle Martha, who watches all with strict attention. "But if I *were* dead, why, a great magician like you would raise me up and I should continue just as I am now. Is this not so?"

Yeshu lifts a concerned hand. "If you were dead, Lazarus, why should you wish to be raised? Would you so easily turn back from the Father?"

Eleazar does not expect this; he grows confused, and if Eleazar is confused, Martha is furious. What kind of talk is this? A proper self-respecting magician does not talk like this. A great magician would not talk at all! He would say certain words, and he would make certain passes with his hands, and those who have been dead are dead no longer. Who is this person she has asked into her house?

But now, the person she has asked into Father's house asks this of her brother, "If a man has reached the span of his days, why should he not die as all die?"

Eleazar thinks this over, then answers, "Why, because . . . well, because first, the span may be too short. And then people grieve. There is much crying and much unhappiness. And what of the death of children?"

"Who can know when a life is too short? Or too long? Who would be the judge of this? A life is as long as a life is. You would have me drag the spirit back from the Father for the sake of the living? Is this not cruel? Is this not without purpose?"

I see the dawn of understanding cross Eleazar's face, and it excites him more than the thought of being brought out from the belly of death. "I see. I do see," he says, "and if a body is left dead for days, crueler still. Or if it is chopped into bits. Or if a man should be eaten by a lion." He shudders in his clutched bedding. "I never thought of this. Besides, the spirit being perhaps a whole four days in Paradise would be quite settled in, and as for the body left behind, why, there would be such a stink, and such a putrefaction. Who would wish to continue in such a body?"

"Eleazar!" Martha has had enough. She did not ask Yehoshua the Nazorean here for such as this. She had rushed out and stopped him on his way to demand he come save Eleazar, from death, from illness, it mattered not which, so long as he was saved. "Sir! As I believe you are the Messiah, who comes into the world to save us, how should you not save my brother?"

And now Yeshu turns full to her. "I would save your brother, as I would save you, as I would save all men and all women, if you would save yourselves. I would raise the Dead into Life. This task is worthy of a man, and not the one you would ask of me. You require only a wonder, but I would require of you the wonder of understanding. I say to you, it matters not that a man sheds his body, not once but many times, for his Life is eternal. And those who grieve and those who would bring him back into the body, cast off as a cloak in summer, do not understand the Father and have no faith."

Martha opens her mouth and closes it. She opens it again, and I know she searches the Law she has in her head for the right Law, for the one that will answer him, and by answering, silence him.

Yeshu knows this. He watches her as she has watched him, as I watch them both. "Even should your brother die, Martha of the Law, he shall rise again. But why wait he for the death of the body when he might rise now? In this moment, in body, he can know the Father, and by knowing him, can live as fully as the Father lives. This is how the true Dead, who are dead not in body but in spirit, are raised into the Life of the Spirit. This is the resurrection and the Life, which I am, which you are. In me is the resurrection, as it is in all men, and in all women, and he that understands this shall never die." He turns back full to Eleazar, and holds out his hand. "And I say to your brother, Lazarus, who pleases me, come forth."

And my cousin, who has listened to this with all the eagerness of his nature, and with all his cleverness, takes the hand of Yeshu, crying out, "I would be raised into this Life you speak of. I would follow you as those others do." Being Eleazar, he must add, "Although I should not like to be killed by Herod or by the Romans." And then he lifts his eyes from the face of Yeshu, where they have rested this entire time, and searches the room. "Mariamne," he calls, "Mariamne, you too come forth!"

Yea Balaam! I would stopper his mouth if I could; I would pass through a wall! Instead, I cling to it, swaying where I stand.

"My cousin, who even as a female is learned beyond most men," Eleazar enthuses, "though I have thought such a thing could not be, would follow too. Would you not, Mariamne?"

I find myself staring directly at Yeshu. Is he surprised? Is he angered? More, is he shamed to see she who was once as a brother? But before I can know, Josephus, who has at some point entered this room with Seth, speaks up.

"Sir!" my father says in his best Caesarian voice. "I have never heard a magician speak better. *If* you are a magician, which I doubt. Come, share food with me. You and all your people as well."

∝

It is a thing of wonder to see Yeshu at Father's table. But he is here, as fully in the flesh as Father is, as Seth is. Eleazar, so excited he has forgotten that he is ill, perhaps dying, is again allowed at table, where he bobs his big head on its thin neck trying to take in so much at one time. And, of course, Nicodemus sits in his accustomed seat, doing as he is accustomed to doing, enjoying his superiority.

Yeshu has brought along Addai and Simon Peter, and Dositheus and hook-nosed blade-giver Simeon, as well as his brothers, the scarred Joses, and the youngest Simon. Here too is bald Jacob, scowling as ably as ever. Jude is as he always is, by Yeshu's side. There is one other, and this one I do not know. This new one is small, so small I might think him yet a child if it were not for his beard. I hear him called Zaccheus of Jericho. I hear he is not only a *publicani,* a tax collector, but the chief tax collector for Pontius Pilate. How varied, and how unclean, those who follow Yeshu!

All others, Father feeds in his north garden, where there is room enough to seat them all on the stone benches surrounding the main courtyard. Father's household is stretched to its utmost to cater to so many at such short notice, but it is being done. As quick as a harvesting mouse, my aunt Rachel scurries from scullery, to hurrying slave, to garden, and back again. As for Father's table, that is served by Martha, Naomi having gone back to bed with a sick headache, as she does most mornings. Martha's face is grim with the burden of welcomed responsibility.

Me? I am seated quietly by the large hearth in Father's morning room. If I say nothing and do nothing, perhaps I will not be noticed. But no matter if I am, I cannot slink away now, cannot have Yeshu in the house of my own father and not listen to what might be said. How often could such a thing happen? And then there is this: when Salome and I are finally gone to Alexandria, it is a certainty I shall never hear him again.

Martha bustles back and forth, bearing all the food Father can offer, such a splendid meal. No household, short of a king's, could offer more. As she passes, the cloth of her robe brushes by me again and again, as does the clothing of an assortment of slaves who assist her; and now and again Martha hisses down at me to get up off my backside and help, or a pox be upon me and a face full of boils be mine. But I cannot and I will not. This is not the time to make of myself a woman but perhaps a last time in Judaea to make of myself a man.

I ignore Martha. But I wonder at Father. If they should see his table this day, how the Pharisees and the Poor would wail! How they should lament my father's choice of table mate. To eat with a tax collector! To share food with an actor and a Samaritan! To sup with a man without sandals! And what of the builders and what of the fishermen—are they not peasants every one?

But if these are merely lamentable, what of the daggermen who share Father's food? For of these twelve, full six are, or were, Sicarii. Father shares bread with those who would destroy him, and would destroy his world.

If I had no other reason to linger and to listen, I would do so to learn my father's purpose. He is not quite a Herodian, and not quite *not* a Herodian, but he lives for the good regard of others. Or he did. By sharing his table with such as these, save Seth, of course, who is welcome in any house, is to risk not only the good regard of his friends, but their wrath. This too: for all that Father knows, he risks his life. Therefore, I admit this crosses my mind, is Father to be trusted? If Father is endangered in the company of such as these, does Yeshu endanger himself in the house of Josephus?

I must know, for no matter the cost, I would prevent either.

Father leans forward. He looks only at Yehoshua the Nazorean of the criminally red hair. I have never seen him more intent on a man, rich or poor. "I do not know if you are a great magician, sir, I care little for magicians, be they great or be they small. And I have less use for wonders, thinking them used to befuddle the ignorant, and so to lead them by the nose." Nicodemus, closely listening, is pleased to agree with this but bristles as Father says more. "But I think you are a great teacher, even as you are a Galilean, and speak with the rough tongue of Galilee. Perhaps you are even one who comes from the Lord, for no man could speak as you do except the Lord be with him." I think I now see why Father feeds a crowd of dangerous strangers, the unclean and the disrespectful and the questionable and the fierce. He does this so that he might question one strange man. I have rarely known Father to question a thing. What is so is what he believes to be so, and what he believes was taught him by the Sadducee. Could it be that now that Josephus the Sadducee grows older, he begins to wonder whether what he thinks is so really *is* so? Poor Nicodemus! Hearing his old friend now will prove the final ruin of his stomach. "Therefore," says Father, "I would ask you, as I have heard you speak of the dead in spirit, and as you say that one might live as fully as he you call the Father lives, how is it that a man who is dead can come alive again?"

Yeshu, who has been listening as he once listened to me, replies, "I would say to you that if you would live in the Kingdom of God, you must be born again."

Clearly, this puzzles Father, as it puzzles Simon Peter, but it so puzzles Nicodemus that he must rudely intrude. "Indeed? And how can a man be born when he is old? Can he enter his mother's womb a second time?"

Even though he eats the bread of Josephus, Yeshu is not careful of him, nor is he careful of Father's oldest friend. He does not pause to smile, but says, "The wind blows where it will, and your ears hear the sound thereof, but cannot tell where the wind comes from nor where the wind goes. What is born of flesh is flesh, and what is born of the breath is breath. Neither the ears nor the eyes nor the tongue nor the hand know the Father, but the soul knows. Can you be a master in Judaea, Nicodemus, and not know these things? Once again, the body is mistaken for the man. Must the body be born anew for the soul to be born anew?"

If this were the house of Nicodemus, perhaps Yeshu would be driven from it, but Josephus hears this gracefully, for my father can be a graceful man, and from my place by his hearth, I am entirely pleased. Father says, "This word you use, 'soul.' Is this not a Greek word and is it not a Greek concept?"

"Are Greeks not men as Jews are men? A Greek can know the Father and the Mother, as a Jew can know the Father and the Mother, for no man ascend to heaven, but that he come down from heaven, meaning that *all* men are of heaven. To know this, is to be born again."

Yeshu turns as he sits, gazes out over the table, looks past all those who look keenly back at him. Though perhaps keen is not the look on the face of Nicodemus. Yeshu seems to be looking for something. At this moment, Martha, who is yet again passing with a large covered dish, chooses to kick my ankle. By all four sons of Ananias—and I have heard there is a fifth on the way, no doubt a son as well—this hurts! But I manage to keep my silence.

Through my clenched teeth, I hear Yeshu say, "I have heard it said that 'all men and all women are angels of light clothed in the cloth of self, but do not know it; not knowing it is the dark in the center of the soul. This is the heart of gnosis, that merely to know this one simple truth is to be set free.'" Here it is that Yeshu seems almost to see me. I make myself smaller. "I speak of 'setting free' as being born again. A greater teacher than I once said that a teacher greater than she taught, 'Ignorance is all there is of Evil.'"

There are two here who stiffen suddenly in surprise. I am one of them. Did Yeshu say that the teacher greater than himself was a *she*? And the other is Seth, for Yeshu has just quoted him as I once quoted him. He means that the greatest teacher of all is Seth! How Theano, who once told Philo Judaeus that Seth could one day be a great philosopher, would preen! And if Theano would merely preen, I inflate with pride.

Yeshu now says this, "For the Father so loves the world that he would not condemn nor would he judge, such as these are the doings of ignorant fearful men. But rather would he call all to his Kingdom. For I tell you, that if you knew the Kingdom, you would not and could not do harm, or imagine the Father did harm. So how would the Father condemn, knowing that all harm is done from ignorance?"

I love how Seth looks upon Yeshu as Yeshu speaks. I love the awe and the pleasure in his eyes as he listens to these words, knowing he listens to a man after his own unusual heart.

Martha has come to stand by Jude at table. She is setting down her bowl, uncovering it, allowing its odor to escape. She busies herself with removing an empty jug; she busies herself with something else and with something else. She darts dark glances at one and all from lowered eyes. I would swear that she would say something, but as she is a woman, she can say nothing. Besides, what would she say?

"Sir!" Martha's voice carries across all else that is being said here, and as it does, all other voices fade away. I am amazed she would hush Yeshu. The men are quite as amazed as I. In surprise, they turn to her; they cannot help turning to her. What does this woman who serves them, this po-faced niece or daughter of Josephus, want? "Sir," again says Martha, and she says this not to Father whose table this is, but to Yeshu, "do you not care that my sister leaves me to serve alone? Bid her to help me."

I cannot help myself. I am overcome with admiration for Martha. She will speak her mind no matter what. And how Father scowls while all other faces but Addai's are varying degrees of red surprise, even Seth's. But then I remember myself, and by this I forget Martha on the instant. Like Eleazar, she has brought attention to one, *me,* who does not seek it, who would actively wish it away. I sink where I sit.

"Martha, Martha," says Yeshu, "you are careful and troubled about many things, save the one thing that is needful. But your sister Mariamne chooses the good part, which no one shall take from her."

I hear no more for I have bolted from my place and am gone.

"John!"

I have taken refuge in Father's *caldarium,* yet am I found. Slipping away from a bench near the pool where I have huddled into myself, I seek steamier shelter. How is he here? I have thought that the heat and the thick steam in the air would hide me; for all that concerns me, all that *consumes* me, is that I should not be seen.

"John. You must not run from me a fourth time."

There is nowhere farther that I can go, being already at the farthest recess of this huge room. There is no exit here, no further room, and I, Mariamne Magdal-eder, must finally turn and face Yehoshua the Nazorean.

I stand and I wait for him to appear from out of the clouds of steam. As I thought he never would, Yeshu has come after me. As I thought he never would, he has come alone.

"Have you forgotten your promise, John? Did you not say you would walk with me?"

My voice is as small as my courage. "John would walk with you, Yehoshua, but I am Mariamne."

"And where is the difference?"

Yeshu walks forward, very slowly, one small step and then another, and I see he thinks he must be careful of me. He thinks me a wild thing. He thinks if he should do or say that which would frighten me, I will be gone. Yeshu is right. Though his voice is as beautiful as the steam, I would flee it on the instant.

As he comes, he says, "I would tell the truth for John the Less would have no less than the truth." Yeshu takes one step forward, and I one step back, coming close now to the edge of the pool. He stops, and by his stopping, I stay in place. "I would have you hear me, John. I would tell you that when first I learned the name Mariamne, the daughter of Josephus of the Sanhedrin, I felt a great anger. Were you not Eve? Had you not tempted me? Had I not been deceived? For days after, though Jude said nothing, and though I said nothing to Jude, how disgraced I thought myself. To be tricked in this way. To think you a man, and therefore like myself and like other men, worthy of regard, and believing this, to speak so to a woman. I would shudder to myself. Had I not told you that which I had told no other?"

I can hear no more of this. Why would he hurt me so? Is it not enough that we see each other no longer? Yeshu must sense this, for he puts out his hand, and though he is not close enough to touch me, yet he is close enough to allow me clear sight of his face. I see the steam become dew on his red beard, see it gather on his brow. I see myself reflected in the soft brown of his eye. I am frightened.

"Mariamne, as you love me, hear me. With this last unworthy thought, I knew my true folly. I had told you what I would tell no other, and why? Because you were a man? If this were my reason, I should have told most of those I meet, for are these not also men? I spoke my heart to you because you were *you*." He steps closer, I step back. I feel the edge of the pool. "Only a man is worthy of my regard? I could think this of my true mother, Anna, and of my sisters? And how was Mary, who bore me in suffering and nursed me in suffering, less than myself? Rather, I should bless her and worship her, for she is my one support on earth. And where came such thoughts of my friend, John, who is Mariamne? Where *came* these thoughts of women? Were they *my* thoughts, and had I come by them through my own fine reason or through my loving heart? I answered myself in this way: they were not mine, but came from others. Repeated by men, generation after generation, they come not with thought, but without thought; I was no more than an echo. And my punishment for such witless presumption? That I would lose my beloved John, to whom I could speak my heart. To lose she who understood me as I could not understand myself. You have not harmed me, Mariamne who is John; it is I who have harmed you."

"Harmed me?"

"I come here to Judaea, where I am not loved, to seek you out."

I have heard him. He has said what I would have him say, and yet I would push him away. Is this my error of cruel pride, as his was the error of cruel thoughtlessness? Would I hurt him for his hurting me? Without humor or pity, I cry out, "Then you know I am called demon ridden?"

By all the stars and by the pure black skin of the goddess Nut they are affixed to—there is his smile! He attacks me with his beautiful smile. I have no defense for this.

"As am I, John. As I am demon ridden. I am ringed round with scribes and with Doers of the Law. I am stalked by the Pharisee who face me, and by the priests who do not meet my eye, but who instead send their spies. And so many of these proclaim that I do what I do not only with the help of demons, but by the power of Beelzebub, which is to say by the very Prince of Demons. They say with the help of Beelzebub, I cast out demons."

In my surprise, I forget my wounded pride. "But where is the logic in this!"

"Exactly! And do I not say as much? I say to them who say this to me, how can Satan cast out Satan, and why? I say that if a kingdom is divided against itself, it cannot stand, and if a house is divided against itself, it cannot stand. If Satan should rise up against himself, and be divided, he too cannot stand. And if Satan cannot stand, there is an end to him."

"And what do they say to this?"

"Their reply is always very elegant. They seek the biggest stones."

And there it is. I am Mariamne, and I laugh. In sweet and honest eagerness, Yeshu also laughs. He takes my hand and he presses it and, through his laughter, says this, "I entreat you. You will walk with me, John?"

Through my laughter, I say, "I will walk with you, Yeshu. But I walk as Mariamne Magdal-eder, named this by Seth, though he has never said why."

Yeshu's grip becomes painful. "It matters not if you are called Mariamne Magdal-eder or if you are called John the Less. What matters is that you will walk with me, for by your loss I have learned this great and terrible thing—no other is more beloved of me."

Lost in Pity

Month *follows month* as we walk, until the seasons come full round again, and the fame of Yehoshua the Nazorean, already grown large in Galilee, grows larger still, until no matter how secluded the place, crowds await our passing. Everywhere the people are near hysterical with the thought they live through the End Times, become all the more hysterical as prophets, competing in holiness, shout, "Repent, or suffer the Wrath to Come!" Yet still they come, many and many more, to hear Yeshu talk of gnosis.

And if fame grows, so too does infamy. There can be no doubt that those in high places are aware of Yehoshua and must lay their plans accordingly. For if John was a danger to the unsound throne of Herod Antipas, so too must this one be. And if John was a danger not only to the high priest Caiaphas but also to the Law itself, this one is equally a danger. And if the people call him messiah, by which they mean king, he threatens even Tiberius, for Rome claims this land, and Rome is Tiberius who is not only called an emperor but a god.

It is through this that Yeshu walks, talking of mustard seeds and marriage feasts, of lost sheep and lost coins, of salt and pearls and the leaven in bread, but always offering his peaceable and perfect Kingdom of Inner Glory to those who might *hear* him.

But it seems to me that those who hear him, hear him only with their ears; and these in their numbers panic that worldly kingdoms fall, and they with them, unless they first be saved by the Messiah.

And if he is met by such as these, so too he is met by those who would be saved in other ways. No matter the season, the ill are taken from their dark and airless homes and laid side by side in the streets so that Yeshu might see them. The crippled and maimed work themselves near us. The deranged and the "possessed" are held up by their kin, while the hysterical or the distraught wail on their knees. Little children, or the very old, are sent to plead a case. The rich and the powerful come to respectfully beg we enter their homes. By the memory of John of the River, there are so many, so many, that no one man can bless them all, and by blessing hope they will know they might heal themselves. It becomes truer by the day that those who come to us come not to enter the Kingdom or to be raised into the Life but to be healed in body or mind. They come to be saved from grievous affliction, not to be delivered into divinity, which, though they know it not, is their natural state.

But who could turn them away?

We are overwhelmed with the blind and the deaf and the mute; with weeping sores and festering boils and with palsy and seizures and with stiffness unto death. Flesh rots from bone, muscle withers away, teeth turn black, and eyes turn yellow. If it can be imagined, it can be found among all these. And above the sight, the stink! Above both sight and stink, there is the utter pathos. The supplications made, the piteous begging, the shame they feel for their own misery. If one does not turn away, one can drown with pity. Yeshu cannot turn them away. And as more come, Yeshu speaks less, for who can hear over the clamor of the supplicant?

And still, we walk. For neither the furious nor the desperate will stop Yeshu. In pity, he heals, and in hope, he counters the accusatory, but never ceases his efforts to teach. Accordingly, we go from village to village: Beth Hakerem, Sekhakha, Naim, Harobah, Duq, Kohlat, Milham, and more, and more, so that I know this land better than I know Judaea, and in the villages of Galilee the Torah is loved. We enter also into its cities, Scythopolis, and even unto Sepphoris, where the Greeks are loved more. But no matter if it be city or village or a crossing of roads, not knowing they heal themselves, the people have come to believe that by the mere touch of his robe in passing, his glance their way, a gesture, breathing in the very air Yeshu breathes out, that this will cure them or save them.

Even those who know him best are not immune. Seeing that so many are "cured," Helena of Tyre would touch the hem of his robe, explaining to Salome, "I would that I too were made whole." And such is the power in Yeshu, the very same he would have others find in themselves, that Helena's need for *rosh* is less, as is the blood that has flowed unceasingly these past twelve years.

In no time, if he takes refuge in a home, people tear holes in the roof to lower down their loved ones. If he begins to speak by a well, the market square will grow so raucous, none can hear him. If instead we choose an open place, so many come and push forward, and push forward, he is in danger of being trampled underfoot. And even should he do what he would do privately, if he will eat with one or two, or if he will sit quietly with his mother, meek Mary, and his sisters, the unmeek Maacah and sweet and solemn Miryam, all of whom he has come to see anew as he sees all anew, or if he would sleep, or seek to be alone in other ways, they will find him. He has taken to rising each day before dawn so that he might have time on his own and so that he might attend to the Father. But there is this, and for Mariamne this is a wonderful thing: the monstrous pain has left Yeshu's head, his eyes remain unbroken. I watch for it every day as a fox at a burrow. So far, it does not return.

⋉

Yeshu, and all who follow Yeshu come in time to stop by the sea of Galilee. For it is only by standing in the fishing boat of the brother-in-law of Simon Peter and Andrew, and having that boat pushed away from the shore, that Yehoshua can speak at all. Jude or Simeon, or any number of others, must climb into Joazar's boat with Yeshu and me and be taken by sea to where the people wait, and there Joazar and Simon Peter and Andrew hold steady the boat while Yeshu speaks to the people. Even then, those on the shore will strain so to hear and to be near him, many are toppled into the water. The Sons of Thunder and their sons are forever fishing them out again.

And so it goes. Each day the teaching grows less and the healing grows more. And so it goes. And so it goes. Now, when Yeshu comes near, a deep awe falls on the people. They call out, saying that with John the days of the prophets are come again, but that now a greater prophet has come among them. As they did John, they call out, naming Yeshu king. If he is touched once a day, he is touched a hundred times a day, and the touching becomes more than this, and more, until Jude must gather his brothers around him, and the brothers gather cousins and friends. So that Yeshu must move now in the center of a group who so love him they will put their own bodies between him and harm, even if the harm is meant only to be healed by the new prophet or to honor him.

I look about me and I wonder, does Salome, who walked with John, not resent Yeshu? As we are as we were, I ask her this and am pleased with her reply. "Is it not possible that Yehoshua is as Herod fears, John risen?" In that case, I say, does she not fear for Yeshu? I know I fear for Yeshu, and my fear, like the Hydra, has many heads, as many heads as those who harbor ill toward Yehoshua the Nazorean.

But as I am Mariamne Magdal-eder, and the beloved of Yeshu, who is beloved of me, I walk where Yeshu walks, and by my side walks Salome, and by hers, Helena. Near Salome and me trots Eio, who goes burdened by Salome's cuttlefish ink and her iron pens and her papers and reeds and waxed notebooks, a great burden, but not weighty. Eio is often companioned by an irritable yellow-brown jack that Tata has come by. Tata's animal carries Tata's *panarion*, a medicine chest so full it must be strapped down to shut it. It is about the use of this chest and its contents, and of the proper dosages, which is learned through the workings of the heavens, that Yeshu and Tata hold intense conversations whenever he can find the peace to do so. As he says, there is much to be said for many of these and a great deal to be said for a select few of them. With them speaks also Salome who talks as she talked to John, and though Yeshu knows she is Simon Magus, he makes no comment. All other women walk behind us in a great and talkative group, but they do not walk as inferiors to men because this Yeshu will no longer allow. Man or woman or child, rich or poor, the clean and the unclean, the learned and the unlearned, Gentile or Jew, would walk how and where he or she will. In this way, Tata, who would not enter Father's house, walks openly with Addai, and Thecla with Dositheus whom she has come to value. Now that he is born again, my cousin, Eleazar, runs after Yeshu as I once ran after Seth on the road to Alexandria, tripping over rocks and asking questions, always asking questions, for Father has allowed Eleazar, ill no longer, to follow Yeshu.

I wonder at this. Josephus of the Sanhedrin cannot follow but imagines he might and therefore sends Eleazar in his stead—is this possible?

As ever, Simon Peter strides as near Yeshu as he can, and if Peter loathed me before as John the Less, what must he feel now that Yeshu prefers the company of a female? I make light of his glares and his growls but make sure that there is, if not Yeshu, then Jude, between the person of Simon Peter and myself. Jude makes no remark, but then neither does he speak to me . . . and yet, there is a comfort near him I did not expect. As for Jacob the Just, who hates the sight of me at least as much as does Simon Peter, he keeps a great distance between his person and mine. Simeon walks with the wife of his heart, bitter Bernice, and Joses walks with Babata. Even Jude, on occasion, walks with Veronica and with his small daughter, Norea, who can walk but must still be carried.

In this way, for the whole of one day, I walk with Mary.

I have fallen away from the chatter of bright Babata, and from earnest Miryam, who are become my favorites, just as Tata is become their favorite. I am near now to the mother herself, mounted, as ever, on a large donkey amid baskets of bread, for Mary tires easily. Her son Simon is, for this rare moment, not with her, and her sister, Martha of the Goiter, is deep in talk with the tedious widow Salome. This elder Salome is the daughter of Zebedee the rich fish merchant from Gennesaret who married her off to Judas of Galilee who would birth the Zealots, not that the father could know this beforehand. It seems this Salome and Martha complain of something or other, but as both are masters of complaint, my small efforts among them would go unnoticed. Accordingly, I turn to the mother of Yeshu, and I open my mouth so that I might say something of value, though what it is I would say, I have as yet not one idea.

But Mary speaks first, and speaking, says this, "Have I you to thank, Mariamne who is called Magdal-eder?"

Surprised, I answer, "You confuse me, Mary. What is it you thank me for?"

She touches my sleeve, the slightest touch, before taking back her small hand. "Have you brought my firstborn to me?"

I stare at her. I do not know my answer, for I cannot say that I have not, yet I know truly it was not I who caused Yeshu to love women, and so I think I will answer one way, and then I think I will answer another way, but Mary, watching my struggle, takes pity, saying only, "I thank you and I bless you."

And with that, we walk and talk together until the evening comes down, and I am content for this one day.

⚭

Yeshu thinks to enter the country of the Gadarenes, for perhaps there, he shall be sought by someone, be it man or woman, Jew or Gentile, who has ears to hear and eyes to see. So it is that we set out by the boat of Joazar for the far shore of the Sea of Galilee, and come along Andrew and Simon Peter and Yeshu's brothers, Jude and Joses. Come Yeshu's cousin Simeon and the two Sons of Thunder: Jacob and Simon bar Judas, and the sons of the Sons of Thunder, James and Menahem. Come also Zaccheus, Pilate's collector of taxes, and the once-follower of Eleazar the Bandit, Timaeus, also a bandit. And as I have never seen Gadarene, I must come as well, which makes me the twelfth of these, and I so squeeze myself between the two who do not hate me, Jude and Simeon, that there is little room left in Joazar's fishing boat. In truth, there is barely room enough for Yeshu. But by dint of much to-ing and fro-ing, space is made in the prow.

And then, in the exact moment we would push off from shore, comes running, breathless, "Lazarus" who pleads to join us, and pleads so long and so winningly that Timaeus is caused to laugh and to give up his place to my importunate cousin, saying as he hikes up his clothing and wades ashore, "I have seen enough of the Land of Hippos. Have I not, in my time, robbed it from one end to the other?"

Thus we set off, on a day I think sharp but not windy, cloudy but not clouded, no more so than on many another day in Galilee. And not more than ten boat lengths from shore, Yeshu seems to fall asleep. Though, of course, he does not sleep, he goes where he goes, into the rapture of gnosis. I sit where I sit and trail my fingers in the water, its surface much nearer than I am used to because we are so many. But not until we are well away does the wind freshen, and small waves lick and lap at the boat of Joazar, and not until we are far out into the sea does it begin to seem that a great turmoil builds overhead, with such a slow roiling of clouds that become weightier and weightier with dark, and such a rumbling and a grumbling of deep voices above us, and the wind catches first one side of our snapping sail and then it catches the other. I have long since huddled into Simeon and then into Jude, and then Simeon again. It is now that Joazar's boat rides up the back of a wave much higher than any come before, reaches its crest, and there it seems for one long breathless moment to hang, when at last it tilts down the other side, slapping its keel hard on the water, and by this, rattling every tooth in my head.

Some of us grow concerned, some of us grow very concerned, in particular, Zaccheus, who is a *publicani*, not a fisherman. As for "Lazarus," poor, pale, green boy, if ever he regretted a thing, he regrets his pleading to sail. In truth, I too am not entirely calm.

There are only two fishermen aboard, and these are Andrew and

Simon Peter. Andrew holds fast to the tiller and Peter works with the sail, skills I understand but little. But by their covert glances each to each, I know this much—they too are very concerned. Yet here is something: in this boat, Simon Peter is become quick and he is become clever. The ropes run through his hands and the sail answers to his will, and if there is a man here who will see us safe, it is Simon Peter. And if there is another, then it is Andrew, for he would not lose his brother-in-law's boat. But even so, even so, we toss and we heave and now and again the sail snaps with a terrible crack on the ear.

More than this, we take on water. Comes a wave that washes over the side, and then another, and another.

I think to look at Yeshu—he still "sleeps"! I am astounded. For now we ride up a larger wave, a much larger wave, and we do not ride up it prow first, but in a sort of a sideways wallow, and all aboard are thrown one against the other, and some cry out. I would not be surprised to know I was one of these. But he who cries loudest of all is my cousin. "Master, save us! We perish!"

And Yeshu comes awake on the instant, to look about and to see the tossing sea, and to see that all eyes are fixed on the prow of the boat in which he sits, at this moment higher than any of us, for at this moment, the boat rides up the back of yet another wave. From here, he heaves a great sigh, almost as great as the sighs of the heavens above us, and looks down on Eleazar, but I know he looks also at us, saying, "Why are you fearful, Lazarus? What is it you fear?"

"Dying! I fear dying, Yeshu'a."

"But as you are alive, you can never die. For the self is eternal, and eternally changing. Where is your faith?"

Eleazar, who now has a grip on James, the son of Simon bar Judas, not even death could break, rolls his eyes. For how can he hear when the only self he knows might be plunged into the troubled waves at any moment? Eleazar cannot swim. Few of us can, and even if we could, we are so far from shore few of us have such strength.

And if I know this, so too does Yeshu. In this moment, he stands, and standing, he shouts out over the sea and up into the sky, "Father! As we hear you, now hear me! Lazarus is in distress."

And now, because of Yeshu or in spite of him, the wind begins to die, little by little, and the skies to clear, little by little, and the sea to settle, little by little. And Yeshu, looking around and finding himself heard, sits down in the prow of the boat once more and returns to rapture.

I am not sure what I see in the faces of some of these who follow Yeshu, even in the faces of his very brothers. Do they think him so great a magician that he might be Pythagoras come again, to raise the dead and still the winds? In this moment, I think some learn even to fear him. And I grieve to see this. If this is what they think of him, how shall they hear what he teaches? And what shall they say of this to others? For they will speak of it, this is certain. If they think he is so unlike themselves as to have power over the sea, how shall they know their own power, and how shall they pass on the teaching?

And so we come to the land of the Gadarene.

Of those who stream out for our passing, there are more and more who clearly mean harm. As Yeshu has already said, out from Jerusalem come the spies of the Temple priests and Father's Sanhedrin. Out from the cities come some of the Pharisee and even certain members of the Poor and the Yahad and whoever else feels a grievance for a man who seems not to follow the Law. These ask themselves, Is this new prophet not worse than John? Does he not walk with whomever he likes? Is he not a glutton and a drunkard? And are there not women who eat with him and drink with him and laugh with him, and to whom he is not related? Does he not preach on the Sabbath?

As example, this: Yeshu sat by a well in Taricheae, surrounded by the clamoring piteous, when a Pharisee had pushed his way to the front. "You there, son of man!" cried the Pharisee. "If you would please God, you would keep the Law! Know you not this is the Sabbath!" Without pause in his healing, Yeshu turned a mild eye upon this one, for he harbored no ill will toward the Pharisees, neither those who followed the strict and rigorous Shammai, nor those who followed the milder and sweeter Hillel. For had they not labored hard for upward of a hundred years to teach people to obey the Law so that they might merit God's favor and salvation? And, according to their beliefs, did they not mean well? Laying hands on a woman who could not walk, he said, "Does sickness keep the Law? Does death honor the Sabbath? I say to you that Jews keep the Law for misunderstanding the Father. But I do as I do as One with him."

By this, the Pharisee was so scandalized, he could not choose between taking a step back, so that he might not be contaminated by such blasphemy, and taking a step forward, so that should he throw one, he might not miss with his stone. "Are you saying you are like unto God? Do you claim divinity for yourself?"

"What I do, shall you do also, and greater things than these shall you do, for I claim divinity for all."

Being only one, the Pharisee could do nothing but stalk away in high dudgeon. But later he could complain bitterly of this man to all who would listen, and there were many who listened. Who was Yehoshua the Nazorean to undermine all they had done, and how could they stop him?

And everywhere there are men sent by Herod Antipas, lately disgraced and defeated by the Arab king and constantly pleading with Tiberius to come kill his once father-in-law. Herod also asks of any who will listen, is Yehoshua, John the Baptizer come again?

There are always these in any crowd, and at any time any one of them might strike. And how should Yeshu not know this, being once Zealot himself? Therefore if Jude is not by Yeshu's side, then Simeon is. Or Simon Peter. Or the Sons of Thunder. Even Mariamne goes armed with the Persian dagger of John the Less. For Yeshu would give the world the Father's Kingdom, which is beyond any price, but what would the world offer Yeshu? All know what it offered John.

And this is why in Gadarene I find my knife in my hand sooner than Jude finds his.

We are making our way up a narrow path from Joazar's boat, Jude as ever in the lead, Yeshu just behind, his head turned as he speaks with his youngest brother, the scarred Joses, and I am talking with Eleazar a few steps behind these, when suddenly, there is a great snarling and roaring, and comes rushing out from the mouth of an open tomb in Gadarene a very beast in the shape of a man. Foam flies from its shapeless mouth, blood streams from long curving wounds on its thighs and on its arms, and all of the man-thing is as naked as the day it was born, but nothing like as hairless, and it would surely have bitten deep into the arm Eleazar raises to defend himself, save for the chain that binds it to the rock of the tomb. I could not see before, but when what is surely a madman reaches the whole of the length of the chain, it is stopped in midair and then is yanked straight back, to fall into a quivering growling thrashing heap at Eleazar's feet.

Frozen to the spot, Eleazar stares down at it, his own mouth open in abject horror. As do I, as is mine. Flushing with fear and with shame, Eleazar turns away, only to catch sight of the knife in my hand, and though his mouth cannot open farther, his eyes can and do. As swiftly as it is out, Simeon's gift is back in my belt.

In a heartbeat, Jude and Simon Peter are also upon us, and upon the poor fierce creature struggling on the ground, chained to an ancient tomb, the skin of its hairy belly and hairy neck abraded away by the rusted links in the chain. With its teeth and its nails, and with the stones near the tomb, the man-thing has cut at its own arms and its own legs.

Before Simon Peter can do whatever it is Simon Peter might do to such a wretch, Yeshu is also upon us. And at the sight of him, the madman ceases its growling and its thrashing, and instead, cringes, holding up its chained and blooded hands to shield the eyes in its head, round and red and running with pus and with tears. Immediately Yeshu kneels down, pushes away the matted hair from its face, traces along the length of the chain with his hand, looks back to where this is fixed, and is horrified at what he finds, the leavings of what is fed the creature, and its own excrement attended by a kingdom of flies. It is only now that the smell of this visits us. Who could doubt the madman has been chained here for many months, perhaps years?

"Why is this?" asks Yeshu. "Why is this done?"

And Zaccheus, looking on, answers, "I have seen such a thing in Jericho."

Yeshu turns on him, eyes flashing. "I too have seen such things. We have all seen such things. But *why* do we see such things?"

"If he were not chained," continues Zaccheus, who does not understand what is being said to him, "surely he would harm others as he harms himself."

"What harm is in this man?"

Zaccheus shakes his small head. Again, he does not understand. "As all can see, there is a demon in him, teacher."

"Is there?" Saying this, Yeshu looks deep into the madman, so that I think it must shatter the poor thing's skull. It pulls away, pushing out its arms, filthy with blood and with dirt and with unnamable muck, so that Yeshu will not come nearer. Bearing its blackened teeth so that Yeshu will fear it, it screams, "What would you do with me? I pray you, by your god, torment me not!"

Still, Yeshu does not take his eyes from the madman. "Is there a demon in you?"

"A demon!" howls the man-thing, "I am home to an army of demons. My demons are legion!"

Hearing this, Zaccheus shows the palms of his hands. By so doing he means to say, you see, I am right.

"Why do they torture me, who am only Yair, son of Akiba? I have done nothing. I wish them gone! You! Get away from me! Leave me and my demons be!"

His screaming tears at my heart, even as he revolts and repels me.

It is now that down the path we have started up, come three men, no doubt from the nearest town, each stopping short when they note what happens here, all murmuring among themselves in exquisite horror. Yeshu does not look up at them, but I do, and Eleazar does, as does Menahem, and I know what it is they murmur. The three push at each other, offer reasons to prove that not themselves, but another among them, must take the lead and voice their surprise and outrage.

"Peter," commands Yeshu, and Simon Peter is there on the instant.

"Master?"

"Break this man's chains. I have come here to meet one who would hear me. I have met him in this man."

Without a word of protest, Peter sets about beating away the chains, no easy task though they are rusted with age. In moments, Jude settles in to help him. All this, while the three at the head of the path are joined by a fourth and a fifth, and all the while, Yeshu speaks softly, but with authority, into the ear of Yair, son of Akiba, who claims his demons are legion. I cannot hear what it is he says, I catch only a word here and there, but I know what it is he intends. He means to set this one free, and not only from his chains. If he can drive away Dread, the demon of Sarah, who is the mother of Perpetua, can he not drive away Legions? But first, he must gain the man's trust, and I see that the limbs of the madman go quiet, and I see that the madman's hands unclench themselves. It seems, if not demons, certainly the fierceness goes out of him.

But the men above us have determined one who would speak for them, and this one takes a step forward, calling down, "We know you. You are Yehoshua of the Nazorean. Why do you loose this man? He is unclean. He would frighten our women. He would attack our beasts. Surely, you would not free him to go on in this way?"

Yeshu does not raise his sight from the face of the madman, but he raises his voice. "I would set him free of all that binds him, as I would set you free. I see what he has done to himself, and I see what you have done to him, but what is it he has done to you?"

But the men hear only that Yeshu would free the madman, and if Yeshu has raised his voice, their voices are raised all the louder. "He is unclean! Demons find room in him. Leave this place!" they call down. "Go home to Galilee where such as you are welcome."

And I see two of them bending where they stand, their hands reaching out for the stones on the path, and I know they will straighten and when they do, they will throw these stones. Simeon knows this too. He stands forth from Simon Peter and Jude who beat on the chains of the madman, and behind Simeon stands Joses and Menahem and Andrew and the Sons of Thunder. Simeon shouts up at the men of Gadarene, "If this man holds demons, you contain swine, for only pigs would treat another man so!"

How this infuriates the Gadarene! They bluster and they threaten with fist and with stick, so that Simon Peter, who has broken the chain with one last blow of stone on link, stands away from the madman, turning to face these men as Simeon, and now Jude, faces them. "As God is just," he calls out, "this man's demons would enter you! Run away from here, pigs of Gadarene, before I come to push you all into the sea."

And they do run. They know true Sicarii when they see them, and they hike up the skirts of their robes and they are off before else is said or done. At which Simon Peter and Simeon laugh so hard the hills ring with the noise of them.

Yeshu gives up his own mantle to clothe the man called unclean, and though the poor thing begs to come with us, back to Galilee where he might be safe from his neighbors, or at least safer, we cannot take him. There is barely room in Joazar's boat for us. "But I hear voices, master. They speak vile things to me. By day and by night, I hear them, so that I hear nothing else, so that I cut at myself to let them out."

"Do you hear them now?"

Surprise crosses the face of he who held legions. "No. I do not hear them now."

"Then they are gone from you, and will not come again. Go to your own house, Yair, son of Akiba. Remember what the Father does for you."

By the evening, we are far from Gadarene, settled once again in Galilee.

∝

Following such things, casting out demons and subduing storms, comes another evening during which Yeshu must endure his disciples sitting near, but not too near for their growing awe, and comes another evening where no matter how clearly he says a thing, he is not heard, not even by those who follow.

Seated at his right hand at table, I watch them. What do they whisper, each to each? Are they as those who call him messiah? Do they too think him king? With good, though foolish, intent, do any speak aloud to others of what, being near Yeshu, they would only whisper? And do these others speak to yet others?

I despair of how this goes, for in whose ear does it come finally to rest?

⌀

Near Gennesaret in Galilee, a great crowd has once again gathered to hear Yehoshua the Nazorean. And once again my beloved is ringed round by those who would protect him from the love the people bear him, and once again he begins with silence, and in silence we all wait, for at such a time there is nothing else in the world, nothing, save Yeshu. But on this day, though the sky is as smooth and as blue as an egg, there is a darkness at the center of things that I cannot name. On this day, even Simon Peter is uneasy, as if a storm were somewhere building and building. I am near to Yeshu. I know he is enraptured. We all of us wait, until there is nothing but perfect quiet and perfect stillness; then, and only then, he speaks, saying, "He who will drink from my mouth will become like me. I myself shall become he, and the things that are hidden shall be revealed to him."

"Ahhhhh," sighs the multitude, looking up at him with such a terrible uncomprehending need that that which is dark in this day becomes darker still. If Yeshu feels this darkness, he makes no sign, but goes on speaking in his quiet way, so that some begin to sway at his words and some begin to moan. Here one is moved to call out, and here another. And by and by, more and more murmur and mutter and raise their hands, and then the day is shattered by the voice of a woman crying out, "This is our Messiah!" and at this, a man stands forth, sweat beading his fervent face, and turning to the crowd, he calls out, "This is he who comes!" And then another man shouts, "This one is our very king! And another cries, "Seize him! This very day, we shall take him to Jerusalem!"

And more and more and *more* of the same, until the crowd presses forward like one great beast, and Jude and Simeon and the Sons of Thunder push them back and push them back, but still they come forward, and it is only by moments that Jude and I manage to catch hold of Yeshu's arms and to pull him back into Joazar's boat. Simon Peter and Seth and Thecla clamber aboard, pushing away those who would also clamber aboard, and then as one they take us away, away. Even so, there are those few who swim after us and those many who run along the shore calling out, "Yehoshua is the Messiah!" and will not leave us, not until we make our way far out onto the sea. And there we remain until it has gone full dark and there are none left to make Yeshu king.

But the day after this day, Jacob the Just goes back to the wilderness, and with him goes Andrew of Capharnaum and Timaeus the Bandit and all those who shave their heads until the Temple is cleansed. "As I love you," says Jacob to Yeshu, "this is not my business. As I love God, I must do my own work."

Yeshu kisses him and, without protest, lets him go.

As we settle to sleep this night, I see the despair in Yeshu's face. I see the beginnings of broken eyes. Reaching out, I touch him, saying, "Perhaps you ask too much, beloved? The people are as children and you must treat them as children."

"What then am I?"

"You are as a father to them."

"In that case, I should beat them for their stupidity."

"In that case, you would be Yahweh and not Yeshu."

Yeshu laughs and laughs. I would seldom hear that laugh again.

Often now, Yeshu is weary. Though he makes no mention of it, it is in his eye and his skin, in the simplest movement of his hand. No matter that I select the best in the markets for his supper, he grows thinner, and I am made uneasy that he will know his pain again. This day, when Hanukkah is gone by for another year, as is the planting of barley and of wheat, he is become shaken in the bone by what has come of his teaching, and would seek solitude.

So it is that today we rest.

There are seven who sit on the banks of the sweet Sea of Galilee just south of Capharnaum. Behind us rise up the mountains of Galilee, coming so close to the sea there is only this narrow strip of land between water and mountain. On this day, Joazar's boat waits quietly at anchor. Others who follow are scattered wherever and however, and if I did not know better, I should think the world a safe and quiet place, and I would think that any time now Salome and I could set sail for Egypt. Perhaps taking Seth, perhaps taking even Yeshu? It is not impossible. It is not an impossible dream, and sitting on the shore of the sweet water sea I dream it, as I still dream of Kush.

Under the nearby mulberry trees, and sheltered by tents from a mizzling rain, Salome sits with Helena as well as with the mother and aunt of Yeshu, though I know she is not truly with them. She is with John, which means she bends her diligent head over her scrolls and her inks and her reeds. Others of us have gone seeking diversion. They travel by boat farther south to Taricheae and some even on to Tiberius. Herod's new city is a mess of timber yards and full loud with the cries of builders and the pounding of mattocks, yet it provides much that should divert them.

Simon Peter has gone home to Perpetua and to Mark, though if he remains the Simon Peter I have come to know, he will demand food of his mother-in-law and he will frighten his son and he will lie with his wife, and he will be gone in the morning. Tata also visits in the home of Simon Peter to see that all remains well with Sarah, but she will not stay the night. With Tata has gone Miryam, for Yeshu's youngest sister has long since become attached to Tata. If Tata remains the Tata I dearly love, and she does, by now the innocent weaver Miryam knows much of honey and of laps and of lifted heads.

Where we sit on the bank, a catfish noses out from the water, then sinks away again. Four turtles are stacked on a sunken log like newly washed bowls in a scullery.

Seated next to Thecla, Addai's old friend Dositheus holds forth on the interesting fact that the god of the Jews does not have sexual organs. Says he, "The priests of the Temple claim this one has created the world by will alone." By now, Dositheus never uses the forbidden name, Yahweh, or even those names allowed, such as Adonai or ha-Shem, but only the name Plato gave his Maker of the Universe, Demiurge, or Craftsman, because, as says Dositheus, "This god has fabricated a copy of the higher world, which by its nature can only be base imitation." But where Plato thought the Craftsman worked to the best of his ability, and therefore his copy is as good as it can possibly be, Dositheus thinks the Craftsman is flawed by self-centeredness and arrogance and the desire to dominate human affairs, and therefore his copy is fatally flawed. He calls him the Jealous God, and sometimes, Sakla, which is Aramaic for fool. Salome has seen the point he makes by this and she has asked, "If Yahweh is the One and Only God, there being no other gods at all, and if Yahweh is good, what is there to be jealous of?"

Dositheus speaks on, "Now this is an interesting thing, calling forth by the will, which is the basis of magic as Joor once taught us, and I would debate it with these Yahwists if their god were truly the Supreme Being, and not the chief material Power, or Archon."

Eleazar, leaning over far enough to fall as he sits near us, though not quite with us, pretends to skip a pebble over the water, and Dositheus follows its course with a gloomy eye. "More and more, I come to believe as it is taught in certain secret sects that there is a realm of the spirit which is Good and is called Pleroma, and over against it there is a realm of matter which is Evil and is called the World. I am entirely convinced that it is not the Supreme Being who calls this World forth, but the Demiurge who is the Master of Matter. And into this evil matter we have fallen, and cannot find our way out again, being tormented by the *nephilim* who mimic the Divine, but who are lesser deities of the chief Archon, and evil in themselves. Enoch's book calls these the fallen angels, and this sits well with me."

Yeshu is staring out at the sea, but he is listening, especially now as Seth is moved to reply to Dositheus of Gitta. "You would have two realms, then? One Dark and one Light, each antithetic to the other, indeed, opposed to the other?"

"I would."

"And therefore you would say that duality is at the root of all things, as is conflict and discord?"

"Yes. I believe this is where my thought takes me."

"As it takes others. But tell me, in this world of Evil in which we take vital part, consciously knowing no other world, have you come to believe that men and women themselves are evil?"

Dositheus holds up his hands, his woeful face wreathed in worry at the very thought. "No. No. I cannot bring myself to think that, though there are surely evil men, or at least men who do evil. But Evil is, as you know, one of my favorite topics, and I have yet to think to the end of it."

"As it is mine, Dositheus. And who has come to the end of it? But it seems to me that rather than use Plato, you might as well call your ignorant Craftsman the evil spirit Ahriman who opposes the god Ahura Mazda, for all this is so much Persian thinking! If we are helpless before Evil, which is outside a man and not inside a man, you take from us our splendor. By this we are no more than creeping things, scurrying from under a sandal; no more than spent leaves, blown this way and that."

Dositheus sighs to hear this, saying, "By this, I have given man his innocence. I have given him the Good as his home."

"It seems to me," replies Seth, "as it did to Parmenides of Elea, that the very thoughts of man and of woman *are* the world, and if there is evil in it, it is *our* evil, and if there is goodness, it is *our* goodness. I maintain there is no battle between Good and Evil that is outside the self. There is only a mastery of the *eidolon,* or smaller self, that leads to Knowing. I believe gnosis is the door to the Kingdom of God, which is the immeasurable Age, or Aeon, of Truth. And it is neither good nor evil, but all things, and felt as love."

I see Yeshu lift an eye at this. I see him regard my teacher Seth, and I allow myself the slightest step beyond his skull. As I admire Seth, Yeshu admires Seth, and how this pleases me! But Dositheus, who has heard all this before, leaps before Seth can draw breath for more of the same. "Just so. Just so. Any day now, sir, I shall finish my book, which I think to call, *On the Origin of the World.* I pray you will read it."

"Dositheus! I should read anything you have written, for yours is a worthy and admirable mind. But, on this, wrong."

And so it goes. And so it goes. This is not a new conversation. Seth and Dositheus once talked like this endlessly. But lately, Seth's heart is not so engaged in such things, nor is his mind. Lately, he has taken to listening to Yeshu, and talking to him, and though Yeshu does not know the half of what Dositheus knows, and not a fifth of what Seth knows, he knows what neither of them know: Yeshu knows Glory. Yeshu has opened the door to the Kingdom. By this alone, Yeshu might be the Perfected Man. And by this, Seth, who follows no one, and would follow no one, follows him.

Since John died, the simple sadness of Dositheus is become dread. This saddens me.

Seth touches Yeshu's shoulder. "Yeshu, what say you? Do you agree with Dositheus the world is a creation of the male Demiurge, who is the chief Archon of Evil, and who does not know his mother, Sophia? Or would you say it was the reflection of Source, which has no gender, and is neither Good nor Evil but endlessly creative?"

Here it is. Dositheus believes the world a thing of a flawed god's evil making, into which we are fallen. Seth believes the world entirely what man would make of it, and a place of magical intent. If Yeshu does not agree with Dositheus, will he have lost him? Beside me, Addai stirs. He knows where this goes. He too fears the loss of his old friend from his days in Sepphoris and his travels with Jael, a friend older by far than any other. Waiting for Yeshu's answer, I think, but what if Yeshu does not agree with Seth?

Yeshu does not move. I know he values Dositheus and listens attentively to his ideas of Dark forces and forces of Light, and helpless fallen humanity caught as the playthings of malevolent darkness. For all his cleverness with the Pharisee and with the Poor, Yeshu is no politician, he must answer truthfully.

This is his answer, one that those who clamor for health or for safety never hear. "I would say that all things must be weighed against the heart. I would say that if I look into my own heart, I see that the Mother and the Father's world is a reflection of man who is a reflection of the Parents and is therefore beautiful even to its most inward parts. To see with the eyes of Glory is to be enchanted. Each thing, animate or inanimate, glows with the force of its own unique perfection, unfolding with the genius inherent in all that is. I would say that it is only man's not knowing his source that is evil, for by his fearful ignorance he does evil."

Dositheus, who has been holding his breath, lets it out slowly. He is relieved; there is room here for maneuvering. But I see also this: Dositheus thinks himself into a place of true sorrow and despair. Step by step, and thought by mournful thought, he takes himself into a tortuous ravine of the mind where all is hopeless and all are helpless and all are beset by ravenous evil. And I think he would not think any of these things if, even for only one brief instant, he could know Yeshu's Kingdom of God. For then Glory would fill him with love for this world, and for all that it contained.

∞

Two men have found us. Both are clearly Pharisee, though the Pharisee are not many in Galilee, nor are they strong. Almost swifter than thought, Jude is risen from his place on the shore of the sea, his curved blade in his hand, though it is a knife unseen if one is not looking. No mystery why, for though one man bears the marks of a once terrible disease of the skin, the other has certainly come for mischief. But Yeshu rises to make welcome these Pharisee, saying, "What would you have of me?"

I hear the sighs of Simeon and of Jude, even of Addai. I sigh as well. Yeshu is forever doing such things, which means we forever find ourselves in many a strange and dangerous place.

So it is that an hour later we are in the house of Simon the Leper, a man in the salt fish trade in the town of Taricheae. And so it is that Yeshu and Jude, Addai and Seth and I sit in the Jewish fashion on Simon's stone terrace as servants hold umbrellas over our heads so that we might not feel the slight rain.

There is, as usual, danger here. And Yeshu, as usual, knows this, but he plays with his fate as he plays with such as Jacob the Just. But no moment has passed that Jude takes his hand from his robe. Nor does Addai, and by this I am suffused with pity, for I know that he could not well wield the knife he carries. As for Seth, his eyes miss nothing, and if there is not a knife hidden somewhere about his person, I should be most surprised.

Simon the Leper of Taricheae, and his friend, the ill-willed Phabi of Nain, have fed us and have talked with Yeshu and, over the course of this long afternoon, have not yet found a single thing to condemn him for. We all of us know this is why Yeshu has been invited into the house of these Pharisee, just as he is often invited into the houses of certain Poor. Though no sect means him more harm than another sect, all would protect themselves. They would find him out, and who could blame them? With the death of John, Herod Antipas has become most irritable on the subject of the Anointed One, the Mashiah. Poor Herod must surely have thought that by his killing of this particular "king," the subject of kings would fade as dye fades, but it has not. It grows darker by the day. If I were the son of the great Herod, or his wife, Herodias, I would be secretly shaking my fist at Yahweh.

But now we sit quietly and sip the wine we have been given, which is as vinegar to the wine Father would serve. And as we do, Phabi of Nain turns to Yeshu and asks if Yehoshua the Nazorean is as John was, why does he eat meat? And Simon the Leper asks if Yeshu is as John was, why does he drink strong drink? And Yeshu tells them he is not as John was; he is as he *is*, but, as usual, they listen only to half of what they hear, and hear only half of that.

Certainly Phabi hears nothing until there comes a commotion at the far end of Simon the Leper's street. Jude is, as ever, first on his feet, and I am not far behind him, so that now we are both leaning over the low railing of worked stone on Simon's terrace looking down on the street below. Around the side of a house as large as Simon's house come two huge slaves, each bearing a silver tray, and on each tray, the petals of roses. In all our travels I have yet to see anything like this. Who comes?

Behind the slaves scattering rose petals, stride two more enormous slaves who call out from side to side and up to the second story and to the third, "It is she who comes among you! All those who would know their fortunes! Come out! Come out!"

I am now as alert as Jude. What fortune-teller is as rich as this one must be? To own such slaves? To squander roses in this way? And what sort of fortune-teller is announced at the top of a slave's voice?

I am not the only one so interested and so curious. Out from their doors come the wives of Taricheae, and out come the husbands. And out come the very young and the very old. For a teller of fortunes, rich or poor, is always a thing of great excitement. Who would not hear of themselves? Beguiled by the litter of "She Who Comes Among Us," there seem as many on the wet street below Simon's terrace as would be on a feast day.

And suddenly, I am as alert as Salome at mention of Pythagoras, for it seems that I might finally see the sorceress of the Pool of Siloam. It *must* be she, because Addai, also hanging over the wall of the terrace so that he might see, fair shouts, "Megas of Ephesus! How Tata shall rue that she misses this!" And I think, even Salome as she is now will rue that she misses this, for there was not a day of our childhood we did not wonder at this Megas, once mentioned by Ananias at Father's table. Is she not a woman who did not then, and does not now, live through a man?

By now, not only Jude, but myself, Seth, Simon and his fellow Pharisee, even Yeshu, have leaned forward so that each might see down into the street a story below us.

Comes a harsh intake of breath from my left, and I hear Phabi hiss to Simon, "By the hat of Zeus, brother! It *is* Megas! I would know her slaves and her litter anywhere. How dare the harlot to show her person here this day!"

Below us, the entire procession comes to a halt under the terrace of the house of Simon, and it does this because the way becomes too difficult. All of Taricheae seems here. No one yet sees the sorceress. For all we know, behind her curtain, she softens her skin with bean meal, or scratches her belly, or is in deep communion with the gods, or her pick of the goddesses.

Her slaves shout out as those who called the wares of Ananias in Alexandria. "You or you! Yes, *you* with the limp. Would you hear what my mistress might say? Or you? You look like you could use a shekel or two. Seek your fortune through the lady! And you there! A sorry specimen like you needs all the help he can get. Or you, you are surely a farmer! What else would a farmer know, but which of these maidens to plow?" Oh! Much blushing and barking. Oh! How the Pharisee whose house we grace bristle with horror. Speaking of such things, openly, before Adonai and everyone! Meanwhile, the litter is set down in the middle of the street, its bearers standing near to keep the curious from harming litter or occupant. And still the shouter shouts, "Come forth! Come forth! For the price of a trinket, whisper your question in the ear of Megas, and hear the answer she gives you!"

At this, so many come forth, the slaves must line them up, first come, first serviced. As for me—the very one once thought a prophet—it takes all of my strength not to run through Simon's house and down into the street so that I too might find my place in line. Think if Megas can truly tell the future! Think of all that I would ask her. Having long since silenced my own voices, I would ask her of Yeshu. I would ask her of Salome. I would ask her of Addai and of Seth and of Tata. I would ask her even of me. What is to become of us all? For surely we cannot be forever walking the roads of Galilee? We should become as Inanna, who was as Isis is, the Queen of Heaven, and who once lived in the Tree of the World with a dragon at her feet and a bird in the branches above her; until the man Gilgamesh cut it down. Inanna was doomed then to wander, saying, "The bird has its nesting place, but I, my young are dispersed. The fish lies in calm waters, but I, my resting place exists not. The dog kneels at the threshold, but I, I have no threshold."

The first of those who would whisper their secret desires and their secret questions into the ear of the sorceress kneel next to her litter on that side which faces the street. But on the side that faces the door of Simon, the cloth is moved slowly away, so that I see clearly and more clearly the face of the harlot. This is more than enough to hold my eye, but I am riveted by what she does next. As I

look down, she looks up. She seems looking for something. But it is
not Simon the Leper she seeks, nor any friend of Simon's. Her
searching gaze has come to rest on Jude and on Yeshu. Immediately
her face goes soft with grief and with yearning. On the instant, it
seems she forgets herself, forgets she would tell fortunes in the
streets of such as Taricheae. Megas the Sorceress, known from Antioch to Gaza, steps down from her litter as Megas, the splendid
whore—for she *is* splendid: tall and slender, proud of bone and of
breast and of bearing—looks neither to the right nor to the left, does
not cover her head or her face, but slips past the worried slave who
would protect her and into the street door of Simon the Leper. And
before I can think more of this, she stands on his terrace.

Yeshu is like Salome, who once showed surprise at nothing, no
matter that she might feel it. He does not speak, nor does he move,
not even when the woman Megas throws herself on her knees before
him without pause or error of choice. Nor does he speak, nor does
he move, when she takes hold of his feet and kisses them. Or when
she looks full in his face, and he sees the tears that flow from her rue-
ful eyes. Her tears flow through the crushed pearl and black antimony of her face paint; they wash over her cheeks and her chin as
the rain once washed over the stones before the House of Thecla, no
less a whore than this one for the taking of five husbands.

Phabi has been quick to reach forward so that he might push this
greater whore away. Simon the Leper has been quick to gain his feet,
and I hear him think to demand of his slaves that they oust this harlot from his house. Jude has not yet moved a hair, nor has he pulled
his hand from his robe and, with it, his knife, but when finally he
moves, it is Phabi of Nain he restrains; as for Simon of Taricheae,
with one look, Jude has caused this one to sit back down on his
bench of stone.

It is now that the woman Megas reaches into her clothing, clothing richer than my stepmother Naomi's, as rich as Queen Helen's,
and from somewhere within, comes forth with a cunning box of alabaster, as pink as the pink alabaster tomb of Alexander. And when it
is sitting on the palm of her hand, she opens it forthwith, and the

whole of the terrace is suffused with the scent of spikenard. How well I know this scent, spikenard from India, as costly as gold, as costly as silk, for did I not carry it for all of my youth in an alabastron I wore round my neck? In that moment, I am a child again. I am a fool for riches again.

Megas would anoint the feet of Yeshu with what is in her alabaster box, though they are coated with the winter's dirt of the road and wet with her tears. She will dry them therefore with the very hair of her head, hair as black as the night goddess Nut, who is the self-fertilizing virgin Neith, the oldest and wisest of all goddesses bringing forth life from herself alone. Megas, who is called whore, wraps her scented hair, as long as the black lands of the Nile, round Yeshu's road-roughened feet, and I watch this as we all watch this, with silent wonder. For clearly she intends anointing his feet with what is not merely spikenard but also the red oil of balsam, and it smells of heaven, and it is the anointing of kings.

Why does Yeshu not stop her? She will place on his person that which is placed on a king, and if Yeshu is a king, then King Herod will kill him.

But Yeshu does not stop her.

I watch the disfigured Simon the Leper of Taricheae watch this as his friend Phabi watches this, their eyes wide with shock and with horror and with the utmost disgust. And I know that word of what happens here will spread throughout Galilee by this very evening, and I know it will reach the gates of Jerusalem in a matter of days. I reach into Simon, only to hear what I do not need my hearing to learn. By this act, Simon the Leper thinks that Yeshu is no prophet nor yet is he a magician, for what son of man would not know who this woman is? Could there be a greater sinner than Megas the Whore, who heeds no man? Could a sinner profit more by her sin than Megas the Sorceress? No man who walked with God would walk with such a one, and that is as sure as the might of Rome.

Phabi cannot stop himself, he blurts, "Have you no sense, Megas? Your waste appalls me. For the cost of such an ointment, much could be given to the poor."

But Yeshu touches her head, as gently as he has ever touched mine. He takes a tendril of her nut dark hair between his fingers and turns it this way and that, and as he does this tender thing, he quietly says, "Is not the first of the Father's works Wisdom, and is not Wisdom a woman? 'The Lord created me the first of his works long ago, before all else that he made / Then I was at his side each day, his darling and delight.'" The beautiful Megas does not raise her head, but scoops out ointment that might pay a man who has labored a year, and with this, she anoints the feet of Yeshu, first one, then the other. And Yeshu, who does not stop her, looks up, saying, "Simon, I would say to thee this—"

Simon the Leper, whose thoughts have run cold and run dark, pulls himself away from the whore that Phabi calls by name. "Sir," he manages, "say on."

"There was a certain creditor who was owed by two debtors. The one owed shekels to the value of an entire cow, and the other owed no more than the tongue thereof. But when they had nothing to pay, he frankly forgave them both. Tell me, Simon, which of these men will love the creditor most for his kindness?"

Simon, who knows what he is being told and is furious to hear it, answers, "I suppose that he who was forgiven most would love him most."

To which Yeshu replies, "You have seen the thing clearly." Then rising, he takes Megas by the hand she has anointed him with and brings her to her feet so that she stands with him. By a glance, we all of us who love him know to stand as well, for it is now that we shall leave this house. "You see this woman, Simon, and you, Phabi?"

Both Pharisee, who have not risen, an insult Yeshu does not acknowledge, nod. Yes, they see the woman. They will be seeing her for a long time to come, such is their shame at her presence and her acts, and such is their fury at the acts and words of Yeshu.

"As guests, my friends and I entered this house, yet you provided no footbath to wash our feet. But she has washed my feet with her tears, and she has dried them with the hair of her head. Therefore, I say that her sins are forgiven, for to those who know love, all is forgiven. But to those who love little, little is forgiven." So saying, Yeshu turns to the whore who, having nothing else—and by men allowed nothing else, save bondage to themselves—might sell the very flesh of her body. "Who am I to place blame if the Father does not blame? Woman, if you would go, go in peace."

Megas, who has looked at no one but Yeshu, looks on his face as if she cannot look enough. It is as a poet would look on beauty or a wife on her most beloved husband. And then she turns and walks away from the house of Simon of Taricheae. It is a thing to see, and I shall remember it so long as I live.

Moments later, when we too would come away from the house of Simon the Leper, my hearing lingers long enough to know how dangerous is the darkness we leave with these righteous Pharisee. They wonder at Yeshu, marvel that he dares to forgive error, which is what is meant by sin. Only Yahweh or the priests of Yahweh can forgive sin. Just as they gnash their teeth at the daring of Megas, so now they gnash their teeth at the blasphemy of Yehoshua the Nazorean.

But Phabi is darker even than this; therefore his fury is darker even than this. Phabi of Nain would have Megas, though married and father to two sons; he would have her even though to him his desire is a *yetzer ha-ra*, an impulse to evil, and he would have her at cost to any.

At the drawing down of the day, we return to our place on the shore of the sea south from Capharnaum and are met by Dositheus and by Simeon and by the Sons of Thunder, and behind these, so many more grim and grimmer faces. And here is Ananias! Though months might pass between his visits, Ananias is always a bearer of news. What has he come to tell us? Even Simon Peter is here and not lying with his wife, the long-suffering Perpetua. By his face, stricken with some grief, I know on the instant there is something terribly amiss.

So soon as he is seen, Yeshu is encircled. There follows much gesturing and whispering, much pointing at the darkening mountains and at the darkening sea, and as it was with the dreadful death of Heli bar Nehushtan and the piteous widowing of Dinah, I do not understand what it is that happens. Or why. All I know is that Yehoshua the

Nazorean is taken away to where more grim men stand grouped near the tents under the shadowed mulberry trees. With him go Addai and Seth and, of course, Jude.

I am left with Salome and with Tata.

I need not beg; they tell me on the instant what it is the men tell Yeshu. There could be no news more fearful! Ananias brings us word not only of Herod but also of Pontius Pilate. Rome's prefect has lately done two disastrous things, one following on the other. First, because he would build a splendid aqueduct to bring more water to Jerusalem, he has used the corban, which is the treasure of the Temple and is dedicated to Yahweh. I well know the high priest Caiaphas, and to do this, Pilate must have worked out something with Father's old friend. But the people, hearing what money was used, came out in their thousands to spit at the prefect, and to shout abuse. Second, Pilate, knowing this might happen, had sent his soldiers among them dressed as Jews. Now, if these had been Roman soldiers, all might have gone well, but Pilate has few Romans under his command. His troops are primarily Samaritans and Idumaeans, if they are not Syrians, and hate the Jews, as the Jews hate them. Therefore, many soldiers carried not cudgels, but daggers, under their cloaks. At a signal from Pilate, these laid about them with a terrible will, so that Jerusalem's narrow streets ran with Jewish blood.

But so too were they awash in the blood of Galilee, for hearing of this latest transgression against the Law, Jacob the Just had come down from the wilderness to howl out his righteousness, bringing the Poor and the Many with him. Sameas, an elder of the Poor, is slain. Andrew of Capharnaum is horribly killed. No wonder Simon Peter grieves. Even I, who have no love for Sameas or for Andrew, am bereft. But the zealous rage in their fury. In Jerusalem they have toppled the Tower of Siloam; everywhere there are uprisings and reprisals as the news reaches more and more ears. Even Samaria rises from border to border, using this slaughter of the Jews to avenge themselves for the killing by Pilate of their own messiah, whom they called Taheb. At this very moment, hundreds lie beaten and bound in the darkness of Antonia, and of these, there are several who are to be made examples. One of these is Timaeus the Bandit.

Here in Galilee, Herod Antipas does, for me, the most terrible thing of all. He seeks Yehoshua the Nazorean. Is not Yeshu now called king by those who riot in Tiberius and Sepphoris? Do the people not follow him as they followed John? And will not the rioters turn to Yeshu should they triumph in this city or that city, and will he not come, gathering around his person an army of Zealots as large and as powerful as the one the Maccabees gathered?

But there is also this, which makes me sit down in shock. This very day Zaccheus has spoken of Yeshu as the coming king in the great marketplace in Tiberius, the very city of Herod. And he has boasted of Yeshu being near. In my own foolishness, I would curse the tiny tax collector. I would call up a spell to still his heedless heart, if I did not immediately think, if not him, then Simon Peter. Or some other.

Salome tells me that a mere hour after our leaving here for Taricheae, Herod's men arrived, as they must everywhere be plaguing travelers, and not finding anyone fitting their idea of Yehoshua, they set to searching our camp. It is easy to see how they have searched by that which is scattered and tossed and ripped open and trodden on. From Salome—because of course it was Salome who set herself between the women and the soldiers—their leader, a Greek with a high voice, had demanded to know the whereabouts of Joshua bar Joseph who called himself the Nazarite, and whose hair and whose beard were red? "Where is he who goes about the countryside causing no end of sedition?" And for once, it was as a woman behind which Salome found shelter. For being only a woman, how could she know where such a man might be found? Who would entrust a mere woman with such knowledge? Enough of this, and the Greek had walked away in disgust.

Tata assures me that no man has been hurt. No woman defiled. So far, the soldiers have not returned. But they might return. Or if not, they will come for us another day in another place, and they will surely find us. And in that moment they will take Yeshu as they took John, and who knows how such an unthinkable thing will end? I am sick with all this. I am frantic. We must leave, and we must leave now.

But where will we go? We are so many. How will this be done?

Within moments of learning that Yeshu would be arrested, this also happens: Where there was nothing but the evening come down and the rustling of night bird and beast, now suddenly there is the woman, Megas of Ephesus, and there are her slaves, more than I saw in Taricheae; and there are her wagons and the mules that draw them. And there are the horses. Persian horses.

The sorceress has come after us.

An hour later, our people are gone this way and that way, fading into the shadows so quickly and so completely, the camp by the Sea of Galilee is as empty of them as if it, and they, had never been. I think of the white storks that each year pass overhead—the people leave less track even than these. One more hour, and the caravan of Megas, famous sorceress, travels openly along the Via Maris, due south to Scythopolis in the Decapolis. But within it, hidden away in the largest wagon of four wheels, is Yehoshua, famous fugitive. Within it also is hidden Jude, so alike to Yeshu, Megas hides him as well so that he is not mistaken for "he who causes sedition." And though Yeshu might protest, he is not listened to. For this once, Jude is allowed his way, and we all of us breathe easier that this is so.

Once again, my beloved Salome and I walk under the stars, and once again, Seth and Helena of Tyre walk with us. Comes also Eio, her foal tucked under her belly, sired no doubt by Tata's testy yellow-brown jack. And this time, Tata and Addai are here. Though Ananias is not. Our merchant of oil and sponges has gone back to Sapphira and yet another son, and he takes with him my cousin, Eleazar. I have entrusted Ananias with returning "Lazarus" to Father in Bethany, for he can no longer be with us, though his protest rivaled Philo for variety and flow. Nor yet do the women come with us. All these have left for Capharnaum to stay in or near the house of Simon Peter, and there to live with Perpetua and her mother, Sarah, who once again busies herself as suits ten women, she is that much a ruby. When I said this, Salome said she certainly hoped so, considering the entire necklace of rubies about to descend around her neck.

My Salome is, once again, a rock in a sounding sea, and her wit and seeming calmness calmed me. By her remark I was prompted to send a sum of money with Miryam so that she might give it to Perpetua, and that prompted Salome to send just as much.

All others, by which I mean the men, sorrowing Simeon and the petulant Simon Peter foremost among them, have begun the journey back to the wilderness, there to await with Jacob the Just whatever there is to await. The loss of the men was as air to me, all but one—Dositheus.

Our mournful friend does not return to the wilderness, for he would not follow Jacob the Just. Instead, he goes north to Caesarea Philippi in Ituraea with those of John's followers who have always loved him and with Thecla who has long since taken the place of Helena. Where would he go from there? He does not know. Perhaps, in time, to Syria, for he has heard the city of Antioch might welcome such ideas as his. He knows only that a world in which the gentlest and the best, by which he means Addai, can suffer so, is insufferable. He knows only that his work in the world has killed John. It has come to this, says our old friend: it is not against human frailty and fear that one must struggle, but against the Sovereignties and the Powers who originate the darkness in this world, the spiritual army of Evil in the heavens. "It is clear to me now that man is fallen and in need of saving."

In parting, he had kissed Yeshu and Seth, had looked long on Helena, on Salome and myself, and grievously wept to leave Addai, who wept to see him go. And then he turned his face from us, and with Thecla and his followers, was gone from this place.

At that moment, I knew Salome's temptation; she also would seclude herself with the John in her heart. And I too was tempted. How sweet to turn away from the poor and the ill and the ignorant. How sweet to leave behind the pain one man causes another, the striving of each over each, the greed that would have one fellow fat as the Temple and all others as thin as a hovel. I would see no more that which would cause a man to forbid the thoughts of another man, even unto his death. And, by Isis of the ten thousand names, how weary I was of the cruel and brutal assumption of man over woman. In that moment, I longed for *ataraxia*. I longed for my studies and the

company of philosophers, and I shivered in my longing, held it close
as a lover. For that moment, it was all I could do to force my mind
west to Phoenicia, and not south and south and south to Egypt.

But at the last Salome turned toward Seth, and toward the road
he would have us take, that one running south to Scythopolis and,
from Scythopolis, another we would follow west through the Plain
of Jezreel. For Seth means us to travel by these to the land of the
Phoenicians.

Herod Antipas does not rule Phoenicia. Nor will Pontius Pilate
look for us there. But best of all is that somewhere, deep in the
mountains of Carmel, we shall come to rest among the secret Society of the Carmelites.

⋖

Once more we are actors, my childhood friend and I, once more we
dress a part. Stopping in the finest market in Scythopolis, a city
famed as a center for the Mysteries of Dionysus, we have chosen
cloth of gold and of silver. We have visited the perfumers and the
hairdressers. As we once did, again we paint our faces, but we do not
laugh throughout and there are no mirrors.

And now we travel away from the great highway that follows the
flow of the Jordan, turning west onto the wide and busy road that
climbs up into the mountainous heights where stands the town of
Jezrael. And beside us, as we wend our way up, rushes a river seeking
the Jordan which, in turn, seeks my Salted Sea. On our left hand is
Pilate's Samaria, and on our right hand is Herod's Galilee, and to all
who note our passing, we make great show of that which Megas is
and that which both Salome and I appear now to be.

Addai, by his seeming status as a poor Samaritan, must sit in an
open wagon with the servants and the slaves. And so too must Tata.
But as Salome does, as Seth, as Helena, as Megas herself, I ride a horse,
a fine beast, red of mane and tail, red of tossing neck and rounded
rump. And I act as blooded as my beast, knowing that no man would
look for a prophet, much less a messiah, among such as we.

In this world, I have presented myself as a male. In this world, I have been presented as a whore. Now I appear not only as a whore but as a sorceress. I sit my red horse and find myself proud to be thought of as such.

How odd I am. How odd my life.

Hours later and we come to the highest of high points, so that once again I look down into the Valley of Jezreel. Checkered with winter fields and ribboned with roads running every which way, the one we will travel lies already beneath our feet. This is a fine Roman road, and it leads ever west, all the way to the Great Sea. Seth tells us it should eventually take us to Efa in Phoenicia, where we could then go north to Ptolemais or south to Caesarea Maritima. But we do not go so far as Efa. In truth, only Seth knows the way we would go, or how far.

Village after village, no matter whether Samaritan or Galilean, Jew or Gentile, turns out to witness our passing. Farmers come in from their fields, artisans rise from their benches, merchants from their mats, women from their hearths, even scribes from their synagogues. For all the railing and lamentations the righteous do, for all the ink they spill spewing forth invective, when "our sort" appears amongst them, they are speechless before us. So too the Roman soldiers.

There is a place where the road curves full into Samaria, and here we pass close under the forbidding walls of a new fortress. Not one of the men who look out at us offers us less than a hungering glance, as what man would not who gazed on Megas or the night-dark Helena? Or on Salome, whose treasures have been buried for years.

But, of course, we are much too grand for such as these.

Somewhere west of the open city of Gabae, which we ride through with much inveigling from eager merchants, much wonder from the poor, and a certain lofty envy from the rich, we pass a small temple to the goddess Astarte. Not far from this, stands a caravansary, and nearby, a small border outpost. Climbing up and up beyond these, we come onto a great height and from there—Phoenicia. Father has enthused over Phoenicia all of my life. For even though they were once the Sidonians, and though they are yet pagans, did they not invent glass!

I am almost too tired to rejoice at the sight of Phoenicia; it is too late in the afternoon, yet I manage a small smile. We shall be safe here if we are careful.

Overhead the sky is an arching vault of chilled white. Helena drifts farther behind, full hooded and dozing on her horse. Riding side by side, and well wrapped in our own cloaks, Salome and I, who have barely spoken these last few miles, are now wholly silent. Even the sight of shy roebuck we startle out from the scrubby oak does not stir us. But here it is, when we would be silent, that Megas urges her horse forward. It has taken her all these many miles, and all these wearisome hours, to find the courage.

The tiny bells at her wrists and her headband ring, and her anxious breath is a white mist on the cold white air. "As you are the beloved of Yehoshua," she asks, and she asks this of me, "I pray you will tell me of him."

I, flushing from neck to brow, rush to protest, though I do not. Megas of Ephesus would know of such things as Cleopas knows wood. For is it not a type of truth that though we do not marry, nor think to marry, Yeshu is truly my beloved, as I am his? And there is also this: Megas asks with such hunger I cannot resist her. I say, "And how should I start, knowing so much, and so little?"

At this, Megas reaches for me, grips my arm. There is desperation in her touch, and I remember her as she was in Taricheae, and I remember her tears. "I have come away from the goodly homes I have made in Tiberius and in Jerusalem. I have come away from all that I knew, so that I too might be near his person. And as I have found him, Mariamne, who is by him and all others, called the Magdaleder, he has forgiven me! Therefore, what is there I might not do for the Messiah? What is there about him I would not know?"

By the moon, I am horrified. Here is another who would make of Yeshu more than a man! Here is one more who would not see who he truly is. But I remember myself. For here is also one who protects him, and without whom, he might well be taken by now. For this, I owe her nothing but gratitude, and for this, I cannot show my distress. Therefore, I begin to speak of Yeshu, moving quickly from his life to his teachings, for there is much of the former that is not mine to say, and the woman listens as if every word were balm.

Up ahead, a track leads off from the fine road we travel. Where Rome's road is wide and smooth; this one is narrow and rough. Where Rome's road continues west toward the sea, running along the valley bottom and beside the river Kishon, this one climbs south up the slopes of a mountain that has been on our left since coming over the pass from the Decapolis. There have been many such tracks on our way, some going up the mountain ridge, some leading further into the valley, but with a turn of his horse's head, Seth indicates that we will take this one, though we cannot take the wagons. There is no one within sight of us on the road, no one to see what we do. In moments, Yeshu and Jude are mounted on mules taken from their traces. In a few moments more, the wagons of Megas are sent back to the caravansary to be sold. In the very next moment, we are lost to sight of the Jezreel Valley, passing under pines and cypress trees and into thickening mists. Here there are still lesser tracks leading away, and out of these Seth chooses the steepest and least prepossessing of all. It is no more than a faint mark in the steeply rising ground—any who did not know it led somewhere, would think it led nowhere at all—and I am become so embroiled in hoping my horse does not fail in his footing that I do not notice I have caught up to Yeshu on the back of his mule.

It comes, then, as a shock to hear Yehoshua's voice speak out from the mist, saying, "Mariamne, I would speak with you."

Yeshu and I have become the last of those who follow this narrow track up through a narrow defile. If I have thought him tired and worn before this day, I now think him near to grievous ill health. But of all that he says as we ride alone in the mist, what he says last is truly the whole of it: "Of what use my life, Mariamne Magdal-eder, if I do not speak of the Father in my own land?"

I am ashamed. While I have marveled at playing the sorceress and the whore, and have sat my horse in vanity and in pride, Yeshu has been bleeding for the poor and the sick and the "Dead." I entwine my fingers, twist and squeeze my hands until I would crack my bones. How does Yeshu continue to look upon me? How does he call me beloved? Of all those who see me, surely he sees best that I cannot feel as others feel. *Eloi! Eloi!* How is it that I continue innocent, when I am surrounded by a world of pain and struggle? How shallow my cup; how empty my heart! For all my questions and all my philosophizing, where is my pity? Why am I not like Yeshu, tormented by pity? Isis knows, I have pity enough for myself. And where is my terror before the sorrows of the world?

It is in this moment that I feel the touch of Yeshu, who pulls my hands apart, saying, "How can I think so of myself and forget my beloved? As the Father is my soul, Mariamne is my heart."

My empty heart breaks yet again.

We have come out of the mist and over a high and hidden pass, and there, lying as white as Jerusalem under the last of the day's cold sun, is the secret Temple of the Carmelites. Far below is the Phoenician coast with its sand of gold, and everywhere before us shines the Great Sea, under whose deep and turbulent waters the sun shall sleep this night.

"You see, Mariamne?" calls Addai. "The Temple Tower!"

I see. There is a tower here, taller than the tower in the wilderness, and finer by far than the ruined tower of Taricheae. Gazing upon it, Solomon's Song sings out in my veins: *Thine head is held high as Carmel, and thine hair is like purple . . .*

This is the tower of the Carmelites Seth names me for.

I am not worthy.

The Secret Temple
of the Carmelites

*C*oming *to a halt before* the one small door in a white wall, not tall and not wide, we were met by an aged and silent man, also in white. Without words, he signaled we were to wait, then took Seth aside. There was a brief whispering, and from that moment to this, we have not seen our friend, nor have we spoken to anyone else. In the days that followed, and from time to time, we catch sight of this one or that one—there must be upward of seventy here, all white-robed and silent, though not all aged. Unlike the Essenes, but like the Therapeutae, some are women, and each goes about his or her wintry day in orchard or garden or vineyards in silence. As they will not speak, we cannot speak. And our own speech, each to each, is become nothing but whispers.

The first night, we were silently shown through bare hall and bare corridor until we came upon two small chambers and, by simple gestures, were given to understand that one was to be used for males, the other for females. Both were furnished with the simplest of bedding.

We were offered water but no food, for we had arrived after the setting of the sun. It seems that here, once the sun has set, nothing else might be done but quiet prayer and quiet reading.

I find this place strange and silent and uncomfortable, but oddly wonderful. For here, before the coming of the Zealot in all his forms, is what Addai has said our settlement in the wilderness once was. It is a *koinos bios,* a place where lives are lived in common and in peace. Here is where, coming away from Adiabene, Seth spent all the years of his young manhood, and for the first time I understand that his bearing, the white of his clothing, his immaculate cleanliness, his love of quiet and solitude—all these were learned here.

As much as I, Salome is enraptured with this beautiful place. For not only was this mountain beloved of Elijah the Tishbite, but it was beloved of Pythagoras. This much she has learned from her poking into every ancient nook and ancient cranny available to her: that Pythagoras once studied here, and that he once meditated in a cave in the flank of the mountain overlooking the Great Sea.

And as she now spends her time, after finding this cave, sitting in it and working on her remembrances of John, and as Helena is with her whenever allowed, and as Tata and Addai remain near each to each the whole of the day and are content with nothing more than this, and as Jude finds work for his hands, mending this and making that—as all these are preoccupied in one way or another, Eio and her colt and I wander everywhere, and we are followed by a raven of formidable size, and even more formidable intelligence. I name her—whether she be female or not—Nyx, after the Greek goddess of the night.

By now, I must know the place of this place as I know the wilderness. It is smaller than the settlement, colder, silent save for the sound of bird or beast or the distant sea. It has no comforts. It has no distractions. It has no ornament. It has beauty but its beauty is as simple as air or water. Few come here. Fewer leave. But as for knowing its heart or its mind? That might take years, if not the whole of a life.

Megas, finding herself a peacock in a farmyard, sends her slaves away free men, bids them take her horses and her mules so that they might have them to make a new life, then sets herself to living as these cenobites of Carmel do. She cannot join them, for this there seems a long wait, and a testing of the will, but she can emulate them. Even so, over and over each day, she contrives to be where Yeshu might be. Salome remarks that the rebirth in Yehoshua of Megas of Ephesus seems quite as extravagant as her life of sorcery and riches. A thing so exaggerated, and so narrowly placed on the shoulders of some other, even if the other be Yehoshua the Nazorean, surely stems from a terrible fear and an empty despair?

As I have ever said, Salome is good at cruel truths.

In these various ways, we all wait for Seth, all save Yeshu. So soon as he saw this place, Yeshu changed yet again. It seems he now lives such a brilliant interior life, it matters not what occurs around him. In the short time since we came here, I have seen him stand on the farthest point of a rocky promontory looking out over the tossing sea for three and four hours at a time. I have seen him climb down to the small coastal plain below and spend the whole of a violently windy day sitting at the water's restless edge. I have seen him kneel at a small flat stone the Carmelites call Elijah's Altar from one day to the next without partaking of food or of water or of sleep. This, and more, we have all seen him do. And it seems even the Carmelites, who eat little and sleep little and speak even less, have never known the like. Both Salome and I think them in danger of becoming reverent.

○<

I intend to spend the ninth of our cold and misted mornings in the Temple. Because I am come with Seth, the shy Carmelite whose task this day is the keeping of the Temple allows me this privilege. But I think it also true that I am welcomed as a curiosity for I am friend to Yehoshua the Nazorean who astounds them. Where they strive to subdue the needs of the body, Yeshu seems simply to forget them. And then, just as they think him the most holy of men, by which they mean the most self-sacrificing, he will suddenly become almost as the Cyrenaics once were. Taking the teachings of Socrates to what many say is an illogical and foolish extreme, these lived for happiness, and what makes a man more happy than pleasure? Yeshu will "wake up" from his raptures of mind or of spirit and call for food or for drink, even for games of skill. More shocking still is his laughter. Yeshu laughs again! The death of John, the terrible trials of his teaching, the threat of Herod—these seem to worry him less and less. Time and again, his laughter will ring out through the hush of their somber halls, and I have seen some few of them stopper their ears, seen others cringe wide-eyed with fear that a demon rages throughout. They do not know what to make of him. And at these times, he will seek me out, and we will sit and talk half a day away. By this, I tell myself that I continue to know his mind.

But on this day, Yeshu is gone entirely—like Salome, I think he has found a secret place, somewhere Megas might not find him. With all others also gone, each to their place, I take myself to the Temple.

Nyx hops along behind me; Eio trots behind Nyx. And the son of Eio—this little one is never quiet, therefore Tata has named him Babel for the Sumerian god of speech—trots behind Eio. I shoo them all away at the door, then stand within the small entry and marvel at what I find.

Inside or out, the Temple of the Carmelites is to the great Herod's Temple in Jerusalem as the home of Thecla is to Father's mansion in the Upper City, yet as humble as this, it is suffused with a deep and abiding sanctity. The altar is no more than a slab of smooth stone; the walls of the Temple are as rough hewn as Elijah's cave, its floor as uneven, and on the interior altar nothing is placed but a cloth of curious design. Yet all this lack is of no matter, for it stands on what the most ancient of the Egyptian writings called the sacred promontory.

In moments, I discover what I knew had to be so, there are no sacrifices of flesh and of blood here. No animal is put to death to placate a god; no money is required, for it is not home to Yahweh, but to Baal Jehoshua, the Lord of Salvation. Yet I am astonished at this. I stand in a temple to Baal, the name forbidden in Father's house. Baal Jehoshua is the very god my Father and his Yahwist friends call Joshua, the Patriarch, so that he is made less than a god, less than

Yahweh who would silence all other gods. Baal is the god who so vexed the prophet Amos, that among all the other unholy horrors he wished his god Yahweh would do, he called out for the top of Carmel to wither. But either Amos went unheard, or Yahweh proved helpless, for here Baal Jehoshua is as he was. Called Iao, called Jupiter, called Joshua, called Baal Jehoshua, this god is the greatest god. Or so believe the Carmelites.

But look at this. I come now to a further room, and I turn where I stand. I am home! I am as I was when yet a child and newly brought to the wilderness. Above me the ceiling is round as the heavens and full of painted stars. And here is the moon and there is the sun, both shining in the sign of Pisces, the Fish. What I did not know then, seeing it for the first time in the small room under the settlement, I know now, having learned it in Egypt. The symbol above my head is the *vesica piscis* of Pythagoras. Two overlapping circles, one meaning spirit and the other matter; when they touch in sacred marriage— reality! It is both a fusion of life's opposites and a womanly portal through which all things come into being. This "touching," or portal, shape is also the Fish. No wonder the Pythagoreans thought mathematics the secret language of God, for in this symbol is also encoded sacred geometrical formulae. It is also the symbol of Osiris who is the Fisher King, and the mark of Joor's Great Year of Pisces, a time marked by the precession of the equinoxes, which, two hundred years ago, was calculated by Hipparchus.

There is nothing between this secret place and that secret place but distance. In the place of the Carmelites, so much is made clearer to me.

I climb the circular stone steps in the Temple Tower, meaning to look from its top over all for as far as I can see, but when I come in time to the very last step, I find Seth before me. I am not surprised. Before ever I took an upward step, I knew I might see him, for it is a long time since I questioned the still and certain voice within me. I no longer love my voices, and I have never loved the Loud Voice, but by now, I assume the rightness of my inner voice, my very *Daemon*, as I assume the pure goodness of Addai.

I have not seen Seth since first we came here. We have not been alone since Japhia. And now we stand together and together say nothing, and though I do not trespass against him, yet I feel his pleasure in this. Just as I feel my own. I say eventually, "Tell me, Seth, how did you leave such a place?"

He answers instantly. "How is it my Queen Bee asks such a thing?" Queen Bee! It seems forever since he calls me this. "Can you, so full of questions, wonder that I, so full of questions, would come away from a place where there are only answers?" Only answers? I do not know what he means, and he knows I do not know. "They have found their answers here, Mariamne. Having found the answers they seek, they ask no more questions."

No more questions? Impossible. I understand him now.

Once again, we gaze out over that which lies below us: sky and sea and cold gray mist. Directly below, Helena crosses a courtyard bearing some bit of undyed cloth. Toward an outcrop of blue stone, Jude has set his hand to repairing the garden fence that keeps the goats and Eio and Eio's son, Babel, from eating all they might eat. Somewhere below Salome writes of John, and somewhere below Yeshu lives his brilliant life, and somewhere below Tata and Addai are complete unto each other. And I am more than content to know this.

How long we stand in silence at the top of the tower, I cannot say, but when Seth speaks again, it seems perfectly timed. "I cannot love Socrates and also believe I know a thing. If I am told 'this is a truth' or 'that is a truth,' I ask always, *Is* it? When yet a youth, I set out for this blessed mountain, which held, so it was rumored, the highest truth of all. I brought with me only the writings of Plato, and I walked the whole of the way from Adiabene." Here, Seth raises his hands as if he would hold in them the Temple and the mountain and the sea. "And I found a world of answers. Ask any man or any woman a question and you will get an answer. But is an answer the truth?"

Say I, "I think perhaps each one is a truth, of many truths."

"Would my Queen Bee hear the answers of the Carmelites? Would she know what I once thought true?" He need not ask, and he knows he need not. "The Carmelites claim they are the Elect."

I think, who does not think this of themselves?

"They say one can only join the Elect by rigorous renouncing of the world."

I think, Yeshu would ask how one can love the Father yet reject what he has made?

"They say, as says Dositheus, that the world is the creation of a foolish god. They say it is they who shall inherit the Lord's Kingdom on Earth."

I think, How can one inherit what is already his? Or hers.

"And here, and in other places like this place, they await the 'wondrous child' who heralds the coming of the Kingdom. They await the Restorer. They will wait forever if need be. For a time, I waited with them. But I, as I was, could not wait long. I must ask my questions."

Over and over, people everywhere await a "herald of the coming day." They await "the One who stands forth." And here, in this place, they wait for the Restorer. In silence, I thank Isis that the Loud Voice is silent within me.

Seth smiles to say this next thing and I smile to hear it: "They were not sorry to see me go."

Nyx finds us. In a great black flapping, my new friend alights on the low stone wall that rings the tower roof, and Seth, watching her as she struts toward me, says, "Only the Voice of the Few, who is the 'wondrous child,' would attract even such a one as this."

I drop my smile as I once dropped my magic pots. I stare at him, horror full in my eyes. *Yea Balaam!* Does he call *me* the wondrous child? Seth knows my alarm but takes no pity. "Have you never wondered why I came again and again to the house of Heli bar Nehushtan? Why I awaited you in the wilderness? Why I name you Magdal-eder, She of the Temple Tower, or why I went with you into the Land of Egypt, and there was so changed, I could not return to the beliefs of my youth?"

I stare at him. Yes, I have wondered. When younger, I wondered often. But as the years passed, my wonder grew less as I grew as accustomed to Seth as I was accustomed to my hand. By now I grip the stones of the wall.

"Did Socrates not hold that ignorance is all there is of evil, mean-ing evil to be that which harms the soul? No matter what it gain a man; if he harms others, he harms his soul. Therefore, how could I follow those who would kill for a god? Or call themselves the Elect, thereby sentencing all others to be outside the love of a god? How could I, knowing John of the River, call myself Carmelite? How could I, knowing Philo, call myself Nazorean? For each of these fears the world and would set themselves apart as God's chosen. Each of these would see the world destroyed so that they alone might inherit its ashes. Even for the love of Philo, I could not call myself Thera-peut. And as for the Essenes, these are more rabid than any, and place no value on mind or the feminine. This is what I have learned, Mariamne: that beliefs are the masters of the world and that all mas-ters are tyrannical. I find therefore that there is no sect, no teaching, in which I might place my heart. There is nothing but what I myself hear within."

"But Seth, you agree there is no *one* wondrous child? Yeshu names us all wondrous."

It is now that Seth looks at me as he has never looked at me. It is as if he gazes for the first time at the Great Library of Alexandria. "Have you never wondered why, when I overheard Tata speak of your Death, and hoping to hear more of it, I asked also the man Yehoshua the Nazorean to hear of it too? And have you never un-derstood the zeal of my affection for you?" At this, I flush and hang my head. For the world, I would not hurt Seth. He lifts my chin so that I must look at him. His touch is as soft as carded wool. "Then learn it now, Mariamne of the Temple Tower. I was mistaken to think we might wed. Because he is called, there is One who appears as the Shepherd among Lambs; but there is one who has come to herald that Shepherd. By the Voice within you and by your very life, *you* are that wondrous child. And though I once thought it John of the River, now I see it is Yehoshua of the Nazoreans who stands forth as a lion. Yeshu is the Messiah. And I pity him."

Turning my head so that I might not see, I look straight into the unblinking eye of Nyx. It is as cold as obsidian, as mad as Herod. She clacks her beak at me, cocks her head and ruffles her feathers of glossy black.

If even Seth believes this thing of Yeshu, surely all is undone.

$\propto$

The Elect have sent for us. They would hear she whom Seth calls the wondrous child. They would hear too Salome who walked with John. But most of all, they would hear Yehoshua the Nazorean.

In this world of perpetual silence, Seth assures us that nothing short of Yeshu being called the Restorer could have done this.

And so it is that on this early day in the month of Tevet, when the hard rains come in the valleys, and soft snow falls on Carmel, we stand before the Carmelites for the first time, and this after descending deep under the Temple. Just as the wilderness, here in this secret place, there is a further secret place.

Despite my cloak, it is cold here. Despite my supper of boiled vegetables, I am hungry. Though deep in shadow, I know this shadowed room holds nothing. The fire would not warm a hand, much less the whole of a person. The lamps do not light more than the small space between us. But I become accustomed to cold and to hunger and to darkness, as I become accustomed to all else. All seven Carmelites, men and women, are older by years than John of the River, save one, who is no older than Seth. This one shares with Yeshu the unusual length of his hair, which falls below his shoulders, though he does not share the color. With Seth, he shares his beauty and his evident wealth. There is a lifting of his nostril as if he might catch our scent and, by this, know us.

Where all these would sit, we four would stand.

The elders have silently taken their places on benches, have silently arranged their clothing, have settled and become more silent still. And when all this is done, still there is silence. The moments stretch behind us as shadows stretch before the sailing moon. We wait. And we wait. Until, finally, there comes a movement. The oldest male among them turns to whisper into the ear of his neighbor. Who then whispers into the ear of her neighbor. And then there is a veritable hiss of whispering. And when all are silent again, the male, who names himself Matthat of Jamnia, lifts a thin finger to point at Seth, holds it for a moment, and then, in a voice as eager and as piping as a child's, says, "This one is always a tumble of questions, and how he would read! So much lamp oil." Matthat shakes his head as if such things were impossible of understanding. Behind him, others shake theirs. But I understand and am amused. As is Yeshu. As is Salome. Could there be four together so capable of such "a tumble of questions"?

From among them another speaks up. This one names herself Ammia, and is older by far than any here, older, I think, even than the age of the Ptolemaic doctor Sabaz. She looks directly at Yeshu. "I hear that you call yourself Messiah."

Not the young man, but every elder in the room leans forward to hear Yehoshua the Nazorean respond, he who has amazed them now for many days. The young man has leaned not forward, but back.

Yeshu does not flush and he does not tighten in all his parts, but answers in the low and musical voice I now so love, "I do not call myself this."

"But others do?"

"So I am told."

"Well, then, are you the Messiah?"

Yeshu smiles. Do I alone see the bleakness in it? "Tell me, old woman, what do you think to call me by calling me Messiah?"

In her person, which is small and as spare as a stool, in the severity of her regard, which is as the iron nails of Cleopas, and in the way she does not turn away from the clear regard of Yeshu, Ammia puts me in mind not of Sabaz, but of Theano. "As for myself, I do not know what to call you, but if I were to name you Messiah, I would mean you were the Restorer of the Elect."

"And what would I, if I were your Restorer, restore you to?"

All but the young man move to protect themselves from such blasphemy. Ammia is made of sterner stuff. "It is written that One comes who will defeat the Archon, which has formed this world, and that he will make the fallen to walk again."

Hearing this, I think: it seems that Dositheus is far from alone in his philosophizing. Hearing this, Yeshu asks, "And are you fallen?"

In my struggle to contain the Loud Voice—in this place of silence, oh Isis, it would come *now* after its own long silence?—I catch the thoughts of Ammia. She asks herself if, after all, Yeshu is simple? Consider what he does each day. Consider his laughter. She decides he is simple; therefore, she will speak to him very slowly. "We are fallen into a world of sorrow and of pain. There is no man and no woman who is not fallen, save the Restorer. What god of goodness would make such a world? What god of goodness would place us here? Therefore, no god of goodness has made this place."

"Is there, then, no goodness here?"

"There is goodness, but it is beaten back again and again by the Archon, and by his lesser deities who are the *nephilim*. We are taught and we believe there is no hope for us until the Restorer comes from Baal Jehoshua. And just as the prophet Elijah, who sleeps under this very mountain, waits, so too do we who are the Elect wait for him here in perfect silence and perfect faith."

Salome moves against me. Though the names change, is this not as the many Nazorean believe? All look to a messiah sent to redeem those who would believe in him, and do his bidding. And the Essenes and the Zealots, do they not increasingly assist their coming savior in acts of violence and outrage?

Yeshu's voice is lower still. "And if your Restorer does not come?"

"If you are not he, still he will come."

"Until then, you do no other thing?"

The old woman shakes her head. "What other thing would you have us do? We would do harm to no man, no matter how odious that man to us. We would not cause the people to suffer more from their oppressors. Until the Redeemer comes, we are trapped in the flesh. Nothing but his coming will restore us. Answer me, then, by your acts, by your words, by your very name, Yehoshua of Galilee, which is as our Jehoshua of Gilgal, which in Greek is Galilee, are *you* the Messiah?"

I close my throat. I bite back the words that would come shouting forth. I will not be a spectacle before the Carmelites, for all Seth thinks me the wondrous child! But Yeshu is stopped before he can answer, and I see he is as grateful for this as I am grateful, though my relief is blunted by some cold thing that chills me as nothing has ever chilled me. Not the coming of the Loud Voice, not Father banishing Salome, nor his calling me whore; not the crippling of Addai or Salome inexorably leaving me; not Yeshu learning my name, not even Herod come for Yeshu, it is this thing: Yehoshua the Nazorean does not know the answer to Ammia's question. Yeshu does not know if he is the Messiah.

I would turn here and now to him. I would look into his eyes and into his mind and into his very heart, but the young man, whose clothing is linen and linen only, and whose hair is loose and long, stands suddenly. Something here has so moved this one, he can no longer sit.

He takes a step toward Yeshu; he holds up his hand, saying, "I know you."

Yeshu turns to face this third speaker. "As you know me, sir, might I then hear your name?"

"I am Apollonius of Tyana."

My jaw has dropped, Salome gives an audible gasp. This is the traveler who calls himself Pythagoras come again? This is the celebrated seer of Cappadocia whose beauty and learning, as well as his healing and his miracles and his raising of the dead, is so great it is proverbial now to say, "Whither do you hurry? Are you on your way to see the young man?" He must be as learned as Seth; certainly he has traveled farther. The lands of Greece, of Asia, of Egypt, even of Babylon: all these have felt his unshod foot.

Yeshu says to him, "I know of you, Apollonius, and I would be as you are. I would be free to wander as the wind took me, but for what the Father would have me do."

Seth and I are as one at this; we would know what Yeshu must do. And so too would the council of the Carmelites. Even Salome, for whom the One was John, must know. But it is Apollonius who speaks. "Though I have never seen you, Yehoshua, yet I knew so soon as you came who you were."

Yeshu lifts his eyes to this one whose own eye is fire itself, and the moment that passes seems forever. The young man, Apollonius, would hold his eye. He is heroic in his attempt but he cannot, for if he is as fire, Yeshu is as deep water.

Yeshu asks in a voice as remorseless as the sea, "Who am I?"

In surprise, Apollonius blurts out, "Do you not *know* who you are?"

Yeshu opens his arms, and does not take his eyes from the face of Apollonius. "Last night I dreamed I stood in the Temple of Herod and all around me it was cast down, stone upon stone. The great men of Jerusalem tore at their beards, they rent the fine robes they wore, and the tears that stood in their eyes blinded them with grief. Yet I did not feel sorrow, but a great joy, greater than any I have ever known, save for breathing in the breath of the Father. As you know dreams, tell me of this dream."

Hearing this, a great shudder goes through Apollonius, and when he speaks, he speaks to the shadows. "Last night I too dreamed, and in my dream a voice came to me, saying, 'Apollonius, though you travel far, and though you learn much, and though you seek the glory of the ages, it will not come to you in this life. Instead, the words and the deeds of another will burn like a living flame deep into the hearts of men, and you will be cursed and forgotten. This is so, even though you share his sorrow, for he will be a thousand times more misunderstood than you, a thousand times worse betrayed. But be not disheartened, for nothing of the good that a man has done, and nothing of the good that he has thought, is lost, even if he is imprisoned or crucified for that good.'"

Apollonius looks at Yeshu, and his face is as if it was burnt away and the bone beneath revealed. "I think you are that other."

And it is now that the Voice rises up in my throat, burns as bile burns, tastes on my tongue as poison might taste—and I cannot stop it as I could not stop my life. The dark room of stone is filled with the sound of me, which is not me. "LO! THOUGH THE WAY BE FRAUGHT WITH DREAD, AND THE WAY BE STREWN WITH SORROW, YET THE ONE SHALL SURELY STAND FORTH FOR ALL MEN. THROUGH HIM, I HAVE MADE MYSELF KNOWN TO THEE. HAVE I NOT SPOKEN AND HAS HE *NOT* HEARD?"

I flinch from the faces of the Carmelites. I shy from the look of Apollonius—it is as if he gazes on a feast and has no mouth. But I could die at what comes over the face of Seth. All that he thinks me, all that he thinks Yeshu, is now justified.

Yeshu steps back. He holds up his hand as if he could ward off what Apollonius has said, as if he could stopper the Voice. And then he turns and he leaves.

I too step back and, without thought and without balance, rush after him, and my white robe sweeps the lamp from the table.

The chamber of the Carmelites is plunged into darkness.

The air is black with night. At the foot of Elijah's Altar, Yeshu has fallen to his knees and clasps himself with his arms, leaning so far forward his forehead would touch the frozen ground. I can see no farther than this, and there is no sound but the soft hiss of falling snow.

How sick is my heart! And how I curse the Voice that causes such pain in my beloved! I sink to my knees beside him, would touch his hand, his shoulder, brush the tender discs of white from his dark red hair. But I do nothing save kneel with him and hold myself in my own arms so that I might not writhe and I might not scream out my horror.

And this is all that we do. Until, by our very stillness, we must seem as brethren to the birds and beasts of the forested night, for they pay us no heed. But I, in my eternal unquiet, cannot stopper my mind. I think of the tower for which I am named. I think of Nyx who seeks my company. I think of the young man of Tyana who dreams he shall be as nothing to he who comes. I think of Elijah, the prophet of Yahweh, who perhaps in this very spot was said to have challenged the four hundred priests of Baal to prove how great their god, and when their god came not, taunted them, saying, "Cry aloud, for he is a god. Either he is talking, or he is pursuing, or he is on a journey, or perhaps he sleeps and must be awakened." But unlike Baal, Yahweh came when he was called, and then he demanded that Elijah slay on the spot all of Baal's priests for the love of himself. Elijah did not disobey. Yeshu's Father is not the jealous bloodthirsty Yahweh, nor is he Baal, nor any other Being man thinks apart from the world and from himself. And Yeshu's Father knows not Death, but Life. And does not need to be summoned, for he is with us always.

By and by Yeshu pushes up from the chill of the earth, and by and by he sits upright. His white breath gathers on the black air, the snow gathers on his shoulders. "If they think themselves saved, John, will they then welcome the Kingdom?"

Something is changed in me. I understand him instantly. He means that if he allows himself to be the Messiah, the people would allow themselves to be "saved" and, being saved, would hear his teaching. *Eloi! Eloi!* I know where he will go with this; I know where it will take him. I would that he not go there. I would that we flee to Egypt. Or to Tarsus. Or to that place John the Baptizer spoke of, Nehardea, the free state of Jews on the banks of the far Euphrates. Anywhere, but where Yeshu will go.

He turns to me; his voice is still no more than a whisper. "In this one thing, I have learned from my brother, Jacob, who said, 'What means it to a man to have faith, but no deeds? I will show you my faith through my deeds, for being good is not enough, *doing* good is what is needed.' But this is a thing I have learned in my own person: most men are Hylics, as your Philo called men of the body. I would name them captives. They do not grow gradually wiser and better and more knowing of God but instead lurch from one blind folly to another, from one superstition to another, from one tyranny to another. This also I have learned in my own person: that not knowing the Father and the Mother, man *will* have a god, and if he cannot find a true god to worship, he will worship the false. Therefore, if we do good deeds, Mariamne who is John who is my heart, then the deeds that we do, we must do well, and there must be no mistaking what occurs."

This too I understand. I kneel beside my friend and a clarity fills me as white and as cold as the snow that falls around us. Yeshu will be the Messiah for a people who are sore afraid, and thereby need to be saved. He will stand forth for a people who cannot see and for a people who cannot hear. He will assume the role of Messiah as initiates of the Therapeutae assume the role each year of Osiris. Like John, if he cannot teach them one way, he will teach them another. But they will not rise up and make him king; he intends that through him they will find the king in themselves. This is what he has been called to do, and nothing will turn him or stop him or sway him.

He lifts his face into the gathering white. "I see now that my life is become the Father's life. I have argued and I have pleaded. I have struggled to wish myself free of this. I have reasoned that if Herod would kill me as he killed John, is this not an end to it? A man might give his life so that others live, but no man can be expected to die so that others might know Life. But I cannot persuade myself. I am what I am and must do what I must do." Stars of snow lie on his lashes, catch in his mouth. He speaks now as if he spoke before multitudes. "If the Messiah comes, he must come as the Voice within you shouts. He must come as a lion, as a king, so that what must be done *will* be done."

What will be done, is already being done. No matter that I have fought it, hid from it, refused it, ineluctably, it has moved, step by step, toward *itself*. And I am as used in this as Yeshu is used in this.

Who uses us? What speaks through me?

Plato taught that the first principle is intellect whose only function can be to think, and the only possible object of thought must be itself. But I must ask: why, then, did it *act*? Does it not seem more likely that the first principle is not intellect, but Consciousness, which being aware, would not only think, but *feel* and, in feeling, would desire to express itself? All reality is that expression. The stars and all they contain, the earth and all that goes on it, man and every movement he makes or thought he thinks. Nothing can be separate from Consciousness, and nothing can be "fallen." There can only be the myriad expression of Consciousness, which is neither good nor evil, but is infinite experience.

God is not a being outside the Self, nor has it gender, nor is it burdened with a desire to find fault, or to test, or a need to command obedience. God is Consciousness—which is All There Is. And we are how it knows itself in all its infinite variety. God is an endless timeless dance of joyous creation. All this, so that God might know itself—and glory in the contemplation thereof.

Yeshu rises, holding out his hand. Our fingers are so cold, his touch pains me. "As you have walked with me, John, will you go with me now?"

Have I really a choice? Would it matter if I did? I say, "There is no other path."

"Then, come. We must prepare for Jerusalem."

✂

In the Valley of the Jezreel, below us to the north, the blossoms of the almond have come forth and have fallen. The flax is harvested. Below us to the west, the Plain of Sharon greens, the winds fold their tawny wings, and the sea lanes are open once more. War biremes and mail boats sail in and away over the Sea of Darkness. And here on our mountaintop, concealed from all but a few, all that is intended by Yehoshua the Nazorean is gone over and over, examined for precise detail or flaw. Messengers come and go, and one of these is the sister of Yeshu, the fiery Maacah, and one of these is Ananias, who has ever been a half-informed Nazorean. Yeshu has learned from the fate of John of the River. He will not do as John did; he will not be taken before his time. Even I can see that the final plan of Yehoshua the Nazorean is worthy of Solomon, that it is tremendous in conception. It is also wonderfully cunning, for it entails not only what we would do but also what Yeshu would have a host of unwitting others do in reaction.

Long are the hours, and many the days, since Yeshu knelt at Elijah's Altar. And throughout, Yeshu and Jude and Addai have talked as they walked from place to place, or sat together in Seth's simple room. Though Seth does not come with us, and Addai cannot come with us—both remaining here to prepare for what will come after— they do nothing more than direct their minds toward that which Yeshu wills. If Yeshu did not know it before, hearing it from me, Seth makes very clear the Midrash of Philo Judaeus, who even now with others creates a godman for Jews. Yeshu questions Seth closely on all that is wanted of a godman, and all that is expected.

And though I would not, I have been drawn into this cool plotting, and there are moments I think we will not fail, that we cannot fail. But many more are the moments I listen to those I love with unutterable dread at my center.

Not so Salome. Salome has a new interest, and even now I feel a new dream forming behind her skull. Hour after hour, she sits at the feet of Apollonius of Tyana and takes what it is he can give. Hour on hour are not devoted to John of the River. My friend has that look in her eye again, the one that even Philo did not dare to defy, and it is all I can do not to think what this means. Perhaps this is why I am so willing to scheme away the nights.

Yeshu, using the skills of a lifetime, is become certain the Jewish godman must come "in body" as their expected Messiah; therefore he must fulfill Jewish prophecy. To that end, Seth, who pours over scripture, most especially Isaiah and Psalms and Zechariah, has chosen six key prophecies, three of which are already fulfilled. First: the Messiah must be anointed by a prophet. Was John of the River not a prophet? And did he not, in some fashion, baptize Yeshu in the Jordan? Second: the Messiah must be proclaimed as such. Do the people not everywhere call out his name, saying he is the Messiah? And has not Megas of Ephesus, once the high priestess of the *zonah*, anointed him as a king? Third: the Messiah will work wonders, most especially the raising of the dead. Do not many believe Yeshu has done just that in the child Matti, son of Ismael the Samaritan, and in my cousin Eleazar of Bethany, and did they not persist in saying so despite his best efforts at the truth?

But there are three not yet fulfilled. Somehow the Messiah must be betrayed by a trusted friend. And somehow he must be arrested by the Jews and tried by the Romans. And somehow he must be crucified, and—as Osiris, as Dionysus, as Tammuz, as all the godmen who are the son of Isis or Sophia or Mariam—he must rise on the third day.

These last three are what is talked of long into the night.

Each new word and each new detail adds to the tremendous fact that we will do as we plan to do. Each moment pushes us forward to the day there can be no turning back. But as I knew that night in the snow, there never *was* a turning back, not from the very instant that John of the River thought to say, "Simon! John! I would have you meet my favored cousin, Yeshu'a."

But now it is far into the month of Adar and we must be about Yehoshua's business, which is the Father's business. As said, Seth will stay on the mountain to prepare a place in expectation of success, as will Addai and Tata. It is agreed that Addai will not show his wonderful flat face in Jerusalem, for he was once caught up in the talons of Rome, and Rome does not forget, and Rome is everywhere. And Tata would sooner live again as a slave than leave him. But Salome will come away, though she will not follow Yeshu.

Apollonius of Tyana means to walk east into the rising sun as his hero Pythagoras did, and Salome as Simon Magus will go with him. They will follow the path Pythagoras took, stopping in secret places such as this place, peopled by such as these secret people. As he names them, there are more than ever I knew, hidden settlements where from time out of mind gnosis has been sought, and where the goddess Sophia still lives. They will travel until they come onto India—India of the Vedas! And there in fabled India, they will live among the wisest of a wise people, learning all that they can.

To be a magician as she was trained to be, to be a seeker of dreams, and to do as Apollonius will do, and do it as Apollonius who also loves Pythagoras will do it, how ravished, once more, is Salome. As I love her, I must rejoice for her.

But Yeshu and Jude and I will go only so far as the town of Cana in Galilee. This is as it must be, for before we would walk into Jerusalem, first we must gather those who would walk with us. And most especially that one who is suited by his or her own character to betray Yeshu.

How ill I feel. How strangely elated.

We stand where the road becomes two, one branch leading north and one leading east. Helena of Tyre, who has ever walked in grace and in silence, does what is in her heart to do: she chooses that road which Simon Magus takes. Megas of Ephesus chooses that which Yeshu takes, as I think now she ever will. And I walk with her, numbed not by *rosh* but by dread and by loss. Salome has said her good-byes, and she has turned her face from me. I hold what she has given me, the tiny vial of Sabaz she has carried all these years. By this, I know that she too has plotted with Yeshu, though only so far. And this one thing she has said so that I understand her choice: "As I love you, my sister, my brother, my dearest friend, it is my desire that you come with me, all the while knowing you will not and cannot. I know you know that men must make themselves ready to 'hear.' I know you know gnosis is not something to be learned, but is something to be felt; it is a change in the very nerve. I know you know no man can bring other men to Life. John could not, though he gave his blood. I know now the Mystery must be kept in some safe place, even if that place be only your heart, until the day they come seeking." She then kissed me, and turning, walked away.

I watched her leaving until she was gone, and still I watched.

I understand the choice Simon Magus has made; in my bones I know it is more than worthy. But I cannot choose it, for I have chosen Yeshu.

And now, as I trail behind he whom I have chosen, birds sing as they sing each spring, the waters of the rivers flow away to the sea, the sun rises and the sun sets. I leave behind my beloved Addai. I leave Tata whom I cherish. I leave Nyx to Tata. Salome leaves me. But to leave Seth who blesses what Yeshu would do, though he cannot share his terrible need, yet begins his own part in Yeshu's plan . . . I could not know how it would feel to leave Seth. I am cut in two.

Yeshu and Jude go with covered heads, and speak to no one, nor catch any man's eye. By this, it is all but certain that Yeshu shall not be found out, for by now the search for him has lost its edge and its vigor. Other matters have taken precedence in the thoughts of Herod, whose troubles with the King of Arabia tax not only his powers but also his mind.

I walk on, Eio under my hand; Babel, almost grown, trailing behind. In the rough warmth of Eio's blessed hide I take some comfort, but nowhere else.

We have arrived in Cana in the midst of a wedding; a large house is taken up with it. And here we find Simon Peter, for the bride is a younger sister, Leah, a frightened young woman who is to marry a fierce young man of this town. We find also Joazar, Simon Peter's brother-in-law, the fisherman whose boat we once so often used, and the Sons of Thunder. Here too is every other Galilean who last year followed Jacob to the wilderness, all, that is, but Leah's second brother, Andrew, who is dead, and the once-bandit Timaeus, who is taken by Pilate. We find also Simeon, who of them all makes little of my being female, and Joses, who, like most, does not allow me to know him. But we do not find Yeshu's brother Jacob, for Old Camel Knees is become strong in the wilderness and gathers his own Judaean followers who are ferocious for the Law.

It seems, though, that even if the Galileans had not come away from Jacob for Yeshu, still, they would have come away. With their rough ways and their rough accents, and without John or Yeshu to calm them, they have felt out of place in Judaea. While we conspired on the sacred mountain of Carmel, they grew homesick by the Sea of Stink and would come home again, for who would choose barren Rome-infested Judaea over green Galilee?

One by one they have learned that Yehoshua the Nazorean intends entering Jerusalem; throughout the wedding in Cana, they talk of little else.

In this house too are the women. It is sweet to be greeted by Perpetua. Sweet to be stared at by young Mark. Sweeter still is the sight of frail Mary; I embrace her. I embrace Miryam and I smile at Maacah. And there is Jude's Veronica, whose Norea reaches now to my knee. I am greeted by Naamah, whose house this is; she is older sister to the bride and therefore to Simon Peter, and her husband is a prominent man of Cana. It pleases me to see Babata, even to see Bernice. It is not pleasing to see again Salome, the daughter of Zebedee and the widow of Judas of Galilee. Though all who intrigue would wish it were, the news cannot be kept from her. Her sons have told her what they understand of things, which, fortunately, is little. So soon as she spies Yeshu, speaking quietly with Jude and myself, she herds poor Simon and poor Jacob away from the wedding wine, calling out, "Master! You must do what I desire!"

Yeshu has what I do not have: infinite pity given to all. He can turn, therefore, a mild face upon the unfavored mother of his favorites, saying, "What would you that I might do for you?"

"Grant that these my two sons may sit, the one on your right hand, and the other on the left, in your Kingdom."

There is a moment, fleeting as a thought, when I look at Jude and he at me, and I know, for once, we think as one. Is the woman mad? By her disastrous marriage to Judas of Galilee, has the loss of her father's money and position driven all sense from her mind? But Yeshu answers her, "You know not what you ask. Have you walked with me these many days, and still you do not know the Father's Kingdom?"

Salome, who suspects a trick, squints up at him. "I know you will be king in this Kingdom, and a king can raise up even a peasant to high place."

Yeshu smiles on the suffering Simon and the squirming Jacob, both speechless with shame, and who each stand a head taller than this mother they must endure. He asks them, "Tell me, are you able to drink of the cup I drink of?" Neither knows what he means, but both glance at the goblets gripped in their hands, and sincerely wish they did. Yes, they say by the nodding of their heads, we are able. "Then it is enough. For a man who *would* drink of the Living Water *will* drink. But as for sitting on my right hand and on my left, this is not for me to give, but for the Father, whose table is round, and all who sit there sit as gods."

Again, neither understand him, but they are satisfied. Their mother is not, and I hear her think to run for explanation to goitered Martha, who is her particular friend.

Simon Peter, the brother of the bride, passing near, has heard this conversation and is much displeased. Simon Peter would not have others take a place he means for himself, and so situates himself behind Yeshu, scowling at poor Simon and Jacob, and I see Yeshu look toward Jude and Jude toward Yeshu, and I know they each of them wonder at Simon Peter, who, so used to the weight of Andrew, is now somehow unbalanced as he is unburdened.

In the house of Naamah and her husband, watching Simon Peter compete for place, I wonder if it is Simon Peter, Yeshu's rock, who must do what needs be done for prophecy? No one of us doubts that Simon Peter in his eagerness and his folly—and now in his loss—can be counted on to be suitably untrustworthy . . . but untrustworthiness can fall either way.

When the Sons of Thunder have required their mother to come away, Jude quietly says, "Brother, after this I will hold my peace, but do we rely too much on what a man *is*? For if that man should falter?"

Ah, they *do* think as I think. Perhaps it will be Simon Peter.

Yeshu answers, "There is more than one who sleeps and, in sleeping, does not dream."

By this, Yeshu must mean there is always another if Peter balks or fails.

Jude sees this, but must still say, "Those who are awake are laughed to scorn, and those who dream are stoned."

For a wonderful moment, no words pass between Jude and Yeshu, but the look they share speaks of more than all that Philo has ever written, or that Dositheus will ever write. Simon Peter, who listens with all of his ears, cannot understand a word of it.

At last, Jude shakes his great head, saying, "So be it. Who am I to think myself, or even you, a pearl cast before swine?"

Here Yeshu laughs and laughs, and what the mother Salome has left of ill taste is washed from my tongue by his laughter.

And now, a worried Mary, so much smaller and so much darker than her firstborn sons, appears from behind Peter, and from behind Mary comes the sour Bernice. "Yeshu'a, so many are come to the wedding, Naamah says she has no more wine."

Yeshu, who still laughs, says, "Mother, what have I to do with this? My hour is not yet come to turn Water into Wine."

Jude and I know what he means. To turn Water into Wine is as

Raising the Dead: it is a way of saying that to experience gnosis is to be reborn into Life, to make what is only water into wine. But Mary does not know this, nor does Bernice, whose brows are beetled with peevish confusion. Mary wrings her hands. "But you *can* make of water wine?"

"Mother, hear me with your heart; if they would have wine, all they need do is ask."

"I ask it."

"Then even this very day you shall have wine."

Bernice rolls her eyes, but Mary does not know whether to smile or to cry. And neither does Simon Peter. And yet, this is the truth of it: understand him or no, they will all follow, no matter that Yeshu leads them to Jerusalem and to certain mortal danger.

And so shall I follow.

The Die Is Cast

For days we walk, many hundreds strong, from Cana in Galilee to Bethany in Judaea, and through all of these days, Yeshu does not heal nor does he teach, asking those who come with him to keep their peace for so long as he should require it. And, for once, his disciples hear him, silencing those who would shout, "Pity me, son of David!" For by this, the people would call him king, and for this sedition they would have Yehoshua the Nazorean taken by Herod, or by the Sanhedrin of Judaea, or perhaps even by Rome, before his time.

Only once as we travel south does he do a thing, and that only because he cannot avoid it.

In the town of Ephraim in Gophna, from which came the bandit Saul, we have stopped to rest at the home of Saul's mother and father. But while we are here, comes to us a group of grim and virtuous men who are certainly Pharisee, if they are not the Poor. In their midst they drag a young woman, her clothing torn and darkened by dirt, her face white with fear. "Master," one among them cries out.

"See! We have caught this woman in the act of adultery. You know that Moses commands us to stone such a one as this. But before we obey, we would ask, what do you say?"

And Yeshu, looking from one to the other of their excited faces, and knowing what is in their hearts and, further, what stirs their loins, says, "He that is without sin among you, let that man cast the first stone." At this, he bends down as if he would find a stone, but instead traces a thing in the dirt, and as he does so, like seducers in the night, each man of them makes his silent escape, until only the poor woman stands before us.

"Woman," says Yeshu, rising up from the ground, "where are your accusers? Is there no one left to condemn you?"

Only then does she lift her head, and on her lovely face is the same loving look Megas had worn, and wears still. "No man remains, sir."

"Neither do I condemn you. Go and err no more."

He then turns, meaning to be on his way, and I look down to see what he has made there. It seems as the letter *Y.* Is it meant, or is it idle? To the Pythagoreans, *Y* is the symbol of the two paths open to man in life and in death. In life, the left hand path leads to dissolution and the right to virtue. In death, the left hand path leads to Tartarus, which is the deepest hell, below even Hades, and then to rebirth. The right leads to the Elysian Fields.

The woman of Ephraim does not leave us. She follows on now as Megas of Ephesus follows, and no one has learned her name.

Those who love Yeshu are quarrelsome with one another, high strung and confused. Many are afraid. In Cana, Yeshu told them little of what he means to do, though he did not disguise where he would go, or what might happen once we got there. This he said for all to hear, "He who comes will be betrayed into the hands of men, and they shall kill him, but on the third day he will rise again."

As we walk, it seems he would push one among them to act, so that over and over he tells them one of his own will betray him. And Simon Peter looks to Salome, the daughter of Zebedee, who looks on Menahem who looks on Bernice who looks on the tax collector of Jericho, who being so small had once climbed a sycamore tree to see Yehoshua the Nazorean, and all who look are appalled, for who would do such

a thing? They could not understand him in Cana; they do not understand him now. Even Simeon seems afraid to ask his meaning. And
though Yeshu has clearly said, "I am not come to destroy men's lives,
but to save them," some are convinced he goes to make himself king.
They believe they shall be part of a violent uprising. Some are sure
he will announce himself the Messiah, that he will punish the priests
who defile the Temple. Many think this is one and the same thing.

And somewhere on the way south, Yeshu pauses by the side of
the road and looks out over a field of stones. All who follow pause
with him, waiting, until beckoning some certain disciples draw near,
he asks them, "Who do men say I am?" And his cousin Simeon, whose
nature would have him laugh, answers without laughter, "Some say
you are John the Baptizer." But his brother Joses says, "Some say you
are Elias, and others say you are Jeremiah, and others say some other
prophet." But Simon Peter, who seems to study each stone in the
field, lifts up his eye, and says, "You are the Messiah." And none but
I who stand near to him, know how Yeshu shivers in his skin, though
he answers Simon Peter, saying, "Until such time as I will it, tell no
man what it is you tell me."

And in time, we come up to Bethany, and though there are those
who began with us who do not finish with us, there came many more
as we walked. It seems there are hundreds now, perhaps tens of
hundreds. Most of these camp now near the village of Bethphage,
Nicodemus's village, waiting—hopeful, anxious, eager, exalted—for
what will be. All around them are the tents and the animals and the
fires of other small groups who come for Passover and find no room
to stay within the walls of the city.

Tomorrow there will be more. And in the week to follow,
more still.

Yeshu will stay in the Bethany house of my father along with certain of us meant to bring about his intent.

❧

On the Mount of Olives stand a mere handful of us and, of these,
fewer still who know what will be. We have come to Jerusalem from
Bethany to do what my beloved will do, and once again, we have

come by night. As before, we approach this sacred city from the east. Above Yeshu, Wisdom, who is the moon, rises as a cobra rises, sending down her cold light. But to the Temple she lends a light so fulgent, we must shade our eyes.

I alone tremble in the chill of early spring, and just as the night we came for Addai, I alone tremble at what we will do. Beside me stands Yeshu, who does not tremble. What he comes here to do I can imagine no man willingly doing. Yet I know we are as set on our path as Wisdom is set in the sky.

But here is something I should never have imagined: my father is with us. Though he would fear to do so by day, Josephus of the Sanhedrin, who is well acquainted with Pontius Pilate, walks under cover of night. Father comes because he can no longer *not* come. Some terrible thing has occurred in his heart since last we saw him, some violence of feeling he cannot put away. My father Josephus struggles with the life he knew, and the Life he would know, and daily the rift grows wider.

As he would not be left behind, Eleazar is brought with him, who is fatter and, perhaps, wiser. Certainly he is become quieter.

So it is that on this night, in the hour past the Sabbath, those closest to Yeshu pause on the flank of the Mount of Olives. In silence, and filled with such thoughts as I would not dream of touching, Yeshu stands between his twin, the faithful and eternal Jude, and Mariamne, who has come as John the Less. Like a wound freshly cut, this thought opens in my mind: Can we not turn back? There is time yet to avoid this thing. For not until Yeshu walks into Jerusalem openly, with crowds acclaiming him, calling out Hosanna! Hosanna!—save us, save us!—will the die be cast.

I do what I seldom do. I seek Yeshu's hand with my own. He takes my hand in both of his, and under their warmth, I feel thin of heart and small of bone. "Have you not been my teacher, John? Have you not taught me the Passion of Osiris?"

"I have, just as Salome taught John of the River, and did John rise on the third day?"

"What need John of rising when he knows the Father?"

"As you *know* the Father, what need you of dying?"

"My need is my brother's need."

There is nothing more to say, and somehow I find the wisdom to say nothing.

All is ready. All the careful planning is done. All that could be thought of, has been thought of. Tomorrow Yeshu will walk through the gates of the city of David. The brushwood on which he will walk is already to hand; the palm leaves, which herald a king's triumph, or a godman's arrival, and taken this day from the great Herod's own groves, are already cut.

But for now, we slip into Jerusalem secretly, make our way quietly through her sleeping streets, so that we might visit the house of Josephus, the home in which Salome and I were children, and there do what must be done by the will of Yeshu.

Long abandoned to the spider and the bat, Father's slaves and his servants have swept and polished and washed, so that the great house gleams as it did when last it was mine. I, who have changed body and soul, see it as changed not at all, and I run from room to room as bedding is renewed and stores put away, remembering.

By first light, we are back in Bethany to prepare for the coming day.

For Eio, it is bad enough to be tied; but to be tied all night and most of the day, surely no ass bore such insult. Eleazar, who has done this tying, tells me she kicked out, that she bit him, but that Babel, well named, brayed at the moon when he found himself tied, brayed until he made himself hoarse. My cousin whispers all this in my ear, as some cubits away, Yeshu selects two recently come with us, the scribes Matthew and Levi of Lydda, both necessarily innocent of what will be, saying to them, "Go to the village you see before you, and soon enough you will find a tethered ass, and her colt with her. Loose them both and bring them to me. And if any man say a thing, say to him, 'The master has need of them,' and he shall let them go."

And, of course, from out of the village of Bethphage these men of Lydda bring Eio, who is unknown to them and they to her, with Babel trotting beside her. And there shines a naive wonder in the eyes of these new followers of Yeshu that he should know an ass would be tied with her colt and that they would be delayed by the "owner" thereof, namely Father's barber, Timothy, who would say to them, "Stop! Why do you untie the beasts?" but who had stepped aside when Levi replied, "The master has need of them."

It is not much, this fulfillment of the prophet Zechariah: "Rejoice, Daughter of Zion . . . for thy King cometh unto thee . . . lowly and riding upon an ass, and upon the colt of an ass." But it is a splendid beginning, and one that any lover of Isis and Osiris would understand. Philo would know what he saw immediately.

As would a seeker of the Jewish Messiah.

All those around us, the many who follow: men, women, and children, these now murmur each to each as in triumph Simon Peter throws his cloak over the back of Eio's colt, then murmur louder as Simeon the Zealot helps Yeshu to mount him. Where once in hope of being healed, the people would push forward to touch or be touched, now they push back so that they might not defile their true king. And it is now that such a thing passes through them, as well as it passes through me, that is like unto strong wine, or summer lightning, or an almost rapture . . . or poison.

Poisoned with joy, I look into the face of my beloved, who looks into mine.

And we stand on the brink of import. We do what we do by intention. In no time, it will be done. Yeshu will have taken the step that cannot be untaken.

Across the Valley of the Kidron, Jerusalem lies like a lover on its ancient mountain, and within and without the people come for Passover fill her as seed fills a womb, and somewhere within the Temple the holy and unblemished Paschal Lamb is readied for sacrifice. Near to hand are all those who love Yehoshua the Nazorean, and in their love have followed after that one that John of the River called the Lamb of God. Laying aside his head cloth, his hair red with bewitchment, Yeshu too makes himself ready. I also lay aside my head cloth and am seen again as John the Less so that none should be disturbed by a woman so close to their "king."

And under the sun of this last late afternoon, Simon Peter, proudly taking hold of the rope round the neck of Eio's colt, shines as brightly as Jude, as Simeon, as Megas, as Eleazar, as the unnamed woman of Ephraim, as do we all—for in this one brief moment there is such a joy among us, such a certainty that all will be as Yeshu wills it to be, that I could weep with it.

Does Eio too know what she does? If not, why then would she reach forward to nip Babel on the rump, so that without gesture from Yeshu all is set in motion?

At the tenth hour of the day, Yeshu descends from the Mount of Olives toward the city of David amid those who long have loved him, and immediately a great babble arises, as from all sides, as arranged, people come forth with their palm leaves, and people throw down brushwood from the fields or the garments from their backs, so that Eio and her colt might walk upon them. And Yeshu's disciples raise up their voices, Simon Peter first and mightiest among them, crying, "Blessed be the king that comes in the name of the Lord, peace be in heaven, and glory in the highest!" Crying, "Blessed is he who comes!" And dozens, hearing this, reply, "Hosanna, son of David! Save me! Save me!" So that by the time we reach the gates that rise over the Gihon Spring, we are mighty in our numbers, and loud with triumph.

It is now that Yehoshua the Nazorean openly enters the Golden Gate of David's city, and all around there are cries of Iao! and cries of Joshua! and cries of Messiah!

By the moon and all the stars—*alea iacta est*—the die is cast.

And when, standing where Seth once had us pause on our way to Addai, which is beside the northernmost of the Pool Towers where the sweet waters of the Gihon Spring are stored, an anxious Pharisee calls out to Yeshu, saying, "Rebuke your disciples, Yehoshua of the Nazorean. Silence the people, or all shall suffer Pilate's wrath." Yeshu answers him thus: "I tell you that if these should hold their peace, the very stones around us would cry out."

Hearing this, Simon Peter and the Sons of Thunder and others like these grow immeasurably larger in their eager righteousness, blazing forth as torches, striding ahead to clear the way, each shouting louder than they had before, "Blessed be he who comes among us! Blessed is the king!"

But to the Few who *know,* these understand what Yeshu has said by this great entrance, for Yeshu could not have spoken more plainly. And to the high priest Caiaphas and all like him, and to Rome itself in the person of Pontius Pilate, it is this, "I am the Messiah who is the rightful king. Do with me as it is prophesied."

But not yet. Not yet. Yeshu cannot be touched just yet, not before the very eyes of the people who love him, who cry out to be saved by him. Not before the youths who dance near, their faces lit with the pure freedom of it, and who would rise up in their futile fury should any come for him now—and by so doing would be beaten back as they are beaten back each time they have risen. The time is not yet.

But I know, and Yeshu knows, as does Jude, that Josephus Caiaphas of the House of Ananus waits for him as a snake waits at the hole of a mouse. Father has told us what his old friend has the day before said in a council convened solely to speak of Yehoshua. "Is it not better that one man should die than the whole nation perish?"

We all know that Caiaphas waits for Rome to rid him of this messiah, for a man claiming to be king is a traitor to Rome, and Rome protects its own.

In triumph, we walk through narrow crowded street after narrow crowded street, up to the very edge of the Temple Mount's western wall, and everywhere it is the same. The people call out, "Hosannah! King of the Jews! Comes our Messiah to save us!" And they pull back in awe if Yehoshua should so much as glance their way.

It seems they will riot in their fevered joy and their fevered hope, and I think we cannot come on the Temple soon enough. But they do not riot; instead they press after Yeshu as we all of us come on the Temple wall. Saul of Ephraim is literally struck dumb by the size of the stones, though not so Simon Peter who cries out above the melee, "Look, master, as I remembered! They are as big as houses, each of them!"

We have stopped in that open space where we might choose to

enter by the gated tunnel used by the common people, or to ascend to the Upper City Bridge above us, which is used by the rich and the Sanhedrin. And here Yeshu halts Babel, and here he dismounts as I gather up Eio and her colt, and certain men among us stand forth as shields against the press of the people. And it is here that slaves sent by Father await us, large men of Gaul with yellow hair. These will hold back the crowd so that Yeshu might be taken away through certain tunnels, clearly mapped for us by Addai, as soon as he needs to be. For all that he would do this day, is now done.

Yeshu has announced himself as the Messiah. He has created a great stir. It cannot have been missed by any and by all. It is enough.

To the people who have come this far, both followers and those caught up in the following, it must seem as if he has vanished into the stones as big as houses.

◇

As planned, we sup tonight in the house of my youth.

Ananias comes to us with news. Zaccheus of Jericho comes to us as well with news. As do the brothers from Lydda, they who chanced on Eio and her colt. By these, and more, we hear that Yeshu has done what he has meant to do. From the Upper to the Lower City, there is talk of little else. From priest to slave, everyone knows Yehoshua the Nazorean has declared himself king. And from Father, who this evening attends yet another special session, we hear that the Sanhedrin is as a beehive in the paws of a bear—as bees, they swarm in anxious confusion. What shall they do? How shall they act?

Nicodemus, who Father sees seldom now, has complained of Yeshu, "The world has gone after him," and all the others rend their clothes. No other messiah has so captured the people as this messiah, not even John of Kefar Imi whose sacrifice by Herod is fresh grief still. This crisis seems as no crisis they have ever known, worse than the murderous zealots come among them, worse than Pilate's slaughter of the people, worse even than the thoughts of Greeks! To enter the city openly, to be followed by a great multitude waving triumphant palms, and in procession to be announced as a king come to claim his throne! From every side, they ask each other, "What does this man plan?" Father himself does not know. This is part of the plan: that so few know, though many carry it out.

Yeshu asks Josephus, "And what do they themselves plan?"

"The Sanhedrin has yet no plan," replies my father, "other than to see you dead, and to see it done without harm to themselves."

Yeshu asks, "Will they go to Pontius Pilate?"

"They would, save for the suspicions of Pilate. He could think it a trap. After all, for months they have petitioned Tiberius for his removal and yet now would come to him for help? They have no proof that an armed rebellion is truly planned. And Pilate might say that it is only Passover, many Jews come from many lands in many ways at Passover."

"But if they should act without Rome?"

"Then the people would revolt not against Rome but against the Sanhedrin."

"And if they should not act at all?"

"Then Rome might accuse them of abetting in treason, and they themselves would be tried before Caesar."

Yeshu smiles. It is all as he said it would be. "Then they must act?"

"Indeed they—we—must. But as yet, we are ignorant of how we might do so and at the same time remain 'innocent' before the people who love you."

"But a way will be found?"

"Oh, yes. A way will be found."

On this second day, Yeshu takes his plan a step further. Today he will goad the priests and the Sanhedrin, provoke them to greater fear and therefore greater effort to do as he wills them to do. For this, he takes with him Simon Peter and the Sons of Thunder, who possess the hottest heads of us all and who will surely do something that will sting the Sadducee and outrage the Pharisee. For this he takes also Jude, who would not, in any case, be left behind; also Simeon, who though zealous, is level of head; and finally me, seen as a youth, John the Less. We seven make our unheralded way late in the day directly from Father's fine house to the Temple Mount, and once there to the enormous Court of the Gentiles. As they do on all Holy Days, the soldiers of Pilate stand above us on the roofs of the colonnaded porticos, and below these, well back under the porticos, sit the dozens of moneychangers. Nearby, as many, if not more, sellers of animals for sacrifice have set up also their living wares.

Yeshu chooses the moneychangers because in Psalms it is written that the Suffering Servant shall take on the reproaches of those who reproach God, and if those who make profit from the Temple do nothing else, they reproach God—most especially the Father and Mother of Yeshu who do not demand blood, or coin, or priest, or even Mount or Temple.

Between the watchful bulk of Simeon on his right, and of Jude on his left, Yeshu throws back his head cloth. At this there is a sudden intake of breath from this one who recognizes him, and from that one, so that by the time he walks across the court, choked with the pilgrims of Passover, he walks through the bustle and din as a king. As a king demands, Simon Peter and Simon bar Judas and Jacob bar Judas go before to clear his way—John the Less walks behind as suits his age, for I am still young, uselessly young—and all around us there is a very Babel of tongues, and all around us the debris of hammer on stone and the scaffolds of masons, for the work on Herod's Temple goes on and on, though it pauses for Passover.

And when Yeshu stands in the thick of those who have come to change their foreign coin for the Tyrian silver shekels acceptable to Yahweh, and when the people, come here from everywhere, are sufficiently aware of and sufficiently moved by he who walks among them, Jude hands Yeshu a whip of small cords. This he has fashioned from the discarded tethers of those poor beasts that each day die in their monstrous numbers to feed the demands of Yahweh.

It matters not which banker Yehoshua chooses; any will do. He selects therefore the nearest to hand, crying out in a voice made loud with righteous authority, "It is written: 'My house shall be called the house of prayer!' But you have made it a den of thieves!" And with this he tips over the table of this first and most astonished of the

bankers, and all the fine coins stacked thereon, and all the boxes con-
taining coin upon coin to the very sum of wealth, fly every which
way, ringing with great clatter on the tiles of the Temple Mount floor.

The people become stunned with awe. No less so the bankers
and the sellers of animals and the man whose "business with God"
lies scattered at his feet. Who is this who would do such a thing?
Who would have the nerve—and the authority? They stare at each
other. They whisper each to each. And I see there is one here who
has an answer; I see three there who also know. It suddenly sweeps
through the crowd: who but a king would do such a thing! An instant
later, as Simon Peter knocks aside a great wicker cage of pigeons
so that the early evening air is full of feathers and the whirring of
startled wings, those among all these come for Passover who are lame
or blind or ill or in despair, and there are many and many, would fall
on Yeshu to be healed. Even more suddenly, Jude and Simeon and
the Sons of Thunder surround Yeshu and push him away.

Before the Temple police can act, and before the soldiers of Pilate on the roofs above us can become curious, and certainly before
the Pharisee can do more than select and pick up loose stones near
the scaffolds, once again we make our way to a tunnel entrance and
are gone from this place.

As we knew it would be, for the second night all of Jerusalem is
agog with talk of Yehoshua the Nazorean. Those who saw tell those
who did not see, and in the telling the acts of Yeshu grow until the
very shadows shrink at his daring. They ask themselves: what does
he do? They ask themselves: what will he do next? If the people were
astonished the first day, this second day they are thrilled. And eager
to be more thrilled still. As is planned.

If the Sanhedrin buzzed with concern the first day, this second
day they hiss with distress.

As is planned.

Tonight, while Father once again attends a special session of the
seething Sanhedrin, only the most trusted of us dine at his table, and
we talk of the morrow. Tomorrow shall be a day of real danger, for
on this third day Yeshu will put himself in the way of not only the

council but of Pontius Pilate—for naturally, the prefect is here in Jerusalem. We should not have come this Passover if he were not; for just as there is needed someone who will betray Yeshu, so too is this Roman needed.

Pontius Pilate comes here but rarely, preferring to act as the eyes and ears of Tiberius Caesar from the cosmopolitan port of Caesarea Maritima rather than in the midst of fearsome Jews whose habits and beliefs are so unlike any civilized Roman's.

Pilate's Jews, as well as his Samaritans and Idumaeans, have proved a horrible surprise to him, never more so than some years ago in the city of Caesarea itself, when, in their thousands, they had come to plead that he take down the Roman shields he had hung in the Jerusalem Temple. Pilate dismissed them, thought them nothing more than a nuisance, but they did not leave. Instead, they went silent and still, staring up at him with tears in their eyes. So then he threatened them, shouted out that he would set his soldiers on them if they would not go home, he would cut them down where they stood, lop off their heads, stick the heads on spikes. But at this, they then did something no Roman could have foreseen. To a man, and in silence, they threw themselves facedown in the dirt at his feet, and they bared the backs of their tender necks to his Roman swords. At sight of this, Pilate stood rigid as the Pharos of Alexandria and as staring as its great lamp. To find a people would die rather than endure the defiling of their Temple—how horrid this must have been to him. And, as well, how curious. To the eye of a Jew, this was devotion; this was righteousness. But to the eye of a Roman or a Greek or an Egyptian, it was fanaticism; it was mindless folly. And there was no answer to it; a man who has nothing to lose is bad enough, but a man who would offer up his life for an idea is terrifying. Such a man cannot be cowed, and if a man cannot be cowed, he cannot be governed. For a governor, could there be a worse man? And yet, this Passover, Pilate is here, resident in Herod's once palace. Why is of no concern to us; it is enough that he is.

"What manner of man is this prefect?" Yeshu has asked of Father. And Father has answered, "He keeps his pride like a wasp in a bottle.

And he bites his nails." By this, Yeshu has already taken the measure of Pontius Pilate.

But this thought worries me, and I take Yeshu aside to voice it. "Please . . . I would that I understood the whole of your thought. If you would teach once you are 'risen,' Rome will see you do *not* die. How, then, can they let you live?"

"If Rome sees that I die, but yet live, how then can they think to kill me? And if the people see also that I die, yet rise, how then can they resist the Father? Loose yourself from these worries, beloved. What will be will be, and what will be is the Father's work." Yeshu taps his brother's shoulder. "Jude?"

Jude, who has eaten every one of a plate of wild German parsnips with three glasses of Father's Setinum wine, looks up from his meal. "Yeshu?"

"Tomorrow when I speak in the Temple, I would have you stay near."

"Have I ever done other, brother?"

There is something in the way that Jude says brother that makes me look full and long on his face. What is it that moves within his heart? What is there of Jude in all this?

Gethsemane

This day our wits must be about us. For surely someone among the Sanhedrin has approached Pilate and has made a first attempt at convincing him of the need to rid not only themselves, but Rome as well, of this messiah, this traitor?

Once more we bathe and enter the Court of the Gentiles, and I must smile, albeit behind a hand, to see that so soon as the red-headed, red-bearded Yehoshua the Nazorean appears, the bankers rise to throw themselves over their coins, the sellers of animals hasten to stand between their pigeons and Simon Peter, and the tenders of goats and of sheep gather them in as best they can. Yeshu, no less than we all, ignores them entirely, making instead for the Temple that stands in the center of the Temple Mount, in which is the Holy of Holies wherein Yahweh lurks.

Behind a low wall is a short flight of shallow steps running along the whole length of this Temple. These are the steps on which stood John of the River the day he came to preach; at the top of which there is a choice of gates, but of them only three are allowed any who are not priests.

Yeshu heads straight for one of these three. As we pass through, I read the signs affixed to the outer wall. In Latin and in Greek, they warn all those who are not Jews, meaning those who do not love Torah, that should they dare pass through they would solicit their own death, and I do not smile to myself to read this. Beyond this door is the Court of Women, and beyond that, the Temple itself whose walls are covered with gold and whose doors are topped with golden vines and golden grapes, and beyond that I do not know. No woman may go nearer the sanctuary than the Court of Women; I have not set foot here since the day I watched in horror as a fearsome Sicarii killed Ben Azar of the House of Boethus. Simon Peter looks about him; he too has not seen this place since that day. Nor has Yeshu, who did not stay his hand, though he would stay it now.

In wonder, we pause, for into this place come all who call themselves prophet and all who would teach. We stand in the very heart of Jerusalem. If in the outer court the air is a haze of death and dying, in the inner court it is a very fog that burns the eyes. And if in the outer court it smells of charred flesh and burnt hair, in the inner court there is a reek so thick it sickens. Am I the only one to think so?

Many who follow Yeshu await us here, having been told he would come this day. So too do the Sanhedrin wait. If Father had not already told us these would be here, still, we should have known, for no sooner do we arrive in the inner precincts close by the Chamber of Nazirites than they advance upon us. Comes a whole flock, elders as well as chief priests, flapping down from the curved steps leading up to the Nicanor Gate—though not, I am relieved to see, Caiaphas. The high priest leaves such things to others. But I sink to see Nicodemus. If he should know me, know that a female stands in the clothes of a man—?

It is pandemonium. If Yeshu's presence were not enough to demand attention from all who come for Passover, the presence of Jerusalem's foremost men would do so. And as for there being both

in one day! It remains pandemonium until Yeshu, by remaining perfectly silent and perfectly still, causes all this to fade and to fade
until it is as if the stink and the noise and the confusion had never
been. Even then he remains silent, and the elders begin to sweat with
the wait of it. By the moment it becomes more excruciating. And
when they can take no more, when even the strongest among them
would speak out, or do a thing unplanned, Yeshu stops them by
spreading his arms as a bird would spread its wings.

Standing on a step so that he is a head higher than the tallest
among them, Yeshu's voice is as it was when first I heard him, low
unto a whisper, and full with Galilee. "Would any among you enter
the Kingdom of Heaven?"

From priest to pauper, a sigh runs through the people. Would
they enter God's Kingdom? At the End of Days, they would do nothing else. As one, they would inhale this messiah, take him deep into
their lungs, and one among them, a small man, but finely made, and
with a look of hard labor about him, speaks out, and his voice too is
not loud, but soft with longing. "Who is it that will draw us to heaven,
Master, if that Kingdom is in heaven? And when shall it come?"

These questions have been asked many times and Yeshu has answered them many times, each time differently. Today Yeshu's answer seems spurred by the burning and the dying all around us.
"The birds of the air and the beasts of the earth and the fishes of the
sea shall draw you to heaven, and all creatures under the earth. For
the Kingdom of Heaven is within you, and whosoever knows God
shall find it, for if you know him, you shall know yourselves. And you
will realize that you are the sons and the daughters of the Father
who is perfect, and you shall know yourselves to be citizens of
heaven, for *you* are the City of God."

Yeshu could not have spoken of gnosis more clearly, but not
"knowing" the goddess Sophia who is gnosis, the faces of those who
hear him are blurred with confusion. He has told them the world
and all it contains is the Kingdom of God if only they would *know* it.
And I pity them so for not having ears to hear, and I pity them for
thinking themselves separate from God, and lost.

But this is what the elders wait for, and one among them, no doubt chosen earlier, and this one Nicodemus himself, has pushed forward and pushed forward so that by now he stands at the foot of Yeshu's step. Nicodemus raises his voice and trumpets out over all those who have listened as they would listen to David come again, "By what authority would you speak of such a thing? Who gave you this authority?" His gray beard is full of rage and his face is free of doubt.

Yeshu turns a mild eye upon Father's once friend. "I too would ask a question, and if Nicodemus should answer mine, I would answer his. Tell me of the Baptism of John? Was it from heaven or was it from men?"

I know what Yeshu has done; I know that Jude does and I feel his flush of admiration. As for Nicodemus, there is no need to touch him; he too knows what Yeshu has done, and is lost.

But now comes forth a certain Gamaliel to stand by Nicodemus. Though a Pharisee, Gamaliel is yet president of the Sanhedrin, and has eaten at Father's table. Just as Nicodemus does not know me, this one does not know me; both are convinced by the person of John the Less. Gamaliel, too, knows what Yeshu has done and his thoughts are as harried as hares, seeking a way to answer. If Nicodemus should say that John's baptism was from heaven, this messiah will say to him in front of all, why then did you not believe him? But if Nicodemus should say that John's baptism was of men, then the people would turn on those he spoke for, would hurl the hard lemons they keep about them for just such moments, since all hold John of Kefar Imi as a prophet. Therefore, neither answer will do. "We cannot tell," is what the president of the Sanhedrin must finally say.

So that Yeshu, who has come here this day to provoke the council and to enrage the priests, answers, "Neither do I tell you by what authority I do what I do. But this I will say to you. If a man asks his son to do a thing and the son says he will not, but afterward relents and does it, and then the man asks a second son to do a thing, and this son says that he will, but does not, which son has done the will of his father?"

Of course, Gamaliel who has eaten Father's bread must answer that the first son does the will of the father, so that Yeshu can say, "Then in truth I say to you that the whores and the tax collectors will know the Kingdom sooner than you shall know it. For John came to you and you believed him not, but the whores and the tax collectors believed him. And neither did you repent. For you are like whitewashed tombs, which appear outwardly beautiful, but within are full of dead men's bones."

Yea Balaam! How the face of Gamaliel darkens! How Nicodemus grinds his teeth! That Yeshu should presume to say such a thing to a teacher of the Law!

By now, the priests and the members of the Sanhedrin have pushed past the people and ring us round with only themselves. I know that Jude fingers his knife, as does Simon Peter, as do the Sons of Thunder. My own blade is no less distant from my hand.

But this pushing forward seems as nothing to Yeshu. Once again he raises his arms and speaks out over them, his eyes on the gathered people behind the wall of priests and of elders. "Hear that the Kingdom of Heaven is like a certain king who would give a feast for the marriage of his son. This king sent out his servants to all just men, so they might be asked to come to this feast. But no one would come, each saying he was too busy with his business or with his farm or with this or with that. And again the king sent out his servants bidding them tempt these just men by speaking of the delights each would find at the king's table, and still none would come. Indeed, some were vexed the servants had come a second time, and made light of them, or set their dogs on them. But the king loved his son, and his wish to share his abundance was great, so sent his servants out a third time. And this time, there were those who were angered by the call and would slay the servants of the king. And the king, when he heard this, was hurt in his heart, so that he sent his servants to the highways and to the wild ways to gather any he could, be they good or be they bad, to come sit at his table. And the poor, not too busy with this or with that, came to his feast. And the bad, humbled that a king's servant would ask them, came to his feast. And those who were like children, and would see such a thing as a great supper, came to his feast. And the king spared them nothing. For I tell you, *all* are called, but few answer."

There are those among these elders who would take up small chunks of masonry; I feel the heat of this terrible desire as it passes through Nicodemus. As for Gamaliel, he could not turn much redder, and how his arm aches to cast the first stone! Gamaliel knows whom Yeshu means by just men—he means the priests and the scribes and the Sanhedrin; he means Gamaliel himself. But in their shock and their outrage, neither he nor the others standing with him can lay a hand on Yehoshua the Nazorean for the crowd at their backs. Only the Romans can touch Yeshu now. And by what he does next, I know that Gamaliel is prepared for this. The movement is slight, and it is quick. Gamaliel has signaled another to come forth, a younger man and a priest of little standing.

It is this one who smiles upon Yeshu, saying, "Master, we know now you are true. We know you care for no man more than another. And we know you teach the way of God. Therefore, tell us what you think. Is it lawful to give tribute to Caesar, or is it not?"

I feel Yeshu stiffen against me. Here is a trap, more dangerous than that which he himself laid for Gamaliel. The president of the Sanhedrin is a clever man and I know it is he who has thought of this. If Yeshu should say that it is not lawful, he will preach sedition against Rome, and—too soon—the Romans will kill him. If Yeshu should say it is lawful, he will show himself a friend of Caesar, and the people will turn away from him. And if he should say, as Gamaliel has said, that he does not know, Yeshu will show himself no more than the elders and the priests who answer as best suits the moment, and the people will be certain he is no messiah. Any one of these answers will put an end to this bold trespasser who speaks in the foolish accents of Galilee.

Gamaliel's thin smile tells me how well he knows this, and how tight his trap. What he does not know is that, according to our plans, there can be no arrest before the right and proper time. Therefore, for his life and ours, Yeshu must answer well.

"Show me a coin."

For the elders, it is the work of a moment to produce any number of such things, and with care and precision a single dinarius is laid in Yeshu's outstretched palm. Yeshu does not look at it, but at Gamaliel, though it is to the young priest that he now speaks. "Whose is this image?"

"Caesar's, Master."

"And this lettering?"

"Caesar's, Master."

Yeshu hands back the coin, as precisely as he was given it, and says so that all can hear. "Render to Caesar that which is Caesar's, and to God that which is God's."

Oh, this is a wonderful answer! Not even Salome could have thought of a cleverer one! And I look out over the faces of the people, and all here, they too think it a wonderful answer and break out in talk of it, each repeating to each what it is the Master come among them has said. By evening, Yeshu's words will be heard in every home, and every place of business, and every fine mansion in Jerusalem. By evening, the sound and the meaning of it will reach the ear of the prefect of Judaea.

Yeshu has done what he need do with the priests of the Temple and the Sanhedrin. If there are any among them who love him, they hold no power now, for he has so turned the president of the Sanhedrin against him the rest would not lift a finger in his defense. Therefore, it is Pilate who is now sought by Yeshu.

Coming away, we know we have played our parts well, and rejoice. Even I rejoice, knowing what I know. But as we pass once more through the Court of the Gentiles, Matthew of Lydda exclaims at how grand the Temple, and his brother, Levi, proclaims at its worth, but Jude surprises us by proclaiming how close Yeshu came to stoning. And Yeshu stops in his tracks, saying, "It is not prophesied that I should be stoned." I need not hear him to know what he does not say, which is: *and blessed be this, for if stoning were prophesied, it could not be survived.*

We stand before the entrance to the Hulda Tunnel but Yeshu does not enter. Instead he asks of us, "You know that in two days it is the feast of the Passover?" Oh yes, all here know this. There is much nodding and much confusion that the question is asked. Yeshu then says, "You know then that the son of man will be betrayed and crucified?"

If I have rejoiced, it is nothing to how I now lament. As for the others, on the instant all joy is gone from their hearts.

Simon Peter tears at his beard, and when he has finished with this, he takes Yeshu by the shoulders and shakes him, crying out, "I would have this thing far from you! This will not be done unto you!"

And it is now, and for the first time, that I see how full of fear is my beloved friend. But Yeshu's fear has made him angry. He takes Peter's wrists in his own hands, and by so doing pulls Simon Peter's hands from off his shoulders, and the look on his face is black. "Get you behind me, Satan, who is ever the angel of doubt. You are an offense to me for you savor not the things of the Father, but of men."

How this strikes at Simon Peter's heart. I would not be him for all the world. His face is as ash as Yeshu walks away. But neither for all the world would I be Yehoshua the Nazorean. Yeshu cannot allow himself to doubt what he does. To doubt is to falter, and to falter is to fail.

⌀

Yeshu sits in Father's inner courtyard eating Nicolas dates, each longer than a woman's finger, with flesh as white as northern skin and taste as sweet as honey. Half asleep, I lean my head on his shoulder and watch him pick among them for the biggest and the sweetest. All around us I hear the murmur of voices talking of this and talking of that, then there comes a moment of silence, and into this silence Simon Peter inserts what he has need of saying, what he has had need of saying ever since leaving the Temple Mount.

"Yehoshua," he begins, and in his voicing of this name there is a world of meaning, "I have tried and I have tried, but I cannot shake your words from my mind. I tell myself you do not mean what you say, that you mean something else, something I cannot grasp, nor can others." Here, he glances round at Jacob and Simon bar Judas and at

Saul of Ephraim and even at Eleazar. "But you say it too often, and I begin to think there is a terrible truth in it. I have thought one other man king, and have I not lost that man to Herod Antipas? How is it you think to tell me I will lose another to the evil ones? How can this be? I am a simple man, Yehoshua, and I live by what wits I have, and by the knife at my belt. I did not come here to have you die. I came here to make you king."

If ever my heart went out to this Galilean, this Sicarii, this gnasher of teeth and hater of women, it goes out now. And in this moment I know as Yeshu knows that Peter will not willingly betray his "king"; therefore, all that is left to hope of him is that he will betray Yeshu unwillingly.

Yeshu says, "Simon Peter, who is it that has created the world?"

"God did."

"And where is God?"

"You teach us he is in man."

"I tell you that men are in God and God is in man. I tell you that there is no God but the God in man who is in all things, and who expresses himself through all things. Therefore, I ask you, who is God?"

And though he would wish to answer, Simon Peter cannot bring himself to say that if God is in all men, then God is in Simon Peter, and if God is in Simon Peter and expresses himself through Simon Peter, Simon Peter is God. Simon Peter stands before Yeshu with all this written in his eye, with his eye full of tears, and though he struggles mightily to speak, he cannot. All that he has ever known of God and the Law stops his voice at its source. With the whole of his being, Simon Peter has made Yeshu his king. But as for the teaching! The teaching is wind in a cave. Where is the black of it? Where is the white? If there are no demons, how then explain the evil that befalls good men? If there is no Yahweh to please, how then can a man shape his fate? If all men are loved, who is there left to hate? If a man cannot love his hatred, what good can he do in this world?

And I, by my gift forced to listen, hear all this roar through his mind.

In pity, Yeshu speaks for him, yet there is a further, darker reason for what he now says. "If I were Simon Peter of Capharnaum and as Simon I were to know the Father, I would then say I was the Light of the World. But as I am Yehoshua the son of Joseph, I say that I too am the Light of the World, and they that follow me shall not walk in Darkness, but in Light. And they shall have the Light of Life and know not Death, but know Glory in Life. For I know from whence I came and I know whither I go. If any man knows these things of himself, he knows all things. By this truth, you shall be set free."

But if Simon Peter has not understood him before this, he does not understand him now.

He is torn by the shame of his ignorance, by his unthinking fear of the Law, by his unthinking need for the laws of man, which do not set him free, but cage him. I watch, and I bleed for him. So too do the tender Miryam and the proud Maacah. Even the Sons of Thunder who understand only with their hearts are here moved to pity. But Yeshu watches him as a farmer watches a planted seed. When will it sprout, and what shall it be? In his love of all men and his desire to save all men, Yeshu is cruel to this one man. Simon Peter cannot bear his pain nor can he bear our pity, but most terrible of all, he cannot bear the look of Yeshu. And he turns on his heel and is gone from Father's courtyard rather than endure another moment of it. And I am flooded with fear. Will Simon Peter go to betray Yeshu out of this pain? If he does, all goes well. But, if all goes well, it is as a pit that opens at my feet.

Josephus arrives, and the look in my father's eye chases all thought of Simon Peter from my mind.

"Yehoshua! They have done it. Gamaliel has gone to the prefect to ask that you be arrested, they accuse you of an attempt to seize the throne. They claim that a whole army of Zealots hides in the city, awaiting your word to rise up. They have rounded up a dozen men who will swear to this and who will condemn you most horribly. Chief among these is Nicodemus, and a certain Phabi of Nain. Do you know this one?" Father, who thinks this the blackest of news, stammers in his horror, clutches at his robe, looks from one face to another. "Have you heard me, Yehoshua? Do you know what I say to you?"

"Yes, Josephus, I know what you say to me. You have told me that what comes is called."

Father does not understand. But then, few do.

When I was very young, younger even than on the day Semne the Egyptian came to live in my house, Father tells me that my mother would walk out from the city so that she might delight in her garden, and when Hokhmah, the young and cherished wife of Josephus, did this, she would take her only child, a daughter, who could yet but toddle.

I do not remember my mother, but I remember her garden.

On the Mount of Olives, there are many olive groves, and of these, Father owns one of the largest. He owns, as well, an olive press, and it is near to this press that Mother made her garden, a beautiful thing, and walled round with stones, flawless in their fitting. In it there are carved benches on which one can sit and look out over Jerusalem. There are leafy myrtle trees that dapple the heated ground with blessed shade. There is a small cave near to which, long ago, Hokhmah would allow me to play. There is a tomb sealed with a large round rolling stone in which she lay for a time. There is a grave nearby in which her bones are buried. And there is an apple tree she planted before ever I was born. All this is tended still by certain of Father's favored slaves.

On this day, as Mariamne, and without chaperone—in so many ways, Josephus lets loose his grip on the Law—I take Yeshu to my mother's garden, named by her Gethsemane for its being so near my Father's olive press. I bid him sit with me under my mother's apple tree. Above us, the young apples are no more than swollen promises. Underfoot, the anemones make a thick red carpet. All around, the bees are busy in their work and the nation of ants tireless.

This day is ours, for on it Yeshu does not intend causing fear or anger or protest. For those who wish Yehoshua ill, this is their day to whisper in ears and to plot cunning deeds, to gather witnesses, and to send messengers running from palace to Temple to private homes throughout the city. But for Yeshu and Mariamne, it is our last day, and it seems we are content to sit, knowing that the other is close by. I push from my mind that which happens or does not happen in the city at our feet . . . Does Simon Peter do what is needed of him? Does he make his way through the streets of the Upper City seeking the home of Gamaliel? Does he fit his body into the shadows near to the great house of the high priest Caiaphas? Gradually I feel a voice rise up within me; it is not one of those that came in youth with Salome, and it is not the Loud Voice. This voice is mine, it is the voice of Mariamne, and what she would say is in her heart to say. "As the apple tree among the trees of the wood, so is my beloved among the sons. I sat down under his shadow with great delight, and his fruit was sweet to my taste."

For my brazenness, I bury my face in the brown cloth of my skirts. But through the heat of my rosy shame, I feel Yeshu's touch on my hair, hear his voice in reply. "You are the rose of Sharon, and the lily of the valleys. As the lily among thorns, so is my love among the daughters."

I cannot look up at him. Does he smile at me? Does he laugh? Does he know the Song of Solomon as I know it, as Tata taught it to me at her knee? Whatever it is that he does, his voice above me speaks on, "Who is she that looks forth as the morning, fair as the moon, clear as the sun, and terrible as an army with banners?" I feel his hand on my heated cheek, know that he encourages me to raise my head. "Who is this that comes up from the wilderness, leaning upon her beloved?"

I cannot help myself, I must look into his face, and what I see there is as tender as the grapes at harvest, and he is my beloved. He is the husband I will never have and the lover I have never known. And there stirs in me something I have never felt, as if a heated thing slept in me and now uncoils itself.

"I raised her up under the apple tree, where her mother brought her forth. Set a seal upon your heart, beloved; set a seal upon your arm, for love is as strong as death."

And I know that Yeshu loves me as I love him, and I kiss his lips.

By all the moments of eternity, how I love him, and in this last place I open to him; I give myself to him as my beloved gives himself to me.

∝

We sit in Father's innermost chambers, Jude and I, and try as we might, it is impossible not to glance at Yeshu now and again. He does not eat and he does not drink. His eyes stare out at nothing we can see.

It is certain. Simon Peter has not and will not betray Yeshu.

Jude, in the sly way of Salome, has learned that if Simon Peter thought John the Baptizer king, he is convinced of Yehoshua the Nazorean. Yeshu is not only his king but his master and his friend as well. How could he be other than a friend to Yeshu? Therefore, we can no longer hope our fisherman will act as prophecy dictates. I stare at Father's floor of agate and lazuli. I think, could he have only known how much better a friend he might have been! But how subtle an idea it is, to lay up heaven's gold, one must steal it here below. Such things are too much for Simon Peter the fisherman. But do I understand it any better? Have I, even once, imagined myself accepting this terrible shame for Yeshu's sake? With this last, I am shot through with the sting of nerves. I cast around for some other. Could the tax collector, Zaccheus, be tempted for money? Or yet again one of the scribes from Lydda be duped into action? Who is strong enough to do this thing? For make no mistake, there would be no end to the suffering such a one would endure.

We wait, Jude and I, for Yeshu to answer us. Am I alone in my secret prayer that even now we might leave this place? That all that Yeshu has planned might be set aside as an unfinished play that no longer pleases its author? It is the work of a moment to know my answer. On Yeshu's face it is writ clear: we will never leave this place, not as we have entered it.

On the couch beside mine, Jude stirs. It seems he would stand, perhaps walk away. Is there some other he has thought of, someone else who might do this thing?

"Yeshu?"

How is it that at the sound of his brother, Yeshu becomes rigid where he sits? Why do his eyes widen as they would at some terrible danger, one he cannot escape? His hands, which have lain unmoving in his lap, slowly clench into fists. "Brother?"

"Let it be me."

I turn to Jude and am struck by clarity. How could I not have known this moment would come? It has been there all along, as stark as a cut throat before the body falls.

The sound of Yeshu as he answers is as a mortal wound. "No, Jude. Not you."

"There is no other. And my betrayal would be the most convincing of all."

"No. I have said it. Not you, Jude."

Jude has stood up. There is nothing about him of the supplicant. He stands before Yeshu, as Yehoshua the Nazorean and coming king stood before Gamaliel and all the elders and all the priests. "It will be me, Yeshu. It must be me. You have a thing to do. How can you think you are alone in it? I too have a thing to do. I am your brother. As I am your double, I am more than your brother. If you have struggled to know who you are, I too have struggled. Yet who have I ever been but the shadow of my brother? If you are the Messiah, I am the shadow of the Messiah. And if you must do as the Father would have you do, so too must I. Therefore, I shall betray you. And when I have done this thing, then I will know who I am. And I will know my own name."

Jude does not wait for further protest, nor does he wait for answer. He walks from this place as Yeshu would walk from it, with Glory at his heels. And I stare at the air he has passed through as if somehow it is changed by his use of it.

Yeshu has closed his eyes as if he would never see a thing again.

I do not sleep this night. Yeshu is gone. Not even I know where. And I walk alone in my Father's house.

I am in torment. How can Yeshu do what he does? For pity of others, men and women he does not know and will never know, he allows his twin Jude, the most loyal of brothers to act the betrayer? He could have risen from his place, could have shouted Jude's name, and forbade him! The Sanhedrin will believe the brother of Yehoshua. Nor will the priests doubt him. Even Pilate will accept his word. For though few can conceive of any man's goodness, many are convinced of his failings.

I have reached the roof. From here I can see all of Jerusalem. Are any asleep? In the Valleys of the Kidron and of Hinnom, by the quarry beyond the Gates of Mariamne and of Phasael, the whole of the Mount of Olives, and near to the pools of Bethesda and Struthion and Israel, there are fires around which the pilgrims have gathered to await tomorrow's feast. There are lamps in niches on the walls of houses from the Upper to the Lower City. Before me, the Temple gleams by the light of the Ogdoad, the starry realm. Behind me, is the palace of the greatest Herod where this very moment Pontius Pilate lies. Or is he as well sleepless, and does he pace as I do, biting his nails? Has he had word of Jude Thomas the Sicarii, who is the betrayer of Yehoshua the Nazorean? Like the Sanhedrin, like the priests, like all those Yeshu would place on a game board and push here and push there, does Pilate all unwittingly prepare even now for what my friend would have him do?

There has never been a moment that Yeshu has angered me, but as I love him, he maddens me now. I am sick with what becomes of us. John of the River is murdered. Salome, the friend of my youth, is lost to me, and I think I shall never, not in this life, perhaps not even in another, see her again or hear her voice. My beloved Addai is crippled. Seth is not here. Dositheus is driven off. Now Jude is gone to play the part of that vilest of things, a man of false heart.

And once this great heart is seen to have done this thing, he too will be lost to me. Lost to all of us. He will be lost to himself. Does no one else rage at this? Will no one speak up?

I must find Yeshu.

I found him where Tata once tended her roses. I did not speak to him, nor in any other way betray my presence, but stood in the shadows as he sat alone on a low wall. What was there to say to a man so anguished it was as if his blood would escape his skin or his bones burst from his back?

I remained near all the rest of that night. Did I think I could stop him if he should rip out his tongue for the words it had spoken, or his eyes for all they had seen?

Later, brief sleep found me, for I dreamed a dream. Yeshu stood under the stars as three fell from the sky, one to land in each of his outstretched hands and one to land on the crown of his head. If this were all, I should have sung in my heart. But it was not all. Around his ankles coiled a man and a woman, both weeping and both blind.

If, as is said, those dreams we dream after midnight are true dreams, what then will I make of this?

⤙⤚

They have crucified the bandit Timaeus. He and all the others Pilate puts to death this day are nailed to their crosses, not roped. I could see them if I would climb again to Father's roof; and though I would not go back for my life, still I see them.

Like men of straw, they are black and broken against the bitter northern sky.

I am sure many think Pilate means the nails as a kindness done on Passover, for by them, the death of all these will come faster. If a man is hung by ropes, it takes him days to die of slow suffocation, sometimes four, sometimes even five or six or more. But if he is nailed, though the torment is so much more, and his agonized body hangs so much lower, often the time can be no more than the passing of two days. By nailing these now, it must also be thought that Pilate means them to die quicker so that they can be taken down before our Passover Sabbath. I would say that this Roman, whom the Poor call the Young Lion of Wrath, has learned a few things about the Jews: there can be no leaving a body on a cross into the Sabbath.

I do not know how I can think of such things. I do not know how I can continue to breathe. And though I read quietly as Miryam mends something of Yeshu's and Mary weaves wool from her small flock of sheep, and I throw down my scroll and I run whenever I hear a sound near the main doors of the largest courtyard, Jude has not yet returned. And if ever I have known disquiet, I know it now. All the comfort I have ever known, all the idle thoughts, all the dreaming of Egypt, are scoured from my skin. I am nothing but drowning, and salt.

Comes the third hour of this terrible day, and the scribes Levi and Matthew arrive with great clamor, what can be seen of their faces around their beards flushed with innocent pleasure. Like discovering Eio and her colt tied in a certain place in Bethphage, Yeshu had told them they would find a man in a certain alley near the rose garden by the Pool of Siloam, and that man would be carrying a water jug. And how could they miss a man with a water jug? To carry such a thing is woman's work. And once they had clearly seen him, they were to follow him and mark the house wherein he entered, for there we would eat our supper this evening. They rejoice, think it another miracle. They do not know it was, and is still, the House of Megas, and that even before they saw her manservant sent to fetch water, it was being readied for the feast of unleavened bread.

I turn away, for to me, the miracle is Jude. If there is any I now revere, and any I now pity, it is this brother of Yeshu. Where is he? When shall he return? Does he already suffer?

We are at supper before I know any of this.

As Yeshu would have it, we are twelve at table. He has listened to Seth and he has listened to John the Less and he has listened to Simon Magus, he knows the meaning of the stars in their twelves. This night, we are as the signs of the zodiac and he is as the sun.

Those who dine in the house of Megas the Whore were chosen long before ever we came up to Jerusalem, and they were chosen very carefully, for these shall go forth to tell of the Last Days. Aside from Yeshu himself, only one here knows what it is that is planned, and that one is I, seen tonight as John the Less. But a full ten are blessed with a luminous innocence. For the first time in my life, I know envy at this; not once before have I understood how comforting is ignorance. I can scarcely speak for worry. As for eating? Not a mouthful. Now and again, I manage a small sip of wine, but that is the sum of it. Yet the Sons of Thunder and Simeon the Zealot, Simon Peter and Joses and Matthew and Levi, these can scarce contain themselves for excitement, and eat and drink as befits a feast. Eleazar, whom they all pronounce as "Lazarus," chatters. Ananias the merchant swells with talk. Zaccheus of Jericho counts not tax money but his blessings. They know so little, understand so little, and what they know least of all is that the Yehoshua who sits among them will never sit among them again.

But in Yeshu there seems neither fear nor excitement. If he has been ill in the night at what he would do, his will has cured him. I know he has not slept. I know this is the first he eats since my mother's garden. I know that he has somehow gathered within himself such a pure and implacable strength that nothing short of the last hour in the last day will now stop him. If, without complaint and without hesitation, Jude can do what is needed of him, Yeshu would not do less. If Jude can find the courage to sacrifice himself, even unto his good name, Yeshu will move the world to ensure it has not been in vain.

I am placed to the right of Yeshu, Jacob bar Judas sits to the right of me. Standing behind us, Simeon tells me some new thing his well loved Bernice has done. On Yeshu's left stands Simon Peter who has yet to seat himself, while my cousin Eleazar stands near him lending an ear to whatever it is Simon Peter is saying to Yeshu. But no one sits on the left hand of Yeshu, and this because there is one of us who is yet to arrive.

Yeshu means this place for Jude.

We are served by Megas herself, and by Maacah and by Miryam, the daughters of Mary and Joseph. Mary has prepared the food, as has Martha, her goitered sister, for Megas has long since freed her slaves, and of her servants, there remain only a very few to maintain her great house.

Wearing the white robe of the Few, I lean my head on Yeshu's breast, who is also robed in white, and I listen for the sound of his heart. There it is, as slow as mine is fast. And I think that there could never have been a stranger feast, made all the stranger by the final coming of Jude. As Yeshu's twin moves among us, as he is greeted by one and by all, my beloved's heart beats now as fast as mine. Jude the Sicarii, so like his brother that even now it astonishes, does not look at us. Yeshu does not look at him. If the ten who are ignorant wonder at this, they make no remark. And Jude takes his place on the left hand of Yeshu, and still there is made no remark.

I feel Yeshu gather himself, and I know he means to speak, but I do not know how he finds it in himself to say this, "In truth, I say to you that one of you shall betray me."

Yea Balaam! I sit up and away from my love. The audacity of it! He will play this thing through! I would touch Jude, but I cannot. I would kiss his mouth, but I cannot. I would throw myself at Jude's feet and wash them as Megas washed the feet of Yeshu, but I cannot. Jude, who knows all this, and more besides, remains as still as the tower in the wilderness, his eyes cast down on the hand he has put forth to take food from a dish. But the others, who know nothing, break out into babble, looking from each to each, uneasy and unhappy, saying, "Is it me, Yehoshua? Is it me?"

"It is one of the twelve who dips into the bowl this day."

All other hands are snatched back from the serving bowls, but not Jude's: his hand is steady. He takes parsley from the bowl Miryam has set before him. He dips the bitter parsley twice in salt water as Yeshu reaches out his own hand for the unleavened bread his sister Maacah has provided us. Slowly and with great deliberation, Yeshu, who must note what Jude has done, breaks the bread he has taken, saying to all, "Take. Eat. This is my body which is broken for you. Do this in remembrance of me." He signals to Megas to fill his cup with wine, and when she has done so, he lifts it, saying, "Take. Drink. This is the blood I shall shed for you. He who will not eat of my body and drink of my blood, so that he will be made as one with me and I with him, the same shall not know salvation. And I tell you now of these things before they come, so that when they come to pass, you will remember, and you will believe in me."

Just as he has chosen his twelve with great care, so too has he chosen his words. Some are words that tell them clearly what it is he does, if they could but hear him. And some are the words of the god-man Mithras, and some are of Seth, and they are meant as symbol, as a way of saying that if they could hear, or "take him in," they would be as he is. But the ten innocents who hear him are as ignorant of this as of all else. Not understanding, these words are sure to ring long in their ears. For if they are not Jews, they are Galileans, and to Jews and to Galileans, blood is a fearsome thing. They are taught it is unclean. They drain it from the beasts they eat. They shut away their women when that time is upon them. They spill it daily on their altars. Yet here is Yeshu talking of betrayal, and here is Yeshu talking of drinking blood. And I feel them shudder where they sit. Yeshu knows full well they will not soon forget these blooded words. Or his deeds. And though each drinks from the cup that Megas fills for them, still their eyes dart from face to face, even to mine as once again I lean on the breast of my beloved, taking what comfort I can there. Yeshu claims one of them will betray him. They wonder, Which one could it be? They have all taken bread this night; they have all dipped their hands in the bowl. But if they are innocent of knowledge, they are also innocent of betrayal. Each knows he has not gone against this son of man who will be their king, and in this sure knowing, they begin bickering. They do not bicker about betrayal but about which among them could be accounted the greatest disciple.

And how is it that once again, the voice of Simon Peter sounds loudest? If Peter is one thing, it is this thing, he is irrepressible.

But this night, of all nights, Yeshu cannot bear to hear them. He raises his hand until they are silent. "And who is the greatest among you? He that sits at meat, or she that serves? If it is he who sits at meat, how then can you call me Master, for I sit among you as he who serves? Sit, Maacah, and you, Megas, and you, Miryam, sit near me, for you are not less than the men who love me."

Though Megas tucks her handsome chin into her handsome neck and goes about her business as one who is deaf, as does Miryam; Maacah would sit on the instant, but decides against it at a look from Peter. This is a look that Yeshu full sees, and though he has seen this same look before, many and many a time when Simon Peter would deign to look on me, this time he will not tolerate it. "Simon, Simon. How often Satan has desired to have you, that he may sift you as wheat, but I have stayed by you, praying that you fail not. I would have you hear me, Simon Peter. I would have you understand what I say to you so that you might be strong, and in your strength you would strengthen the others when my time is come."

Simon Peter is all contrition. "Master!" he cries. "I am ready to go with you, both into prison and into death."

Yeshu shakes his head slowly, saying, "I tell you, Peter, before the cock crows this day, you will have denied me thrice." Wounded, Peter points to his own breast, mouthing, "Me, Master?" But my beloved friend lifts now his head and looks out at all of us, and this time his voice is strong and firm and does not brook contradiction. "I tell you this also, that which is written will be accomplished in me. Therefore, it is time we began this night's business. Jude, go and do what it is you must do."

I do not know if any see but me, yet see I so clearly I know the sight will burn in my brain for all the rest of my life. I see a tear fall from the eye of Jude.

Jude's tear is as a pearl I wear in my heart.

His Will Be Done

All those Yeshu would have wait for us are even now in the shadows of the great supports of the Bridge of the Red Heifer in the Valley of the Kidron. They too have feasted in the homes of friends, or by campfires. Some have supped this night at the table of Josephus, and of these, we find first Veronica with her delight, the prattling Norea. And here are all the rest of the women who have not been to the House of Megas, or of Josephus, and as ever among them is the nameless woman of Ephraim. And there are the men: Saul the Bandit and Menahem the son of Simon bar Judas and James the son of Jacob bar Judas and more and more, and more even than followed us from Galilee, for word of Yehoshua the Nazorean has spread like fire through straw.

Though Father is not here—for it is not planned that Josephus of Arimathaea be in this place at this time—my cousin Eleazar keeps near me. And I am near to Mary the mother of Yeshu and of Jude, and I hold her, though she does not know why. *Eloi! Eloi!* How soon this timid one will be put to a test not even Job could bear. Not one son, but two, to die this night, each in his own way.

Our torches hiss and spit, as did the torches of the Feast of Osiris once spit, as all these wend their way from bottom to near top of the Mount of Olives, and Yeshu's robe is as unearthly white as the robes of the Therapeutae. At our head, he leads all these up to the very gate of Gethsemane, my mother's garden and tomb. But when I think we will all pass through the gate in the stone wall, he turns and holds up his hand, saying, "Wait for me here, for I go now to speak with the Father. But you, Simon Peter, will come with me, and I would have also the Sons of Thunder." He says nothing to me, but it is understood that I do not leave his side.

And so it is that we five would make our way up into Hokhmah's garden of the olive press, but Mary reaches out and takes hold of Yeshu's mantle, and by this, she slows his going. She says not a word, but all of scripture is in her eyes, and all of living and of dying, and Yeshu knows that in some way, she understands. He cannot help but smile upon her. "Let not your heart be troubled, Mother."

And here he lifts his face to all who listen. "Little children, yet a short while, I am with you. You will seek me, but where I go, you cannot come. So now I say to you that I bring a new Law, that you love one another as I love you. By this, shall all men know you. For all who believe in the Father believe also in me, and understand that in my Father's house are many mansions. If it were not so, I would have told you. I go to prepare a place for you. And if I do this, I will come again, and where I am, there too you will be. For no child is shut out from the house of the Father and the Mother."

But his cousin Simeon, whose great smile is washed from his face by what it is he hears, cries out, "Cousin! Show us the Father, so that we know where it is you go."

Yeshu loves this man, whose strength of body far exceeds his strength of mind. "Have I been so long with you and still you do not know me? He that sees me sees the Father. I am in the Father and the Father is in me. The words that I speak and the acts that I do, these are the Father's words and the Father's acts. Any who believes this of me, should he also believe it of himself, for the works I do, *you* shall do, and greater than I have done, shall you do."

It is Veronica, Jude's wife, who speaks now, and I see that she grapples with what is being said to her with the whole of her mind. "But you say you will come again?"

"You have heard me say this. I go away and come again to you. For greater love has no man than this, that he should lay down his life for his friends."

And there are those who begin to hear him, and those who begin to understand. In the face of Veronica a knowing comes forth. Yeshu smiles on her, raises his hand to her face. "Because I tell you these things, I see sorrow has filled your heart, but here is a truth. If I do not go out to what has been prophesied, how then can I return to comfort you? You sorrow now, but I will see you again, and your heart will rejoice, for in that time I will speak no longer in proverbs and symbols, but plainly, for in that time you will hear me."

Veronica is awash with tears, as is Simeon and many others. Do they know now what is to come?

"Where, Yeshu'a?" Simeon is hewn at the knees by his under-standing. "Where and when will we see you again?"

"You shall see me in Galilee, after my three days are past." At this, he turns to me, saying, "John, take us to where we might wait for what comes."

And so we enter again into the garden of Gethsemane.

We walk up the path I know well, not for having followed it at my mother's heel, but for following Father when my mother had left this world. Now I am at the heel of Yeshu, at mine are Jacob and Simon bar Judas, and at theirs Peter. And we go on in this way, silent and purposeful, moving under the black branches lit white by moonlight until we come to the stone bench where stands Hokhmah's apple tree. Here, where he and I tarried the whole of a day, each opening unto each, Yeshu stops, saying in a voice as grievous as my heart, "Sit you here, and watch with me. I would go farther for there is a sorrow in me, even unto death."

Hearing these words, John the Less would sit with Simon Peter and with the Sons of Thunder, but Yeshu makes a small gesture that calls only me on with him. For this, I am gifted with a look of baleful hatred from Peter. But as he, in his way, suffers so, I cannot begrudge him his jealousy. Simon Peter shall ever be as Simon Peter is.

So we leave them to sit and to keep watch, each with his hand under his cloak, for all three, being seasoned Sicarii, know that something tremendous is afoot, though none knows what. But Yeshu and I go on, climbing a narrow path through carven rocks, some tall as a tower, some wide as a house, that leads to the door of my mother's tomb. And here it is that Yeshu places his palms on the wheel of stone that covers the whole of the entrance. It would take but a strong shoulder against the stone to roll it away, but Yeshu does not push. He stands and he presses his hands flat to the surface, a surface I know is as cool as death. He presses his forehead against the stone. "Will I do this, beloved? Will the Father have me do this?"

Only now, as I move to his side, do I notice the sweat that flows down his face, mingled with tears. I have never seen such agony. Not on the face of the Samaritan father whose son was lost. Not on the brow of the madman who contained Legions. If ever I had words of comfort, or something of wisdom to teach, it must be now—but I am wordless. If ever Mariamne the prophet should speak ringing words of meaning and challenge, it must be now—but the Loud Voice is silent, as it has been since the Chamber of the Carmelites.

"Father!" my friend cries out to the stone, as silent as I am silent. "Take this cup from my lips!"

Oh Isis and all the gods, would that I could take it from him! Would that I could find the words or the way to turn him from what he has set his face to do, but I would sooner find a way to stop a great wave in the sea, or the sun in its path. And all around it is as quiet as death, and the Father neither speaks nor howls nor lights up the world with the crushing Glory of his Kingdom. That trick of the eye, that way of looking at what is always there, but rarely seen, is not mine this night nor is it Yeshu's. Not since he walked out from the wilderness with Glory in his red hair and in his red beard, with Glory coiling like shining mist about his person, has he been like this. The Light has fallen from him. He stands unrevealed in the darkness. And he is afraid.

I sink down beside him, and clasp his knees in my arms. And I think I will die of weeping. Or that I will weep forever. But he has lifted me up again so that once more I stand beside him. My face is not wet with tears but awash with them, as the delta with the Nile, and he traces my flooded cheek with a fingertip, touches my wet and salty mouth. And then he smiles. Can it be? Could his Glory come again, and come greater than ever? Does Yehoshua the Nazorean have this one bleak moment of unutterable darkness, but banishes the Dark in knowing the Light? I feel a tremendous stirring uncoil through my spine and throughout my limbs and behind my forehead, and it seems I am thrilled by joy. I am made rapt by Yeshu and by the snake that unwinds within me. Will I walk once more, as I have not walked since a dying child, in the Light of Perfect Peace and Perfect Knowing?

I am afraid and I am not afraid. I walk in Glory again—but this time I go with Yeshu. And being truly alive, Yeshu and I who am once more enraptured, meet in the Bliss of Being as it was meant in the Beginning of the End and the End of the Beginning. We are not selves at all; we are not two but one. For have we not been husband and wife, always?

It is still dark, the stars still shine, but the moon rolls along the edge of the sky, so that I know the sun is no more than an hour from the east. I feel Yeshu stir beside me; his voice a whisper. "Rise, beloved, my time is come." And immediately I rise up in full knowing and I no longer tremble and I no longer rage, for I am no longer afraid. All is as it should be. We walk down the path between rocks that we walked up, and it is the same path, changed in no way that the eye can see, yet it is a different path, so changed it seems of another world. And there at the end of it are the Sons of Thunder, and there is Simon Peter, and they sleep tumbled each against each. For a moment, Yeshu stands before them, looking down on the innocence of his disciples with great fondness.

From below us, farther than the gate to my mother's garden where all the others wait, far enough to be yet near the waters of the Kidron,

I hear a faint clamor, and I look out into the dark. Torches flare, a great number of torches, all weaving their way over the Bridge of the Red Heifer from out the Temple Mount, all coming toward us. There is no need to tell Yeshu this, for he knows as surely as I.

He shakes Simon Peter, whose head is on the shoulder of Jacob. "Cephas, why do you sleep? Could you not watch one hour with me? Rise for those who will come, have come."

Our Sicarii are on their feet in a trice, sheepish with guilt. And immediately we take the path that leads down to my mother's gate.

The people are rising from where they have slept, some already on their feet, some already aware of the torches and the growing tumult that comes at us from out of the dark. Children cry out; women enfold them in their robes. Everywhere men slip *sicae* from their belts, and like sly smiles, the waning moon gleams on the blades. If it should be asked of these, some of those who climb the Mount of Olives with torches and with staves will meet an unhappy fate.

The men who follow Yehoshua look to see if it is asked of them.

But Yeshu, circled whether he will or no by Simon Peter and Simon and Jacob bar Judas, and now by Simeon and Saul and others, does not ask it of them. Even, he goes so far as to say, "Put up your knives, for they that live by them, shall die by them." And some put up their knives, but not all.

I know what is coming, and I know why, so that I stand in my white linen tunic and I am wrapped round with my white linen mantle against the cold of this new day, and I face what Yeshu has willed. He that has fulfilled prophecy three times, fulfills it now a fourth. He is betrayed by a friend.

Jude Thomas the Sicarii is the first to reach us, his well-loved face stiff with what he will do. Jude, who has done so much for his brother, in this moment will now do the last of it, for so soon as it is done, and it is seen to be done by Simon Peter, by Simeon, by us all, he will be allowed no further thing. If he does not die by his own hand, he will die by another. And if he does not die, but lives, his life will be as the life of a lost lamb. And though I am enraptured and am enchanted, still I know the sorrow and the pity, but so too do I know the great triumph of it. Greater love has no man for a brother than he that will lay down his good name.

Behind him I see the face of Nicodemus. I see the face of the steward of Gamaliel, who is named Ellem, and next to this man is Malchus, who is servant to Josephus Caiaphas. They have both supped in Father's house. There are a handful more such as these, Jews out of the city, Sanhedrin and priest, enough to begin to fulfill what is needed by the fifth prophesy, that Yeshu be arrested by Jews. These carry torches, a handful carry staves, but following on seems an entire cohort of Pilate's men. Hundreds! Syrians by the looks of them, and these many hundreds carry swords. Pilate sends hundreds! The man must be convinced of armed rebellion. As is planned.

Jude makes no turn or pause, but walks to his twin as he has done all the days of their lives, to stand before him and to look his last into the face of Yeshu. "It is done, brother," I hear him whisper. "It is paid. I know my own name. Pray for me."

I hear Yeshu whisper, "As you will pray for me. No matter what occurs, no matter if I fail or I do not fail, you and I will meet in the Kingdom, for we have much yet to do with the other."

There follows a moment like unto no other moment, as if all other clamor and tumult fade away, as if the showering sparks of the pitch torches do not land on their red hair, and burn, and in this silent, sweetly scented place, Jude steps forward and kisses Yeshu full on the mouth. It is his good-bye, his greeting, his love, and his trust, and he has sealed it with this kiss. But I hear a hiss behind me, and it is Simon Peter who makes this noise, and I know what it is he thinks, but it is of no matter.

For Yeshu knows. And Jude knows.

And I know.

Yehoshua, turning away from his brother, faces those who have followed on after Jude. He looks into the eyes of Nicodemus, of Malchus, into the eyes of Ellem. In body, he makes himself as large as Simeon. He says, "Whom do you seek?"

And though I know him hideous inside with fear, Ellem answers, "Yehoshua the Nazorean. Him we seek."

"You have found him, for I am he."

And here should be the end of it, for Yeshu has no plan to lose any of his, or to have them harmed in any way. There is no plan for any to strike back, and this plan would hold—save for Simon Peter. In his howling fury, Simon Peter of Capharnaum would slay Jude, but instead he collides with the first to hand, which is Malchus. In a trice, this man's ear is gone from his head and his hand is clapped to the bloody hole, and he himself is howling and down on his knees.

And Yeshu, appalled and turning, gifts Simon Peter with a gaze like to burn, saying, "The cup the Father gives me to drink, shall I not drink it?"

So by Peter's foolish act of foolish violence, the many soldiers of Pilate that come with the few Jews of the Temple, rush forward, some to take Yehoshua the Nazorean, but most to cut down those who follow Yehoshua. By the flaring light of the torches, by the heart-rending sounds of fear and pain, I watch Saul of Ephraim put himself between Yehoshua and Pilate's men, only to be knocked to the ground and there set upon by a dozen Syrians. I watch as the Sons of Thunder would urge Yeshu away, and when he will not go, they would pull at him. I watch as those who are not Sicarii, Ananias and Eleazar and all the women and children, gather themselves up, and flee.

Is Norea safe? Is Mary? Am I?

Suddenly, there are two huge men of the north, their eyes made pale and dreadful by torchlight, who would run me through as I stand, and I seem as stone for all that I move. But Simeon the Zealot places himself between me and these, and though one has reached me, and grips my mantle with his fist, by the love of Simeon, I have time to wrest away, leaving only the long white cloth as a ghost in the dawn, before I too, as all the others, even Simon Peter, even Simeon himself, have fled.

Where is Jude? It is planned that we meet under my mother's apple tree. It is planned that together we will then do all that must still be done. I have come, breathless and numbed. He is not here. Must I act alone?

Below me, the torches move away. Like a snake of fire, they descend back down to the Valley of the Kidron. With them goes my heart, but not my sense. This is as it was meant to be. This is what Yeshu wills. I will wait for Jude . . . but I cannot wait long. The sun comes; even now the eastern sky opens so that Ra may pass through, and with it comes Yeshu's "death." In two hours, perhaps three, Yeshu will have caused Tiberius's prefect to condemn him. No matter that the Roman does or does not believe him guilty, Yehoshua will have forced his hand. This I do not doubt, not for a moment. Pilate is a proud man, he is hasty to act and regrets at leisure. As prefect, he has made many mistakes with the Jews. He is afraid he will make his last mistake. All say he is terrified of Tiberius—though who is not terrified of this cryptic and unpredictable emperor? Ananias has told me that a certain man once visited Tiberius; before his eyes this man broke a glass cup, but a moment later, passing his hands over it, made the cup seem whole again. It is an easy trick, one Addai taught me early on, but Tiberius was appalled—not even an emperor could control this!—and before another moment passed, he put the man to death. My beloved is like that man who visited Tiberius Caesar. Pilate will fear he cannot control him.

But when it is done, I must be ready. Where is Jude?

I can wait no longer.

Yeshu and his tormentors have reached the Gihon Spring Gate. In moments, they will have disappeared inside the city walls. There is much that I must do. I am up and running back down to the garden gate I have so lately fled. There is no one here. If any have fallen at Yeshu's arrest, they have crept away, or been taken. Like unmelted snow, my mantle lies where it was thrown, but I cannot bear to touch it.

Above the rooftops, the sun is moments old. And I am on the steep and narrow street that climbs past Father's north wall and up to the Upper Market. It goes also to Herod's palace where Yeshu will soon stand before Pilate. But I have no time to think of that now. Here is Father's side door; the very one I hid behind as Josephus forbade Salome and Ananias to ever again enter his house. In moments, Jose-

phus of the Sanhedrin will be called to his last special session, and
before that happens, I must speak to him. As planned. It is left to me
to persuade my father to do what only he can do—or we fail. But as I
open this small door, the door that Father seldom used, I am stopped
by a strong grip on my shoulder and I whirl in place. Though not before I have the knife of Simeon in my hand.

It is Jude. He has come!

He says nothing. There is a madness deep in his eyes, and though
I am wholly afraid, I reach inside and find his center holds. But only
because he, like me, must do what is planned. Or he must try to.
Without word, we enter the house of Josephus.

At sight of Jude, Father would call his Germans to seize him. He
would drive him from his house. But as Simeon the Zealot did for me,
I do for Jude. I step between them, crying, "No, Father! Hear me!"

"Daughter, I have accepted much from you. This I will not accept!"

Behind me, Jude makes no sound or movement, but I am desperate in mine.

"Father, you must hear me! We have no time to argue or to reason! As you love me, hear me! As you love me, as you love Yehoshua,
know what I will tell you is true. All that Jude has done has been
done for his brother. Can you think for one moment, this could not
be true?"

"Not be true? I have had word of it. His own wife has told me!"

"Father! If you drive him away, you will kill Yeshu."

"Kill Yehoshua? *Me?* It is *this* one, this—"

"Listen to me! Yeshu will be crucified this very morning."

"You think I do not know this? I am summoned to the council.
Caiaphas examines your Yeshu as we speak."

"Yes. And he will send him on to Pilate, and Pilate will do as Caiaphas wants and Yeshu wills: he will order him crucified. This will
all be done in as much secrecy as can be managed, so that the people
will not hear of it and, in hearing, come for him."

"You know this? And yet you do not fill your mouth with ashes?"

"I know this, Father, for it is what Yeshu *intends*. He intends to
hang on their cross. He intends to be seen to die on it."

"You are insane. You are making me insane."

Would that Yeshu had told him beforehand, but for Josephus to know was to risk his worry and his hindering, and perhaps his undoing with the Sanhedrin. Josephus must hear me, and he must understand me! It was planned that someone of standing and wealth come for Yeshu's body so that it might not be thrown into a ditch for the dogs, as is the fate of most who are crucified. For all that Megas is wealthy, for all that I am rich in my own right, it could never be any who is female. All along, Josephus has been in the mind of Yeshu. Josephus of Arimathaea must go to Pontius Pilate and beg to have the body, and he must succeed in his petition and be granted it! My father must make all the arrangements to have it taken to our tomb in the Garden of Gethsemane. Jude was to have gone here and there in Jerusalem, to warn of Yeshu's trial and dying so that it might not be the secret the authorities hope it will be. He cannot now do these things, for who will heed a betrayer? Therefore, he will do what I would do—he will gather the medicines to tend to his brother and he will wait for him in my mother's tomb. And I will alert those who will alert others.

It takes time, perhaps too much time, but in the end Father hears me. And when he does, he looks long and hard at Jude Thomas. Father shakes his head at the wonder of it. Who knows another such man?

And there is one last thing I must do: follow Yeshu on his way to Golgotha and to stand beneath him so that when his time comes, I will be ready.

What I need do is done. I have gathered the witnesses.

What Yeshu does, is almost done. And now it is gone the second hour. As has been agreed, I stand near the Hasmonaean palace, the bulk of which looms at my back, shading me from a sun grown fat with the day. Near to hand is the Gennath Gate, that which is closest to the palace of the Great Herod and I wait. Yeshu shall pass by here, this is certain, for it is the surest and fastest route from where Pilate this day governs, to Golgotha, the Place of Skulls where

Timaeus hangs as he has hung since this time yesterday, slowly dying on his cross. With me are the women, every one of them. With these women, I too am a woman. I am Mariamne Magdal-eder, and I dress as becomes a Jewish woman of the Law, and I comport myself as becomes a Jewish woman of the Law. My head is covered, as is my face, and my eyes do not flash with understanding. No male stands near me. The males who have followed Yehoshua the Nazorean have fled the city. It seems they hide themselves in the hills beyond. I have nothing to say about this. I think nothing. I stand with the women, and every part of me is intent on what I must do. If the men have fled, they have fled. What they would do so soon as Yeshu was taken was never our concern. I have only one concern, and it consumes the whole of me: Yeshu is coming. And I will be his rock.

There is a disturbance to the west. The gates of Herod's palace open. As it has already begun for Yeshu, it begins for me.

Comes now Yehoshua and comes those who surround him, at the very first sight of which Mary sways against me, her breath gone shallow and ragged. Behind me, Miryam would choke on the sobs that convulse her. Megas stumbles into the road, and would fall but for Maacah. Around me are sent up the wails of the children and the keening of the women. But I do not wail and I do not keen. Mariamne Magdal-eder does not weep and she does not cover her eyes and she does not cry out to God in her anguish. She does nothing but watch Yeshu. Before him and behind him march Pilate's soldiers, but they are only six in number, which can only mean that another thing is as Yeshu said it would be. Neither the prefect nor the Sanhedrin mean to make a show of this killing, nor do they expect most to notice, and Pilate will not give them cause by sending out more than six men. But I am here and the women are here, and more come now, and also comes now men of the city appearing in the doors of the houses, from out of the side streets. Some stand on their roofs. Others throw open their shutters for all inside to see out. There come more and more of them, from all over Jerusalem.

There will be those who see this.

He who is dearly beloved of me has been scourged. He has been spat on. The white of his linen tunic is splashed with the blood of his body, redder than his hair is red. My beloved is bent double by the weight of the *patibulum* he carries, which is the crossbeam they will hang him from, and around his neck he wears a sign on which has been crudely written KING OF THE JEWS. Yeshu cannot see for the blood in his eyes. I think about his eyes. I think about his sight. I think about what he has seen and what he has felt since last I saw him. He breaks my heart. I cannot watch. And for one moment and only one moment, I turn my face away, and in this moment there is a quick intake of breath behind me, and I am jostled by someone who pushes past.

Veronica has run out into the road. She pulls the cloth from her head, the one she must wear by Law. She exposes her beautiful black hair. Jude's wife hurries to her brother-in-law's side so that she might cleanse his face with the soft blue head cloth, so that she might wipe away the blood and the sweat and perhaps even the pain. And I know, as all the women know, Veronica carries within her body another child by Jude, and I know too that she carries within her soul the burden of his betrayal.

My beloved lifts up his face as he feels her touch, and I see him smile. He cannot see her through the swelling and the blood, but he smiles. Then, abruptly, a soldier nearest shoves Yeshu with the hard flat palm of his hand so that my beloved falls forward to his knees, and another rips the blue head cloth from Veronica's hand, and yet another grips Veronica's hair and by it propels her away from Yeshu, so that she stumbles on the cobblestones and would also fall, but she does not. She does not fall, for now, from out of the gathering shocked and silent crowd comes a big man with a rage as black as a Cyrenian, his white teeth set on edge.

Yehoshua's cousin Simeon has not run away.

He has not hidden himself in the wilderness. He is here, and he catches Veronica before she would hit the stones, and when she is once more safely away from the soldiers who surround Yeshu, he lifts the hundredweight of crossbar from Yeshu's back and places it on his own. And when a soldier would stop him, Simeon the Zealot says, "Let me be about my business."

I have followed every cubit of the way. Every step Yeshu has taken I have been witness to. Every movement of his body, of his head, of his hands. Simeon carries his crossbeam but speaks not. Here and there someone from the crowd would call out the name of Yehoshua but is hushed. Now and again someone offers Yeshu drink. He does not take it. He does not look around. He does not speak. Our last walk is made in this strange silence. Only the leather of our sandals sounds, the loose rock underfoot, the breath of so many on the chill morning air. Only the crows cawing on Golgotha, what care they what men do? And though Yeshu is beaten so that he might be weakened and, by weakening, die quicker on the cross, he is yet strong enough to do this thing. I see that he is strong. By the act of Simeon, he is spared using the strength he will need to endure what he must soon endure. I bless Simeon as I bless Veronica as I bless Jude.

And I follow.

Out from the Gennath Gate, the road leads west past the limestone quarry from where the great stones were cut for the Temple Mount. The earth is raw here, it is wounded. But we take this road only until it comes on a rutted path that wends its way to the top of a rise above the quarry, and on this rise Timaeus awaits us. As do all others crucified with him. Every moment we have walked, I have felt them above us, and now that we climb the slight rise to meet them, I feel them more palpably still. Their presence hangs in my mind as their bodies hang slumped on the crossbeams.

At the last moment, something has moved Pilate to be merciful to Yehoshua the Nazorean. A man he is told is a rebel, a pretender to the throne of David, a seditionist, and a nuisance who has caused him to be rousted from his bed early on the morning of a feast, is granted what mercy is left a man who would condemn others to their deaths. Pilate has decreed this latest messiah be crucified with nails—as Yeshu knew might happen. My friend has all along steeled himself for nails instead of ropes knowing his death will be hastened by them, that the pain will be that much more, the trial that much harder, and the risk that much greater. For me, it means I must not take my eyes from him or my hands from Tata's leather purse at my waist. When the signal comes, I must be ready.

We come to the crest above the quarry; we come now to stand under the Tau crosses of the crucified men. I have no heart to count them. And here, to my increasing horror, I see that one of these is Saul of Ephraim. Saul is also pinned like sacrifice on a cruel altar of rough worked wood. Above his head is nailed a *titulus* that says BRIG-AND. Above the head of Timaeus is nailed also BRIGAND. Timaeus seems almost gone from this place, but Saul is yet fully with us. The flies have found all these. They feed from their blooded mouths and their salted eyes, and from the waste they cannot help passing. They creep along the stiffened, stretched, and broken limbs. I look away. So they might not be shamed, I look away.

From among the many upright *stipes,* no more than poles, one is chosen. Bluntly, Simeon is ordered back into the crowd where he comes to stand by me, and the crossbeam he has carried full half the way is laid on the ground. Quickly now, so that it might be over and done with, the soldiers rip the blooded tunic from Yeshu's body; they require him to lay himself on the ground and to stretch out his arms against the length of the crossbeam. He must hold his arms firm so that first one wrist is fastened to the wood by a nail, cruel in its thickness and length, and then the other. The man who would hold the nail against Yeshu's flesh chooses that place between the two bones of his arm above the wrist, and even here Yeshu does not cry out as the nail is driven home, though he closes his eyes and turns his pale face from the crowd to seek what small privacy is left him. Yeshu has known pain; there is always more pain.

Mariamne, who has seldom known pain of the body, knows now searing pain of the heart and dizzying pain of the mind. She would drop to the earth with it, lie on her belly and howl with it. She would grind dirt into her hair and into her face. But John the Less must not move—he must watch and he must remember. And Mariamne must comfort Mary. Yet there is more mettle in the mother of Yeshu and of Jude than ever there has seemed. Mary, the second wife of Joseph, is quiet by my side. It is her hand that steadies my shoulder.

It takes all six soldiers to pull up and place Yeshu's crossbeam in the notch at the top of the *stipes,* to fasten it so that it does not tip or tilt or fall, and to nail upon it the sign Yeshu has worn since leaving

the hall in which Pilate gave out his decree: KING OF THE JEWS. It takes
two to drive the tremendous nail through his heels. Even Yehoshua
cannot bear this without sound. His shriek of agony fills my mind
with terror. It takes all that I have not to scream. And to scream.

It is just gone the third hour of the day.

There comes the slightest touch against my back. Who would take
my attention from Yeshu? I turn my head only far enough and no
farther, for I cannot cease my witnessing. It is Jude! Jude has come up
behind me. His head and half his face are covered so that none see
the telltale red hair and beard. Jude Thomas stands at my back, his
eyes fixed on Yeshu. I should have known Jude could no more wait
alone all these hours in my mother's tomb than I could. I allow myself one look round. All eyes are on Yeshu. None concern themselves
with this stranger among us. I allow myself one small movement
against him so that he might know I know.

The hours pass. And I, who the whole of my life have thought
this and thought that, questioned all I might hear and then questioned my questions, think nothing.

And now that Yehoshua dies before them as all their messiahs die,
some others drift away, first one and then another; then a small group,
and then another. I remain without movement. Jude remains without
movement. The soldiers who have done this thing sit nearby playing
at dice, but I do not sit. Neither sits his mother Mary nor his sweet sister Miryam, who stand closest to me and to Yeshu. Nor does the sister,
Maacah, or Megas of Ephesus or the unnamed woman of Ephraim.
And though she is with child, Veronica stands as we all stand; even
Martha and the widow Salome stand. We are a small group of women
who witness that Yeshu dies so that others might know Life.

Aside from the soldiers, only two men stand with us: Simeon the
Zealot and Jude. It is not impossible that Simeon knows the man
who keeps the whole of his head covered, but if he does, he says
nothing, does nothing. Jude is as still as the death all around him.

I stand and I listen to the horrid song of the flies and I wait.

Is it now? Does Yeshu call me? I start from my place, gripping Salome's vial, the one given her by the ancient Sabaz who once tended
to the children of Mark Antony and of the seventh Cleopatra, only

to find that Yeshu is not speaking to me. He has turned his head to Saul who is crucified on his left hand.

None who hang can easily breathe; it is this loss of breath that slowly kills them, and as for speaking, it is almost impossible, yet Yeshu would speak to Saul. I reach out to know what he would say and find I know this: It was not meant for any but Yeshu to feel the fatal grip of Rome. No other was to be crucified. Yeshu grieves for Saul and would atone, but Saul stops him before his words can come. By gesture only, for Saul has hung so much longer and is so much closer to death, he forgives Yeshu who I know cannot forgive himself. The price he pays for what he does is more costly than even the King of Lydia could summon, but to know that others pay as well, by Isis, what a thing is done this day. With great effort, Yeshu says, "This very day you shall know the Kingdom."

Shadows stretch across the stony ground, each shaped as a thin black cross and on each cross: black flesh, black blood, black pity. The sun is lowering itself into the west; by this we know the Sabbath nears. Yeshu must die by the Sabbath. If he does not die, then the soldiers will kill him as they will kill all the others. There will be no bodies on crosses to defile the Passover Sabbath; it is certain that Pilate will not cross the Jews in this. Even now the soldiers make ready to break the legs of those who have hung here much longer than Yeshu. If their legs are broken, they cannot push themselves up against the small block of wood placed at their feet and thereby suck air into their agonized lungs. Without this moment of blessed breath, they must now die quickly.

I move closer to the foot of Yeshu's cross. I cannot call out. I can do nothing but stare up at him and, by the strength of my need, somehow touch him. Yeshu! Yeshu! The time comes! Call out. Tell me I must do what I must do. My own breath comes quickly; my own heart beats without rhythm. I have feared this, always. Beforehand, Yeshu could not know what it would be truly like; he could not account for everything. Months ago, Salome warned me on the mountain of the Carmelites that anything might happen to a man who was hung on a cross. All die if they are not taken down, and few are ever taken down once they are condemned. But some die quickly, as little as two days. And some die slowly, as long as the whole of a week. And some, before dying, go mad. What if Yeshu has lost himself? More terrible than all else on this terrible day, is this thought: what if he has forgotten what he intends?

Before I see it, I feel Yeshu gather himself, and then he opens his eyes.

I am closest. As I stand at his very feet, he sees me first before all else he sees. And then he sees the sun, and he too knows his time is come and he must act. Therefore, my time is come.

At the ninth hour, my beloved cries out, "I thirst!"

He has not forgotten, nor has he become lost in his mind. This is what I wait for. But now it is come, I tremble that I will fail my friend. The blood of my body, hot as the blood of the lambs spilled on the altar this day, seems suddenly to drain away and, with it, my very purpose. I am afraid. I am afraid. What do we do here? Yeshu is as good as dead; would I die too? If any should suspect me, could I withstand the scourge and the sword? I am nothing but a woman. I cannot do this thing! I was not made to do this thing! And I would turn and I would run. And I do, I turn. And there before me stands Jude who has given the whole of himself to Yeshu. And there before me stands Simeon who does not understand what is done here but who has not run and will not run. And there is Veronica and Mary and Megas and all the others who do not fade nor faint nor fail, though they see Yeshu die before their eyes. And I am ashamed. Long ago, John of the River said I was as a man. By all that I have ever said and all that I have ever done, I will do this thing. I am not a man, but a woman—yet I will not fail.

This is what I know to do. Before dawn, before ever any were in this place save the already crucified men, there was sent here Miryam who has ever had a steady hand and a steady heart. The youngest sister of Yeshu placed within sight a slender pole, and near it one of the sponges of Ananias, and near to that a small jug of vinegar. I slip the vial of Sabaz out from my purse and the stopper from the vial. Inside is a tincture made from the skin and the liver of a tiny puffed-up ball of a fish. None but the most informed poisoner would know of this fish, and of this small number, only the richest could afford it. Quickly, I shake out a few drops onto the sponge. Salome has been careful to show me how much to use: too much and I might kill Yeshu myself; too little and he might rave, but just enough and he will appear so convincingly dead no one shall doubt it. To this I add vinegar in case any would stop me, for the crucified are often offered gall, which is *rosh* and vinegar, to ease their suffering. And when I have done these things, I affix the sponge to the pole.

Once again I am under the cross of Yeshu. I lift the pole so that the sponge reaches his lips. He knows what is on the sponge; he knows that he must trust that I have made the potion well. He knows if I have not, this will be the end of it. Knowing all this, he sucks at the sponge, takes within himself as much as he can swallow. Salome swore it would work quickly. She had seen such things in classes with Sabaz, and she did not lie. It is but a single moment since I offered up the gall and already his head slumps on his chest; already his skin grows pale and there comes a lifelessness throughout his limbs. Could he be truly dead? Have I misjudged the potion?

No time for my incessant questions. I must play my part. I must cry out that he dies so that the soldiers will see this for themselves. I must cry out loudly so that Father, who has stood for the last hour some way down on the road to Emmaus, will hear me and will run now to Pilate. I must cry out so that all the women will believe he dies, and the air will be shrill with it. By this, the soldiers will be sure it is so. And though they cannot believe it—What man dies within only six hours? No man dies before even a day; who has ever heard such a thing?—and though they mutter among themselves, they will decide that this one was beaten too hard, or they will decide that this one was too weak. Whatever they decide, they will believe he is dead. They *have* to believe it. I will them to believe it. If I can receive a thing, I can send a thing, and this I send into them with all that is within me: Yehoshua the Nazorean is dead. There is no need to hasten his end, no need to break his legs, first one, and then the other so that he cannot lift himself to breathe. There is no need. No need.

It works. It works! They too see that the sun soon passes into the Sabbath. And taking up their swords, they walk among those who still live—all but Yeshu still live, though all have hung now for the whole of one day and one night—and one by one, they break their legs. Pilate would have all these dead before Passover, and they will do as Pilate has ordered. It is a gruesome and fearful thing. I weep for Timaeus, for Saul, for a man I have heard is named Yehoshua Barabbas. I weep for them all, but as I have seen so many gruesome and fearful things, I stand steady. And when they come to Yeshu, they put away their swords. At this, I stand steadier still. I hear what they do not say: why make the effort when no effort is needed? They put away their swords, they put them away—all but one. And my heart thinks to leap from my breast. This one is old; he has seen many deaths done in many ways, but he has never seen a man die so soon. He cannot believe what he sees here. He cannot believe a man of Yeshu's age and Yeshu's condition could be so weak; not even a woman would die this soon. I hear him mutter: "Something is wrong, here. Something is not right." And so muttering, he comes to stand under Yeshu's cross and to peer up at him.

Yeshu is dead! I shout it in my mind. Yeshu is dead! But this one lifts his sword to poke the point of it into Yeshu's foot. There is no movement. And still this is not enough for the man. He stabs Yeshu's thigh. I gag where I stand. Behind me, Mary looks on appalled. Her son is dead. Rome has killed him. Must it also dishonor him? And still this is not enough. Drawing back his arm, the seasoned soldier makes a short powerful thrust into Yeshu's side, and from this wound flows Yeshu's blood. My breath is lost to me. I cannot breathe. By this, the man must know the condemned man lives, for no dead body bleeds. Yet, for some reason, he is now satisfied. Perhaps because if Yeshu did not die before, he will certainly die now.

The old one struts away. By his going, all the soldiers have gone. There is nothing here but dead and dying men and weeping women and crows cawing at the waning sun.

And I would faint but for Jude. Jude, who has stood all along, silent, as Yeshu is now silent, comes up behind me to keep me from falling. But when I have recovered myself, and I turn to him he is gone from this place.

I have done what Yeshu willed. We have all done the will of Yeshu, who does what he is certain is the will of the Father. All has gone as planned. Save for the part that Jude would play. And for the soldier who would not believe.

Now that the raw red sun sits on the far edge of this day, people I have not seen before begin gathering. They have come for the bodies the soldiers leave on the crosses. Some come for a son or a brother or a father, and some come for those who have no kin here, for by Law all bodies must be gone from the crosses by the Sabbath, mere moments away. If it were not the Sabbath, most especially the Passover Sabbath, they would not be allowed this caring. If it were not the Sabbath, the bodies might hang until they rotted, and only then would the soldiers take them down, to throw them like waste into shallow uncovered pits for the scavenging dogs to take in the night. This is why Yeshu has chosen to die on this day of all days. This is why he could not be arrested sooner than the night before this day. It was planned that he be no longer than needed on the cross. It was planned that he be seen to die as he hung before the people. It was planned that he be taken away by friends and by kin. And it was needed that Pilate be in Jerusalem when Yeshu proclaimed himself king, for if he were not, none could hang until Pilate came. Only Rome crucifies and only Rome can legally put to death a seditionist. If Yeshu were arrested without the personal presence of Pilate, he would wait, like poor John under the Fortress of Machaerus, suffering agonies in the lightless cells under the Antonia, where anything could happen to him, and none would know. For Yeshu, there could be no other time to die than this Passover.

In the last of the light, and as my skin thrums like the strings of a lyre, comes finally Josephus of Arimathaea. And with him, he brings the barber Timothy. Beside them, and without protest, Eio draws a cart, and in the cart there are linen burial clothes.

Father has succeeded. He has somehow persuaded his acquaintance Pontius Pilate to allow us Yeshu's body. I would embrace him, tell him how dear he is, but we must be about our business here.

With the help of the dauntless Simeon, Yeshu is taken from his cross, tenderly, carefully. Eloi, but the nails are cruel! Any would think my beloved dead, would swear he was well and truly departed from this world. As the dead, he is wrapped in the linen. As the dead, he is placed in Eio's cart so that his limbs are straight. And his mother will sit with him, will touch the white cloth that covers his face, will smooth the white cloth that covers his body. Mary will weep over her son the whole of the way to the Garden of Gethsemane and the tomb of my own mother, over whom I have never wept.

There is only one prophecy left.

Yehoshua has been baptized by the prophet John of the River and been anointed as a king by Megas the Sorceress. My beloved, who is called Messiah by the people, and who has worked wonders even unto the raising of the dead, has now also been seen to be betrayed by a trusted friend, the best and closest and most trusted of friends. He has been accused by the Jewish priests and by the Jewish Sanhedrin. He has been tried by the Romans. Yehoshua the Nazorean has been crucified. And now he must fulfill the last of the needed prophesies: he must rise on the third day as Osiris, as Dionysus, as Tammuz, as all godmen rise on the third day. Even as Horus rises on the third day. Horus, the son of Isis and the son of Osiris, was born in a cave at winter solstice and his birth was announced by a star in the east and was attended by three wise men. As an infant, Horus was carried out of Egypt to escape the wrath of Typhon; as a child he taught men in the temple; as a man he walked with twelve disciples. He fed multitudes with bread and with fish, he walked on water, he raised the Dead. He was called the Lamb of God, the Messiah, the Good Shepherd. He was crucified, buried in a tomb, and resurrected on the third day.

It is Mariamne Magdal-eder who must set about fulfilling the last of this terrible plan, who must begin now to play a part that Jude was to have played, but first we must care for Yeshu. The blood still flows from the cut made by the old soldier's blade. It is a frightful wound, deep and damaging. It was not meant that he be stabbed. It was not

planned that he be wounded beyond the anguish of the Roman torture and the Roman cross, and be wounded so grievously. But no one
was fool enough to discount it might happen; therefore, there is to
hand all that we might use for such a wound.

But here is a thing we did not anticipate. Though all others are
long since persuaded to leave us, Mary will not go. I reason with her,
I plead, I demand: she will stay near the body of Yeshu. I grow frantic. Yeshu has insisted no one be told, yet his wound is grave. How
can we tend it if Mary believes him dead? There is nothing for it.
She must be told.

As he has ever taken such unspeakable burdens, Jude, who is as
he should be, waiting by my mother's tomb, will take yet another.
Jude Thomas the supposed betrayer tells his mother Mary what has
been done this Passover.

Any mother would rejoice her child was not killed, but to hear
that he has caused his own death? Any mother would rejoice her
child has not betrayed his brother, but to hear that it must always be
thought so? Why is it that Mary does not seem surprised? Do I only
imagine her quiet pride? Again and again, she gives me pause.

For prophecy, and to assure Pilate that the King of the Jews is well
and truly killed, Yeshu had need of being seen taken to Josephus's
tomb in the Garden of Gethsemane, and this we have done. But he
cannot stay here. It was never planned that he remain here. So soon
as it is entirely dark, and so soon as Jude is entirely sure there is
none to see, Eio's cart must take him away to Father's house. Father's
house is where he will stay until all that need be done is done.

As Timothy the barber and I muffle the wheels of the cart so that
we might go quietly, Jude rolls back the stone of the tomb. And
Mary, who understands now and understands quickly, so arranges
Yeshu's burial linen that it might seem cast away.

And then we leave this place.

Could the world turn blacker? Could the air turn thicker so my breath
comes harder? Can I bear more? For all whom Yeshu has healed,
would that he might heal himself.

He is hidden in an inner chamber of Father's house, far from the airy central courtyard and the public rooms. There is nothing here but a bed and a lamp and thick draperies and thicker rugs to soften the sound. It is deep into the night, full halfway between the sun's leaving and the sun's return, and only mere moments ago did Salome's poison wear away so that my beloved seems not dead, but sleeping.

Yeshu returns to me. But he does not return as he left. And it seems he will not stay. My friend is dying.

Father's slaves and Father's servants run every which way, bringing me this and bringing me that, but still he dies. I am become frantic. If Tata were here, could she save him? If Seth were here, could he? I am here. Can I?

Jude does not weep. Save when I have need of him, Jude does not move. If Yeshu is dead, so too is Jude.

Mary tends to her son's ankles, to his wrists, to the lashes on his back, to the great gaping wound in his side. Mary does not cease in her work, and by this, has no time for weeping. Nor for speaking. All this goes on around me in a silence made dreadful by the sound of Yeshu's breathing. Harsh, erratic, difficult, sometimes stopping altogether.

But yet he breathes.

And so long as he breathes, I will not leave him. I do not leave him. I have arranged myself so that I might rest my head on the pillow near his head. With the very best of the sponges of Ananias, I have washed his face and his limbs. I have carefully combed his red hair and his red beard. His linen is the finest Father owns. I have mixed spikenard into the lamp oil so that in this way he is soothed by the odor of God. I have done all these things, and more, and can think of nothing else I might do. So that now, by the soft light of the scented lamp, I stare at him, drink him in with my eyes, commit to memory all that I might of him. Every line so precious, every color so perfect. My beloved is as beautiful in his dying as in his living, more beautiful, for the threat of his being no more.

I sink into sleep as I watch him. I must sleep, for I start awake with the sun full on my face. In surprise and alarm, I find I am no longer in the hidden room. While I slept someone has carried me into a small courtyard where there is room for a small pool, and near the pool, room for me, and for Yeshu on a pillowed divan, and for Mary. Mary is slumped on a stool pulled close to Yeshu's divan where she now sleeps. I would wager all I own that he who carried me sits at the courtyard's entrance, keeping close vigil.

Jude has not slept. Jude has not slept for days now.

Slowly, slowly, I raise my head from where I rest it, afraid of what I might find.

By the full and rounded moon! Yeshu is not dead! He is awake and he stares at me just as half the night I have stared at him. I am on my feet in an instant. I would run to Jude, to Father. I would awaken his exhausted mother, but he stays me with the slightest movement of his bandaged arm. He would have me sit again. I will sit again. I will do anything he would have me do, only that he would live.

But he cannot speak aloud, cannot make sound enough so that I might readily catch his words. I must lean my ear close to his mouth. "Do you know what the Roman said to me?"

"No, I do not know. But please, do not speak. Rest." I am so afraid. His life drains away as I listen.

"I have all eternity to rest in the Father and the Mother. Hear me, Mariamne, for I would say these things to you. As the Roman condemned me, he asked, 'What is Truth?' Of all that was planned, I did not plan to answer this question." Even now, he sees the foolish joy of things, and more than all that has gone before this tears at my heart. He beckons me closer. "As I was crucified and hanging on the cross I had chosen, I thought of Pilate's question. What is Truth, my beloved?"

Does it come to this? Do all the questions come down to this question? It is asked by Seth. It is asked by the man sent to rule the Jews by the demented tyrant Tiberius, a Roman, a soldier, a stranger. It comes again from out the mouth of Yehoshua who is so full of truths, he whose very Truth attracts all others.

What is Truth?

Yeshu cannot move, but he can turn his head, and behind his eyes I can see the light that shines there, undimmed. It is as the light that shone in the eyes of John of the River, half mad, yet wholly sane. "I will tell you all I know of Truth," he whispers in my straining ear, "and I will be done with it. There is no one Truth: there is only Life. There is only the Kingdom that holds many Truths, as many as the sea holds fish, or the sky holds stars. Therefore, each man holds a Truth, holy unto himself. If I should live, I would ask a man to look to *me* who is outside himself for what is his. But if I should die, a man who would look for me must look within and, by so looking, would find not me, but himself." Yeshu seeks my hand, grips it with surprising strength. "You see what I must do, Mariamne, who is as wife to me?"

I cannot breathe, cannot see, cannot live. "I see it, husband."

And here, before me, Yeshu drops his head to his pillow and is gone from me. Back to that place where he does not sleep, nor does he yet awake by dying, but hides himself in darkness, waiting for what comes by his perfect intent that it do so.

I do now what Jude was to have done. I do the last thing.

Deep in the darkest part of the night, Jude and I have made our way to my mother's tomb—Jude, so that he might roll away the stone and, having done so, return to keep watch over Yeshu. And I so that I might be here when the god sun rises on this, the third day.

Now I sit just outside the entrance, alone. And at my feet is my bowl of spices, and by my side is the blooded white linen that covered Yeshu's body. Any moment should bring not only the sun, but two, perhaps three, perhaps more, eager, wondering, frightened men. I await them not as John the Less, but as Mariamne Magdal-eder, the *myrrhophore*, the ointment bearer. I await them as she who has come to do that which women do for their dead. I await them as she who has come in all piteous sorrow and has found the stone rolled back and the tomb empty.

There is one other besides Jude who helps me this last day of Yeshu's Last Days. More than an hour past, Eleazar is sent out into the city to find any he can of Yeshu's disciples; it matters not which they are. I have told him he must bring them here, to the Garden of

Gethsemane where they, as well as he, are sure their murdered Messiah still lies. Yeshu's "Lazarus" knows nothing but what he has seen, and what he has seen is what the magician Yehoshua the Nazorean has caused him to see. Therefore, he does this thing in perfect innocence and with unfeigned grieving and full bursting with wonder. I have told him that no matter they will not come for fear of the Romans, or for fear of some unnamed trickery, he cannot fail me. No less than two must come. There must be at least two, so that each will believe what he sees by the other's also seeing it.

I hear them come before I see them. From where I sit, I might see full half the length of the high stoned path leading back to my mother's apple tree. Those who approach are farther still, but they are coming quickly.

Immediately I rise to play my part. I pinch my cheeks so that I seem flushed with awe. But I need not summon tears; tears are with me now always. They are as Yeshu's blood; with them, my wounded life flows away. But I hold myself steady before what I know will be said and will be done. No man wishes news from a woman. No man bears well that a woman knows first, and I make myself humble before them. Meekly I stand, and submissively I wait, and humbly I look up, and they are upon me. *Yea Balaam!* Comes now someone I did not expect to see, nor did Yeshu, and just behind this one—both running as fast as they are able and both seeking to outrace the other—comes the man I never had doubts of seeing. Not only is Yeshu's fiercest brother, Jacob the Just, more righteous than Simon Peter of Capharnaum, he is faster.

Jacob, as he has done since first ever I saw him, does not look at me. I am nothing to him. I will never be other than nothing to him. His skull as bald and as blue skinned as when last I saw him, Jacob stares at the stone rolled back from the door of the tomb. He stoops to peer into the darkness inside. He sees the linen that Yeshu had lain under. He notes the bowl of spices that I would use to sweeten the body. But he does not go in. That is left to Simon Peter, who does look at me, and the look is grievous in its envy and painful in its hatred. But this does not matter now. I do not matter now. What matters now is what Simon Peter will see and what Simon Peter will make of what he sees.

He enters Hokhmah's tomb. There no more than a moment, he is back again. At this, and perhaps because no demon has seized Simon Peter, nor fit come over him, nor any other terrible thing happen, Jacob goes in. And is quickly out again.

"Woman," says Simon Peter in a voice he can use now that Yeshu is gone, "what has happened here?"

I look at Simon Peter as a woman is required to look at a man, saying, "I found it as you see it, Simon Peter. Just as you see now, save one thing. I also saw an angel, I saw—"

Simon Peter thrusts his face into mine, grinds his broken tooth, stuns me with his breath. "Why would a woman see an angel? If there is an angel to be seen, I will see this angel."

"As Yeshu loved you, Simon Peter of Galilee, you will see an angel. But it is gone from this place. It was here and it shone as white as rime, it shone as bright as fire, and then it was gone. Yet before leaving, it spoke as clearly as you or I."

The color drains from Simon Peter's cheek. Jacob's back stiffens.

Simon Peter asks, "What did it say?" Simon Peter demands, "Tell us what it said."

"The angel said that Yehoshua is risen."

Simon Peter could not become paler, nor could his eye become rounder. "It said to you that he is risen?"

"Do you doubt it, Simon Peter? Did Yehoshua not say he would be betrayed by a friend, and was he not betrayed? Did Yehoshua not say he would be arrested by the Jews and tried by Romans, and has this not come to pass? Yehoshua said unto you that he would rise on the third day, and has he not risen? And did I not turn from the angel, and did I not see him?"

Simon Peter hisses, "See who?"

"I saw Yeshu who stood where Jacob stands." And now I am certain that Jacob hears me, for though he does not seem to listen, the bulk of his body jerks away from its place to settle in another. "I saw him in a vision, and he said to me, 'Blessed are you who do not waver at the sight of me.' But I did waver. And I wept to see him so, for I could not touch him. But he said to me, 'Mariamne, why do you weep? Do you not see I ascend unto my Father.'"

And here I falter. My throat is as sand. I cannot do this. I cannot say these things Yeshu would have me say for I am stricken with arrows of grief so sharp and so killing that my limbs tremble and the tears roll down my face. All this was to be done as Yeshu lived! It was planned that he returned in body so that he might open the Spirit! But Yeshu will not live. He will not remain in body. These things are no longer his intent.

In this moment, as I resist his will, surely my beloved stands before Glory. Surely he speaks with the Father. Surely the Mother opens her arms to him. And if this is so, then as Yeshu himself once said to Eleazar, "Who would easily turn back from the Father?" And in this moment resisting his will, suddenly I see before me the face of the old soldier who would not believe. If ever a man played his part, this man did. By his disbelief and by the strength of his sword, he has done the will of Yeshu who intends that all men who look for him will find the Father by finding themselves.

I gather myself. I shake off the doubt that weakens me. I too will play my part.

I speak on. "This too he said to me: 'Tell the others I rise from the dead this day and I go before them to Galilee. There shall they see me.'"

Jacob will listen no more. Yeshu's righteous brother is off down the path he has just come up as if a demon drove him. I think he will run to Galilee. But Simon Peter stands his ground for one moment longer. Simon Peter is torn between great joy and great anger. Only he is here and only I am here. There is none to temper his rage at my sex, nothing to stay his loathing of Mariamne the Magdalene. But what care I of this? I am lost in sorrow. I am lost and I am forsaken. Simon Peter's rage cannot touch me.

I speak in the face of it as a sapling stands in the wind, "As you are his rock, said he also this, 'Where two or more are gathered in my name, there too I shall be.'"

Simon Peter draws back as if I have struck him. "Gathered in his name? Does he mean to have us speak out?"

"He would have you remember him so that you will find yourself."

But Simon Peter does not hear what I say, for he is pulling on his beard and he himself is saying, "But if they did not spare him, how will they spare us?"

In this moment, I have had enough of humility. I think of what was reported to me, that three times as Yeshu stood before Pilate, Simon Peter denied him. So thinking, I stand forth as my very self, the beloved of Yeshu. I stand forth as Mariamne, the very Magdaleder. "Be resolute, Simon Peter. He has made you a man as I am a man, and what is hidden from you now, in time will be shown to you. Depart this place and do his will."

Simon Peter has stepped back from me, his uncertainty of self replaced by execration of me. Under the skin of his face, the muscles twitch with venom. "Woman, I will go to Galilee. I will speak of Yehoshua who is the Messiah. But I shall erase all thoughts of you from the minds of men."

"Do what you will."

And then Simon Peter, like Jacob, is gone. Moments later, so too am I.

It is done.

It took three days more for my friend to die. Never again did he open his eyes nor did he call me beloved. And when it was over, Yehoshua the Nazorean was placed in my mother's tomb, and when I had accomplished all that must be done for him, I left Jerusalem. With me traveled Mary and Jude, and with us traveled Eio and Babel, the colt of Eio. I took nothing with me for there was nothing left to me, though Jude took less than this. His heart had died when his brother died. We set our feet on the road leading west out of the city of David that would take us to Joppa, but somewhere in the land of Lydda we found ourselves turning north, and in time came unto Galilee once more. And there, though I would have him stay with me all the days of our lives, Jude walked away. And from that day to this, I do not know what became of him.

But Eio and her son and Mary and I continued on to the Mountain of Carmel, for finding myself in Galilee, I knew nowhere else to go. There with the Carmelites, Addai and Tata still lived, Addai mending their walls, Tata growing roses over the stones. And there with the Carmelites lived Seth who had been waiting for us, and for Yeshu who would never come.

I left Babel with Tata and Addai but took with me Nyx.

And for many a year after, Seth and Mary and I walked where we would and stayed where we would, and behind us walked Eio and on Eio rode Nyx. We heard all who could teach us. We taught all we could teach. For a time, we lived in the city of Pergamum, where there stands a library as wondrous as the Brucheion in Alexandria. And from there the fame of Seth of Damascus began to spread until we feared they would make a god of him. Men and women will forever make gods of others rather than see the god in themselves.

By this, we determined to go farther, far enough to remove us from the world of men and from the sorrow of men. But more, from man's fear of Life, and his need to be saved from it. So came we here to this far place from out the town of Massiliot where the Phocaeans were, and where everywhere there are statues of the Black Virgin, who is Isis.

In time Father joined us, bringing with him Eleazar. It is here Mary died in my arms. As Salome meant to do for John, here I have built her a tomb, and in it are lit lamps by day and by night so that she might be remembered for mothering such as Yeshu and such as Jude and such as Miryam. Even such as Jacob, for Jacob was a remarkable man.

And it is here, in a cave overlooking a Gaulish sea, I too shall die.

Here on our mountainside, all is still and all is fruitful under the western sun. Far below, I see that Father's garden is in bloom, I see men leading a team of oxen from one fine field to another. Farther toward the sea, there sits on its rocky prominence the town of steep roofs and steep streets Seth and I have made our home. And there is our house of blue stone with a door of mossy green and beside it the small stable where Eio's granddaughter will soon foal.

Eio has lived on. She who carries me each day to our cave stands even now in the sun, flicking her tufted tail.

Over these thirty years, Simon Peter has kept his word. I am as nothing in the stories they tell of Yeshu. But as it was not then, it is not now of any importance. I am a woman and women are used to such things.

Though we did once meet a certain Paul of Tarsus—a story in itself. In him, it seems the Mystery of gnosis lives and perhaps grows. In him, Yeshu becomes Osiris/Dionysus—as the Daemon *of Yeshu intended.*

I tire now. My story is all but told and the words within me fade. Write you now, Seth, my last truth.

The eidolon *of Mariamne does not know if Consciousness is God. It does not know if there is a place beyond this place. It does not know that if when it dies, Mariamne is no more. Mariamne of the body, who has lived a life of mind, knows nothing, but this thing. She knows pity and she knows sorrow, for in their deepest heart, all men are as she is. All men are as lost and as hopeful of being found.*

But this the Daemon *of Mariamne Magdal-eder knows, and this the* Daemon *of Yehoshua the Nazorean taught: as he IS and will always BE, so too I AM and will always BE. We are all Consciousness. We are all eternal. There is no Death. There is only Life.*

Selected Bibliography and Source Material

The author wishes to thank all those whose invaluable work is listed below.

Allegro, J. *The Dead Sea Scrolls.* Harmondsworth, Middlesex: Penguin Books, 1956.

Alter, R. *The David Story.* New York: W. W. Norton, 1999.

Ambrosini, M. L. *The Secret Archives of the Vatican.* Boston: Little, Brown, 1969.

Apuleius. *The Golden Ass.* Translated by Robert Graves. New York: Farrar, Straus & Young, 1951.

Ariel, David S. *What Do Jews Believe?* New York: Schocken Books, 1995.

Aristophanes. *The Clouds.* Translated by William Arrowsmith. Ann Arbor: University of Michigan Press, 1962.

Armstrong, K. *A History of God,* New York: A. A. Knopf, 1993.

Baigent, M., and R. Leigh. *The Dead Sea Scrolls Deception.* New York: Summit Books, 1991.

Baigent, M., R. Leigh, and H. Lincoln. *Holy Blood, Holy Grail.* New York: Delacorte Press, 1982.

Baring, A., and J. Cashford. *The Myth of the Goddess: Evolution of an Image.* New York: Arkana, 1993.

Barnstone, W. *The Other Bible.* San Francisco: Harper & Row, 1984.

Begg, E. *The Cult of the Black Virgin*. Revised and expanded edition. New York: Arkana, 1996.

Blavatsky, H. P. *Isis Unveiled*. Pasadena: Theosophical University Press, 1998.

Borg, M. *Jesus and Buddha: The Parallel Sayings*. Berkeley: Ulysses Press, 1997.

Brandon, S. G. F. *Jesus and the Zealots*. Manchester: Manchester University Press, 1967.

Budge, E. A. W. *Egyptian Magic*. New York: Dover Publications, 1971 (orig. pub. 1899).

———. *Egyptian Religion*. Avenel, NJ: Grammacy Books, 1996 (orig. pub. 1899).

———. *The Gods of the Egyptians*. New York: Dover Publications, 1969 (orig. pub. 1904).

Cahill, T. *The Gifts of the Jews*. New York: Nan. A. Talese, 1998.

Campbell, J. *The Hero with a Thousand Faces*. New York: Pantheon, 1949.

———. *Occidental Mythology: The Masks of God*. New York: Penguin Books, 1976.

Canfora, L. *The Vanished Library*. Berkeley: University of California Press, 1989.

Carse, J. P. *The Gospel of the Beloved Disciple*. San Francisco: HarperSanFrancisco, 1997.

Casson, L. *Libraries in the Ancient World*. New Haven: Yale University Press, 2001.

Crossan, J. D. *The Birth of Christianity*. San Francisco: HarperSanFrancisco, 1998.

———. *The Historical Jesus*. San Francisco: HarperCollins, 1991.

———. *Jesus: A Revolutionary*. San Francisco: HarperSanFrancisco, 1994.

Cullman, O. *Jesus and the Revolutionaries*. New York: Harper & Row, 1970.

de Boer, E. *Mary Magdalene: Beyond the Myth*. Harrisburg: Trinity Press International, 1997.

Dimont, M. I. *Appointment in Jerusalem: A Search for the Historical Jesus*. New York: St. Martin's Press, 1991.

Doherty, E. *The Jesus Puzzle: Did Christianity Begin with a Mythical Christ?* Ottawa: Canadian Humanist Publications, 1999.

Doresse, J. *The Secret Books of the Egyptian Gnostics: An Introduction to the Gnostic Coptic Manuscripts Discovered at Chenoboskio*. Rochester, VT: Inner Traditions, 1986.

Ehrman, B. D. *Lost Christianities: The Battle for Scripture and the Faiths We Never Knew*. New York: Oxford University Press, 2003.

———. *Lost Scriptures: Books That Did Not Make It into the New Testament*. New York: Oxford University Press, 2003.

Eisenman, R. *James, the Brother of Jesus*. London: Faber and Faber, 1997.

Eisenman, R., and M. Wise. *The Dead Sea Scrolls Uncovered*. Rockport, MA: Element, 1992.

Eliade, M. *The Myth of the Eternal Return*. New York: Pantheon Books, 1954.

———. *The Sacred and The Profane: The Nature of Religion.* New York: Harcourt, Brace, 1987.

Ellis, N. *Awakening Osiris: A New Translation of the Egyptian Book of the Dead.* Grand Rapids, MI: Phanes Press, 1988.

Empereur, J. *Alexandria Rediscovered.* New York: George Braziller, 1998.

Epstein, P. *Kabbalah: The Way of the Jewish Mystic.* Boston: Shambhala, 2001.

Euripides. *The Bacchae.* London: Longmans, Green, Reader, and Dyer, 1871.

Fox, E. *The Sermon on the Mount.* New York: Church of the Hearing Christ, 1934.

Freke, T., and P. Gandy. *Jesus and the Lost Goddess.* New York: Harmony Books, 2001.

———. *The Jesus Mysteries.* New York: Harmony Books, 2000.

Friedman, R. E. *The Disappearance of God: A Divine Mystery.* Boston: Little, Brown and Co., 1995.

Funk, R. W., R. W. Hoover, and the Jesus Seminar. *The Five Gospels: The Search for the Authentic Words of Jesus.* New York: Macmillan, 1993.

Gibbon, E. *The Decline and Fall of the Roman Empire.* New York: Modern Library, 1995.

Golb, N. *Who Wrote The Dead Sea Scrolls?* New York: Scribner, 1995.

The Gnosis Archive, http://www.gnosis.org.

Grant, M. *The Ancient Mediterranean.* New York: New American Library, 1988.

———. *From Alexander to Cleopatra: The Hellenistic World.* New York: Collier Books, 1990.

———. *The Jews in the Roman World.* New York: Scribner, 1973.

———. *Twelve Caesars.* New York: Scribner, 1975.

Graves, K. *The World's Sixteen Crucified Saviors, or Christianity Before Christ.* New Hyde Park, NY: University Books, 1971.

Graves, R. *I, Claudius.* New York: H. Smith and R. Haas, 1934.

———. *King Jesus.* London: Cassell and Company Ltd., 1946.

———. *The White Goddess.* New York: Octagon Books, 1972.

Gullaumont, A., H.-C. Puech, G. Quispel, W. Till, & Y. Abd Al Masih, trans. *The Gospel According to Thomas.* San Francisco: Harper & Row, 1959.

Hamilton, E. *The Greek Way.* New York: W. W. Norton, 1930.

———. *Mythology.* Boston: Little, Brown, 1942.

Haskins, S. *Mary Magdalen.* New York: Riverhead Books, 1995.

Helms, R. *Gospel Fictions.* Buffalo: Prometheus Books, 1988.

Herodotus. *The Histories.* Translated by W. Blanco. New York: W. W. Norton, 1992.

Hoeller, S. A. *Gnosticism: New Light on the Ancient Tradition of Inner Knowing.* Wheaton, IL: Quest Books, 2002.

Hornung, E. *Conceptions of God in Ancient Egypt: The One and the Many.* Ithaca: Cornell University Press, 1982.

Johnson, S. E. *Jesus in His Homeland,* New York: Scribner, 1957.

Jonas, H. *The Gnostic Religion: The Message of the Alien God and the Beginnings of Christianity.* Boston: Beacon Press, 2001.

Jones, D. E. *Women Warriors: A History.* Washington, D.C.: Brassey's, 2003.

Josephus. *The Complete Collection of Josephus, Antiquities of the Jews, War of the Jews, The Life of Flavius Josephus.* www.giveshare.org/library/josephus/.

King, K. *The Gospel of Mary of Magdala: Jesus and the First Woman Apostle.* Santa Rosa, CA: Polebridge Press, 2003.

Knight, C., and R. Lomas. *The Hiram Key: Pharaohs, Freemasons and the Discovery of the Secret Scrolls of Jesus.* Rockport, MA: Element, 1997.

Lamsa, G. M. *The Holy Bible from the Ancient Eastern Text.* San Francisco: Harper & Row, 1985.

Layton, B. *The Gnostic Scriptures.* Garden City, NY: Doubleday, 1987.

Lockhart, D. *Jesus the Heretic.* Shaftesbury, Dorset: Element Books, 1997.

Mack, B. L. *The Lost Gospel: The Book of Q and Christian Origins.* San Francisco: HarperSanFrancisco, 1993.

Malina, B. J. *The Social World of Jesus and the Gospels.* New York: Routledge, 1996.

Mead, G. R. S. *Fragments of a Faith Forgotten,* 2nd ed. London: Theosophical Publishing Society, 1906.

Merkur, D. *Gnosis: An Esoteric Tradition of Mystical Visions and Unions.* Albany, NY: State University of New York Press, 1993.

Meyer, M. *The Gospels of Mary: The Secret Tradition of Mary Magdalene, the Companion of Jesus.* San Francisco: HarperSanFrancisco, 2004.

Meyer, M., and R. Smith, eds. *Ancient Christian Magic: Coptic Texts of Ritual Power.* San Francisco: HarperSanFrancisco, 1994.

Miles, J. *God: A Biography.* New York: Alfred A. Knopf, 1995.

Mitchell, S. *The Gospel According to Jesus: A New Translation and Guide to His Essential Teachings for Believers and Unbelievers.* New York: HarperCollins, 1991.

Murphy, C. *The Word According to Eve: Women in the Bible in Ancient Times and Our Own.* London: Penguin, 1999.

Pagels, E. *Beyond Belief: The Secret Gospel of Thomas.* New York: Random House, 2003.

———. *The Gnostic Gospels.* New York: Random House, 1979.

———. *The Gnostic Paul.* Philadelphia: Fortress Press, 1975.

———. *The Origin of Satan.* New York: Random House, 1995.

Philo of Alexandria. *The Contemplative Life.* Translation by D. Winston. New York: Pavlist Press, 1981.

Philostratus. *The Life of Apollonius of Tyana.* Edited and translated by C. P. Jones. Cambridge: Loeb Classical Library, 2005.

Phipps, W. E. *Was Jesus Married?* New York: Harper & Row, 1970.

Picknett, L., and C. Prince. *The Templar Revelation.* New York: Bantam Press, 1997.

Plato. *Collected Dialogues.* Translated by L. Cooper. Princeton: Princeton University Press, 1961.

———. *The Last Days of Socrates.* Translated by H. Tredennick. New York: Penguin Books, 2003.

———. *Timaeus and Critias.* Translated by D. Lee. New York: Penguin Books, 1972.

Potok, C. *Wanderings: Chaim Potok's History of the Jews.* New York: Alfred A. Knopf, 1978.

Potter, D. S., and D. J. Mattingly, eds. *Life, Death, and Entertainment in the Roman Empire.* Ann Arbor: University of Michigan Press, 1999.

Price, R. *The Three Gospels.* New York: Scribner, 1996.

Price, R. M. *Deconstructing Jesus.* Amherst, NY: Prometheus Books, 2000.

Renan, E. *Life of Jesus.* Boston: Little, Brown and Co., 1924.

Robinson, J. M., ed. *The Nag Hammadi Library.* New York: E. J. Brill, 1996.

Rubenstein, R. E. *When Jesus Became God.* New York: Harcourt Brace & Co., 1999.

Rudolph, K. *Gnosis: The Nature and History of Gnosticism.* San Francisco: Harper & Row, 1983.

Saint John of the Cross. *Ascent of Mount Carmel.* Brewster, MA: Paraclete Press, 2002.

St. Augustine. *The Confessions.* Translated by H. Chadwick. New York: Oxford University Press, 1992.

Sandars, N. K., trans. *The Epic of Gilgamesh.* New York: Penguin, 1977.

Schneider, M. S. *A Beginner's Guide to Constructing the Universe: The Mathematical Archetypes of Nature, Art, and Science.* New York: HarperCollins, 1994.

Schonfield, H. *The Essene Odyssey.* Shaftesbury, Dorset: Element Books, 1998.

———. *The Passover Plot.* London: Hutchinson, 1965.

———. *Those Incredible Christians.* New York: B. Geis Associates, 1968.

Schweitzer, A. *The Mysticism of Paul the Apostle.* Baltimore: John Hopkins University Press, 1998.

Shanks, H., ed. *Understanding the Dead Sea Scrolls: A Reader from the Biblical Archaeology Review.* New York: Random House, 1992.

Shorto, R. *Gospel Truth.* New York: Riverhead Books, 1997.

Smith, M. *Jesus the Magician.* Berkeley: Seastone, 1998.

Star, J. *Tao Te Ching: The Definitive Edition*. New York: Jeremy P. Tarcher/Putnam, 2003.

Starbird, M. *The Woman with the Alabaster Jar*. Santa Fe: Bear & Company, 1993.

Szekely, E. B. (claimed as a translation). *The Essene Gospel of Peace*. San Diego: Academy of Creative Living, 1971.

Tubb, J. N. *Canaanites*. Norman, OK: University of Oklahoma Press, 1998.

Tullock, J. H. *The Old Testament Story*, 3rd ed. Englewood Cliffs, NJ: Prentice-Hall, 1981.

Vermes, G. *Jesus the Jew: A Historian's Reading of the Gospels*. Philadelphia: Fortress Press, 1981.

Wilkinson, J. *Jerusalem as Jesus Knew It*. London: Thames & Hudson, 1978.

Wilson, A. N. *God's Funeral*. New York: W. W. Norton, 1999.

Wilson, I. *Jesus: The Evidence*. London: Weidenfeld & Nicolson, 1984.

Winter, P. *On the Trial of Jesus*. Berlin: De Gruyter, 1961.

Wise, M. O. *The First Messiah*. San Francisco: HarperSanFrancisco, 1999.

Wroe, A. *Pontius Pilate*. New York: Modern Library, 2000.